BOUND TO THE SHADOW KING BOOK 1

FELICITY HEATON

BOUND TO THE SHADOW KING SERIES

Book 1: Wolf Caged

Book 2: Wolf Hunted

Book 3: Wolf Crowned

POOL OF STARLIGHT
EVENING STAR COURT
CELESTIN CASTLE
KINSORROW
FELWYDDEN
FARHOLD
SUMMER COURT
DAWN COURT
GREENCROSS
EVERGREEN CASTLE
HIGHBORN GROVE
VALESTAR CASTLE
GREAT WALL
APPLERUN
FAEONOR CASTLE
ARGENT MTNS
HIGH VELLSWATER
FOLGUNSIL
AURIEN
ARGENTYR CASTLE
AURELIAN COURT
VALENTHIR CASTLE
SILVER COURT
AETERNUS COURT
NARROW SEA
CARDINAL KEEP
TITHESWYLL
GREENSWATH HARBOUR
AUREUM CASTLE
GOLDEN COURT
WATERS RUN
HALLOW WATER
VELSFALL TEMPLE
WHITE FALLS
FELGRADDON FOREST
FELCROSS SPIRE
DREAM COURT
LAST WATCH
SOMNIRYN CASTLE
FELGRYN CASTLE
HARROWDOWN HOLD
SPRING COURT
WRATHSWORN CASTLE
DRYBELYN HARBOUR
DREAMSAND QUARRY
FAELON'S KEEP
DREADSFALL CASTLE
LIGHT'S END
INFERNAL COURT
KAERHYN TEMPLE
DEADLANDS
KAYBR'S MAW

FAE REALM OF LUCIA

RHYNSGARD CASTLE
WINTER COURT
BROKEN RIDGE
SCORCHED ISLE
FORGOTTEN WASTES
STYGIAN ISLES
DRAGON'S CLAW
WANDERER'S KEEP
KING'S WATER
WRAITH WOOD
FALKYR CASTLE
SHADOW COURT
RIVERWRAITH
PENWYTHN ESTATE
SCARRED WASTES
BELKARTHEN
TWILIGHT COURT
VOLGUR'S HOLD
FOREST OF BLOOD
TALONRAITH CASTLE
ASHWAKE
NIGHTSWANE
WRATHBORN SCAR
KING'S CROSSING
DUSK COURT
JAGGED FANGS
VELTARTH CASTLE
FORSAKEN COURT
HUNTER'S CHASE
WRATHBORN SCAR
NIGHT'S HOLLOW
FELDARK CASTLE
HIGH KING'S WATCH
FALLOW'S SILENCE
TRAITOR'S FALL
NIGHT COURT
RE CASTLE
OBSIDIAN TOWER
CROW'S WOOD
SCARNYX CASTLE
NIGHT'S END
DARK COURT
KARNDOWN

CHAPTER 1
SAPHIRA

I was born into this world with one purpose: to mate the new Hunt alpha and keep the truce between our two wolf shifter packs strong.

Fate made me for him, and tonight I will become his.

But what I don't know right now is my future isn't all sunshine and roses, and white picket fences with two-point-four pups like I've been led to believe.

My future is shadow and blood, and destiny has grander plans for me...

And so does my fated mate.

My fingers danced over the heart-shaped pendant as Everlee draped it around my neck, a smile playing on my lips as I gazed down at the twin silver wolves set against a clear, bright blue stone. A colour Lucas had told me reminded him of my eyes when he had gifted me the necklace last year for my birthday, and then he had kissed my cheek and murmured how beautiful I looked and that he couldn't wait for the day we would be mated.

Fate couldn't have picked a more perfect mate for me, and I counted my blessings daily for the fact he was the son of the former alpha of the Hunt pack, and that it had bound our lives together at such a critical moment. My birth and the discovery of the tie between us had spared my pack the full wrath of the Hunt pack in those dark days following my uncle's foolish attempt to overthrow the Hunt alpha and take control of both packs.

Everlee stepped back and I released the long braid of my platinum hair, letting it fall against my spine, and turned towards my best friend. Her emerald eyes glittered with her proud, if a little wobbly, smile.

"Don't start." I glanced at the summer dress laid out on the bed behind her, a flimsy thing I was sure I would regret once I stepped outside and felt the cold bite of early spring air, and drew down a deep, steadying breath. "You'll get me going again."

I had spent most of the morning torn between tears of happiness and sorrow, and had barely managed to stifle them when I had stood before my pack on the deck of my family's cabin as my parents went through the formalities of my leaving for another pack. Looking down at all the familiar, friendly faces, and hearing their congratulations and heartfelt wishes that I would have a beautiful future with my new mate, a sensation of dread had stirred inside me and now it was growing with each minute that ticked past.

Time marched onwards, despite my attempts to slow it down by dawdling and dressing at a snail's pace.

Everlee sniffed and nodded, and her expression pinched as she took me in. "You're sure you don't want to wear it down?"

She was talking about my hair. It had become her

favourite topic the moment I had asked her to tie it back in a braid—my usual choice of hairstyle. I had distracted her by twisting the unruly waves of her russet hair into a knot at the back of her head and not-so-subtly hinting that my cousin, Chase, had once said she looked pretty when she wore her hair that way. It had been enough to quiet Everlee for twenty minutes while she had lost herself in thoughts I was glad I wasn't privy to. I really didn't need to picture my cousin like that.

"You're going to have to get dressed at some point. The sun's getting lower." Everlee crossed the small wood-walled room to my tiny single bed and picked up the dress. She ran her hand over the sky-blue fabric, a faraway look in her eyes.

I'm never going to see her again.

That thought drove through my head like a nail, jarring and painful, and I swallowed a gasp as I pivoted away from her, ridiculous tears burning my eyes.

I would see her again. I would.

I was supposed to be happy today, and I had been in the month leading up to this moment. I had daydreamed about what life with Lucas would be like. With my fated mate. With the man I loved. I had watched my parents, how they touched hands when they thought no one was looking, or shared a secret smile, radiating love that I could feel in my bones. In my soul. I would have that kind of love with Lucas once we were mated. I was sure of it.

As I had approached maturity, Lucas had started visiting more and more often, making excuses to stop by my pack whenever he was passing or going as far as bringing supplies for us that someone other than the alpha's son should have been delivering. We had spent every possible minute together, sneaking away to the lake to be alone, to sit and talk about anything and everything, or just laze together in the sun.

He had been visiting less frequently since the death of his parents.

Losing them in such a sudden and brutal way and stepping into the role of alpha while still grieving had been difficult and hard on him.

I closed my eyes, still able to see him as he had been at the funeral, his gaze hollow as he stared at the pyre as flames engulfed and devoured his parents, releasing their souls to their ancestors. I had wanted to speak with him, my heart breaking for him as I felt him slowly withdrawing from the world, but too many words had filled my mouth and heart, and before I could sort them into order and find the right thing to say to him, something that wouldn't make him feel weak but would show him that he wasn't alone, he had been walking away.

A solitary male with hunched shoulders and a bent head.

My heart had screamed at me to follow him into those dark woods, but his cousin, and beta, Braxton had stepped into my path, blocking my way. One look into his stern, dark eyes and I had known he wouldn't let me near Lucas—near my own future mate.

But now he wouldn't be able to stand between us.

Lucas would be mine before the moon had set.

A smile tugged at my lips, warmth unfurling through me as I thought about what this night held for me, even as that trepidation continued to build. Nerves. It was just nerves. Any woman about to start their forever with their fated one would feel the same.

Tomorrow, my life would be completely changed.

I would have a mate, and a new pack.

"Are you wearing this?" Everlee turned away from my dressing table and I glanced at her hand, at the silver chain cupped in her palm, with a solitary charm hanging from it.

A gift Everlee had given me close to a decade ago. She had

even had it enchanted, so I could wear it whenever I shifted and wouldn't lose it. It was the same spell Lucas had used on my necklace, performed by a witch in Quesnel, the nearest city to our pack lands.

"Of course. Why wouldn't I?" I reached for the charm bracelet, eager for it even as my hand shook a little, my nerves rising again as I stared at it and then felt the links beneath my fingers. I lifted it before me, studying it, and that feeling of unease grew within me, tinged with something like regret.

Everlee took the bracelet from me and set it back down. "Time to get dressed. If you delay any longer, people are going to start talking."

"Can't a wolf show up late to her mating? Brides do it all the time in the human world." I stripped off my fluffy white robe, letting it pool at my feet.

"And humans talk about it. Arms up." Everlee motioned with her own arms and when I dutifully raised mine, she was quick to snatch up the summer dress and pull it on over my head for me. She pulled a face at it before moving around to my side to zip it up. "I still think you should be wearing something more suited to a princess."

I laughed, couldn't help it.

The act alone lightened some heavy thing within me, and I was grinning when I looked over my shoulder at her. "Are you ever going to stop calling me that?"

Everlee grinned right back at me. "No. You're a princess, whether you want to be called one or not. Or maybe a queen. Alphas are like kings, aren't they? That makes you a queen." Her expression turned serious and she came around to stand before me and took hold of my arms. "You're going to have an amazing life, Saphi. You'll be treated like a queen. You'll want for nothing, and you'll be deeply loved by your fated mate. Your future will be bliss... like your parents have."

She loosed a long sigh as her gaze drifted to the window of my bedroom, growing distant and sombre.

"You're one of the lucky ones," she whispered. "I wish I knew who my mate was."

It was my turn to take hold of her arms, and my hands lowered to lock with hers. I squeezed them and smiled. "You'll find him."

But I wasn't sure it was the man she hoped it was.

Chase showed no sign that Everlee was his fated one.

I held on to hope that it was because Everlee hadn't matured yet.

Usually, wolves only knew they were fated once both were sexually mature, something which occurred at around a century old. I was different. A witch and a spell had revealed I was Lucas's mate soon after I was born. I had known all my life who my mate was, without all the worry I would never find him, or that he would be someone cruel and terrible.

So many wolves never found their fated mate.

Everlee was right. My future would be bliss.

But my eyes strayed to the charm bracelet on the dressing table, a gift Everlee had given me when I had found the courage to confess my secret desire to see the world, to have adventure and experience life beyond the boundaries of the pack. I loved my life and my role within the pack, but for the last thirty years, my gaze had started to stray towards the edge of the Harper pack lands, towards that horizon filled with unknown sights, sounds and so much promise.

She had told me she had seen online how some people who travelled had charm bracelets and they added one for each place they visited.

Mine still only had one charm on it—a wolf to symbolise me—despite how long it had been since Everlee had bought it for me in Quesnel.

A city that was close to my pack territory in Wells, yet I had never seen it with my own eyes.

Just like I had never seen the ocean.

And deep in my heart, I doubted I ever would.

"This will be a beautiful adventure." Everlee took the bracelet and wrapped it around my wrist, fastening it for me.

I wasn't sure this was the adventure I really craved, or that stepping into a mate bond wouldn't be like locking myself into a life I wasn't quite ready for yet.

As the mate of an alpha, I wouldn't be free to travel and see everything beyond the boundaries of our pack lands. I would just be trading one life of duty for another, one set of walls for another.

I wouldn't see beyond those walls as I longed to, to see what else was out there, and see how others lived. I wouldn't know the scent of the sea or the feel of sand between my toes. I wouldn't know the infinite horizon.

I would know another set of trees. Another group of people who would need my help with day-to-day chores, and if I was lucky, maybe Lucas would let me help with the running of the pack, or at least let me work as a healer, as my mother had taught me.

"Saphira," Everlee started, but I held my hand up, silencing her as the weight of everything pressed down on me and I struggled to push it all away, all the doubts and the fears. She sighed. "If you ever need to get away or need a change of scenery, you can always come visit."

I looked at her now.

Could I?

Would Lucas allow it?

I had a sudden urge to be outside, to explore every inch of my home and the woods surrounding it one last time, as if I would never see it again. I wasn't sure that I would. It wasn't unusual for mated females to remain with their new pack and never return to their old one, especially those females who mated an alpha.

Would this be the last time I saw my pack lands? My friends? My parents?

My stomach tightened, twisting painfully at the thought tonight might be my last moments with them, that voice in my head so loud it drowned out the one that soothed and whispered I was overreacting, letting fear get the better of me. I was being foolish, I knew it deep inside, but I couldn't shake the dread and the fear I would never see this place or these people again, that my mate would order me to remain at his pack—*my pack*—and cut me off from this world.

The pressing need to drink it all in and savour it, to make memories I would cherish for the rest of my life, had me moving to the cabin window, my wolf instincts tugging me there, towards all that freedom I had taken for granted.

"Saphira?" Everlee's soft voice tried to soothe the sharp edge of fear that felt like a knife poised over my heart, but it pressed closer nonetheless, the tip of it piercing my chest as I struggled to breathe. "Saphi?"

Her hand on my shoulder was a balm, an anchor I clung to as I placed mine over it, pinning it to me and clutching it tightly.

"Lucas isn't like that. He's not like other alphas, and not all alphas are so controlling. Look at your father." Everlee squeezed my shoulder and I tried to take comfort from those words, but it was hard.

My father, who had never even entertained my requests to go to Quesnel with Everlee, or even with Chase and my protector, Morden. Who had looked close to laughing the one time I had asked whether I could make the long trip to Vancouver. He had always reminded me that my time was better spent here at the pack, carrying out my duties and taking care of our people. My mother had always looked as if she wanted to argue, and then she had agreed with him, shutting down my attempts to seek out adventure even in its tamest forms.

Yet even though part of me resented them for keeping me caged within the confines of the pack lands, my eyes still burned and throat still clogged up as the bedroom door opened and my mother poked her head into the room.

"It's time." Her eyes—eyes I had inherited—warmed as they took me in and she pushed the door open fully to enter the room. "You look beautiful."

She bustled across the room, opened the closet and pulled out a thick cream shawl.

"But you're going to freeze your backside off. It's April, Saphi. You're lucky there isn't six inches of fresh snow on the ground right now." She handed me the knitted shawl and I took hold of it, but she didn't release it. She stood there, clutching it, her hands close to mine, so near I could feel their warmth. Her lips trembled as she forced a smile, her blue eyes glittering with unshed tears as she released the shawl and lifted her hand to sweep strands of my matching pale silver hair behind my ear. "It was snowing the day you were born. I told your father you looked as if you had come from the snow, had been born of it, with your hair and your eyes... as if you had come from another world. He had chuckled in that way of his and told me you looked just like me, and I was too warm and kind to be made of frigid winter. Just like you. I knew the first time you laughed and smiled how warm, kind and beautiful you were."

"Mom." I rolled my eyes, aiming for dramatic effect. "We've heard this story a thousand times."

She released me and raised her hands in surrender. "I know, I know. But forgive me this one time? It's not every day a mother lets her daughter go."

Those words hit their mark.

Let me go.

Like I was being released into the wild, into unknown and uncharted lands, rather than into the hands of another person, like a possession.

I shunned that dark thought and focused on the positives, on the happy moments that were ahead of me, and on Lucas. I pictured his bright smile that would soften his glacial blue eyes and would draw my gaze down to his lips. He had never kissed me on the mouth, but tonight he would do that and so much more.

A buzz tripped down my arms, shimmering through my veins as my blood heated.

Suddenly, I was itching to see him rather than itching to be out in the woods, running wild and free as a wolf.

I pressed the backs of my fingers to my heating cheeks, and my mother smiled knowingly.

"It won't be long now." She sounded as proud as she looked as she wrapped the shawl around my shoulders. "Maturity can hit a female hard, but Lucas will take care of you."

"Oh my god!" I nudged her in the shoulder, sure I looked as mortified as I felt inside. One moment she was talking about when I had been a baby, making me feel younger than my ninety-eight years, and the next she was hitting me with talk of my first heat. I wasn't sure which was worse. Actually, I was. I would take her speaking about me as if I was still a little pup over her talking about my impending maturity. "I am so not having *that* conversation with you."

Everlee laughed, the sound bright and warm, and my mother chuckled with her, and as I was escorted out of the room, out of the cabin and ushered into the back seat of my father's red SUV, I couldn't bring myself to laugh, even when I wanted to.

Lucas occupied all my mind, my heart, and that ache to stay here in my old home with my old pack transformed into an ache to see him.

An ache to take hold of him.

Kiss him.

And mate him.

CHAPTER 2

SAPHIRA

The barn in the centre of the communal green deep in the Hunt pack lands had been beautifully decorated with white lights that shimmered as dusk began to fall, making the compacted snow around the building twinkle like diamonds. I had thought we would celebrate the coming together of our two packs in the street that ran through the middle of the small town that served as an outpost for humans passing through the area. Lucas had mentioned it happening that way in the last message I had received from him. Maybe the lingering cold weather of early spring had forced a change of plans.

I relished it.

I had never felt comfortable visiting the Hunt pack, mostly because Lucas's father had always held the gatherings in the heart of the town they had built, one filled with stores that catered to tourists and the few locals that lived out on remote properties in the area. None of my pack had failed to see his actions for what they had been.

A show of power and wealth.

My pack—the Harper pack—lived in a small community of cabins in the middle of the forest near Wells in Canada, far away from civilisation. We scraped by, growing food and hunting, living off the land as best we could. But for most of the supplies we needed, we had to travel to the nearby Hunt pack or make the journey to Quesnel.

We were few in numbers, and they were many.

Our two packs couldn't have been more different, and the old Hunt alpha had loved pointing it out to us.

Even going as far as bringing up how easy it had been to defeat our former alpha and two of our pack's protectors.

My gaze sought out Chase and Morden as I exited the SUV.

Chase pulled his black Jeep up behind us, looking deeply at ease as he chatted animatedly with Morden's younger sister, Danica, who sat wedged between him and a very grave Morden. My former protector's grey eyes shifted to me, as stormy as ever as they locked with mine. I sensed the movement of people towards me before his gaze snapped to my right and narrowed.

Lucas.

If I hadn't been able to feel him closing the distance between us, hadn't been able to recognise his earthy scent, that look in Morden's eyes would have told me who it was.

While Morden had felt no love for his father, he had loved his brother deeply, and Lucas's father had taken both of them from him that night Chase's father had foolishly challenged him.

I gave Morden a look that warned him to be on his best behaviour.

Morden merely shoved the car door open in response and

stepped out, unfurling all six-foot-five of his powerful body, and gripped the top of the door.

Lucas stopped beside me, his deep blue eyes fixed on Morden rather than me.

Where Lucas was light and elegant, with his neatly styled blond hair and pressed jeans and shirt, and charming as he smiled at my former protector, Morden was darkness incarnate, his black flannel shirt and jeans, and his dark brown hair making him blend into the falling night beyond him, and his lips were set in a grim line that made it perfectly clear he wasn't happy to be here.

Before the two of them could ruin the night, I stepped in front of Lucas, capturing his attention.

His gaze dropped to mine, and then fell further, raking over me in a way that heated my blood and had my mind racing forwards to after the celebration, when we would finally be alone.

When we would mate.

"You look beautiful," he murmured for my ears only and leaned down to brush his lips across my forehead in his usual greeting.

I lifted my head instead, tipping my chin up, and his smile was wicked as he shifted course and swept his lips across mine in the barest whisper of a kiss.

A shiver bolted down my spine and my wolf side urged me to growl, to claim this male as mine now rather than wait another few hours. My fingers trembled as I stood before him, as he gazed down at me, right into my eyes, the corners of his kissable lips still curved into a faint smile. Heat coloured his eyes, heat I could feel beating off him as he inched closer, as he trailed a hand down my arm beneath my shawl.

His fingers locked around my wrist rather than twining with mine.

"Come. Everyone is waiting." He tugged on my arm and I stumbled after him, confusion flashing through me as I looked at his hand on my wrist. His grip was firm, and I could sense agitation in him as I focused on him.

He was probably just as nervous as I was, or maybe excited to see where this night would take us.

I walked faster to keep up with him and fell into step beside him. He angled his head towards me, his smile warm, no trace of unease in his eyes. That agitation I had sensed in him faded as he walked beside me, his grip on my wrist loosening as we reached the threshold of the barn. Warmth swept around me as I crossed it, and not only from the candles set in the centre of each wooden bench table.

A cheer went up as all eyes turned towards us, murmured greetings and hollered welcomes following it, together with a few remarks about how eager we probably were to get to the mating part of the evening. My cheeks heated despite my efforts to keep my embarrassment hidden.

They warmed for a different reason when Lucas looked at me, hunger I had never seen before shining in his eyes.

Fire that scalded me.

I couldn't pull my eyes away from his as he led me through the room, towards the long table near the back wall. A smile lit up his face as he eased my chair out for me, as I sat in it and he took the seat beside me. It had been a long time since I had seen him this happy, and the thought that it was because of me warmed me right to my soul.

Lucas leaned towards me, draping his arm across the back of my seat, his earthy scent filling my senses as he poured me a glass of chilled white wine. His smile was easy and charming as always, a feat I always marvelled at. I had never met a male who smiled so easily, who could charm all around him as Lucas could, no matter how dire a situation might be. Even when he had been mourning his parents, he had been able to smile just a few short weeks after their deaths. If I lost my parents, I was sure I wouldn't be able to smile for a full year.

He grazed his fingers down my spine, sending a chill tumbling down it as he pushed the glass towards me.

I almost spilled the wine as I picked it up, fumbling with it as my hands continued to tremble.

He noticed, his focus shifting to my fingers, and then back to my face.

He eased closer, his breath tickling my ear as he whispered, "No need to be so nervous. It's not as if we haven't known this moment was coming for years. You really do look beautiful tonight, Saphira."

He dropped a kiss on my neck and I growled, the rumbling sound slipping from my lips before I could stop it as my instincts roared to life, making me restless with an urge to push and goad him, to tempt him into biting my nape.

Binding us as mates.

His raspy chuckle tickled my senses and my skin, making the hairs on my nape stand on end, hyper-sensitive and aware of how close he was to where I needed him most.

That ache that had been building from the moment I left my pack lands reached a crescendo as I glanced at him, catching his gaze rooted on my nape. His eyes were unfocused, his pupils blown. Was he thinking about marking me too?

I squeezed my thighs together as all that wicked heat pooled there, the ache too strong now, almost overwhelming.

Lucas pulled back and clinked his glass against mine, a mischievous light in his eyes as he said, "Drink. It'll help with the nerves... and the heat."

He could sense it. Maybe even smell it on me. I died a little inside, cringing internally at the thought he was deeply aware of how badly I wanted him.

I gulped my wine and the moment I set the glass down, Lucas refilled it. I gulped that too, because it took a lot for a wolf shifter to feel even a mild buzz from alcohol.

I had experimented with it once, when Morden had brought a box of six whiskey bottles back from a trip to Vancouver and we had celebrated his birthday on a bitter November day when the snow had been falling so thickly that we had struggled to get out the door when it was time to head home. Chase had ended up staying over at his place, and I had stumbled back through the snow with Everlee. She had slept in my bed next to me, complaining it was too cold to trek the additional distance to her cabin.

Lucas kissed my shoulder, regaining my attention, and chuckled at something Braxton said to him. The big dark-haired beta rivalled Morden in his height and build, making me feel small as I looked up at him. He ran a hand over his shorn hair and smiled, but no trace of warmth touched his dark eyes. I wasn't sure Braxton would ever approve of me, but I was determined not to give him any reason to dislike me. I knew how easily one wolf could turn others against a female, even the mate of an alpha, especially when they wielded power in the pack, like Braxton. Wolves listened to their betas as much as their alphas. Even an alpha listened to their beta.

I turned my gaze on Lucas.

Although I was sure he wouldn't be easily swayed by his cousin.

"Sit. Have some wine with us." I pinned Braxton with my best smile and gestured to the seat beside me.

Braxton grunted at it and moved on, drifting into the crowd.

"Don't mind him," Lucas breathed into the shell of my ear and nipped at my lobe. "He just thinks I'm rushing things."

I looked at him. "And what do you think? Are you rushing things?"

He shifted closer. "No. I think this is the right time. I don't want to wait any longer."

I blushed, the colour climbing my face before I could stop it.

Lucas took my chin between his thumb and forefinger, his smile dazzling. "So innocent. So perfect. You could charm any male with a look… a reaction like that."

I brushed his hand away. "I don't want to charm *any* male."

"Shame." He refilled my glass. "Countless men would part with good money just to have a beautiful female blush for them like that."

I scoffed. "Did you start drinking before I arrived? I'm not that pretty, nor that innocent."

That last part tasted like ash on my tongue, a pitiful attempt to pretend I wasn't as innocent as all my blushing and unconcealed eagerness declared I was.

His eyebrows lifted. "Really? Tell me, Saphira, who have you been not-so-innocent with?"

"Morden," I blurted.

Lucas barked out a laugh, as if that was the most ridiculous thing he had ever heard. "Morden Snow?"

Morden scowled over at us from his seat at Chase and Everlee's table near the door.

Lucas suddenly stopped laughing when Morden's grey gaze moved from him to me. His arm tightened around me, pinning me to his side, his fingers pressing in hard enough to hurt.

"You lie." His voice pitched low, laced with a growl.

"I do not." I dragged my focus from Morden and settled it back on Lucas, a smile curling the corners of my lips as my wolf rumbled in approval of the jealous look on Lucas's face. I wanted more of that look, of that possessive hold he had on me, so I confessed, "He's seen me naked."

Lucas looked as if he might laugh again as he relaxed a notch, his grip loosening. "We're shifters. We see each other naked all the time."

I frowned at him. No, we didn't. Males often stripped before a shift, not caring who was looking, and some even walked around nude afterwards, but pack females didn't tend to do the same. At least, females at my pack didn't. My gaze darted around the room, singling out all the females of the Hunt pack. How many of these females had Lucas seen naked?

How many had seen him naked?

Now I was the jealous one.

So, I snapped, "It wasn't during a shift. We went skinny dipping at the lake."

Lucas's face darkened.

Claws pressed into my arm, threatening to break my skin.

"It was just once," I stammered, my heart pounding as fear rose within me. I had taken this silly game of making each other jealous too far, pushing him too hard.

Fated males didn't like others looking at their mate, especially before their bond was completed.

I wanted to blame the buzz of the wine, opened my mouth to do just that, but then the darkness in his eyes faded, melting away as a breathtaking smile curved his lips, a charming mask falling into place but not convincing me his anger was gone.

"And never again." Lucas swept his fingers down my cheek and took hold of my chin again, keeping my gaze on his. "You're mine now."

My breath hitched, lodging in my throat, and I nodded, my voice lost to me as I stared into his eyes and their wicked promise of things to come.

He brought his mouth to my ear again, his lips brushing it as he said, "Skinny dipping sounds good. Let's do that."

"Now?" My eyes widened. "It's freezing out there and we're in the middle of a celebration for us… which means we should probably be here."

He shrugged. "We'll shift and run to the lake. It'll warm us up. And believe me, no one will care if we slip away. They're probably all expecting it."

My heart pounded, accelerating at the thought of Lucas chasing me through the dark forest in his wolf form. Instinct howled at me to agree, to make him chase me and fight to catch me. To make him work to win me.

Make him hunt me.

I nodded, and before I had come to my senses, still lost in that fantasy of running with him, he had me on my feet and was pulling me away with him.

The two packs jeered as they spotted us making a beeline for the exit. I glanced back at my parents, my gut twisting at the thought of leaving without saying goodbye to them, but I caught sight of their smiling faces. They waved me on, and I smiled shakily back at them before Lucas tugged me out into the crisp night.

I needed to say my farewells to Everlee, and Chase and Morden.

Lucas released my arm and pulled his shirt off, making me forget my need to say goodbye to my friends as my wolf howled in response to the delicious sight of his carved chest and abs. He toed off his boots and shucked his jeans, and that howl became a growl as I glimpsed all of him.

Only glimpsed.

He shifted into his dark wolf form before I could drink him in, robbing me of the pleasure of gazing upon his perfection.

The sight of him letting his wolf out beckoned me to do the same, instinct driving me to run with him, with my fated mate.

I wanted to take my time stripping, letting him see all of me, but he growled, impatience ringing through it, and it was so cold that I found myself rushing to ditch my shoes and dress, and my underwear.

I shifted the moment I was naked, payback for what he had done to me, and took off towards the nearest lake, the scent of water telling me where it was. It wasn't a far run through the snowy forest, the distance short enough that it wouldn't satisfy my need to be chased by Lucas, hunted by him.

My paws flew over the leaf litter, the cold lost on me as I raced through the night, the chill air kissing my fur.

Lucas broke off to my left and my sharp senses tracked him.

Curiosity rolled through me as he came across me, herding me towards my right, making me change course as he brushed against me. He pranced around me, yipping and nipping at my flank. I nipped back at him, nudged and rubbed against him as we ran, and then broke away from him, trying to run back towards the direction I could smell water.

He came up beside me again, loosing a growl this time, a command I felt all the way down to my soul. He wanted me to go somewhere else. I glanced at him, my heightened vision easily making him out despite the pitch darkness. He pointed his snout towards somewhere in the distance.

Towards his home.

Eagerness rolled through me, hunger sweeping me up in it and making me turn towards that direction. My paws pounded the dirt track as I picked it up, one that wound through the forest and was familiar to me.

Lucas nipped at my heels and I ran harder, streaking ahead of him, a thrill bolting down my spine as he gave chase.

My breaths fogged in the air as I put on another burst of

speed, increasing the distance between us, and Lucas snarled and redoubled his effort to capture me. He closed the gap, narrowing it down to only a few lengths of my sleek body.

Each leap over a fallen branch, or dance around a tree in my path, heightened my awareness of him and that hunger that was close to shredding my restraint as I imagined him catching me, shifting back and pinning me beneath his powerful body on the ground and taking me.

Lucas used my distraction against me, closing the distance down to nothing and smacking my rump with his head. He nipped with his fangs, the sharp sting of them against my flesh sending heat skittering through my veins. So hot I almost tripped and face-planted into the dirt.

When he tried to nip me again, I dodged, leaping to one side, and he almost hit a tree that came between us.

His eyes flashed with irritation and amusement.

And then he took off past me.

Into a clearing.

I slowed to a trot.

I didn't recognise this place or the ancient barn that stood in the centre of it.

Lucas didn't slow until he was at the open door of the towering dark wooden building. He stopped and looked back at me, jerked his head and disappeared inside.

My breaths came faster, my heart pumping harder as I listened and focused my senses, stretching them as far and wide around me as I could manage. I couldn't sense any movement nearby or hear anything above my heartbeat and rapid breaths.

We were alone.

Excitement coursed through me, making my head a little light as I eased towards the barn. My vision wobbled and I shook my head, clearing it. Heat prickled down my spine, and my limbs tingled. Maybe I should have listened to my mother when she had wanted to tell me what my first heat would be like, because this giddiness wasn't at all what I had expected.

I trotted into the darkness, shaking off my nerves as the gloom embraced me and my eyes adjusted to it, revealing the enormous open space and a large box covered by a cloth.

Lucas stood near it, snagging my attention as he shifted back. I growled, hunger rushing through me at the sight of him in all his glory. My shift came over me without me even thinking about it, my bones elongating and fur receding as I straightened to my full height.

I stood before him, feeling a little dizzy as his gaze raked over me, scorching a trail down my bare body that made my blood thrum with need.

I had never been so aware of someone's eyes on me.

He stalked towards me, a predator in human guise, and I bit back a groan that bubbled up my throat as his hungry gaze drank me in and his penis twitched, beginning to grow hard. My body hummed in response to the sight, heat pooling low between my thighs, and I squeezed them slightly, savouring the ache building there.

When he reached me, he ran his hand down my arm and took hold of my hand rather than my wrist. "Come with me."

I eagerly followed him, my vision shifting again, and I squeezed my eyes shut and opened them again. This time, the haziness didn't clear. I tried to focus on Lucas's bare back, on the delicious globes of his bottom, and how his muscles shifted as he stalked forwards into the gloom. He swept his arm out, and I didn't notice what he had revealed at first, his body a distraction that held me under its spell.

Until he pulled me forwards again.

My gaze leaped to my right.

A cage.

I took a step back, panic blaring like a warning horn in my mind, and instinct screamed at me to run, that this wasn't right.

Lucas's hand locked around my wrist before I could bolt and he yanked me forwards.

The scent of damp earth hit me, but it didn't cover the other things I could smell. Blood. Urine. My eyes widened as I struggled against Lucas's cruel grip, leaning away from him, a feeble attempt to gain some leverage and break free. My limbs trembled, turning rubbery as I spotted claw marks on the iron bars of the cage.

My chest tightened painfully.

I kicked at Lucas's leg, slamming my heel down on it, and he growled and tugged so hard on my arm that I cried out as fire lashed at my shoulder, shooting outwards from the joint.

The look on his face.

I didn't recognise this dark male before me, who was looking at me as if I was filth as he seized hold of me, pinning my arms between us as I fought him. I wasn't strong enough. Not in this form.

I tried to shift.

And nothing happened.

That panic morphed to full blown fear, to crippling terror as it hit me that I wasn't strong enough to escape whatever Lucas had planned for me, that something was wrong with me, inhibiting my ability to shift. My mind reeled, thoughts spinning and colliding.

"Lucas?" I blinked at him, at the cage, my eyes leaping between them as he manhandled me towards it. I managed to twist my hands around and pressed them to his bare chest. "Lucas... *stop*. I don't know what this is, but I don't like it. Please. Let's go back to the celebration."

He didn't react.

Was he even listening to me?

His glacial blue eyes remained fixed on the cage, his face etched with grim purpose as he dragged me towards it.

Something in me snapped.

I twisted my head and bit down on his arm, sinking short fangs into it and gagging as blood flooded my mouth.

"Bitch." Lucas released me and staggered back, his eyes darting to his bleeding arm.

The sight of it startled me too. My wolf side howled in rage and agony at the sight of my fated mate injured, even when I had been the one to inflict the wound. What had I done?

Before I could shut down my instincts and run, Lucas back-handed me, striking me hard across my temple, and my vision swam with stars. I sank to my knees, gripping the dirt with both hands as darkness loomed, threatening to pull me under. Bile rose up my throat.

Lucas seized me and dragged me across the floor, and hurled me into the cage before I could recover and fight him again. I grunted as I hit the wall of bars on the other side of the cage and fought to shake off the dizziness that was invading every molecule of my body.

The metallic sound of the door slamming closed felt like a death knell.

"Lucas." I moved as quickly as I could manage to the door, grabbed it and rattled it. It didn't give. My head spun, my stomach rebelling as a dull throbbing ache spider-webbed across my skull. "Lucas, what is this?"

Lucas acknowledged me at last as he crouched before me, still nude, and reached between the bars to seize my face in a vicious grip.

"Stay awake." He shook my head so violently I wanted to vomit. When I blinked several times, trying to stave off the dizziness and the looming darkness, he muttered, "I told Braxton the dose was too high."

Dose?

It hit me that it wasn't the mating heat making me feel dizzy. It wasn't the wine either.

Lucas had drugged my drink.

I looked at the lock, cold realisation sinking in. That was the reason I wasn't strong enough to fight him or break the lock on the cage door. That was the reason I hadn't been able to shift to my wolf form again.

My fated mate had drugged me.

"Lucas," I whispered, my voice failing me as I took stock of my situation and realised the only way out of this was to appeal to the one man who looked happy about it.

He looked so much like his father. Cold. Callous. Cruel. Where was the man who had smiled so easily at me, who had been warm and kind to me, charming me into falling for him? Had it all been an act, a mask to conceal the truth of him—that he was as vicious and cold as his father, as seduced by power and with a heart only big enough to love himself?

"Good." He almost smiled, satisfaction that I wasn't about to pass out written all over his smug face.

I wasn't sure why he was so pleased about it, until a female stepped into the room, one I recognised from the party.

"I wanted you to be awake for this moment." He did smile now, a grin that held no hint of the affection he had shown me over the years. It was as cold and brutal as his next words. "I wouldn't want you missing me rejecting you."

I gasped and reeled backwards, that word like a slap in the face.

Rejecting.

"Y-you're re-re-rejecting me?" I stammered, my ears ringing as I felt as if I was losing my mind. My wolf side howled in agony as fiercely as my heart screamed in pain. "I don't understand."

I wasn't sure I ever would.

I stared at him, struggling to make sense of the world and Lucas now, unable to recognise any shred of the male who had smiled and called me beautiful, who had lifted me up and was now tearing me down in the worst of ways.

"My stupid father made me wait—made me loyal to you—some female I've never known and never wanted." Each word that left his lips was like a knife in my chest, cleaving away another piece of my heart, bringing another memory of him into my mind to shatter together with my reality. "I've waited almost half a century for this moment, wasting my maturity. I should have killed the bastard sooner."

Shock knocked me on my backside. "You killed your own parents?"

Their deaths had been an accident, a fatal error while they had been running in the mountains.

The cold edge to his eyes and the satisfied twist of his lips chilled my blood.

It hadn't been an accident.

It had been planned, by their own son.

Who was this male before me? Had I ever really known him?

I had been wrong. He wasn't as cold and cruel as his father. He was worse. So much worse.

I couldn't bear to look at him as the fragile pieces of my heart broke, as my instincts and my wolf side grieved, and everything I had known shattered before my eyes, revealing bleak reality that I had been blind to, and a future that was going to be far different from everything I had dreamed. The chairs spaced around the barn, all facing the cage, and the grim scent of bodily fluids, told me my future would now be a nightmare.

People gathered here. To watch what?

"Don't worry. You'll fetch a nice price. One last big sale. Maybe you'll even bring in enough to get my pack out of this hellhole." Lucas reached through the bars and patted my cheek, the action condescending, as if I was just a pet to him now.

An animal he intended to sell at auction.

Just as he had sold others.

Tears welled, even though I fought them back, not wanting him to see how easily he had broken me as dread pooled inside me, so bleak and black that I was sinking into it, drowning as my mind filled with images straight out of a nightmare. My throat closed as numbness swept through me, as some part of me receded into the darkness, curling inwards to protect itself. This wasn't happening. This was all just some terrible dream. Not reality.

Not reality.

Lucas loved me. He was my fated mate. He *loved* me.

No matter how many times I told myself that, the broken part of me refused to believe it, and something dark stirred within me in response, held back and muted by the drugs that blurred my vision and stole strength from my limbs.

"But we're fated." My words were weak even to my own ears, a foolish and desperate attempt to make him change his mind or maybe to make him wake up and realise what he was doing.

Part of me wanted to tell him this wasn't funny, that he had taken this joke too far—the part of me that couldn't comprehend that he was serious, that he was rejecting me, and that the love he had shown me was a lie.

"We're fated," I whispered, my voice strained as my brow furrowed and my throat closed. Tears streamed down my face. "We're destined for each other. I'm meant to be your mate."

"Fuck fate. I don't want a mate." He scoffed and pushed to

his feet, coming to tower over me. "I reject you, Saphira Harper. You are not my mate and you never will be."

Something inside me broke and I screamed out the pain, the fiery agony that had that scream coming out as a howl as my wolf side pushed to the surface, as instinct tore me apart.

He bent down and for a moment, I thought he would open the cage, but instead he seized my arm and ripped the bracelet from it. "You won't be needing this anymore. Not where you're going. It's not like you'll be travelling much. You'll be lucky if you even leave the bed of whoever buys you."

Bile rose again but I swallowed it, refusing to let Lucas see my terror as that dark, malevolent thing buried deep in the layers of numbness bared fangs at him.

"You can keep this though." He tapped the pendant he had given me.

A token of his *love*.

A lie.

I wanted to rip it off, but I didn't have the strength to lift my arms now. I didn't have the strength to move. Numbing darkness slowly rolled up on me, and I wasn't sure whether it was the drugs or the pain of rejection, but I welcomed it as Lucas clicked his fingers and the female approached him.

Naked.

He stood and seized hold of her by her nape and pushed her over, bending her towards me. His eyes held mine as he moved behind her, filled with hatred and anger, and so much heat as he thrust into her. The female moaned and gripped the bars of my cage as he pounded into her.

I tore my gaze away and slumped over, squeezing my eyes shut and pleading with fate to end this, to stop my suffering.

Every thrust my fated mate made into the female broke the ties that bound us a little more, stretching and snapping them, leaving me raw inside, howling in pain and clawing at my bare skin as I sobbed and rocked.

Lucas grunted and stilled, and the last thread twisted and snapped.

The female moaned and something heavy hit the dirt near me. I cracked my eyes open and stared at her as she lay on the ground, breathing heavily, her gaze glazed. Blood smeared on her trembling thighs.

Lucas crouched before me, grabbed my hair and jerked my head up, forcing my eyes to meet his as he smirked.

"Pray the male who buys you treats you half as nicely."

CHAPTER 3
KAELERON

It was a dance I had executed countless times.

I slipped through the shadows, twining with them one moment and releasing them the next as I closed the distance between myself and my prey unseen. The full moon shone down on the frozen forest, glittering on patches of snow, turning them to diamonds beneath my silent feet.

The stench of the hooded males ahead of me strengthened, choking my lungs, pulling a smile onto my lips. It would be so easy, so very easy, to slip among them unnoticed.

To slip a claw across a throat or two.

To watch pandemonium erupt in a flash of fear.

And taste it on my tongue.

My grin stretched wider, the intoxicating urge to unleash on the unwitting shifters, demons, and other breeds who made their way towards the solitary barn almost pulling me under its spell. I tugged back on the reins as my claws emerged, black and sharp.

Now, now.

I flashed jagged teeth at the moon as my shadows faltered

and reached a hand towards it, a fistful of claws that closed around the orb.

But I held little sway over it here.

So I wrapped shadows tighter around me and stepped back into the kiss of gloom beneath the trees, savouring their inky welcoming embrace.

There would be no crossing the expanse of open ground between the forest and the barn without someone noticing.

The muttered comments of the males ahead of me revealed this was the right place.

My key was right where Neve had told me it would be.

My grin returned, wider now as I sensed impending victory. No moon could snatch it from me.

"Lucia," I murmured to the stunning orb, "By thy great goddess's heart, grant me silence and stealth. Seal shut your eyes. Breathe darkness before me."

I stretched my hand to the sky again, blotting out the moon, and the earth grew still and the air trembled. The males fell silent, the scent of their fear swirling around me as they stiffened. When I lowered my hand, darkness so thick even I could barely see through it descended around me. I tilted my head back, raising my face to the heavy blanket of night, and slowly smiled as weak pinpricks of light gently bloomed into sparkling waves of stars that coated the sky.

One of the males stepped back, his fear striking me, speaking to me. "No. I am leaving. Nothing is worth this. I suggest you do the same."

He twisted this way and that, wild eyes scanning the shadows.

Seeking me.

Fae filth.

Traitorous heathen.

Two of the men chuckled, as if the male had lost his mind and was overreacting.

If only they knew.

"He who turns his back on his beloved goddess deserves nothing less than my wrath." I stroked my claws over the rough bark of the tree beside me, contemplating all the delicious ways I would carve this male up for daring to live beyond the lands of Lucia. Beyond the sphere of his goddess's grace.

The male swung towards me, golden eyes bright, and his hood fell back to reveal hair as gold.

A hiss ripped from me.

"Seelie," I snarled.

Recognition flashed across his face and then he was gone, only glittering air remaining where he had been standing.

My claws cleaved deep into the tree.

Foul wretch.

Neve had failed to warn me I would find one of his ilk in my path. For that, the dragon would pay.

The remaining five men hurried towards the barn, granting me silence and stealth.

I stepped out from beneath the tree, and a moment later, I stepped out of the shadows, the pointed tip of my right boot emerging first, cleaving through the darkness like a blade. The shadows slipped away, lovingly clinging as they went, caressing with tendrils that fell away to writhe like snakes across the frozen ground.

At my shoulders, they clasped me tightly, pressing into the plates of my black pauldrons to form a cloak behind me.

A sigh escaped my lips as I tilted my head towards the night again, as endless starlight seared my eyes and bathed my skin. I breathed it in, savouring the calm as my claws retracted and the earth stilled again, time seemingly suspended around me. But my mind continued to race, my thoughts drawn to the barn, to what awaited within it.

What form would my revenge take?

A flicker of excitement dared to dance in my veins, tempered by ironclad calm.

Patience.

I had waited too long for this to rush now. Such a tactic had not worked in the past and was the reason I was here now. I could not risk war, and war is what I would have if I disobeyed my high king.

My revenge needed to be swift and silent.

And merciless.

To do that and not break the pact between my breed and the seelie, I needed to find a more subtle approach. Success must be assured before I made my move or the high king's retribution would be swift and merciless in return.

My seer had foreseen that silent vengeance could be mine, without consequence, as long as I possessed the key. Without the key, I would fail.

For decades, I had waited and watched, had tested the boundaries of the pact and learned patience, tethered to my kingdom and my sanity by her vision, awaiting the next one that would bring me the information I needed to secure my key.

Each night I had asked Neve what she had seen.

And each night she had told me the same thing.

My key would take the shape of a babe with an animal's heart.

It had not made sense until close to ten years ago when Neve had experienced a clearer vision.

It was a wolf with a human heart.

A shifter.

My eyes slipped shut and I drew in a breath, drawing in the

night and power with it. Strength to remain patient, to remain still and calm, in control as I neared my vengeance.

I had searched my kingdom, and then beyond its boundaries, and when Neve had a vision that the wolf was female, I had searched even harder. Every clue she had given me, I had used. Landscape. Buildings. Even faces. I had scoured fae towns and far-flung places, beginning to feel as if my vengeance would slip through my fingers forever.

Until that fateful day when she had awoken me with a roar that had shaken my castle.

Phantom cold sweat rolled down my spine beneath my onyx armour, my heart galloping as it had that morning when I had run to her, when she had told me the wolf would die if I did not act now. That I had to secure my future *now*. She had been pale, shaking, her eyes glazed as the vision held her captive, as she had frantically babbled what she had seen, details that had finally led me to this place.

I stalked towards the dark wooden barn, a wraith in the night, my senses on high alert, pinpointing the five males who had remained, and three others within the building. One heartbeat was more frantic than excited and I singled it out, unsure what to expect as I wrapped concealing shadows around me and entered the auction house.

The males gathered before me, huddled around a velvet-covered cage, obscuring it. Snarls and growls emanated from it, interspersed with flesh and bone striking iron. The scent of fear was strong in the room as I made my way to a vacant seat and I held my curiosity at bay as I casually relaxed into it, allowing my shadows to fall enough that others might see me.

But not the occupant of the iron cage.

The blond male who reeked of wolf glanced my way and then back again, a wary look crossing his face. He leaned back and to his left, and glanced at the other wolf, this one a larger, dark-haired male I supposed was meant to be intimidating.

I inspected my nails.

Neither male were a threat to me.

Little in this world was.

Magic rose within me, tendrils of it spreading outwards, leaping in jagged motions towards the cage, unseen by the uncouth males.

And met with a powerful ward.

I held the ringleader's gaze. He feared someone would snatch his prize and make off with it before they parted with their gold. The occupant of the cage rallied and attacked again, rattling it. Or he feared she might escape and he would meet with her fangs.

The spell also rendered her struggles useless.

Even I would need more time than she had to unravel the ward and break out of such an infernal cage.

Yet she continued to try, banging against the bars and snarling.

Admirable.

"Everyone, take your seats." The blond clapped his hands and the males broke apart and filtered away into the shadows, each taking a seat and leaving several empty between them.

The largest gap remained between myself and what appeared to be a vampire. At least I smelled blood on him. No trace of red in his eyes as he glanced at me several times, revealing his nerves.

I kept my expression bored as I studied my opponents, adding more details to my mental catalogue of them, discerning their breeds and strength, in case one of them decided not to take defeat lying down.

Spotlights fell on the cage, all very dramatic and apparently impressive to the eager males who leaned forwards in their seats. A murmur of anticipation ran through the room, but I remained where I was, still and calm, revealing an unaffected fae king who had seen this kind of thing countless times in my long life, even when it was new to me.

That mask almost slipped as someone pulled on the thick rope attached to the velvet cloth and it lifted to reveal my prize.

My blood thrummed as my eyes landed on the frantic little female and I found myself leaning forwards, pulled towards her as she bashed the cage with her fists and snarled, flashing fangs at the males groping her bare curves with their lustful eyes.

And when she lifted her head, chin tipping up in defiance...

By the Great Mother, the sight of her hit me like a punch in the chest.

This was no mere wolf shifter.

She was beyond beautiful, and had I not known her breed, I could easily have believed she was fae, with her long silver hair and unearthly blue eyes.

I could not tear my gaze from her, but I somehow managed to conceal my shock, carefully schooling my expression into one of indifference as my shadows kept her blind to me.

Her bare breasts swung as she pivoted on a male who had dared to stand and flashed her fangs, hatred burning in her eyes. Such ferocity. Such beauty. Such defiance even when she was on her knees, the cage too small to allow her to stand.

She roused my body and captured my attention as no other had before.

I hid my grimace as I eased back into my seat and lifted one leg to rest my ankle on my knee, concealing her effect on me so the other males would not see it.

Her vicious gaze snapped to me, as if she could see me through the cloak of shadows, the feel of her eyes on me a danger I had not been prepared to face. It threatened to rip at my control. I clamped down on my unruly desires, chaining them and shattering them, and coolly stared at her, revealing nothing to the males now watching me.

Not a shred of interest.

I was not here for what they were.

This female was not destined to warm my bed.

She was a tool, a key that would unlock my vengeance.

And that was all.

She continued to peer at me, the stillest she had been since I had entered the room, but that quiet fierceness remained, bewitching me. I had never imagined such a delicate creature could be so ferocious. So fae like. That glow in her eyes spoke of terrible thoughts.

Dark desires.

If I were to unlock her cage, I had no doubt that she would rip out the throat of the other wolf with her fangs and then she would turn on everyone else.

Even me.

"One hundred thousand." The possible-vampire raised his hand, gaining the attention of the ringleader of this auction, his bodyguard and the female in the cage.

A paltry sum for what this despicable wolf was selling—the virginity of such a charming creature.

"One fifty." This from the male who had kept his hood up, concealing his face. He carried the scent of magic.

"Two." The vampire apparently did not want to be outdone.

"Four hundred thousand." A third bidder made things interesting, gaining the attention of the other two and a sour look from both.

Was it not the done thing to double the bid so quickly?

I was not sure of the etiquette involved. I had imagined that the point was to win the bid, not play a game of chase.

The fourth male, this one definitely another shifter judging by his scent and the claws he was digging into the wooden arms of his chair, barked, "Five."

"Six." The fifth male glared at him. A demon. His horns grew, curling around from behind his pointed ears, a sign of aggression in his breed.

One to watch.

Demons were notoriously stubborn and did not like losing.

I knew that from experience.

"Seven fifty." The bloodsucker had found his voice again, much to the sickening glee of the ringleader wolf, who looked as if he might drool at any moment.

What poor breeding.

I checked my nails again, inspecting the rounded clear tips that concealed any hint of what I was, and sensed the ringleader staring my way. I lifted bored eyes to meet his. He wanted me to bid too. I would. When the time was right. Now was not the time. Things were only just getting interesting.

How much would they pay to secure the female?

"Eight." The demon looked ready to snap fangs at anyone who went higher and grinned at the little wolf in the cage, his gaze filled with hunger as if she was already his and he was already planning the ways he would take her.

The female snarled at him, flashing fangs as she bristled.

Perhaps it was the thought of breaking her that had so many of the males willing to pay so much for her.

"Nine," the vampire put in.

Just as the magic user said, "A million."

Everyone glared at him.

Except me. I was too busy watching the female as she stilled, as her skin paled and her striking eyes widened, as if the reality of her situation had just hit her and only now was she aware that this was happening. One of her own kind was selling her to slavering males with wicked intentions.

Her shock was fleeting, quickly morphing back into rage as the vampire countered, and the demon followed suit, and her price rose to close to one point five million dollars.

"One point nine." The vampire shirked all civility, jumping the price up by half a million, much to the irritation of two other males.

The ringleader looked to the three no longer bidding. All shook their heads.

"Two million," the demon growled.

The blond wolf male almost grinned, satisfaction flickering in his eyes as he lowered them to the female.

She spat in his direction.

"Two point two." The vampire would not be outdone.

"Two five." The demon proved him wrong.

I waited, watching the two males as they engaged in a silent battle. Would the vampire bid again?

His now-crimson gaze shifted to the cage and I could almost sense the moment he decided she was not worth the outlay.

Which was my signal.

I lazily raised my right hand, snaring everyone's attention, because the vampire and demon were not the only ones unwilling to let another win her.

"One million," I drawled, my bid met with laughter from some and a muttered comment from the demon that questioned my intelligence as the bid had already surpassed that figure, and calmly finished, "gold coins."

The room hushed.

Incredulous stares all aimed at me.

Even the female fell silent halfway through a particularly vicious series of growls and snarls.

"That has to be worth a hundred million dollars at least," the vampire said, his gaze questioning my sanity as much as the demon had questioned my intellect.

The magic user lifted a hand, and a skinny male dressed in tight-fitting black clothing appeared behind him.

The servant dutifully bent towards his master.

"Who is he? He was not on your list." Displeasure rang in the master's voice, threaded with an unspoken spell that had the servant twitching as he struggled to answer.

"I do not know. My deepest apologies for my failure, my grace." The servant was a spymaster then.

Perhaps I should have employed my own spymaster to investigate the auction and the attendees, but then it would have alerted my sister to my intentions and nothing good could have come from that.

The bodyguard showed something in his palm to the ring-leader. I presumed it revealed the dollar equivalent of my bid judging by his reaction.

"Sold!" The disgusting wolf's eyes lit up, so grossly eager to take my coin.

Perhaps I would kill him once I had secured my prize.

I lowered my gaze to that prize.

She sat in the centre of her cage, peering in my direction, squinting to see through the glare of the harsh spotlight, as if it would allow her gaze to pierce the shadows.

Fear radiated from her, but it was tinged with the curiosity that glimmered in her eyes as she tried to glimpse me.

And then the bodyguard hit her in the back with a feath-ered dart.

She flinched and her luminous eyes widened, edging towards her shoulder. Before she could even spy the dart, she swayed and slumped, hitting the ground hard, out cold.

I barely held back the snarl that rose up my throat, and the claws that wanted to punch from the tips of my fingers. The urge to let them out, to give in to the darkness and rip apart the male for treating her with so little respect, was strong.

I wanted him to bleed. To beg for mercy.

Just as I wanted to utterly destroy those males who dared to approach me as I stood, vilely offering coin in exchange for time with the wolf female once I had claimed my prize—her virginity.

I stared them all down, silencing them with only a look as I straightened to my full height. Impudent wretches.

I stalked to the cage, gaze fixed on the unconscious female in the centre of it, and summoned the chests I had prepared, pulling them to me through the void.

They slammed down with a rattle of coins between myself and the blond wolf as he thought to approach me, forming a wall between us and halting him in his tracks.

"If you're ever in the market for another, you know where to find me," he said, already flipping the lid of one wooden chest open to inspect his fortune.

"This one will suffice." I kept my tone emotionless and measured as I held his gaze and reached for the cage door.

The iron was cold beneath my touch, the ward fighting me as I reached into it, pouring my shadows down the corridors between each word of it, but it surrendered easily enough. I yanked the door open in one brutal movement, shattering the hinges and the lock, and tossed it away from me, savouring the startled gasp of the male wolf.

My shadows tore it to shreds and the wolf swallowed as he watched them destroy it before his gaze shakily met mine again.

I grinned, flashing my jagged fangs as my darker side rose to the fore. "But yes, I know where to find you."

I reached into the cage with clawed, black-tipped fingers.

And took what was now mine.

CHAPTER 4
SAPHIRA

Pain was the first thing I was aware of as the world slowly dawned on me again, the darkness receding in my mind but not in my heart. My wolf side bayed mournfully and instincts pulled at me to return to my fated mate, neither understanding that he had rejected me.

Not like the human part of me could.

The rage burning within that side of me didn't stop the pain from tearing into my soul, shredding it to pieces, or the crushing sorrow from threatening to devour me whole. I wallowed in it, drifting in the lightening night that enshrouded me, not ready to return to the world yet.

I wanted to remain here, far away from it all.

Far away from reality.

Nothing good awaited me on the other side of this soft darkness I clung to, too afraid to let it go and break to the surface. I wanted to stay here forever, where the pain was muted, because I knew when I woke, it would get worse.

So much worse.

I pined for the bastard who had crushed my heart and soul, and then sold me.

I fucking *pined* for him.

And it sickened me, angered me so much that the black smoke around me became tinged with crimson, with the colour of my rage as my instincts did a one-eighty, flipping around to despising Lucas as he deserved and making him want to pay. I wanted him to suffer just as he had sentenced me to suffer. I wanted to watch him beg and break as I had in that cage.

I had been so stupid. So blind.

The potential mate-bond had made me weak to Lucas and I had fallen in love with him, and all he'd had to do was smile and tell me I was beautiful and pay attention to me. It had all been an act.

He had only been acting how people had thought he should—his parents, our packs, the world. He had been pretending and I hadn't seen it. I had been blind to the truth, so eager to believe he meant every look and every word. So eager to have my fated mate and that foolish dream of a perfect future with him.

Through the endless night, I smelled a faint hint of storm, like snow or windswept mountains.

It transported me back to the cage, and for a moment, I thought I was back there, under that spotlight, exposed and vulnerable.

I knew that scent.

It had been there, muddled among the others, had caught my attention the second I had smelled it and I had tried to pinpoint who it was coming from, but then the auction had begun and it had all been a blur of terror and despair, and rage. So much rage.

I had never felt anything like it.

If someone had opened my cage, I would have launched from it to kill every person in that room.

And that shook me still.

It wasn't like me to want to harm anyone. In that moment, it had felt as if someone else had been inside me, in control, a person I didn't recognise. A person who had craved violence and bloodshed, and wouldn't have felt an ounce of regret in the aftermath.

I wasn't that person.

I wasn't.

I curled into myself, slowly realising that I was on my side on a scratchy surface, and things were jabbing at my bare flesh. Things that itched and pushed that comforting darkness further away from me, pulling me up towards the world I didn't want to face.

Together with distant voices.

I tugged the blanket over my shoulders, warding off the chill, and huddled into it, hoping I might disappear and whoever was coming wouldn't see me. Anger at Lucas morphed into anger at myself. I was stronger than this. If I had to face my *owner*, I would face him knowing where I was and all possible escape routes.

I cracked my gritty eyes open and a growl almost burst from my lips as fur rippled over my bare skin.

A cage.

I was in another cage.

I sat up, the swift action jarring and making my head spin. When my vision settled, I quickly scanned my new surroundings. Not quite a cage.

It was a prison cell.

Or maybe it was more of a dungeon.

Damp dark stone made up the wall behind me and pillars between the cells, together with the wall beyond the thick metal bars ahead of me. To my left and right, more bars divided the room into more cells. The one to my right seemed to veer around a corner in an L shape and was larger than mine, with another solid wall on the other side of it rather than bars.

Torches flickered and guttered on the wall of the corridor, the only source of light.

The bed beneath me was nothing more than a sack of hay.

Not quite the bed I had expected to find myself chained to upon waking.

I glanced at the cage again.

Maybe my owner was into darker things than I had imagined and this was some sort of twisted sex dungeon.

I pushed away from that thought, because I was already scared enough without throwing dark fantasies into my panicked mind. Instead of letting fear get the better of me, I studied the barred door, seeking a possible way to escape.

Not that I knew what I was looking for.

I didn't have much experience with cages and cells, or things beyond lighting campfires and healing and taking care of others.

That deep pining returned, but not for my bastard mate this time. My family. My pack. Did they know what had happened to me or was Lucas lying to them too, telling them I was devoted to my new pack and no longer wanted to see them?

Gods, the thought of my parents thinking I didn't want to see them again had a heavy weight settling on my chest as my eyes burned.

I needed to contact them, warn them somehow, because my fear also returned, and this time it took the shape of Lucas doing something to them, planning something for my pack. He might have lied to my face about his feelings, but he had never concealed his feelings about my pack. He had told me once that

I was the only reason the Hunt pack didn't slaughter my own. That I was their saving grace.

But now he had sold me into servitude.

Where did that leave my pack?

My throat closed at the thought they might be in danger, panic lighting my veins and urging me to take action, to do something.

What?

What could I do?

I didn't even know where I was, and I doubted my new owner was going to let me go, even if I asked nicely. They had plans for me too.

That panic threatened to turn into all-out fear and a meltdown of epic proportions, so I closed my eyes and drew down a deep breath, holding it for five seconds before slowly releasing it, trying to calm my shredded nerves. In. Out. Slow breaths. Calming breaths.

Harder than I imagined when voices travelled towards me, my sensitive ears picking up two sets of footsteps—one heavy and one lighter. A male and a female.

Not wanting them to know I was awake and sure I would be more vulnerable if they knew I was, I rolled onto my side on the scratchy hay bed, putting my back to the corridor, and did my best attempt at looking as if I was still unconscious, remaining perfectly still as the two sets of steps grew louder.

Controlling my heart was far harder than controlling my body as they stopped and I sensed their presence behind me, on the other side of the bars. I willed it to slow, to remain steady, trembling a little as I waited, unsure what was about to happen. Wolves weren't the only species with heightened hearing and I wasn't sure what kind of male had bought me. I hadn't been able to make him out at all during the auction.

"What have you done?" The female sounded not angry, or disgusted, but perhaps disappointed.

"What was necessary." That male voice was sword-sharp, cutting the thick, tense air, as commanding as I remembered it.

My new owner.

The female huffed and I felt her gaze on me, the weight of it heavy and immutable, before carefully chosen words reached my ears. "He will not forgive you for this."

Who? I almost said that aloud. Who wouldn't forgive this male for purchasing me?

"He will understand." Such confidence from the male.

The female didn't sound so sure, her tone taking on a hard edge as she bit out, "How *convenient* that he departed on business for you just yesterday and will not return for some time."

A smirk in the man's voice. "Yes, it was rather."

"You cannot leave her in that cell. It is not right. None of this is right. Are you sure this is necessary?" Whoever this female was, I already liked her. This male clearly outranked her, might even be her master, but she stood up to him, and was standing up for me, a stranger.

Maybe this all wouldn't be as terrible as I thought it would be. For the first time since Lucas had drugged and rejected me, I felt a small kernel of hope take root in my heart. This female sounded as if she was against whatever this male planned for me, and perhaps I could turn her into an ally, one that might keep me safe from him.

But hope could be a dangerous beast.

One I might be better off killing now in case it only savaged me later.

"It is necessary." His tone could have cut iron and stone. It was as hard and unyielding as both, his words almost a silent order to the female to let it go as he added, "Everything I do is necessary, or did you forget that?"

Tension simmered between them and I wanted to burrow deeper into the velvet blanket.

Anger radiated from the female, and I swore she wanted to snap at him, that she wanted to fight him, but then she calmly said in a resigned tone, "At least do not treat her like an enemy. She does not belong in a cell."

No response.

She sighed, as gentle as a summer breeze, and her voice softened further.

"This is wrong." Those words were met with silence that felt tighter—thicker—*heavier*. "Is she human?"

"No." His voice had grown colder, deeper, and more commanding. Sharper than a blade. Although I wasn't sure how that was possible.

"Return her to her world."

I braced, sure the female had pushed too far by issuing an order to this male and he would put her in her place, as a wolf male in a position of power would have.

My eyes widened a heartbeat later, when her order repeated in my mind, echoing there.

Return me to my world? Panic lanced me. Where was I if this wasn't my world?

"No." A male of few words, and not the retribution I had expected.

"Why is she here?"

"That is none of your concern." He was definitely her master, or at the least, her superior. He spoke like an alpha.

"None of my concern?" She did snap now. "I beg to differ. As your second in command—"

"A position you wish to keep?" he growled low, a cold threat and one that silenced the female for a full minute.

But then she muttered, "At least give her some clothes."

I had the feeling she either wanted this male to strip her of her position, or she knew his threat had been an idle one, something he wouldn't do no matter the circumstances. They were close then. Shared some kind of bond that made me pine for my parents, for Everlee and Chase and Morden.

The female huffed. "I do not know your plan, brother, but it would not kill you to make her more comfortable."

Brother.

They were siblings.

Silence, and then light boots on hard stone and the weight of his gaze on me, searing through the blanket to leave me feeling exposed as she moved away from us.

"See to it." His voice was darker than midnight as he issued that order.

The steps halted and then she responded.

A muttered, almost sarcastic, "Yes, my king."

I drew down a steadying breath as the sound of her steps drifted into the distance, the weight of his gaze on me unbearable, making me squirm and struggle to keep still.

The scent hit me again. A wild storm.

This male.

It was his scent, one that filled my lungs and some hollow spot inside me, speaking to me on a primal level, where my animal soul met my human heart.

He huffed, the sound beast-like, and snarled, "You can open your eyes now, little lamb. You are not fooling anyone."

I cracked my eyes open and rolled towards him. Only I couldn't see anyone. Just darkness on the other side of the bars, as if someone had snuffed out the torches. I held the blanket to my chest, and brushed my fingers over the soft material, and dread accompanied each stroke of them as it dawned on me. This was the blanket that had covered that terrible cage before Lucas had lifted it to reveal me to all those greedy, wretched eyes.

Eyes like the ones watching me now, drilling into me.

I wanted to throw it away from me, but doing so would expose me to this male.

So I clung to it instead, just as I clung to my courage.

I straightened my spine, refusing to let him see my fear as I clamped muscle down onto bone to stop myself from trembling. He hadn't cowed the female who had confronted him, and he wouldn't intimidate me.

"I'm not a lamb. I'm a wolf." My voice came out surprisingly strong, and a bit loud in the musty dungeon, as I bared my fangs at the shadows before me.

"You are a lamb in wolf's clothing. There is a difference, little lamb."

Weak.

He was calling me weak.

Bastard.

I growled low, keeping my fangs bared, despising how that word made me feel and how right he was. I was weak. Coddled. Nothing in my life had prepared me for not only being rejected by my fated mate but being thrust into this dark situation I now found myself in. The primal instincts of my wolf side warned I was going to have to fight if I wanted to live, and I was woefully underprepared in that department.

Female wolves didn't train.

We didn't fight.

"Where am I?" That question echoed as it bounced off the cold stone walls. Maybe if I knew where he had taken me, I could start planning my way out of this mess.

"The answer to that is simple." He paused and my breath halted as I waited, sure he had done it for dramatic effect. His deep voice rumbled through the darkness. "*Lucia.*"

The way he said that, drawing out that name, and the way

he stilled in the shadows, waiting for a reaction, told me I was somewhere I should fear.

But I was tired of being afraid. Too tired to care or participate in whatever game he was playing. I couldn't keep up with everything that had happened and deep inside me, my soul was howling, raging, grieving... still unable to believe my fated mate had betrayed me.

This male couldn't do anything worse to me than Lucas had in rejecting me.

I shrugged. "Never heard of it."

He scoffed. "So uneducated. I expected as much."

I scowled at the darkness before me. "So haughty. I expected as much—from a king."

He chuckled, but it was a deadly, hollow sound. "We shall see how long that tongue remains sharp when you realise where you are and what I am."

Not who. *What.*

He was of a species he believed I should fear then.

I tried not to let it shake me, but it was hard. This male had bought me. Paid handsomely for me. Playing a game with all the other bidders, letting them think they had won before he had casually thrown in excess of a hundred million dollars down on the table. For my virginity. And now I was in a cell at his mercy.

Not that he seemed to have much of that particular quality.

"Do you know of the faerie?" A direct question, laced with a hint of amusement that said he thought I didn't and was as uneducated as he expected.

I was too busy wrestling with how ominous that question was to snap at him, found myself stilling and holding the blanket closer to keep out the sudden chill as I peered into the shadows where he stood.

Shadows that seemed unnatural the more I looked at them.

I glanced left and right, and it was lighter in both directions, the torches still flickering brightly to warm the cold space.

It was only dark where he was.

"A little," I murmured and looked back at the gathered shadows, my pulse picking up as the full gravity of my situation hit me.

"Tell me what you know." A gentle prompt, but that amusement was still there, lending a cruel edge to his bass voice.

"That there's good and bad fae—and this is their world, isn't it? I'm in the faerie realm." Not my world. What that female had said came back to me and dread sank through me. I was in the land of the fae, as far from my home as I could get, and even if I did escape this dungeon and whatever building it belonged to, I had no way of getting back to my pack.

Unlike the fae, I couldn't teleport or use magic.

I was trapped here.

"Perhaps not so stupid after all." There was almost a grin in those words. "And tell me..." He moved, voice a low rumble as he stepped closer and the shadows fell away, revealing him at last. "Which do you think I am?"

I couldn't breathe.

He was darkness made flesh. A warrior from another time in black armour and with an onyx spiked crown curving across his forehead. Shadows streaked across his eyes, below pitch-dark eyebrows, making his silver irises as bright and sharp as moonlight ringed with night. The twin braids he wore tucked behind pointed ears tipped with silver metal and adorned with rings fell to one side as he canted his head, studying me.

Not me. My reaction.

Apparently, my shock was satisfactory, because his lips, a shade darker than his pale skin, curved at the corners.

But it wasn't fear that had me reeling.

No male should be beautiful, not when they wore an air of cruelty and darkness like those words had been made for him, but he was *breathtaking*.

Otherworldly.

Beautiful.

Every feature was perfection, from his chiselled jaw to his striking molten silver eyes, to his glossy black hair that reached his nape and had been pulled back into a half ponytail.

I struggled to find my voice, to muster some witty and scathing retort as he towered over me, elegance incarnate in his fine armour that hugged a body I felt sure would also be perfection.

His smirk widened.

Because he thought fear had me stunned into silence, not some sort of misplaced awe that bordered on a dangerous attraction that had my pulse quickening at just the sight of him.

I shut it down, because this was probably a trick, a lie. Fae could use glamours and magic, altering their appearance as they pleased. That was what the story books had taught me.

I would be a fool to fall for his charms, for his looks, just as I had been a fool to fall for Lucas's.

And I was sure if I did, if I lowered my guard for even a second around this fae king, my fate would be far worse than what my mate had done to me.

"A bad fae." I pushed the words out, part of me wanting him gone so I could breathe again and find some balance, his presence seeming to tilt my world even further off its axis.

"A very bad fae," he corrected and angled his head the other way, a predator sizing up his prey. "You would do well to remember that, little lamb. You are in my domain now."

The shadows that clung to his shoulders like a cloak rose again, swirling around him, and as he melted backwards into them, he left me with parting words that rattled me to my core.

"Entertain me and you might live to tell the tale."

CHAPTER 5
KAELERON

The moment I entered my study on the second floor of the castle, Jenavyr was barging through the ornate black wooden doors, her anger a living thing as she stormed towards me. Perhaps the moniker of 'the wrathful' fitted my sister better than myself.

Now I had two forthright and fierce females to contend with, a headache I did not need.

The little wolf had shown far too much spirit for a female locked in a cage in a world she did not know. Her courage had made me recklessly reveal myself in some spiteful attempt to rattle her, to shake her and make her fear.

It had only made her bolder.

Her gaze had been scalding as she had raked it over me, taking me in from head to toe, lingering on my face for far too long.

So I had shaken her harder.

And it had worked.

Better she remembered her position. I did not need her getting too comfortable. She was here for a purpose.

Perhaps it was better I remembered that too.

I stopped by the grand arched window on the right of the room that filled the space between two arched bookcases set into the black stone wall, my gaze on the formal gardens that lined the lake on the left side and the cliffs on the right. The waterfall that separated them, plunging into the bay below the cliffs, threw mist into the air that sparkled with hues of the aurora. I normally found this view calming. But not today.

My sister glared at my shoulders, silently ordering me to look at her.

I refused.

This vengeance was something we both needed, even if she would not admit it.

"Do not push me, Vyr." I remained with my back to her and clasped my hands behind me, my gaze drifting to the horizon, to the wide expanse of ocean beyond the jagged black mountains that edged the high lake.

If she did, my council would hear of it, and they would push me too, demanding I strip her of her rank for her insubordination. Something they were prone to do whenever she spoke out of turn. It was the last thing I wanted for her. I had trained her for a purpose, had fought for her to join my commanders so she would know how to fight and how to protect herself. I had wanted her to be strong.

What I had not wanted was this female who challenged me at every turn and had found her passion in life as a warrior.

It was not meant to be.

Another life awaited her.

She had forgotten that.

Perhaps we both had.

"You need to let her go, brother. Return her to her world. This is not right. This is not you." Jenavyr slammed the doors closed behind her with such force I was surprised the gold metal inlaid into the black wood in the form of trees and elkyn did not fall out.

"This is me." I turned on her, shadows swirling outwards with the motion to blot out the natural light. The candles and lamps guttered out, leaving only the motes of golden magic that danced and gathered near the vaulted wooden ceiling to illuminate us. I stared her down as anger rose within me, the pain of what had happened as raw within me as the night we had lost our parents. I growled, "Would you have me do nothing? Would you have me give up on our brother? Our blood?"

Vyr held her ground, almost masking her flinch but failing to mask the pain that glittered in her silver eyes a moment before she concealed it. She tilted her chin up and flicked her sleek black hair over her shoulder, defiance shining in her fierce gaze.

"Leave me, Vyr." I went to turn away from her, in no mood for arguing with her when I needed to figure out why Neve believed the little wolf was vital to my vengeance and what her role might be.

My sister proved just how stubborn she was as she stepped further into the room instead of marching her backside out of the door, the click of the heels of her black leather riding boots loud on the onyx marble floor.

"You tried to infiltrate the Summer Court many times, starting battles that always ended with you having to pull your forces back. Battles that almost got you killed. The high king had to intervene to stop you and I thought you were done with this... but here we are... with you doing something I truly thought you would never be capable of." She stalked towards me, passing the large black desk, not stopping until she was only inches from me and her anger buffeted me. She folded her arms across her chest, pulling the navy material of her long-sleeved blouse tight across her arms as she stared me down. "You *bought* another living creature. You paid for an innocent female who now believes you intend to use her body as you please. This is not you, Kael."

I shot her a warning look; one she did not heed.

Darkness writhed around me, my shadows reaching for her as my anger rose, as my blood pounded and her words echoed in my mind, the reproach in them cleaving great grooves into my calm veneer and provoking a response. I bared jagged teeth at her, something which would have made most in my court back down.

But not my sister.

It only made her bolder.

She stood her ground and bared fangs right back at me. "Our own high king went as far as creating new laws and forming an accord with the seelie high king to prevent you from going to war. You cannot cross into the Summer Court. If you do, the full force of Ereborne will come down on your head... and this court."

I growled at her for that one. She dared suggest I was placing my court in danger when all I had ever done was try to protect them?

"When you were young... I thought things would be different." Disappointment rang in her soft voice as she gazed at me, as if she was seeing that boy I had been when our parents had been wrenched from us and I had been thrust onto a throne, too young to keep hold of it and too naïve to know how to run a court. "But then you began plotting the demise of those who had ordered our parents' deaths, and then it was the destruction of the entire Summer Court you wanted, and it took both myself and Oberon to talk sense into you when you wanted to march over the border and invade that land on a crusade that would have ended in your death."

I bared my fangs again, despising her for reminding me of that day. "I should not have listened to either of you."

She scowled at me. "You do not believe that."

I did not.

She and Oberon had been right to stop me. Anyone who had come with me would have been either slaughtered by the Summer Court or executed by their own high king for treason. That day I had realised I needed to find a subtler way to carry out my revenge, and I had gone to the Forgotten Wastes to clear my head with a little slaughter.

And I had found a weakened, starving dragon.

And when I had touched her, she had seen the death of the seelie king of the Summer Court—not at my hands—and that there was an heir as wretched as him now vying for the throne.

Infighting in the Summer Court had stolen my vengeance from me, but there was still my brother to save, and a court to make pay.

"And let me remind you of the time you crossed the border through the tunnels in the Black Pass and broke into the Great Library of the Summer Court, seeking information on their strongholds. You were lucky you were not seen!" Jenavyr wisely stormed away from me across the gold-veined black marble floor, my shadows snatching at her heels.

If it had been anyone else speaking to me with such disrespect, I would have allowed my shadows to rip them to shreds, but I held them at bay, despite the dark urge to silence her and put her in her place.

"I was seeking a location where they might be holding our brother. I was careful. The ancient tunnels are not warded to the unseelie, so none of their breed would see me, and I expended great magic to shield myself and slip through the shadows. Any who might have sensed me were put to sleep."

A feat that had taken great restraint.

I should have killed them all.

Death was what they deserved.

"And how did that work out for you?" Jenavyr planted her hands on her black-leather-clad hips.

"I retrieved valuable books, records of their kings and bloodlines, and maps of their strongholds."

"And almost got yourself killed when you made the rash decision to check one of those fortresses without support!" she bit out, her eyes brightening as her skin paled, her darker side coming to the fore as anger got the better of her. "This obsession is unhealthy and dangerous, Kael. You no longer risk the Shadow Court, but the entire unseelie courts. If you break the accord—"

My shadows struck at the desk between us, cleaving long grooves in the wooden surface as they lashed at her but I pulled them back in time to stop them from reaching her.

She snapped her mouth shut, her shoulders going rigid.

For a moment, I feared she might continue the argument and risk my wrath, but then she pivoted and stormed away from me, heading for the door.

She yanked it open with enough force that the hinges creaked and barked over her shoulder, "I am not speaking with you until you do the right thing!"

"I am trying to do the right thing!" I barked right back at her, patience wearing thin and close to snapping as memories tore at me, as that night roared up on me and I could hear their screams of pain, could smell their fear, and their blood. "Can you imagine the torment our brother might have suffered in the decades we have been apart? What the wretched seelie might be doing to him right this moment?"

Jenavyr turned on me, hurt flaring in her damp silver eyes, and bit out, "Our brother is dead. He is *dead*, Kael. You are trying to save a ghost and hurting everyone in the process, including yourself. Can you not see that?"

I curled my fingers into tight fists at my side, my emerging claws cutting into my palms as I reined in my shadows, and quietly, as calmly as I could manage, ground out, "He is alive. I can feel it."

Bitterness coated her voice as she glared at me. "You only feel what you want to feel. What will justify this reckless hunger for war. You only feel what will justify the cold, callous male you have become. Maybe both of my brothers died that day—"

"*Jenavyr*." Her name was soft on my lips.

She locked up tight, regret flashing across her face, and opened her mouth, looking as if she might apologise.

Because she knew the things I had done for her sake and that of my people.

She knew the price I had paid to keep them safe.

Her shoulders sagged, and her features softened, that look cutting me deeper than her vicious words had because I could see the despair that lived in her heart in it, the hope she clung to and the pain that haunted her too. We had both paid too steep a price.

"Let the wolf go," she whispered, gaze imploring me to listen this time. "This is not like you. This is... this is too much, Kael. Believing in visions and buying innocent people. I do not like where this is heading. I do not like what is happening to you. I do not like that I am finding it harder to recognise the brother I once knew in you."

"Enough!" I slammed my hand down on the desk, the force of the blow cracking it in half, and shadows erupted from me, filling the room and chilling the air, striking at everything and obliterating it.

Only a small space around her remained untouched.

Because no matter how hard she pushed me, how deeply she angered me, I would never—*never*—harm her.

"Do you remember what happened the last time a gentle king sat on the throne of the Shadow Court?" I straightened, shadows writhing around me as they slowly receded, forcing myself to look at my sister as she struggled to remain still and standing tall. The tremble in her fingertips she could not quite control tore at me, had my rage turning inwards, towards myself for losing control, for frightening my beloved sister.

My blood.

She averted her gaze.

Afraid to look at me.

Shredding what little remained of my soul.

Regret swept through me, because it was not like Vyr to withdraw from me.

She had understood once, long ago, when the throne had become mine that bloody night and in the years that followed it. She had understood that I could not be weak. I could not be kind. A king did not remain in control of a court by being a friend to his people. He needed to rule it. He needed to keep everyone in line.

He needed to be firm.

Unyielding.

Our father had tried to rule with gentleness, with kindness, and it had gotten him killed.

Yet apparently I had not quite destroyed all gentleness or kindness I had once possessed because I still lined up an apology.

But she turned on me, darkness branching outwards from her bright silver eyes.

"How can I forget when you drag it behind you, chained to it, as if your sole purpose is to carry the weight of it like a burden for all eternity... When you are obsessed with chasing ghosts. Our brother. The seelie who killed our parents. They are all dead, Kael." Tears glistened in her eyes, born of pain that chilled one part of her even as rage made the other burn hotter than the fires of the Forge. Her sharpened teeth flashed between her lips as she hurled the words at me. "How can I ever forget what happened and move past it when you constantly punish yourself for what happened when it was not your fault?"

She disappeared in glittering black smoke.

I stood there, as still as the night sky, because every word had hit its mark far more accurately than mine ever could, lodging deep into my heart.

This burden *was* mine to carry.

She just did not know it.

I turned from the scattered remains of my furniture, towards the window and the world beyond, slowly clawing back control over my darker nature. Shadows twined around my hands, threading through my fingers, and I focused on them, soothing them as I let them soothe me too, seeking comfort in the darkness.

One day I would tell her.

Once this was all done.

Then, we would have a reckoning.

I turned my mind to the wolf in the dungeon, to the things Neve had told me, using them as a distraction as I continued to toy with the shadows and struggled to let the rage and anger Vyr had provoked in me fall away. Thoughts of my brother kept it strong, slipping in whenever my guard was down, flashing images that haunted my sleep.

My older brother, broken and bleeding, at the mercy of the seelie.

Jagged shadows clawed at the stone walls, hungry to sink into those responsible.

He was not dead. I knew it. But he would be better off that way.

The seelie were as cruel as my kind, and took pleasure from harming my breed. The things they might have done to him in the decades since they had snatched him from the castle in Belkarthen.

I did not want to contemplate them.

I pulled the silver-haired wolf into my mind instead, attempting to banish my dark thoughts, unsure whether it was her image or my vengeance I was using to distract me from them. A growl curled from my lips. It was my vengeance. She was the key to it, and that was all the delicate little wolf would ever be.

Neve had called her vital to the future I desired—and the only thing in this world I desired was Summer Court blood coating my claws.

The wolf was a tool to be used.

A weapon I would wield to carve out my vengeance.

Nothing more.

CHAPTER 6
SAPHIRA

Rather than what I had imagined would be revealing clothing, I was given leather pants and a cream blouse—almost human clothing, albeit a little antiquated in their style—that covered me entirely. I ran my fingers over the supple burnished black leather, taking comfort from being covered after feeling so exposed.

I felt safer.

Protected even.

Despite the fact the fae around me, even the servant who had delivered the bundle of clothing to my cell, were strong enough to rip the clothes right off me if they wanted.

"You think too loudly."

I started at the female voice, not one I recognised, and my head whipped towards the cell to my right.

A huddled kneeling figure emerged from the shadows, peeking out from behind the corner in the L shaped cell that I had decided looked as if someone had made it larger, removing two of the barred walls. Holes in the heavy, worn stone floor and the ceiling matched the spacing of the bars that separated me from the newcomer.

She blinked large deep amber eyes at me, the gold around her pupils shimmering as if fire burned inside her, her look inquisitive as she took my measure. And I took hers. She was pretty, delicate almost. Like a doll with her clean porcelain skin and braided gold hair.

I wasn't sure of her species, but I knew she wasn't human. Perhaps fae. I hadn't sensed her or smelled her before she had made her presence known, and even now I couldn't detect her. It was as if she wasn't there.

Concealed by magic?

Maybe she was a witch.

She didn't resemble the dark fae king.

Her ears were rounded and there was a warmth to her that beckoned me, as if she wasn't a danger in this dark and wicked world where I had found myself. Another potential ally. I decided to befriend her and perhaps broaden my limited knowledge of this world at the same time.

It certainly beat being alone in the dungeon.

I shuffled towards the bars between us, shifting my hay bed with me so I wouldn't have to sit on the chilly stone floor, and the female eased back into the shadows, almost disappearing behind the walls.

"Wait," I said, desperate for her to stay. If I couldn't see her, I wouldn't know she was there, and I would be alone again.

I didn't want to be alone.

Wolves weren't made to lead solitary lives, and I had been raised in a pack, surrounded by others. I had thought my captivity would be the thing that broke me, but I was beginning to suspect it would be the loneliness.

She edged forwards again, those strange eyes curious as she waited.

How could I tell her that I needed a friend in this land of monsters?

"They are not monsters." The female moved further into the open, her pretty face blank as she stated that fact as if it was undisputable.

I was more hung up on the fact she could either read my mind or my thoughts were that obvious and written all over my face. Maybe it had been my desperation that had clued her into my dire thoughts and fears.

She inched closer to me, and I noticed she wore a dark red dress that reached her ankles and her wrists and was fitted to her torso, looking about as medieval as my own outfit. It was clean, as if she had changed into it recently, but that knowing look in her eyes said she had been here some time. Was at home here in this dungeon.

"Despite your ordeal, you are safe from the real monster here. The young wolf will never reach you."

I startled, flinching back at her words. "How do you know so much about me?"

She tilted her head up, peering at the ceiling, as if seeing straight through it. "Anger rattles the old bones of this castle. She pushes him too hard."

"Who? The king? He deserves to be pushed." The last few words came out more bitter than I had expected and I froze up when the female angled her head towards me and clucked her tongue.

"Speak like that and discover why they call him 'the wrathful'."

"He's a monster." I didn't need to know him well to know that about him.

Now that the drug had worn off, I was beginning to remember things about the night of the auction. The darkness I had felt when in that cage. The way his presence alone had silenced the other men. I might not have been able to see through his shadows, but I had felt his strength, and could feel it even now.

I could feel his darkness just as the female had said—in the stones of this castle.

She shook her head. "He is not the monster. Not one to fear."

I scoffed, doubting that. "Are you here to warm his bed too?"

Her amber eyes widened, and then she did something that shocked me.

She threw her head back and laughed.

Laughed so hard that she had to fight for breath and the sound echoed and bounced around the dungeon, out of place in such a dreary location.

I could only stare at her as she struggled to regain control of herself.

"Good gods, no." She wiped a tear from her eyes and gave one last chuckle, nailing home that feeling she thought the suggestion was ludicrous. "I am not a concubine, and he would not wish me to be one. I serve King Kaeleron the Wrathful in another way."

King Kaeleron the Wrathful.

Delightful.

I had craved adventure, but this was too much. Captive of a fae king who had earned himself a title straight out of a nightmare.

"And you are?" I had the feeling she already knew my name, but I wanted to be polite, so I added, "I'm Saphira."

"Neve." The woman shuffled closer, and that was when I noticed just how fine her dress was, glittering with gold thread laced with crystals, and that she was using her finger as a bookmark in a leatherbound hardback that looked new. "I serve as King Kaeleron's seer."

"And he keeps you in a prison cell. How lovely of him." I was starting to suspect I was destined for his bed and this was to be my own personal quarters. Whenever he was bored of me, he would toss me back into this hole. I pushed the thought of what was to come from my mind and focused back on Neve, using her as a distraction I badly needed. "Are you a witch?"

It had been a magic user who had foreseen that I would be Lucas's mate, scrying the future for us. She could have told us he would reject and condemn me to a miserable life. I might not have fallen for him and might have denied all my instincts and my parents to strike out into the world in search of adventure.

Neve stared at me, expression blank as she said, "I am a shifter, much like you... but not like you."

I could do without the riddles. I was tired and my head was starting to ache, and my stomach had been rumbling for the last thirty minutes. Neve looked in good health, so hopefully someone would remember to feed me too at some point.

"Not a wolf," she said, as if I was as stupid as the fae king believed and couldn't work that out for myself. She cheerfully tacked on, "A dragon."

"A dragon shifter." I might have gawped at her a little. "Of course. If the faerie realm is real, then why not dragons too?"

While I was still taking that in, Neve gracefully stood and went around the corner of her cell, and returned carrying a heavy upholstered wooden chair in one hand as if it weighed as little as a twig. She set it down near the bars, sat down, rested her book on her lap and folded her hands over it.

Looking for all the world like the teachers back in my pack had when I had been a pup, eager for story time at the end of the school day.

"I will tell you of this world... for a price." She smiled widely, her gaze going glazed as it lowered to my breasts.

"Not you too." I clutched my blouse over my heart, and felt like an idiot as my fingers brushed cool, hard metal.

"It is a pretty thing," Neve cooed, swaying a little as she continued to stare at the pendant still hanging around my neck.

The only thing Lucas had left me with.

Another cruelty from him, the male who was supposed to be devoted to me, his fated one.

He had taken my precious bracelet and left me with this trinket he had given me—a token of his devotion and love.

I scoffed as I took hold of it and yanked on it, snapping the chain, and tossed it to Neve. "Take it. I don't need it anymore. In fact, if you could burn it with fire, I'd really appreciate it. I want it destroyed."

She gasped, horror flashing across her delicate features, and snatched the necklace up, tucking it against her chest as if to protect it from my wrath. "It does not deserve such treatment. Save it for the one who betrayed you. Take not your vengeance upon this precious item, but upon the one responsible for your pain."

Vengeance.

That word lingered in my mind, echoing there, tempting me even as Neve slipped the necklace into the pocket of her dress and patted her book, apparently satisfied with her payment.

"I do not have long, so I will need to fill in the details later, when we are alone again." Neve smiled almost fondly at me, as if we were already best friends and having a pleasant conversation over coffee rather than through the bars of a cell in a dank dungeon. I was starting to suspect her captivity had worn away some of her sanity, and maybe that was the reason she thought the king wasn't a monster to be feared and I wasn't in any danger.

"There is a world beyond these bars, Saphira. A world far different from your own, filled with things you could not conjure into your imagination if you tried. You have fallen down the rabbit hole, little one. This nightmarish world of courts, of light and dark, play dangerous games with each other, and if you are not wise, not willing to still yourself and listen to the whispers of the Great Mother through the sighing trees and the crashing waves, to open your eyes and see without the opinion you cast in iron the moment you woke colouring your vision, you will not last long nor will you find a path to a future far beyond your dreaming."

She leaned closer, and hissed.

"Look between the cracks."

More riddles.

"Between what cracks?" I stilled as the hairs on my nape rose.

Chilling darkness swept along the corridor and then it receded and he was there, a towering wall of graceful wickedness.

His sensual lips curved into a parody of a smile, practiced to perfection, with no warm emotion behind it, only a dark brand of amusement. "Little lamb."

I stood on trembling legs, denying him the pleasure of looming over me and making me feel small.

Weak.

Although, the son of a bitch had to be bordering on seven foot tall, because my eye level was the broad expanse of his chest. I wasn't the only one who had been given a change of clothes. Rather than the black armour he had been clad in when we had met, he wore a fitted black tunic decorated with silver thread that hugged his honed physique, soft black leather trousers, and knee-high boots.

"King Kaeleron the Wrathful." I mocked him with a curtsy.

He slid an unimpressed look at my neighbour.

Neve just gave him a blank look in return, completely unruffled by his glare, as if she didn't fear his wrath, and started reading her book, as if he wasn't there.

Either the dragon was crazy, or she had no reason to fear the fae king.

His power wrapped around me, dark and crushing, making my wolf side shrink back, but I still felt nothing from Neve. Was she stronger than Kaeleron?

The fae king swept his right arm around with a flourish and a silver tray appeared on his upturned palm, filled with a grey metal pitcher and cup and a plate of what looked suspiciously normal food.

What a neat trick. I might have been impressed if the sharp tang of magic hadn't hit me and his power hadn't increased to the point of it pressing down on my bones.

I grimaced.

"It is not poisoned." He eyed the food and then me.

"Wouldn't matter if it was since I'm being squashed like a bug and will likely be a splatter on the floor any moment now," I bit out from between clenched teeth and braced myself, upper body slowly inching forwards towards my buckling knees despite my effort to remain upright.

He arched a fine black eyebrow at me.

"Your majesty is not taking into account that the little wolf is delicate." Neve didn't even look up from her book as she flipped a page.

Great. Now Neve thought I was weak too.

Both of his eyebrows hiked up.

And then the weight of his presence lifted, as if he pulled all that terrible power into himself, and I could breathe again.

I drew down great gulps of air into my aching lungs and

sagged a little, bracing my hands against my trembling legs as I slowly recovered my strength.

He placed the tray down and toed it towards me. "Eat."

I pulled a face at the meat and vegetables laced with a thick gravy. "It might be poisoned."

"I said it was not poisoned."

I was aware of that, and it was the reason I had said it, so I could see that irritated flash in his silver eyes and for a brief moment feel I had some power in this arrangement even if it was only the power to annoy him.

"That sounds like something someone who poisoned my food and wanted me to eat it would say." I smiled brightly up at him.

"I have no desire to kill you right now."

Right now.

"Well, that's comforting." I toed the tray right back to him. "Not poisoned then. Drugged, so you can get what you paid for."

Rather than his face darkening with delicious irritation, he smirked.

And it was salacious.

And far too cocky.

"If I wanted that, little lamb, I would not need to resort to drugging you."

I wasn't sure what he meant by that. Did he mean he would simply overpower me, which he could easily do, or something that felt far more unsettling and dangerous?

Like seducing me into wanting him.

I wanted to say I wouldn't fall for it, that I could never want this male, but my pulse picked up as he stood mere inches from me, his dark presence wrapped around me and that scent of wild winter storm teasing me as those stunning silver eyes locked with mine, holding me immobile. That tug I had felt towards him when I had first set eyes on him returned, pulling me closer despite my fears, making my gaze chart his handsome face and wicked smile, and more.

And my traitorous body responded to him, heat coursing through my veins to pool low in my belly.

My eyes drifted to the silver-covered pointed tips of his ears, and I wondered if beneath those adornments they were actually pointed. I wanted to brush my finger along one to feel the cool metal and then gently ease it away from his flesh to reveal it to my eyes.

I had lifted my hand before I caught myself, locking it around the bars of my cage instead and gripping it tightly as I slammed the gates on my unruly feelings shut and pulled back control of myself.

He blinked, shattering whatever spell I had fallen under, and his gaze lowered to his boots, his scowl returning.

Had he felt that pull between us too?

I wasn't sure and I didn't want to know the answer to that question. Of course, he had to find me attractive to a degree because he had bought me, or he found one aspect of me attractive. Maybe he just preferred virgins and once he had taken that from me, he would grow bored of me, or worse—change his mind and hire me out to those other males. As the darkness of the drug had devoured me in that cage, I had heard them appealing to him, offering money in exchange for time with me once he had claimed my virginity. I hadn't been awake to hear his response.

He sank to his haunches, used the fork to stab a chunk of meat, and ate it, surprising me.

His eyes narrowed on me. "I demand to know your thoughts."

"You eat food… like me." Which sounded ridiculous now I said it aloud.

That eyebrow lifted again. "What did you expect me to eat?"

I shrugged, unsure now and feeling awkward, and a smidgen of stupid, as I weakly offered, "Blood?"

He laughed, but there was no humour in it. It was a cold, steel-sharp sound that rang through the dungeon, and where Neve's laugh had warmed the chilly space, his only made it feel more frigid.

And then he was deadly serious as he stared at me, his gaze cutting, and said, "My kind are not monsters... nor vampires."

"Could have fooled me on the monster part." I knew I was pushing my luck when Neve looked at me, that warning back in her amber eyes.

Push him and find out why they called him 'the wrathful'.

Sense said to dial it back, to apologise or at least back down, but I was hungry and tired, and hurting. That part of myself I was growing to hate still howled for Lucas, refusing to accept what he had done, and I wished I could take a dagger and cut out my soul.

"Eat. I need you strong if you are to be of use to me," he growled, silver eyes flashing.

I didn't particularly feel inclined to eat when he wanted me strong so I was useful to him. I would sooner starve myself if it meant I avoided my inevitable fate and his bed.

But then he slid a black look at Neve.

And demanded.

"You are sure she is necessary?"

Neve inclined her head. "To tread this path, you must not tread it alone."

He huffed, sounding like a beast, and regarded me, gaze cold and calculating as it drilled into me. "Risking my court is sounding more appealing every moment I spend in the company of this wolf."

"Why am I necessary? What path? Don't tell me you're looking for a virgin sacrifice, because I am not onboard with that." I snapped my mouth shut when his eyes narrowed and he looked as if he might flay me alive if I uttered another word.

"Vengeance tastes delicious," murmured Neve, her gaze glassy and fixed on the ceiling.

Kaeleron turned his frown on her.

Vengeance.

It sounded delicious to me.

That buried, dark part of me latched onto that word with a fervour I never knew I possessed. I clung to it, to the delicious fantasy building in my mind, a hunger so fierce it consumed me and bent my desire to take a dagger to my chest to carve out my soul to rid myself of the pain of Lucas rejecting me towards a terrible, tempting need to turn that dagger on him instead.

If he was dead, I would be free of this pain.

"The little lamb bleeds darkness," Kaeleron murmured, curiosity ringing in his deep voice, the sound of it pulling me further into that wicked fantasy. His gaze was heavy on me, that shadowy power curling around me, invading my every pore, building that fantasy in my mind, as if he had power over it and me. His breath fanned my face as he whispered, "Do you crave vengeance on the wolf, little one?"

My breath hitched.

By the gods, did I.

I craved it with all my being, was near mad with a need of it, lost in the awakening of this side of myself I never knew existed, one that responded so sweetly to the dark fae king before me and his gentle coaxing.

"What if you could have it?" His power brushed my limbs, making me tremble. "What if it was yours to take? Would you take it, no matter the cost?"

I was ready to nod, so eager for it, but no matter the cost?

"No," I whispered, the fires of my blood cooling in an instant as my mind filled with all the things I could lose. I shook my head and focused on the fae king, catching the flicker of disappointment in his eyes before his cold mask descended once again. "Some things are not worth risking."

"Wise words," Neve said, earning a vicious scowl from him too. "Some things *are* not worth risking, my king."

He looked ready to devour us both, shadows caressing his shoulders and black hair, darkness radiating from him to press against me as I stood my ground.

I needed to learn to hold my tongue around him, but it had been impossible. The thought that he might want vengeance too, that he burned with the same fire as I did, had me wanting to press him more on the subject, to make him help me.

"Eat." He shoved the food towards me again, spilling some of the water in the pitcher. "I will not order you to do so again. Disobey me and you will be punished."

I bit my tongue as he pivoted away from me, but it didn't stop the words from escaping. "You're sounding more like a monster with each passing second."

He turned on me, shadows dancing around him, his silver eyes as bright as the moon but as cold as the stars.

My body locked up tight as he stepped right up to the bars, as he reached through them and seized my throat in a grip that was both hard and soft, rough and sensuous, and a little alarming.

"A *monster*. I am no more a monster than you, little lamb." His thumb pressed to the underside of my chin, forcing my head up, and our gazes collided. "The unseelie feast, fight and fuck very much the same as your breed. In fact, we do one of those things better than those in your world. I will let you decide which."

I got stuck on the word 'fuck' and how his regal accent only made it sound dirtier, more wicked, and I couldn't help wondering which one he believed the fae did better.

My cheeks burned up as my mind supplied that word again.

Fuck.

His smirk was pure dark amusement as he turned from me and disappeared into the shadows, his parting words lingering in the air between us to torment me.

"If you wish to find out, you only need to ask."

CHAPTER 7
KAELERON

Four days had passed since I had brought the wolf to the Shadow Court and I was still no closer to deciphering her role in my vengeance. The day after the wolf's arrival, I had summoned my sister to speak with her about it, and rather than answer my call, Jenavyr had immediately left to take her legion to the west to prepare for the Beltane celebrations in that region.

Each day, servants had delivered meals to the wolf, and each day she ate barely a mouthful before calling the servant back and telling them to take it away. I was not sure whether she was starving herself, or striving to make a point about refusing to eat any significant quantity of it in case it was drugged.

My boots were loud on the pale flagstones as I crossed the garden, heading for the edge of the patio where it met the cliff rather than my usual route towards the lake. Stretching my legs had turned to mulling over what use the wolf might be to me, and that had slowly devolved into facing a truth I had been avoiding.

I could not keep the wolf caged.

Jenavyr was right about that, even when the shifter female was safest down in the dungeon, close to Neve and the wards that protected her. Neve had inspected every inch of my castle when I had brought her here from the Forgotten Wastes, and had made her nest in the dungeon, declaring the ancient stone of the mountain that formed the foundations of the castle and walls of my dungeon was the safest place for her, a conduit for magic powerful enough to keep her hidden.

Releasing the wolf would be dangerous, but if it were to happen, I would put restrictions in place and guards at her back to watch her and report back to me. It might be worth the irritation of her presence if spending time with her outside the confines of the dungeon would help me discover her purpose.

While also silencing Jenavyr.

I needed my sister as my ally, not my enemy. Vyr's stubborn streak and disobedience had opened her to comments from my council once again. There were already murmurings, whispers circulating about removing her from her post. I could not afford to let her carry on like this. If she did, I would have to punish her.

Or slaughter those in the council who had spoken out against her.

To avoid that, I would consider what she had asked of me.

But first I would consult with the one who had spent the most time with the wolf—the female responsible for her presence in my court.

I teleported to the dungeons, wrapping myself in shadows and stepping out of them closest to Neve's cell.

My gaze instantly darted to the cell beside hers, to the prone form of the silver-haired female, tucked beneath a dark silver blanket that had once belonged to Neve. She slumbered, her face peaceful and soft. No feigned sleep this time. She was deep asleep.

An unnatural sleep.

Neve's presence pressed against mine through the wards that protected her home, a bare whisper of her power as she came to a halt beside me on the other side of the bars.

"Is this your doing?" I tried to pull my gaze from the slumbering wolf, but she was stronger than my will, keeping my eyes rooted to her.

"Saphira is exhausted, and so I used a little magic to give her a push."

My gaze snapped to Neve, the spell shattered, and I frowned at her. "Saphira?"

The little wolf was called Saphira.

Neve caught my look, her amber eyes bright and clear today rather than clouded from fatigue born of her visions, and nodded. "Yes. Saphira. A pretty name, is it not?"

I hiked my shoulders. "No prettier than yours."

She chuckled, but then sobered, her gaze challenging as she came to face me, Saphira forgotten. "I must side with Jenavyr on this one. Keeping the wolf caged will not help you with your vengeance."

Vengeance. That word had cast a spell upon the little wolf. Lust for violence had shone inside her, so dazzling that it had been irresistible, had drawn me to her and bewitched me. It had spoken to something deep within me, just as I felt it had spoken to something deep within her, forming a strange bond between us for a heartbeat of time.

I stared at the wolf. "Have you seen that in a vision?"

Neve shook her head, her fall of golden hair caressing her slight shoulders in tumbling waves today. "No. It is simply common sense. You need this female to help you, and to trust you. She will do neither of those things while she is a prisoner."

"I take it you are also responsible for her new luxuries?" I eyed the blanket, and then the one that lay discarded in the corner, almost pushed into the empty cell next door.

"She despises it, and when I learned of the reason, I offered her one of my own blankets. I have enough to spare... and really, my king, you thought it adequate to leave her with that trinket of her past?"

"A blanket is a blanket. It was better than leaving her naked. I am sure she did not mind it that much."

The look on Neve's face as she glanced at the wolf told me the female had minded it, had possibly even been upset by its presence. I was not sure I would ever understand the wolf if that was the case. It was better to have some modest form of covering and warmth rather than freeze to death, was it not? The blanket had been adequate, whether the wolf or Neve believed it or not.

"I will take your advice about her containment under consideration." I went to leave now that I had a clearer bearing and decisions to make about releasing the wolf, but Neve caught hold of my arm.

"Kaeleron. She is in pain." Neve looked from me to Saphira as the wolf twitched and moaned, her sleep not as settled or deep as I had believed.

"How do you know that? Did the wolf tell you?" I studied that wolf now, watching her more closely, reaching out with my power to wrap her in tendrils of shadows that would allow me to sense more from her. I felt no pain, but her sleep was troubled, darkness clouding her mind that seeped from her and tangled with my shadows.

Neve slowly shook her head again. "No. But her soul does... Like calls to like. I know a soul in pain when I see it."

Pain.

I sought it, pressing deeper into my shadows, using magic to heighten my senses enough that I caught a glimmer of it, the barest whisper of her feelings.

It was deep and dark, as cold and jagged as a blade as it twined with my power, but it was hot and violent too, as if two kinds of pain were tearing her in different directions. Strong despite the fragile connection between us. If I could feel the full wrath of it, it would be devastating, a storm of emotion that would batter and break even the strongest soul.

"She has lost much." Neve looked at me again, her grip on my arm tightening as her voice softened. "Do not think to take more from her."

I snatched my arm back and glowered at her, anger curling hot in my veins as I pulled my shadows away from the wolf before they could snap at her by accident in response to my rage. "Do I have to tell you that I am not a monster now?"

Neve held her ground, her expression unapologetic. "This is not like you."

My shadows lashed at the boundaries of her cage and she was fortunate that the ward that concealed and protected her prevented even them from reaching her.

I growled, "You are beginning to sound like Jenavyr. She will be punished for her insubordination by training new troops with Riordan. I will need to think of a fitting punishment for you. Would you like me to see you returned to the Wastes?"

She stiffened and paled, genuine fear flooding her eyes and dulling the fire in her irises.

Regret punched me deep in the chest.

"I am sorry. I would not do such a thing." Because it would be the death of her. I pinched the bridge of my nose, a headache building there as I withdrew a step. "I am tired."

Neve whispered, "You have been tired for a long time."

"I have not." My denial was weak, breaking easily under the knowing look that Neve gave me. I looked at the wolf rather than her now, unwilling to let her see how easily she had seen through me and how tired I truly was. I had no time to be tired. I could rest when it was done. "I will not take more than what the wolf will give me willingly."

Her glare scalded the side of my face. "That is not good enough."

"What is her purpose?" A change of subject seemed like the most appropriate choice given the darkness that emanated from Neve. It provoked the darkness within me, the shadowy part of me that wanted to toy with this wolf, to push her and delight in how she pushed back. "If you could tell me that, I would not need to discover it through my own means."

"I still do not know, but I seek visions whenever I am strong enough." A sigh escaped Neve and I could sense her irritation and sorrow, her desperation to help me and despair that she was failing as a seer.

Part of her still believed that I would turn her loose and take away my protection if she could no longer complete that work for me. Despite her fears, I was not a monster. Or at least, not that much of one. I would never subject her to the terror she had felt before I had met her, to the daily struggle to survive that had seen her skulking from cave to cave in the Wastes to the north of the Shadow Court, hiding from the beast that hunted her.

She was part of my family now.

The grace I had shown her, I had failed to show the wolf.

"It will reveal itself in time." Neve moved to the bars that kept her from Saphira and gazed at her slumbering form, a distant but warm look in her eyes, one I had not seen in a long time. Neve liked the female. I was not sure any good could come of that, because the dragon was fiercely protective of those she cared about, even me. She sighed, her fine eyebrows furrowing. "It will reveal itself in time, if you keep the wolf close."

Keep her close.

I stared at Saphira, so innocent in her sleep, the words of those men clanging in my ears. One of her kind had auctioned her virginity. She was as innocent as she appeared.

Innocent and beautiful.

"I do not like that look," Neve murmured.

"Your order was to keep the wolf close to me." I stalked towards the female's cell and halted before it, my eyes locked on her. "And that is what I shall do."

"What is it you plan?" Neve sounded concerned, and ready to fight me. So protective of the little wolf already. The female must have worked her charms on my dragon, luring her over to her side, attempting to pull her away from me.

"I plan to take what is mine. I paid for a servant—for entertainment. That is what Saphira will give me."

My mind whirled, a plan forming as I studied the sleeping shifter, sensing that dark seed that was growing within her. While I waited for Neve to have a clearer vision of Saphira's role in my vengeance, I would attempt to discover it by myself, by spending time with the female.

I would enjoy my time with her until her usefulness was revealed and my revenge was done.

"I will offer her a choice."

I grinned as I sank into the shadows, wrapping night and starlight around me, eager to set my plan in motion.

"Rot in this cell... or earn her freedom."

CHAPTER 8
SAPHIRA

Neve had gone awfully quiet.

Since I had awoken from strange nightmares of running in my wolf form through a darkened wood where trees glowed with violet veins that ran down their bark and their blooms glittered like stars, she had refused to come around the corner to where I could see her.

Either that, or she had been taken away.

With whatever magic that made it impossible for me to sense her in place, I couldn't really tell.

Was I alone?

"Neve?" I tried again, because I needed to ask her something, and the longer I went without an answer, the more my imagination ran riot and panic set in. "Neve, please. Come where I can see you... or at least answer me. I fell asleep so fast after eating a little and I'm afraid—"

"It was not Kaeleron." Neve's soft voice was a blessed relief, soothing my fear, but she still refused to move into the open where I could see her. "You needed rest."

I frowned at the empty cell. "You made me sleep."

I had been fighting so hard to remain awake, afraid that something would happen to me if I slept. That the fae king would choose that moment of vulnerability to enter my cell while I was unaware of him and take me. When I had come around, I had checked myself over ten times, desperate to convince myself that he hadn't.

"You needed rest," she repeated. "Though you sound as grateful for my expending my limited magic as Kaeleron did."

"He was here?" My blood chilled and warmed at the same time, the strange combination spinning my thoughts in several directions at once. Dangerous. I was already on dangerous ground with the fae king. I pulled my shields back up, forming a thick wall around me to keep whatever dark desire he roused in me away. I was not going to fall for his charms. "What did he want? How deep asleep was I? Did he—"

My voice hitched, lungs tightening as I threw aside the blanket Neve had given me and checked my clothing again, even though the sensible part of me knew I had already checked and found none of my clothing out of place and no evidence the king had touched me.

Neve did appear now, her face a dark mask as she glowered at me. "You think so ill of him."

"He hasn't exactly given me a reason to think any other way about him," I snapped back at her, the relief I felt upon finding my clothing intact short lived as my anger spiked right back up again. "He bought me for sex!"

"And has he enjoyed what he paid for?" Neve's expression only hardened, her amber irises smouldering around her pupils like fiery embers.

"It's still early." I wrapped the blanket around myself again, a shield against the cold of the dungeon and the chilling thought of the fae king taking what he had paid a hefty sum to enjoy.

Since our last meeting, my traitorous mind had become fixated on the way he had looked at me, the feel of his hand on my flesh, and how drawn to him I had felt when he had uttered that filthy word—*fuck*.

His parting words had remained with me, a challenge I had felt deep in my flesh and my bones.

When I had lost the fight against my fatigue later that day—or night, I wasn't sure what time of day it was anymore—I had replayed that moment over and over again.

How his eyes had shone with a mischievous light, how his smile had been seductive and his look searing as he had told me that I only had to ask if I wanted to find out which the unseelie did better—fight, feast or *fuck*.

My dreams had twisted that moment, unfurling it into several different endings, ones where those hadn't been his parting words, but ones said while he still faced me.

My cheeks heated as I recalled several of the ways that replayed moment had ended in my dreams, and my body thrummed and ached, my clothes suddenly feeling too tight and restrictive.

The reason for my reactions and my heated dreams dawned on me.

"I don't need this now." I curled forwards into my knees, burying my hands in my matted hair, and cursed my maturity as it taunted and tormented me, and my mind flashed back to the night of the celebration at the Hunt pack and how hungry I had been for my mate.

My first heat was approaching, rolling up on me fast by the feel of things.

"Do not need what now?" The deep masculine voice swept over me, crashing against me like the waves of a raging, wild sea.

I drowned in it for a heartbeat, unable to fight it as it

surrounded me and pulled me under, back into those dangerous dreams.

And then I kicked upwards, battling the strength of the waves, fighting for my life and refusing to succumb.

"None of your business," I bit out as I emerged from my knees, lowering my hands to rest on them, and glared at the one male I really didn't want to see right now, while my maturity was messing with my mind and my body.

Making me want him.

Not him.

Any male would probably trigger the same pounding, relentless need in me right now.

I would probably pounce on one of the gaunt skin-and-bones servants that brought me my food if I had the opportunity to scratch this itch building within me.

Neve stared at me, the weight of her gaze demanding I look at her, and it took only the briefest glance in her direction to catch the concern in her eyes as she watched me.

She knew.

I wanted to bury my head back in my knees.

Could this moment get any worse?

"I have a proposition," Kaeleron said, proving that it could.

Proposition.

That rang through my mind, sounding dirty and alluring.

I shook my head, dislodging it. Propositions could be innocent.

He unrolled a piece of parchment and turned it towards me. "Sign this, agreeing to my terms, and I will allow you to leave this cell."

That didn't sound so innocent.

Not when the corners of his profane lips were curling in that wicked way of his.

I rose to my feet and crossed the cell, slowly approaching

him and the contract he was offering, several thoughts hitting me at once. One, he owned me, so technically I had to do whatever he wanted, like his servants and his other concubines probably did. So why offer me a contract at all? Two, gaining my freedom from this cell meant I was one step closer to finding a way back to my world and to my vengeance.

Three, the lettering on the parchment was precise and neat, and crimson, as if it had been written in blood.

Four, I couldn't understand the elegant marks that I presumed were words.

Except I had to scratch off that last one because as I neared the scroll, the lines of the symbols shifted and suddenly I was reading English.

I looked up at the fae king towering before me, his expression neutral now, almost bored as he waited, as if he didn't give a damn whether I signed the contract or not and had better things to do.

"How can I read this?" I frowned and searched his eyes, and then added, "Come to think of it, how can I understand you? You're speaking English, right?"

He cocked an eyebrow at that, an amused twist to his lips. "I can, but I am not."

"He speaks the fae tongue." The closeness of Neve's voice startled me and I looked to my right, where she now stood close to the bars, peering at the paper Kaeleron offered as if she was trying to read it. "This... infernal contract is written in the same language."

The fae king turned his arched brow on the dragon. "The contract is fair and more than the female deserves."

I was inclined to agree with him on the latter point, but I would be the judge of whether it was fair or not.

Once I discovered something.

"And how is it I can understand both your spoken and

written words?" My gaze snagged on the top line and my name there, so close to his. He knew my name. I looked at Neve, sure she had been the one to give it to him.

"Magic," Neve offered.

I looked at the king.

"Magic," he echoed. "An easy enough spell to cast and maintain."

"Why even bother letting me understand you... or this?" My role in this castle could have been fulfilled without me knowing their language. I didn't need to be able to understand him, or his sister, or Neve in order to warm his bed whenever he was bored. "I mean, unless you bought me for my stunning conversational skills."

His smirk widened just a little, as if he enjoyed my sniping at him. "As I have told you. I am not a monster."

I eyed the contract. "We'll see about that."

What I read as I went through it line by line three times seemed innocent enough, and more than a little tempting. He was offering me a chance to earn my freedom. Every task I completed for him would reduce my debt to him by a varying degree, the recompense determined by the level of task he assigned me. If I worked hard enough for him, I might be able to return home.

But I had taken Neve's warning words to heart and I looked between the cracks—between the lines. This contract looked innocuous, but it gave the fae king far too much freedom to interpret the words of it in any way he wanted.

"I want to add a caveat." A bold demand, and I braced myself as I waited for him to react, sure he would shoot me down. He was offering me a chance to pay him back and be free, and I was probably about to ruin it. If he didn't rip up the contract in my face, I would be surprised.

He regally waved his free hand. "Speak it."

"You can't ask me for sex." My voice trembled a little despite my efforts to keep it strong and steady as I issued an order right back at him. "This says I have to serve you as you please. I have to do as you order. I cannot agree to that when doing as you please could be anything from serving you drinks to serving in your bed or the beds of others. I'd rather remain here in this dungeon than sleep with you."

I waited for him to laugh in my face or take this chance to earn my freedom away from me. It was more than I deserved, and I wasn't sure why he was offering it, and I wanted to know but feared if I pushed him too hard, he would rip it up and leave me in the dungeon. I wanted to see that world Neve had told me about, to experience whatever waited up those stairs behind the fae king. A fae king I was sure was playing some kind of game with me. I didn't care. Hope bloomed dangerously, barely tempered by common sense. If it was a game he was playing, I would play too, giving him as good as I got.

His silver eyes revealed nothing.

I knew he could do as he wanted and I wouldn't really have a say in it, that sensible part of me whispering that this contract was likely just the first play in his game, a ploy to comfort and subdue me, a lie I would believe to calm my fear and leave myself open to him, but my breaths shortened as I waited, needing to hear him agree with my demands.

"Very well." His roguish smile roused something inside me, stirring heat in my blood. "I will not ask you for sex."

Suspicion tinkled warning bells in my mind as he smirked at me, so quick to agree to something I had believed he would rail against. Maybe he wasn't attracted to me after all, or he hadn't bought me for that purpose. I had been here days after all and he had only visited twice, or three times if I counted the one where I was sleeping. And he had talked to Neve about whether I really was essential and about vengeance. Maybe he hadn't bought me for my virginity. Maybe I had another purpose, one I might discover if I signed this contract and played his game.

He held his free hand out and a black and gold feathered quill appeared on his rough palm, the contrast of its elegance against his calluses holding my focus. He wielded weapons as well as magic. Some of the protectors at my pack and the males who worked to keep the cabins sturdy and the fires burning had hands as rough and strong as his.

I looked from the quill to his face, trying to see the warrior within him. I didn't need to look hard as his gaze gained a calculating edge and he pressed his hand towards me, a silent demand to take up the feathered weapon he offered me—one that might be my doom.

But my pack.

Lucas.

I needed to return to my world, to my family, and make my mate pay for what he had done to me.

The only way to do that was to gain my freedom.

I grabbed the quill and flinched, hissing as pain lanced my finger. The white stem of the feather darkened and I almost dropped it as I realised it was my blood filling the space and beading on the pointed gold tip.

A contract signed in blood.

My fingers shook as I stared at the parchment, at the dark crimson words inked on it, most likely in the fae king's blood. This was more than a simple contract like the ones I was used to, typed up on a computer and printed out in triplicate.

How binding were the words he had written so carefully and elegantly in his own blood?

"Well?" He stared down at me, his handsome face bored, but that challenge shining in his eyes. "Sign it or do not sign it. I have matters more important that require my attention."

Veiled words. I didn't need to peer too hard between the cracks to know he was covering, acting bored and pretending he wasn't on the edge of his proverbial seat waiting to see whether I was willing to cross this line—to subject myself to his mercy and play whatever game this was to him—in order to gain my freedom.

He went to pull the contract away.

I seized hold of it, stopping him, and read it one last time, my eyes widening as the words changed before me, as if my touching it had altered it. My caveat appeared on the page, close to the bottom, just above where my name had been printed.

Was I really going to do this?

Subject myself to the whims of a dark fae king in order to earn my freedom?

My revenge?

I sure as hell was.

I scribbled my signature on the parchment, gritting my teeth as the quill pulled on my blood with each letter I added.

And it was done.

I waited, sure I would instantly regret what I had done, that something terrible would happen to me, like the fae king laughing and seizing hold of me to drag me away into whatever dark world was beyond the dungeon.

But nothing happened.

Kaeleron pulled the contract back to him and the quill disappeared from my hand only to reappear in his. He eyed my signature, and then immediately signed his beside it.

I frowned at him as he rolled the parchment up and it vanished, together with the quill.

His silver eyes danced my way, bright with amusement. "I have no caveats. Nothing is out of bounds for me."

I believed that.

The lock on the cell door clicked, making me jump.

The fae king turned his back on me, shadows lovingly caressing the shoulders of his black tunic jacket, and I inched my hand towards the door, unable to believe it really was unlocked now and I was about to take my first step towards my freedom.

Towards seeing what lay beyond the walls of this dungeon.

Would it be as fantastical as Neve had made it sound?

As dangerous?

"Your handmaidens will be here shortly to escort you to your new accommodation, where you will be bathed so you no longer smell like livestock and dressed in a manner more befitting of your new position." Kaeleron paused and angled his head towards his shoulder, revealing a sliver of his profile, when I growled at him for insulting me.

"May I remind you who kept me in this musty dungeon with no access to fresh water or soap?"

He chuckled. "Keep your fangs sharp, little lamb. You might need them."

"What does that mean?" I halted with my hand almost at the metal bars of the door, nerves rising as I considered all the possibilities and what Neve had told me of this world. "Am I liable to be attacked?"

I had never been allowed to learn how to fight or even how to defend myself.

He pivoted to face me, all darkness and wrath as his silver eyes darkened a shade, and I swore fangs of his own flashed between his lips as he spoke.

"Only that my first request is one that will require all of your wit if you are to successfully complete it and earn a gold coin or two towards your debt."

His grin was fiendish, sending a shiver down my spine even

as it roused the aching hunger of my primal instincts as a maturing female wolf.

I was starting to think I would regret this.

Because now I would have to be on constant guard against him and this dark pull I felt towards him.

And my first test?

He melted into shadows filled with glittering gold stars, his invitation a sensuous caress across my skin.

"You will dine with me tonight."

CHAPTER 9

SAPHIRA

Apparently, the fae king wasn't the only one who thought I needed a bath.

The two females who had taken me from the cell and led me to a room on the third floor of the castle had immediately pushed me into a copper clawfoot tub of steaming water laced with rose petals and other dried flowers and scrubbed me raw. My reddened skin still burned a little, but not as much as my scalp as the taller of the two dark-haired females pulled at my silver hair, yanking a comb through it and twisting the strands into an elaborate nest of curls at the back of my head.

The other female knelt beside me on the black marble floor, jabbing under my fingernails with a stick that looked disturbingly like a smooth piece of bone.

"Ouch!" I snatched my hand back and scowled at her. "Is all this prodding and poking really necessary? It's only dinner."

They both looked at me as if I had lost my mind, or perhaps my grasp of the situation I was in. I locked eyes with the one attending my hair in the beautiful oval mirror on the dark red dressing table. Her wide gaze and parted lips relayed her shock as much as the way her hands had stilled in my hair, a reprieve from her torture that I savoured.

"Our king rarely dines with others." The one who had been attempting to pry my nails from their beds looked to her companion and then me. "It is a great honour."

I scoffed at that.

An honour?

It wasn't as if I had been invited to dine with him.

I had been *ordered*.

And if I didn't comply with his demand, I would probably find myself back in my cell before I even had a chance to explore my new accommodations.

My gaze strayed to the enormous black-stone-walled room reflected in the mirror. I didn't know whether I had a view beyond the arched shuttered windows that flanked my bed or the one in the curved annex to my right that hinted at being part of a tower, close to the door to the bathroom, and I wanted to live here long enough to discover what lay beyond them.

So far, the only thing I had really noticed in the room behind me was the huge four-poster bed made of the same glittering lustrous cherry-coloured wood as the dresser before me.

Whenever I dared to look at that spacious bed with its black covers and pillows edged with fine gold embroidery, my mind raced forward to imagine what I might expect tonight from this dinner with the king, and in the coming days of my new servitude.

He had so easily agreed to my clause about not asking me for sex, and suspicion still lingered in my mind over that.

I wasn't sure what I was to expect from him and these tasks he would set me, but I supposed I would find out tonight, or at the very least get a taste of things to come.

The two females continued their work, looking almost like

twins with their dark brown hair pulled back in a severe bun that revealed fae really did have pointed ears and plain black fitted dresses covering them from neck to ankle and wrist. A thousand questions bubbled to the tip of my tongue, each bursting before I could voice it. Neither seemed inclined to talk to me, and when I had tried asking them things while they had been scrubbing the skin from my flesh in the boiling bath, they hadn't even acknowledged that I had spoken.

I drew down a steadying breath as they finished with my nails and my hair, staring into my own eyes in the mirror as my nerves slowly built. I wasn't sure what to expect from the king or this dinner tonight, but I was beginning to feel I was meant to be some kind of object for him to admire while he ate, a form of entertainment to amuse him while he unwound after his work.

Like a doll.

Or a concubine.

I felt like one as one of the servants daubed crimson on my lips and added a sprinkle of pink to my too-pale cheeks, and the other female went to the bed and returned with the dress that had been laid out on it.

"Rise." The one who had done my make-up took hold of my arm, pulling me onto my feet when I hesitated, and I tensed as she tugged the dark cloth robe off my back, exposing my bare body.

Before I could protest, I was being stuffed into a dark silver strapless dress with a corset studded with a swash of diamonds that swept from my right breast to my left hip and then curled around the back of the skirt, growing wider as it glided towards the hem. The twinkling gems reminded me of the Milky Way and my view of it from home, a pang lancing my chest as I looked at them.

The dress was beautiful, but far too revealing for my liking as I tugged at the heart-shaped front of it, trying to pull it a little higher so I didn't feel as if my breasts were about to fall out.

"Isn't there something a little less... I don't know what." I went to look at the servants in the mirror as they selected matching silk slippers and placed a diamond diadem against the tangled knot of my hair on my crown and stilled as I caught my own reflection.

I wasn't sure I had ever looked so beautiful.

I whispered, "I look like a princess."

All the times Everlee had teasingly called me one came back to me in a rush and tears pricked my eyes as that hole in my heart opened up again, that emptincss at the other end of the bond I shared with my pack tearing at me.

Were they okay?

Had Lucas done anything to them?

I needed to know.

And I needed them to know I was fine, that I would find my way back to them.

Reluctance to attend the dinner and have the fae king staring at me as if I had been made to amuse and please his eye swiftly morphed into a burning need to see him and a determination to ask him about contacting my pack.

I didn't protest as the servants slipped the shoes on my feet and led me from the room, down a series of fine black marble corridors lit by strangely glowing lanterns. When we entered a grand vestibule with an elegant curving stone staircase that swept downwards, following the walls of what I felt was another tower illuminated by a large crystal chandelier, the female behind me lifted the skirt of my dress and I hitched up the front.

Not a chandelier, I noted as I descended the gold-threaded black marble stairs.

The glowing crystals weren't attached to anything, and a similar one hung higher up the circular structure.

They bobbed and hung in the air, the crystals moving slightly and changing colour as I followed the staircase down and the angle between us altered.

Magic, I presumed.

Fascination gripped me as I watched the muted hues of a rainbow chase across their facets.

Incredible.

Perhaps Neve was right about this world I had found myself in, one so far from my home. It *was* beyond my imagination, and the part of me that longed for adventure wanted to bravely step out into it and discover all it had to offer.

While the part of me that longed for my pack wanted to beg the fae king to let me return to my world.

I settled on asking him to let me tell them that I was fine and about what had happened. He didn't owe me anything, but I had to believe that beneath all those shadows he wore so well, there was some remnant of a heart.

I had to believe there was some shred of kindness within him that I could appeal to, some part of him that felt a bond with his own family and might understand my pain and fear over what might have happened to mine.

I was stuck with him after all.

The servant left the curving staircases at the second floor and led me along another fine corridor of black stone walls and a black marble floor. Warm light glowed from the lamps set between the inset columns that supported the wooden ceiling, punching back the darkness and gloom. I was so caught up in trying to discern if the lamps were magic too that I almost walked right into the servant as she stopped before a set of black wooden doors beautifully carved with vines and roses. She looked from them to me as she pushed them open, revealing a long wooden table in an elegant marble-walled gothic dining room.

And Kaeleron.

Light from the large onyx fireplace on the left of the room warmed one side of his face and threw the other into shadow, making him look like light and dark melded into one far-too-handsome male.

Being stuck with him wasn't difficult when he wasn't a chore to look at and when I was teasing him, like I wanted to now as I stepped into the room, the sole object of his attention as the door closed behind me and I faced him.

For some reason, this fae made me feel confident and bold, even when I knew I should fear him and that he might hurt me.

Some reckless part of me believed he wouldn't.

Even now, when his expression took on a dark edge and his lips thinned, as if the sight of me displeased him and he would rather I hadn't interrupted whatever he had been looking for in the bottom of the glass he held in one hand.

He looked me over as he eased back to lounge in his high-backed chair, a sweep of his shrewd silver gaze from my head to my toes and back again.

"You look as if you don't approve of my appearance," I sniped, the way he was studying me raising my hackles and making me want to storm right out of the room regardless of how angry he might be with me for disobeying his order to dine with him.

Or shift and sink my fangs into him.

Just moments ago, I had felt more beautiful than I had in all my life, even when Lucas had called me it. I had felt a strange kind of lightness and warmth unfurling within me when I had looked at my reflection. And now Kaeleron was looking at me as if I was far from that, and gods, it rankled, even when I knew it shouldn't because I didn't want his approval or compliments.

I didn't want him to find me beautiful and didn't care if he did or didn't.

"It was not what I was expecting," he muttered and lowered his glass to dangle from his fingers at the end of the armrest.

My eyebrows lifted. "It wasn't what I was expecting either, but it was on the bed in my room, waiting for me. You didn't order it for me?"

His grin was feline. Wicked. A little thrilling. "Oh, I did. I am just surprised you chose to wear it."

I huffed. "Chose? What *choice* did I have?"

"The choice not to wear it." He gestured to the seat closest to him. "Sit."

I picked the seat at the opposite end of the long table to him, keeping my distance, and his eyebrows pitched low as I made a big show of sitting in it, delicately arranging my dress he had apparently ordered for me but hadn't expected me to wear.

"If I could have chosen to dress differently, could I have ignored your demand that I dine with you?" I needed to know the rules of this game we were playing, so I could avoid any potential pitfalls as I chipped away at my debt. There were things I wasn't willing to do, things that had only come to me after I had signed the contract, so I wanted to know whether I could refuse if he asked me to kill someone, or commit any other terrible act like it.

"No." Darkness rolled off him, his voice firm and almost chilling as his gaze narrowed on me. "Some things are not optional. I issue an order and you must follow it." He pulled the contract I had signed out of thin air and waggled it at me. "It is all here, signed in your blood. Whether or not the things I request are orders or suggestions is down to you to figure out... but know if you get it wrong and refuse an order, you will be punished."

He was teasing me again, amusing himself with my fear and my ignorance as I fumbled my way around his world and him, trying to learn what was right and what was wrong in order to survive.

If he wanted to be amused, I would happily entertain him with the wit he had requested I bring with me tonight. I would show him how sharp my fangs could be.

I gestured to the empty table. "What kind of dinner am I attending anyway? An invisible one? There is no food."

Kaeleron angled his head towards the double doors in the wall behind him that were as beautifully carved with scenes of nature as the ones I had entered through.

Servants marched in. Many servants. Each carried a silver tray ladened with dishes they set out on the table and two carried a huge gold soup tureen between them. Platters of roasted meats, bowls of boiled... potatoes... I thought, but they were a light purplish colour, together with dishes of vegetables and other things I did easily recognise were laid out between us. Carrots. Peas. Golden-crusted pies. Some kind of cabbage. Jugs of the rich gravy I had secretly enjoyed while shut in that awful cell.

"This is all very... human... food." I salivated as the aromas hit me, my stomach gurgling in anticipation as the servants laid out cutlery and plates before me and filled my long-stemmed glass with what looked like red wine.

Oh gods, I hoped it was red wine.

Another servant placed a bowl on the plate before me and ladled a cream-coloured soup into it that smelled faintly like parsnips and spice.

I pulled the glass towards me and subtly sniffed it as I lifted it towards my lips, pretending to take a sip as I checked to see if it was wine or blood, but of course he noticed.

The king gave me a bland look, dismissed his servants and

poured himself a healthy glass of wine. "I do not dine on blood or the entrails of my enemies."

"That's not what I heard. Neve said entrails of your enemies was your favourite dish when she was giving me the run down on your majesty." Would it be rude if I just grabbed several of the platters of meat and dragged them to my end to devour them before he could select a slice or two?

I squirmed in my seat, finding it hard to remain as civil as my clothes made me appear as my mouth watered and my wolf side snarled at me to claim every scrap of meat for myself before he could steal any of it.

He canted his head, watching me like a hawk watched a mouse. "I doubt that. But... I am curious. What did my seer have to say about me?"

I had lost myself in staring at the roast beef—or I hoped it was roast beef because it certainly smelled like it and I wanted to dive into it—and only the weight of his stare pulled me back to the world and it hit me he had said something.

"That you're not a monster. I haven't made my mind up about that yet. The jury is still out, I'm afraid. But this," I gestured to the sumptuous food spread before me, half of which seemed familiar while others were new, like the sweet cakes and sticky buns that sat beside a clear pitcher of glowing violet syrup that smelled incredible as I pulled it towards me to get a closer look, "is a good step towards improving my opinion of you."

A deep, rumbling chuckle escaped him. "Feast, little lamb."

That word halted me in my tracks with a spoonful of soup halfway to my mouth.

Feast. Fight. *Fuck.*

This certainly was a feast, every inch of the table covered in delicious looking food, and I wanted to taste every item, to eat my fill until they had to roll me back to my room.

My gaze drifted to the male at the other end of the table and my wolf side growled at the sight of him, lounging in his high-backed chair, firelight dancing across the angular planes of his sculpted face as he watched me with a glimmer I couldn't decipher in his cold silver eyes.

Was this the thing unseelie did better than my kind, or was it one of the others?

Fight?

Or fuck?

My cheeks began to heat and I scrambled to cover the reaction, grabbing my glass of wine and lifting it to my lips as I turned my head away from the light of the fire to conceal part of my face. I drained half the glass, not caring how I looked. If I blushed now, I could blame the alcohol.

I studied the long wooden side table that occupied the entire right side of the room as I calmed myself, gaze dancing over the silver trays of crystal goblets and decanters filled with liquids in shades of amber to crimson. Inset pillars added interest to the plain black marble walls, both accented with pure gold. Warm light from the chandelier suspended above the dining table chased over the gold and the facets cut into the glassware, drawing my gaze up to it.

Beautiful.

Not just the chandelier made of globes of golden magic that drifted among gold vines and leaves, but the ceiling above it.

I had never seen a ceiling like it.

Elegant golden cornicing surrounded it on all sides, like a frame for the stunning masterpiece someone had painted on the ceiling. A fresco that made me feel I was deep in a forest, surrounded by trees and gazing up at a sky filled with aurora and stars. The more I looked at it, the more I noticed the details. Dragons flying over faint jagged mountains beyond the trees. A stag-like creature grazing among the rugged trunks.

Night birds perching in the branches. Motes of glittering gold light drifted around the ceiling, almost as if the stars were moving.

Kaeleron's gaze bore into me but I refused to look at him or end my perusal and enjoyment of the room. The most elegant room I had ever set foot in. A room fit for a castle and its king.

"Eat," he growled.

I somehow made it through the soup with all the genteel manners a fae king might expect, but the delicious warmth of it didn't satisfy the deep craving for something more substantial—for meat. I set the empty bowl aside and longingly looked at the platters just beyond arm's reach.

While Kaeleron was watching the fire rather than me, I stealthily leaned over the table and reached for the nearest platters of meat, my senses focused on him as I snared my prize. I piled what looked like beef and chicken onto my plate, together with a pie that smelled of pork and herbs.

It was only when I sat back, my prize secured, and had stuffed an overly-ladened forkful of meat into my mouth and bit back a moan at the juiciness of it, that I noticed Kaeleron was now staring at me.

I chewed and swallowed, hating how vulnerable and exposed I felt as some part of me waited for him to comment on my behaviour.

When he said nothing, simply continued to stare at me, I bit out, "What?"

He swept his hand out towards the vegetables with a regal elegance that only made me feel the difference between our table manners even more fiercely.

"You're welcome to them," I sniped, feeling it was too late now to act civilised so I might as well act like myself rather than trying to please a male who had sunk so low as to buy another person. I was better than him, even if my manners weren't quite as refined. "Don't hold back on my account."

I jabbed my fork into another slice of beef and devoured it as I stared right at him, my wolf side rumbling in approval.

"I should have presumed a wolf would prefer meat." Kaeleron eased back to lounge in his chair again, as if it were a throne and he was holding court, a challenge in his eyes as he swirled his wine. "I have something you can wrap your pretty lips around if you like the taste of meat."

I didn't miss a beat. "I'll bite it off."

I snapped short fangs for emphasis.

His throaty chuckle was alarmingly thrilling as he held my gaze, the bold challenge in his eyes joined by a glimmer of amusement, and then his focus shifted to his drink, freeing me of his hold. I wasn't sure how he did that. Was it some kind of power he had? His gaze was magnetic and demanding, holding me fast at times, even when I wanted to look at anything but him.

Silence stretched between us, pulling something inside me taut as I struggled to find something to say while shovelling more meat into my mouth. He had brought me here for conversation, and if I failed to provide it, he might deem tonight a failure and not reduce my debt.

"You've barely touched your food." I waved a fork at his plate and the terribly balanced meal he had selected for himself. Far too many vegetables. Not enough meat. I had thought someone with so much honed muscle would be packing in the protein at mealtimes. I cut a piece of the pie, placed it in my mouth and almost moaned as the salty pork hit my tongue, denying it so he wouldn't get the satisfaction of hearing it. As I chewed, I looked at all the food on the table, enough to feed my entire pack. "This is wasteful. At my pack, we never waste anything."

I hesitated as words rose on my tongue, my heart demanding I voice them.

"Speak." Ever the king, Kaeleron waved regally in my direction.

I added observant to his list of qualities, ones Neve had failed to mention, mostly because she had spent a lot of our time together trying to make me believe he wasn't a monster.

"I need to contact my pack." The sound of my fork hitting my plate was loud in the heavy silence, jarring me, and I struggled to hold his gaze as his eyes darkened and his fine brows lowered, narrowing them on me.

"No."

I bared fangs at him and shoved back from the table. Or I had intended to shove back from it. Rather than my chair moving, the table did, shooting towards the fae king as the legs scraped loudly over the marble floor.

He braced one hand against it and arched a brow at me.

It hadn't been an act of retaliation.

My body locked up tight anyway, bracing for his wrath.

Rather than punishing me for apparently trying to hit him with a table, he gently eased it back into place and continued to study me, the scrutiny making me want to squirm in my seat.

"I will not allow you to contact your pack." His words were careful, coming out slowly, as if he was considering what he would allow as he spoke and hadn't quite decided which course of action to settle on yet. "But I will consider writing to them to let them know you are safe."

It was more than I expected, but I still said, "Will you let them know where I am?"

"No." That word was hard and unyielding, a flat denial that I knew I wouldn't be able to bend into a maybe let alone a yes. He set his glass down on the table, shadows forming across his broad shoulders as he gazed at me, his expression as cold and firm as his denial had been. "I will not disclose your location. I will not be responsible for your family attempting to navigate Lucia to reach you and getting themselves killed."

I hadn't even considered they might try to find me, but as I absorbed those words, it hit me that they would. My parents would do as I asked if I told them I was fine and safe for now and would return to them, and explained the dangers of where I was.

But Chase and Morden.

They would seek out a way to reach this world in order to take me back.

Morden in particular.

He took his position as my protector seriously, and if he discovered what had happened to me, what Lucas had done to me, he would feel responsible for my predicament. He would want to save me, even when I wasn't sure I needed saving. I had a way back to my pack, and I could do it. No matter how long it took to pay off my debt to Kaeleron. It was time I learned to stand on my own two feet and take care of myself rather than relying on my family and my pack.

And some small part of me that was growing louder each day wanted to stay here and see more of this world.

"The little lamb grows quiet," Kaeleron murmured, canting his head to his left. "Do you tire of my company?"

"No." My denial came out quickly, and it wasn't a lie.

This evening with him had been pleasant, almost normal, and I wanted more of it, wanted to stay right where I was and see what happened next.

Was that selfish of me?

That deep-rooted part of me that missed my pack said that it was, that I wasn't where I belonged and I should be finding a way to escape and return to them. That part of me that craved adventure, had longed to see beyond the borders of my family's lands, wanted to scream a denial and plant my feet to the stones of Lucia and refuse to leave until I had seen what was out there.

"Would you answer some questions for me?" I asked.

He poured himself another glass of wine.

I took that as permission.

"The chandelier in the stairwell... is it magic? It was beautiful. Like all of this above us." I looked there, watching the flecks of golden light dancing across the ceiling and the globes of the chandelier wind around the vines. "This is magic, isn't it?"

His eyebrows lifted, as if he was surprised to hear I found something in his world beautiful.

"A simple use of the power of this land. We often use magic to illuminate our homes, especially those in the highborn families, where magic runs stronger in our veins." He pressed the tip of a pale finger to the rim of his full glass and I gasped as the wine drained from it only to appear in my empty one. "Magic has its uses."

"And it comes from the land?" I couldn't imagine what kind of world had magic laced through everything in it, there for people who could wield it to use as they saw fit. Witches had innate magic, a limited well of it inside themselves that they could draw on, but Kaeleron made it sound as if there was magic for the taking here and the fae could draw it to them.

He nodded. "Lucia grants us power, and we feed that power in return, performing rites that restore some of the magic to the land and also to us."

Rites. I wanted to know more about those, and would ask about them later, because in my head, I was picturing him in a white druidic robe chanting at the sunrise over monolithic stones. I highly doubted that was the kind of rite he was talking about. Another image flashed in my head, this one of him bare-chested and stood before an altar, and upon it was a bloody sacrifice.

I shoved that right out of my head, refusing to let the vision unfold, not wanting to see what my mind put in the position of sacrifice.

"And highborn families have more of it? Does that mean you have the most?" I sipped the wine and it tasted the same as it had when I had poured it from the jug. "Is the magnitude of your magic the reason why the aura of power that surrounds you grows so strong at times that I feel I can't breathe and I'm being squashed?"

He slowly nodded.

"I have the most in this court, and Jenavyr is second to me." His gaze narrowed on me, a flicker of curiosity in it. He wanted to see where I was going with my questions and it was amusing him.

I had the feeling not many people in his court bothered talking with him like this.

Or he didn't allow them to speak so freely with him.

"The most in *this* court." I frowned at his choice of words. "Other kings are stronger than you?"

"Our high king is the most powerful," he said and refilled his glass. "But few others match my strength."

"How many courts are there?" I leaned towards him and rested my elbow on the table, propping my chin up on my palm. "I take it a high king reigns over all the other kings?"

"So curious. I could believe you a cat if I did not know you were a wolf." He smirked and sipped his wine. "There are nine courts of the unseelie and the high king presides over all."

"And how many do the seelie—"

His scowl and the sudden shadows that loomed behind him, sucking some of the light and warmth from the room, and turning those motes of magic near the ceiling into tiny shards of glittering darkness, halted my tongue.

I filed away that he didn't like anyone mentioning the seelie and tried to think of a different topic of conversation. "You bespelled me so I can understand your language. Is that a permanent thing? You said it was easy to maintain. So you could stop renewing it and I wouldn't be able to understand anyone?"

He inclined his head.

"So if I want to remain able to talk to you and Neve, I need to remain on your good side."

He grinned, flashing straight white teeth. "I have no good side, little lamb. You simply need to remain obeisant to me."

"Fine. This spell of yours, does it work both ways? Like... is what I'm saying coming out as fae rather than English?" I hadn't considered it when I had been in the dungeon, but both the king and Neve, and my servants could understand me too.

"I speak your tongue, but for others, they would hear your words as if you spoke fae."

Fascinating. "So it's kind of like a universal translator?"

Chase had made me watch several different Star Trek series during one *very* long snowy winter and when I had asked how all the different species understood each other, he had explained about universal translators. I doubted this fae king knew about them, and secretly enjoyed knowing something he didn't and idly bringing it up in conversation.

"I would suppose so." He swilled his wine, watching it run around the glass, and then his eyes lifted to lock with mine, the corners of his lips curving. "Imagine what it might be like to have that taken from you."

A chill skittered down my spine at the thought of being here in this strange world, unable to understand anyone or have anyone understand me.

Except for him.

"Do you like threatening people?" I pushed my plate away, my appetite gone, and leaned back in my seat, mimicking him.

"Threatening would insinuate it is done to intimidate. I merely state facts."

"To keep me obedient. Feels like a threat to me." I was half-tempted to hurl my wine glass at him as the air between us took a turn I didn't like, but it seemed like a waste, so I drained the contents instead. "I'm tired. Are we done?"

"So curt." He tapped the pitcher of wine and my glass refilled. "We are not done."

"Fine." I folded my arms across my chest and glared at him.

The fire crackled and popped, showering sparks up the chimney, and silence stretched between us. His gaze remained fixed on me, sharp and focused, as if he was attempting to slice and peel back my layers to discover how I ticked. Or he was waiting for me to break.

When I had been a pup, Chase had mocked me over something I could no longer remember but had cut me to my heart, and I had given him the silent treatment for close to five days. It had taken him apologising in front of my parents and half the pack for me to speak to him again.

Minutes ticked past, neither of us willing to break the heavy silence that began to feel oppressive the longer it went on and I realised why I had stuck to my guns with Chase as a pup. It was because this unnatural silence and battle of wills made it harder and harder to speak as it dragged on, as if it was a living thing that was wrapping around my body and constricting me.

"I intend to take a swim in the lake tomorrow." Kaeleron pushed back his chair and rose to his feet, looming like a shadow at the other end of the table, his striking silver eyes as dark as storm clouds. His deep voice wrapped around me, more crushing than the silence had been as he stared me down, his handsome face cold and devoid of emotion. "You will join me."

A clear-cut order rather than a suggestion.

Suspicion jangled those alarm bells in my mind again.

A swim in a lake.

The last time I had swum in a lake, I had been naked.

"I want a bathing suit," I blurted.

His eyebrows pitched low. "A bathing suit?"

"It's a covering mortals wear when bathing to protect their modesty." And would probably require someone to make a trip to the human world to get me one judging by how confused he looked.

He inclined his head. "I will see to it. Your handmaidens will bring you one and you will meet me at the lake before the light reaches its brightest."

So agreeable. Those alarm bells rang a little louder, but I muffled them, sure that a swim wouldn't be the death of me and doubting he would try anything at the lake given the clause he had added to our contract for me.

Not only that, but I would be allowed to leave the castle.

To see beyond these walls.

And the part of me that was sure he was up to something was drowned out by the part of me that grew excited at the thought of seeing what was out there.

Kaeleron strode for the double doors behind me, shadows sweeping outwards like a living cloak, brushing against me as he passed me and sending a shiver down my limbs.

His deep voice reverberated within me as he growled.

"Do not be late, my little lamb."

CHAPTER 10
SAPHIRA

Birdsong pulled me from turbulent dreams about those strange trees with their glowing violet veins and beautiful shimmering blooms, surrounded by boulders draped with thick dark moss and the clearest stream I had ever seen. Despite how familiar the sound was, it was still foreign to me, the song not one I knew. I lay with my eyes closed beneath the thick but feather light black covers of the bed, drifting in that song, strange warmth slowly filling me as the melody rose and fell, growing closer and fainter at times.

What did those birds that sung so beautifully look like?

Curiosity pulled me from the comfort of the bed and I grabbed the black robe from the chair near the dressing table, where I had left it when sleep had finally rolled up on me.

Last night came flooding back as I tied the belt, cinching it tight around my waist, and stared at the dark fireplace near the door. I couldn't figure this fae king out. I was normally good at understanding others, the training I had undergone as a healer teaching me to observe people closely so I could tell if something was wrong with them without them telling me. It was surprising how many wolves didn't like to confess they had an ailment or had hurt themselves. But this male. I couldn't keep up with his changes in mood.

Was he the dark, scary unseelie king?

Or the gentler male who had laughed at things I had said, the warmth of it reaching his eyes at times?

Which king would await me today when I joined him at the lake?

Wanting to see if I could spy that lake, and if I had a view, I drifted to the arched window in the tower area of my room, kneeled on the pillows covering the seat that followed the curve of it, and unlatched the heavy wooden shutters, drawing them open.

Muted sunlight greeted me.

Together with the most breathtaking vista I had ever seen.

Shivers danced down my spine and arms as I unlocked and pushed the leaded windows open, an urge to immerse myself in that view and be closer to it controlling me. A cool salty breeze swept around me, laced with the scent of flowers, and the birdsong grew louder as I took in the scene before me.

It was incredible.

Below me stretched a formal paved garden with arbours and statues and a large fountain together with a long white wooden pergola dripping with spears of lilac flowers and a beautiful gazebo. Raised flowerbeds bordered the paths that intersected at the fountain and the ones that led towards the gazebo and pergola, filled with blooms in so many colours that shock rippled through me.

Some foolish part of me had expected the flowers in this kingdom of a dark fae to be sombre hues and shades of night or blood.

Between those blooms, fist-sized bees bobbed and buzzed, and I had to blink to be sure I wasn't imagining them. Pretty jewel-toned birds flitted past them, darting through the stems of some of the taller flowers and the branches of a tree, their song now familiar to me.

But what really stole my breath were the black mountains that rose like jagged teeth beyond the crystalline lake that nestled among them and lined the edge of the half of the garden to my left.

Mist from the waterfall that fell over the rim of the plateau glittered in the air directly in front of me, shimmering with not a rainbow but an aurora of purple, blue, green and red. My gaze tracked the water as it plunged downwards, some of it hidden behind the garden where it continued around to my right, hugging the top of the cliff, and then trailed along the vicious line of the black mountains that jutted beyond the waterfall, forming a bay below where they crashed into an azure sea.

The sea.

I couldn't take my eyes off it as it glittered and sparkled beyond the mountains, stretching far to the horizon, calling to me—eyes that had longed to see it since I had been a pup.

By the gods.

It was beautiful.

A shiver danced over my limbs again.

I had wanted adventure, and here it was, in a whole new world!

One that now I saw it I finally believed was real.

This wasn't my world.

It was too beautiful, too dreadful, and the air glittered with faint motes of gold, as if laced with magic.

And the sky...

It was twilight kissed with aurora, threaded with stars, as if night never really left this land.

Another bird called, this song different and harsher, and I looked for it. Great black gulls hovered and played on the breeze rolling up the cliff from the ocean, their wingspans as long as my arms.

The door behind me opened.

My heart shot into my throat and I whirled towards it, placing my back to the stunning scenery.

My *handmaidens*, as Kaeleron had called them. I had servants apparently.

I had spent my entire life waiting on others, taking care of others, and now I had two strangers devoted to my care. It was difficult to process that. I squirmed a little as they entered the expansive room that was all mine and was far larger than my family's entire cabin, both carrying a silver tray. One had a delicate fine china cup and teapot on it, and the other had more very-human food. A full toast rack, a pot of butter, and what looked a lot like one of preserves, but it was the bacon and eggs that snared me in their spell, making my mouth water.

I didn't fail to notice there was more bacon than eggs, the rashers piled in a mound that beckoned me.

The bastard fae king already knew my greatest weakness and was employing the knowledge with deadly aim. If he kept this up, delivering me delicious meat to devour, I might be tempted to change my opinion of him and downgrade him from monster to something closer to a male.

The handmaiden with the tea set her tray down on a wooden table near another set of doors in the wall to the left of me, beyond my bed. She turned and opened the heavy wooden doors and I caught a glimpse of sea. They weren't doors to another room after all, but rather another set of shutters hiding arched glazed doors that led to the outside world. She opened those doors and returned for the tray.

"King Kaeleron believed you might prefer to take your breakfast on the balcony this morning." The one with my food glanced at me before she disappeared through the doors.

I had a balcony.

I tried to act demure and not rush to see it or what lay beyond it. It looked out on the other side of my room and I wanted to see the view in that direction, because I was sure I could spy other buildings and possibly distant hills there.

"Where is the king this morning?" I presumed it was morning anyway. The light was muted and the sky star-kissed, and if this was morning, then I wanted to get a better look at it too now.

"King Kaeleron is holding court this morning, but he expects you to meet him at the lake early this afternoon. We will come to help you dress and escort you there when it is time." The one with the tea returned with her empty tray held downwards before her hips, the flat of it resting against her legs.

They both bowed and headed for the door, while I nodded and drifted towards the balcony.

My balcony.

This whole experience was only getting stranger as it went on, but it was a wonderful distraction, pushing what Lucas had done to me to the back of my mind and burying the pain that still throbbed in my heart.

It was easy to forget I was a servant myself as I stepped from my luxurious quarters onto a balcony that overlooked a land just as Neve had described it—one far beyond my imagination.

I felt as if I had been transported back in time as I looked down on this new world, at the layers of the castle town tucked within several great black stone walls complete with parapets. Elegant stone townhouses packed the space between the wall that surrounded the main castle and one that was thinner and less fortified. They looked expensive, each beautifully crafted with their columned facades and tiled pitched roofs, and smoke billowing from their chimneys. Every single one of them had their own small garden too, neatly divided by low walls laced with greenery, and an avenue dotted with trees separated them.

But they didn't hold my attention or pull at me to get a closer look.

It was the buildings beyond that thinner wall that tugged me towards them. The half-timber houses that spilled down the terraced hill looked as if they had fallen right out of a medieval history book, and the busy thoroughfare that snaked and branched between them captivated me as my eyes followed its trail. I tugged the stone table on the balcony towards the balustrade that embraced it and sat on it as I sipped tea and nibbled my breakfast, watching the world in motion below me.

Carts trundled between the distant large arched gateway at the end of a dirt road flanked by two colossal statues of armoured knights riding some kind of beasts and a smaller gate set into the thinner wall, and some even navigated the fortified castle gatehouse to pull up outside it below me. The great black or white stags that pulled them huffed and shook their double sets of antlers, the front of which were little more than sharp horns, their pointed ears flapping. They looked as big as a horse but as elegant as the deer I had often watched and hunted back home. Men dressed in leather breeches and loose shirts tended to them while shirtless muscled males hefted the goods from the back of the cart. Barrels. Wooden boxes. They carried them on their shoulders as if they weighed nothing.

Within the castle walls, and even within the city beyond it, people came and went, their clothing far different from what I was used to back home. They all looked antiquated to me, many of the females wearing dresses similar in fashion to what I had worn last night, albeit more suited to the daytime, while others dressed more plainly, in clothing made of a more rugged material. There were finely dressed males too, wearing dull coloured embroidered tunics and trousers and riding boots, either escorting some of the beautifully dressed females or talking with other males of their standing.

I chewed on a piece of bacon as I studied the ones I suspected were the highborn Kaeleron had mentioned last night. The females walked with elegant precision, their posture perfect, acting as if they were unaware of the way the males watched them as they passed, or how they were silently judging each other as they pleasantly nodded in greeting to every female they met.

I hoped to the gods the fae king didn't expect me to act like these females. No amount of lessons could transform me into something akin to them and I didn't want to be like them. Even when watching them made me feel even more like a fish out of water.

I didn't belong here.

Or at least, I didn't belong in this castle.

My gaze tracked back to the town that hugged the hill, each building different in scale and design, and I ached to explore it and be among those people who looked as if they were greeting each other, hands waving at whoever they had spotted or being shaken by men who saw someone they knew. This place of lofty highborn wasn't me. That place of warmth and laughter, of smiles and joyful greetings was me.

An ache started deep in my breast, my eyes stinging as my wolf instincts howled for my pack. For that comfort and warmth, and being surrounded by friends and family.

I looked back at my room, with all its lavish finery and carved wooden doors and black marble floors that were inlaid with patterns of gold metal that reflected the magical lights. I bet it was real gold. I traced my fingers over the edges of the table I sat on, feeling the carvings there too. Everything here was finely crafted, even the table and chairs I had seen in the dining room last night. The king's craftsmen were incredibly talented, but I doubted they lived in the fine houses below me.

I shifted my focus to that town beyond the highborn houses, to the smoke that rose from some of the chimneys and the sound of metal striking metal ringing out. People moved between buildings with small carts of goods, and one of the houses closer to the gate to the highborn area was putting out what looked like baskets of bread as people gathered there, a mixture of the finely dressed and the others.

The heart of this castle town was there, among those craftspeople and commoners.

I wanted to go there.

Maybe I would ask Kaeleron to allow me to visit it.

I needed to get in his good graces first though.

I nibbled at a piece of buttered toast as I shifted my focus to beyond the walls of the town, to lands that called to me more fiercely than the bustling streets below.

A great swath of farmland and forests stretched as far as my eyes could see. Hazy mountains rose beyond them like great onyx teeth. And above them… the most incredible sky I had ever seen. My handmaidens had called this morning, but the sky did resemble twilight, with faint shifting aurora that stole my breath. If I had needed proof I wasn't in my world any longer, if the landscape and the shimmering air wasn't evidence enough, this sky was it.

My eyes tracked the rippling hues of green and purple.

I had seen aurora before, but not like this. Golden stars glittered among the dancing ribbons, moving with them, and if someone had asked me to paint magic, and I had been capable of creating something so beautiful and bewitching, this is what I would have drawn for them.

I watched them until my food was stone cold and my teapot was empty, and then I watched the town, but as the minutes ticked past, I found myself drawn to the window that overlooked the lake again, my mind turning to the one thing I had on my agenda today.

Swimming with the king.

Trees lined part of the lake and bordered the garden, and gathered thickly off to my left, where there seemed to be an entire forest within the confines of the walls. Those trees called to me, pulling on my instincts, filling me with an urge to shift and explore them. What scents would be in that forest? What new creatures might I encounter? How would the leaf litter feel beneath my paws?

There were clearings in places where the dark canopy of the trees fell away.

I frowned.

Stared harder at that dense canopy, trying to peer through the leaves to confirm I wasn't imagining things. I lowered my gaze to the nearest trees and my eyes widened. The bark of the trees were lined with violet glowing veins, just like my dreams.

Neve.

The dragon held some kind of power and she had influenced my dreams. The more I thought about them, the more certain I felt. I had seen glimpses of the aurora in my dreams, of mountains and the great crashing sea. She had shown me these things.

Teased me with what I would find beyond the bars of my cage.

My gaze remained rooted on the trees, something about them speaking to me, not just calling to me but actually *speaking* to me, as if they wanted me to run among them. They beckoned. Filled me with a sense that I belonged there, among those stunning but strange trees. Not just the trees though. Everything in this place spoke to me on some primal level.

I had never felt more as one with nature than I did now, here in this strange new world.

Something about this land whispered to my wolf side.

Made me feel light and warm.

Comforted.

As if I had been born to be here and had finally found my way home.

I shook off that sensation, because my home was back in Canada with my pack, far away from this court of dark fae and this world of magic and shadows.

Yet I wanted to go out there and explore it all, to soak it all in and fly free of my pretty, gilded cage.

And that was the reason I was excited about meeting the fae king for a swim. Adventure. Not Kaeleron.

I needed to break free of these walls and breathe for a moment, to immerse myself in nature and let the pain and the fear and all my feelings fall away for a time while it filled me up. My quarters might be bigger than my family's cabin back home, but the more I looked at those trees, the smaller it felt, until the black stone walls were closing in on me and I couldn't breathe.

I needed to run.

I needed to be out there.

Whether or not it was allowed, I no longer cared. I needed to run and feel the wind on my face. I needed the space and the freedom, because I couldn't breathe in this castle. I needed to be outside, among nature. If Kaeleron punished me for it, so be it.

I washed up in the bathroom and dressed in the leathers and blouse I had been given, and strode back into the bedroom to find my boots.

There was a black box on the foot of the bed.

I frowned as I went to it, unsure when someone had

entered my room to place it there because I hadn't heard anyone enter and my wolf side was on high alert, so eager for freedom that it was hyper-focused on the world.

Unless someone had used magic to put it there.

I slowly inhaled, catching the scent of a wild storm on the black cardboard.

Kaeleron.

He had sent it to my room.

My heart picked up pace, drumming rapidly against my ribs as I edged closer to the box, bracing myself for what might be inside. I had asked for a swimsuit but hadn't specified what kind, and now I imagined it would be a flimsy and revealing bikini.

I whipped the lid off.

Revealing a boring black one piece.

Surprise swept through me as I stared at it, together with a little thread of disappointment. I shook that off. A one piece was perfect. I wasn't looking to expose myself to the fae king or put ideas in his head with a revealing bikini. Although, showing a little skin might have encouraged him to agree to my request to see more of the castle town or those woods.

I shut down that line of thought. It would also encourage him to think he could order me into his bed or that I wanted him.

Beneath the plain black swimsuit was a matching black sarong, as if Kaeleron wanted as much of me covered as possible. Or perhaps the moody fae king was trying to give me some modesty while I walked through his castle. He probably thought I was delicate and afraid of others looking at me.

A brittle scoff escaped my lips.

He had a lot to learn about wolves.

I changed into the swimsuit and didn't bother bringing the

sarong with me as I marched towards the doors and opened them.

One of my handmaidens, the younger of the two, appeared before me, as if she had been somewhere in the ether, waiting for me to emerge from my room. Or she had been guarding it and ordered to stop me if I attempted to leave, which seemed far more plausible.

The servant gave me a once over and then glanced into the room behind me, at the bed—at the discarded sarong.

I tipped my head up and strode down the hallway, heading in the direction we had taken last night when I had gone to dine with the king. She hurried ahead of me, taking the lead and guiding the way down to the curving staircases to the ground floor and out into the garden. Curious gazes tracked me as I paraded through the neat formal garden, my chin tipped up and shoulders squared.

Let them look.

Let them see what their king had brought into their castle.

I earned a few scowls from the highborn females as I strode past them, not even bothering to acknowledge them as I made a beeline for the lake, my handmaiden struggling to keep up with me now.

The pale stone flags were warm beneath my bare feet and despite how muted the light was, it kept the chill of the sea breeze off my bare skin.

"This way." The handmaiden managed to get ahead of me at the lakeshore and guided me towards the left side of the rippling body of water.

Towards the trees.

The haughtiness in me faltered as I headed for them, overshadowed by eagerness to step into their shadows and feel them around me. My pack lands were heavily wooded mountains, and I had run in the forests daily since I had been old enough to shift. That hour of exercise had been my only true freedom and adventure, and I had been missing it in the time I had been here.

I shivered as I slipped into the shadows of ethereal trees and felt them around me, as their leaf litter and the earth cushioned my feet, and the urge to run was strong. It bubbled through me, making my steps feel lighter as I almost danced through the trees that clung to the foothills of the mountains, fascinated by how they glowed and how those violet veins reacted to my touch as I brushed my fingers across them. They dimmed and the area beyond my touch brightened, as if the tree had pulled whatever magic or sap ran through them away from me. When I broke contact, the veins filled again.

Mossy boulders tumbled close to the path that had been worn into the dirt, the scent of them lacing the air together with the earth and the water, and the flowers in the trees. I breathed deep of it, filling my lungs, letting nature flow into me as it swirled around me. Bliss. This was bliss.

And it was beautiful.

To my left, a dark cliff came into view above the canopy of the forest, trees sprouting from it, clinging to its cragged face, and long grass tumbling down it, together with a creeping vine with blood red blooms that reached their faces towards the twilight sky. The path rose over a series of timeworn boulders and packed dirt at the base of the cliff, the canopy of the trees to my right, their roots buried deep in a small beach below, close enough that I could reach out and touch the shimmering flowers. A small waterfall tumbled over one part of the cliff, trickling down to the earth below and forming a stream that rushed beneath a small wooden bridge that spanned the gap between two boulders, carrying me over the beach to where the path began to descend again.

My wolf side bayed for freedom and I fought it, struggling

to hold it at bay because I wasn't here to run, even when I wished that I was. I was here to swim, and while I could do so in my wolf form, some petty part of me wanted to keep that part of me hidden from everyone.

I wanted to deny him something.

This male who stood ahead of me on the pebbly shore, his backdrop fierce black mountains and waterfalls that thundered down their faces. I hadn't noticed them before. I looked back towards the castle and couldn't see it through the trees. We had come further than I had thought. Perhaps they had been hidden from view by the curving mountains.

The servant bowed and disappeared.

Leaving me alone with Kaeleron.

He raked cold silver eyes over me, not at all shocked to see I hadn't bothered with the sarong. The curve of his lips said he was pleased I had forgone using it. I stood my ground, unfazed by the way his eyes danced over my body, because he had seen far more than this already.

He had seen me at my lowest and most vulnerable.

He gestured to the lake, sweeping his left hand towards it. "After you."

That eager glint in his eyes warned he was up to something, but I was already lost in how clear and inviting the water was, and how freeing it would feel to be in it and get a look at this place from another perspective. Maybe I would be able to see the castle and my room, and later when I stood in the window, I would be able to recognise where I had swum and could recall how the water felt or how free I felt right now, out here in the woods, almost alone.

It was hard to shut out the presence of the fae king.

His power ensconced me, his gaze heavy on my face, as he waited to see what I would do.

I stepped towards the lake, eyes darting over the crystalline rocks and boulders that lined the bottom. They glittered beneath the turquoise water, each a hue of grey but tinged with other colours. Some were purplish, some had a hint of crimson, and others captured shades of green and blue or gold. It was as if someone had poured glass beads into the water, only they had been made by giants. If I had been in any danger of forgetting how different and magical this land of Lucia was, this would have reminded me.

Kaeleron continued to watch me like a hawk.

I didn't dare glance back at him, even when I wanted to know if he looked as disappointed as I was sure he did by my swimsuit. Whoever had bought it for me from the human world had probably made a mistake, purchasing me something far less revealing than the king had had in mind.

I stepped into the surprisingly warm water, letting it lap at my ankles, and risked a look back at Kaeleron.

He looked fascinated rather than disappointed.

Strange male.

I wasn't sure I would ever understand him even if it took a decade or more to earn my freedom.

A decade or more.

My breath hitched and I took in the lake that stretched before me, embraced by those forbidding black mountains, and kissed by that twilight aurora sky, and rather than crushing fear and loneliness at the thought of being separated from my pack for so long, I felt only calm.

The steady, gentle touch of nature against all of me that comforted me and made me feel at home here.

I strode into the water, watching glowing green bugs lift from the surface as I disrupted it and how they danced among the reflected aurora.

It was beautiful.

I was so caught up in trying to absorb it all and put it all to memory as I dragged my fingers through the water at my sides, attempting to capture it in my heart forever, that I forgot all about Kaeleron.

Until water splashed behind me.

I twisted to look at him.

And gawped.

He was utterly naked.

By the gods.

Some divine power had carved this male from marble, every honed muscle on his exquisite body lovingly crafted and deeply cut, a study in raw, masculine power. His long legs flexed with each step closer he took, water splashing up to caress his lean thigh muscles and the wicked vee that arched over his hips. Abs like rocks shifted as he prowled towards me, a bewitching dance that I tried to look away from, dragging my eyes up to the broad slabs of his pectorals.

He wasn't a mere king.

He was a dark god.

And some primal part of me wanted to worship him.

The sight of him flustered me, and not because I was shocked to see a male naked, because I had seen plenty of that at my pack—wolf shifter males didn't really have any shame when it came to preparing for a shift. They just stripped off in front of anyone, even total strangers.

No, what shocked me was the heat that blasted through me in response to seeing *him* naked was like an inferno, ratcheting up my temperature to an unbearable degree.

Something inside me responded to the sight of him, something fierce and hungry that made me want to howl and had my claws coming out, ready to sink into him and hold him in place while I devoured him with my gaze.

My traitorous body roared with need.

A hunger only he could slake for me.

And my eyes dropped to his groin.

I plunged headlong into the water, trying to cool off and escape him, struggling for control over my unruly body and that pressing, wicked heat that filled me and had me wanting to swim right back to the fae king.

This wasn't good.

It really wasn't good when he didn't let me get far. He swam after me and by the time I had broken the surface, he was within a few feet of me again. My cheeks felt as if they were on fire as he treaded water before me, blocking my route.

The water was so clear that I could see everything.

Everything.

He was temptation incarnate as his carved muscles danced beneath his pale skin with each gentle kick of his long legs, water droplets rolling down his face from his slicked-back wet hair, and his silver eyes brighter than I had ever seen them.

The reason he had been so damned quick to agree to my caveat hit me.

Why I had felt suspicious of him in that moment.

His sensual smirk rocked me as it dawned on me, cranking my temperature higher, rousing that hunger in my veins until it was close to overwhelming me.

He had no intention of asking me for sex.

He intended to make me want him so badly I would be the one asking him.

That was the game he was playing.

He wanted me to beg for it.

And by the gods, some part of me wanted to do just that.

CHAPTER 11
KAELERON

The little wolf's innocence might be bewitching, and her lightness refreshing, but she was a bold creature. All morning, as I had held court, meeting with my advisors and hearing requests from my people, I had considered her reactions to me at dinner, and how curious she had been about my world. I had thought she would be afraid of it, but with every question I had answered, she had only grown more curious.

I was still no closer to unravelling her purpose and role in my vengeance, and it irritated me, but this wolf had a strange way of making me forget the pressing need to find my brother and make the Summer Court bleed. Amusing myself with her was a glorious distraction, one I willingly plunged myself into while I found ways to discover more about her, sure in time either she or Neve would reveal her purpose.

She strode towards me through the trees, chin jutting upwards the moment she noticed me, her wandering and flitting gaze locking onto me. Her aquamarine eyes darkened a touch, losing some of the shine of fascination that had been in them as she had taken in her surroundings. She liked nature. It made sense, given her breed, but I had been unprepared for how strongly she liked it. Even now, she struggled to keep her eyes from the trees and the lake, and the mountains that loomed above us, fighting to keep her focus locked on me.

As if I might strike like a snake and bite her if she did not watch me closely.

Saphira halted in front of me, bold and a little courageous even as I raked my gaze over her, appraising her shapely form and how the swimsuit she had requested hugged her curves, the black material fitting snug to her body and revealing more than it concealed. My servant had returned from the human world with several choices, some more revealing than others, and this had been the most modest of them. I had selected it and another garment I was told mortals often used to cover their legs while they were out of the water.

I had wanted to see what she would make of the offering that played up her innocence.

Would she hide as much as possible from me and others, shielding herself as best she could with the garments, or would she be the bold female who had stood up to me on more than one occasion?

This female before me, her blue gaze challenging me to say something about her attire, was as bold as they came.

It had been a long time since I had courted a female, but there were few in this world who were as brave as this little wolf as she faced me, standing her ground despite the tremulous beat of her heart that betrayed her nerves.

I swept my hand towards the lake. "After you."

She lingered a moment longer, looking as if she was trying to soak up the scenery that surrounded her, and then stepped into the water. Fascination played across her face and my senses as she studied the water and the glow bugs that took flight at the disturbance, and I wanted to ask her what she thought of this world.

My world.

I held my tongue, sure whatever would leave her lips would be adequately scathing if I demanded to know her thoughts rather than letting her offer them up to me of her own accord. She would snap fangs at me and bite with her words, attempting to wound me. Amusing little wolf. She wielded words like weapons, as if she had no other defences.

Perhaps she did not.

I was not particularly informed on the behaviour or societal structure of wolf shifters. They rarely entered Lucia. But in this world, females were often treated as inferior to males, held back from activities the males could pursue—such as fighting. It had taken threatening my council, and dealing with several of the less malleable members in a manner that sent a message to the others, in order for me to allow Jenavyr to join the ranks of my army and train in the art of war.

Had the little wolf been subject to such ridiculous restrictions in her pack?

I would find out.

But first, I would set out to complete the plan I had set in motion last night at dinner.

She strode deeper into the water, so it lapped at her slender thighs, and I peeled my tunic off, following it with my boots and then my pants, leaving them in a neat pile on a smooth boulder on the shore.

Like the little wolf, I had few qualms about being seen in a state of undress.

Yet, a strange fluttering feeling began low in my belly as I waded towards her, my pulse hitching as she started to turn towards me.

And her mouth hung open.

Crimson painted her cheeks, and hunger flared bright in her eyes, the scent of need perfuming the air as she stared.

And then she dove into the water.

Attempting to escape me.

"That will not do," I murmured and followed her, diving deep towards the crystal boulders at the bottom of the lake before kicking upwards, enjoying the feel of the warm water and the sight of the little wolf as she tried to swim away from me.

I came up before her as she broke the surface for air and that blush on her cheeks deepened as I treaded water before her, letting her drink her fill and enjoying the feel of her hungry gaze devouring me. Innocent, but not shy. Afraid, but courageous. This female was a delicious blend of contradictions.

There was not a female like her in my court.

Perhaps that was why I was drawn to her, wanted her as I had wanted no other. She was different. Alluring. Tempting. And I liked teasing her, trying to crack her cool reserve and rattle her a little.

She was a challenge.

And I would be the victor.

I would break her.

No trace of fear coloured her eyes as I swam a lap around her. She turned in pace with me, blue gaze lifting to the mountains at times, or perhaps the sky. When she was facing the castle, I lost her. She ran her hand over her wet silver hair, clearing it from her delicate face, and stared at the castle.

"Do you like it?" I husked, watching her reaction as she took it in, that irritating fluttering returning as I waited to hear her verdict.

She shrugged. "It looks like the Addam's Family and Disney had a baby."

I was not sure what that meant or who these two families she spoke of were.

She glanced at me as she wiped water from her face, a little smile teasing her lips. "Now who's stupid?"

It only took a scowl to make that smile wobble. "I know little of your human world."

"Not human world. Plenty of shifter breeds live there, and vampires, and witches and even demons. It's just not *your* world." She rotated to face me, but her gaze drifted back to the castle. "I just meant it's a little grim with all that black stone, but something out of a fairy tale too."

I had never thought of my castle as like something from a fairy tale. "What makes it so?"

She lowered so the water met her nose as she studied the castle for long seconds, and then kicked upwards, her shoulders breaching the surface. "It's the towers, I think. The rest of it looks a bit... medieval military. But those towers and the cone-shaped roofs. Very Disney."

"Who is this Disney?" Someone she knew? I needed to know and while I could have feigned knowledge of what she spoke of and asked one of my servants to investigate it later, I found I wanted to hear it from her soft, pink lips.

"They make kids TV and movies... like pictures that move and have sound. Although they've branched out a bit now. But when I was younger, they were really known for entertaining children, and pups like me." She waved a hand towards the castle. "Their logo is a castle. Towers like yours, but it's more... light... fake. Towers that look too thin to be of any real use, taking up valuable space. Your castle is more... real. Functional."

I looked at it too. I had built it as a fortress, one strong enough to protect all within its walls if it came under attack. It was not beautiful by any stretch, but it was beautiful to me. It represented safety and security, and strength. Designed to strike awe and fear into those who saw it.

"The towers are functional," I assured her. "Men use the upper levels to keep watch. The vantage point from so high is such that they can see movement across a great distance, and even up into the mountains."

"See." She spun to face me again. "That makes total sense."

It struck me that she was far too at ease with me despite my nakedness, that she had easily overcome it and now acted as if it was nothing. Not the reaction I had desired when devising this plan. I had been sure she would blush constantly and attempt to evade me, too ashamed of her own feelings and desires to gaze at me as boldly as she was now.

I kicked onto my back and then rolled and dove beneath the surface, heading away from the castle and along the shore, feeling her gaze tracking me as I went. More than her gaze tracked me. She swam after me.

Curious little wolf.

I broke the surface and swam for the waterfall.

I reached it before she caught up with me and hauled myself out onto the slippery boulders in the midst of the spray close to the thundering water. The sound drowned out all other noise, and my senses sharpened to compensate for the loss of one of them, centuries of training and experience kicking into place. None would dare attack me here, but I refused to lower my guard.

The little wolf caught up just as I finished traversing the stretch of wet stone and stepped beneath the edge of the waterfall, letting it rain down upon me and batter my shoulders and back. The chilly water numbed my skin, but by the Great Mother, there was nothing quite as invigorating.

Well, perhaps there was something.

The feel of Saphira's gaze scalding me.

I tipped my face upwards towards the rushing water, letting it engulf me, and then lowered it again, looking at her as I ran both hands over my hair, slicking it back from my face.

Sure she would look away now I was watching her, obviously aware of her staring.

The bold little wolf continued to gaze at my nude form.

"You seem to enjoy looking at me." I meant the words as a challenge, to make her blush and look away, but they came out teasing and light.

Strange how she did that.

I tried to snap and bite and bare my fangs, to keep her in her place, to shake and rattle her, and she somehow softened me.

It was a desire to bed her that kept me civil, that was all.

A frightened or angry female did not make a good bedfellow.

She shrugged. "You're not the first male I've seen nude. I'm a wolf shifter. Male wolf shifters have little shame and we would go through a lot of clothing if we shifted without undressing first."

My eyebrows pitched low as I stared down at her as she floated on her back, as if she did not have a care in the world.

She should.

She had just announced she had seen many men naked.

Shadows curled through my veins, staining the tips of my fingers as my nails began to transform into claws and the darkness that lived within me snarled at me to find those males and end them, because this female was mine now.

The only naked male body she should know was *mine*.

Something corrosive scoured my insides, pouring like acid through me, a feeling I was not accustomed to and did not want to examine too closely.

"That's an odd look," she murmured as she studied me,

slowly rotating in my direction with nothing more than a gentle wave of one hand through the water. She pursed her lips. "I might even say you don't like that I've seen a *lot* of men naked."

"Ridiculous." I ran my hands down my body and her gaze followed them, cheeks pinkening and not from the cooler water near the falls.

She might have seen many nude males, but I was sure not one of them compared with my physique. Fae were blessed with strength. It was etched into our bodies. There were many tales of fae who travelled to the mortal world being set upon by the opposite sex of all species because we were so alluring to others, our vitality and beauty craved by all.

Oberon had told me of several of his conquests over the years, how desperately the females had wanted him. So desperately they had fought among themselves until Oberon had kindly offered to share himself with them all.

Saphira's blue eyes drifted back to me, running over my body, rousing awareness of her. If she had not been sold as an innocent, I might have believed her otherwise. Although, the wolf might have been lying.

There was one way to find out.

"Are you a maiden, little lamb?"

Horror flashed across her face and she swept her arm around, spraying me with water as she loosed an embarrassed squeak.

"Apparently so," I husked.

"Oh, you—" she muttered, anger rolling off her, and flattened her lips, holding back whatever salvo she wanted to launch at me.

I chuckled as she swam away from me, kicking her legs hard, as if she could not get away from me quickly enough.

It was only when she neared the other end of the lake that my amusement faded into sharp, cold terror.

The falls.

She turned and began frantically kicking back towards me, but she made no headway, was slowly being pulled towards the waterfall that fell over two hundred feet to the lagoon below.

"Saphira," I whispered through the shadows as I teleported.

I plunged into the lake a short distance from her.

The moment I hit the bottom, I sought her, gaze rapidly scanning the hazy bubbling water, and kicked off when I spotted her flailing form, shooting towards her as she was pulled towards the falls and spun around in the current.

I reached for her, shadows bursting through the water, slicing it apart to reach her, and wrapped her in them, yanking her to me. The second she was in my arms, her small body shuddering against me, her fear wrapping around me, I teleported us back to the shore.

And held her close as she coughed and spluttered, as she shook and slumped, her legs giving out beneath her.

She nestled in the shelter of my arms, her heart a rapid drumming against my stomach, the scent of her panic rousing something dangerous in me, something vicious and dark that had my shadows slicing through the rocks and water of the lake, lashing out at everything in it, as if it were to blame for what had almost happened.

The little wolf was immortal, in the sense she was long-lived, but tumbling over the waterfall would have been the death of her. There was no way she would have survived the impact with the water, and even if by some miracle of the Great Mother she had, she probably would have been knocked unconscious and drowned in the sea before I could find her.

Her trembling slowly subsided and she shifted in my arms, her palms scalding my flesh as she pressed closer to me. The feel of her leaning on me, seeking more from me, bewitched my shadows and calmed the darkness that writhed within me, demanding someone pay.

If anyone were to blame, it was me.

I smoothed my hand over her tangled silver hair, my chest tightening as I felt her beneath my palm, in my arms, tucked close to me. Safe. My mind flashed with images of her falling, of what might have happened if I had not reacted so quickly, and I found myself holding her more tightly.

"Foolish little wolf," I murmured against her hair, unsure whether she was the one shaking or I was too, and tried to banish whatever softness was building inside me, building between us as she clung to me, and made light of the moment by adding, "If you wanted my naked body pressed to yours, you only had to ask."

She tensed.

And then did something that altered something fundamental inside me.

Something that felt too dangerous.

Too bewitching.

She laughed.

Her breath bathing my skin.

Warming me.

Soothing me.

Lightening me but making me feel weary at the same time, as if it stripped all my strength from me and I was in danger of crumpling under the weight of all I bore on my shoulders.

I growled and teleported away from her, slamming shut the iron doors around my softer emotions—my useless emotions—she had somehow pried open.

Because I had no use for them.

I had no use for her beyond my vengeance.

And it was time I remembered that.

CHAPTER 12
SAPHIRA

The muted sunlight was warmer today, and I wondered whether it was spring here as well as back home as I stood on my balcony, fully dressed in my blouse, leathers and boots, longing to be down among the townspeople seeing more of this world.

Kaeleron had kept me shut in my room the last two days. The only people I had seen in that time were my handmaidens, who I had annoyed with so many questions during their brief visits to bring me my meals that they had eventually surrendered a few crumbs of information.

Firstly, I had learned that the younger of the females was called Thalina, and the older one was Beliana, and I had apparently insulted the latter by believing their ages to be vastly different. It turned out that there was only a twenty-year gap between them and that was nothing when you were talking about ages in the hundreds. I had believed Thalina younger than me, but she was close to two centuries older, and had been working for the castle for longer than I had been alive.

That had left me wondering how old Kaeleron was. Neither had been willing to disclose that information, so instead I had asked where he was and whether I was being punished. My captivity certainly felt like punishment. He had given me a glimpse of his world and a taste of freedom, and then he had snatched it away again, and a small part of me couldn't help but feel it was my fault.

It had been stupid of me to let my emotions get the better of me and my angry thoughts steal my focus away from the world so much that I hadn't been paying attention to where I was swimming, especially when I knew there was a waterfall at both ends of the lake.

And how far that water fell to the sea below.

That moment reared up on me as it had so many times in the last two days, and my throat closed as jumbled memories barraged me, stealing the world from my grasp until I felt sure I was back in that frigid water, fighting for my life.

Desperate to live.

I looked down at myself, at my violently shaking hands as I held them before me, and curled my fingers into fists. I owed Kaeleron my life, and he hadn't even given me a chance to thank him for what he had done. He had saved me, risking his own life to protect mine, and then he had held me so damned close.

So damned hard.

And by the gods, it had felt good.

His arms around me had felt more than good. They had felt strong. Comforting. *Right.*

That revelation had shaken me and I had tried to blame it on my instincts, that I was still struggling to grasp what Lucas had done and being held in powerful arms against a honed masculine body in an intensely protective embrace had made me think of my fated mate.

That was the only reason Kaeleron's arms around me had felt right.

But no matter how many times I told myself that, I couldn't bring myself to believe it. I hadn't been thinking of Lucas when Kaeleron had held me. I had been soul-deep aware of whose arms I had been in, of who was holding me close and shielding me from the world. I just didn't want to admit how deeply he affected me.

I had wondered time and time again since that moment whether holding me had shaken him too, because no matter how I looked at things, his words to me hadn't been wicked or teasing. He had been trying to lighten the moment. To break the hold we had on each other, clinging so fiercely to the other, as if they were a lifeline.

As if letting go meant greeting death.

A cold, slow and torturous death of the soul.

Maybe it had rattled him as violently as it had shaken me, and that was the reason he was keeping his distance from me. Ignoring me.

Was this to be my life now? A doll he would remove from its box whenever he was bored and wanted to play? An object of entertainment and nothing more?

I would be anything but that.

Ignoring the breakfast Thalina and Beliana had so kindly laid out for me on the balcony, I strode for the door, my confidence wavering and my boots sounding increasingly loud in the room as I approached it. I could do this. I wouldn't go far. Just a walk around the grounds for some fresh air and to test whether I was allowed to leave my room without permission from the king.

I eased the door open.

Glanced both ways along the elegant corridor.

A guard stood at either end, both dressed in matching thick

black leather tunics, trousers and boots, and both resting one hand on the hilt of the sword that hung from their waist.

Would they cut me down if I tried walking past them?

Or force me to return to my room?

There was only one way of finding out.

I stepped out into the corridor, closing my door behind me, making sure it made a noise so they were aware of me. Neither reacted. I took the only route I knew led to the garden, heading towards the vestibule, and my ears twitched as I sensed the male behind me moving, trailing after me. When I reached the second male ahead of me, he allowed me to pass and then fell into step behind me.

Apparently, I didn't just have handmaidens. I had guards.

But they weren't stopping me from leaving.

Although, I was sure that would change if I dared to venture beyond the inner walls that surrounded the castle. What areas would be off limits to me? If I walked to the lake, would they try to stop me? Could I visit the forest?

Deciding I would test all these theories and learn the boundaries of my confinement, I stepped out into the beautiful garden. Bees ambled around the blooms, and birds flitted between the trees I had taken to watching yesterday, once I had realised they were growing fruit as purple as the veins that marked their trunks and branches. The delicious sweet syrup I had tasted at dinner with Kaeleron had to come from these trees. I glanced at one of them, noticing small notches in the bark near some of the veins, as if they had been tapped.

I was so absorbed in it that I didn't notice there were others besides my two shadows in the garden.

Ahead of me, lounging on the pale grey stone benches under one of the arbours, were several finely-dressed males and females. Highborn. The name suited them. They barely hid their sneers as servants offered them refreshments and they spied more tradespeople delivering barrels to the castle through a side entrance. I changed course, wanting to avoid them, and wanting a closer look at the great stags that pulled the carts. This pair were so black they were like a void and had a shimmer to their fur that reminded me of raven wings.

"I do not understand why our king would pay so much attention to a *mutt*."

I tensed at the snide female voice that cut through the birdsong and barely bit back a growl as my hackles rose. She could only be talking about me. I peeked at her out of the corner of my eye, not wanting her to know I had heard what she had said. The tall, dark-haired beauty wasn't even trying to be subtle as she turned towards the female beside her, disgust written in every line of her sneer.

"Look at her." She shook her head. "She wears the garb of commoners, so I suppose she at least knows her position."

I liked my buttery-soft leather pants and loose blouse, and was much happier wearing these common clothes than restrictive dresses like the one Kaeleron had dressed me in for dinner —like the ones these women wore.

"Perhaps she is his servant." A pretty, petite brunette female in the trio looked me over, more curious than disgusted by my presence.

The haughty one scoffed. "And she serves him how?"

Maybe they didn't know I could understand them. They were being so open with their remarks. Or maybe they knew I could grasp their words and that was part of the fun for them.

Mock the little wolf.

The third female, this one as tall as the first, muttered, "Perhaps she is his mistress."

The haughty one's dark eyes widened and her face paled before crimson splotches coloured her cheeks and she scowled at me. "Impossible. Our king would not sully himself with such a lowborn female. I will speak with him about it at our next meeting. I am sure he will set our minds at ease. I can barely tolerate her presence. Perhaps we should move away to somewhere that smells less like dog."

I halted when rather than moving away, she led her little group right towards me, holding my ground and aware where this was going. Sense said to walk away, but my wolf side and my primal instincts told me to stand firm and not let them win by scaring me off.

This fae wanted me to run with my tail tucked between my legs and it wasn't going to happen.

As she was passing, she dropped a handkerchief.

"Oh, how terrible. Be a dear and do your duty and pick that up for me." She regally waved towards the piece of lace-trimmed white cloth.

I stared at it. "No."

"It speaks back to me." She fluttered her hand over the chest of her rich violet silk gown and looked at her two companions. "Did you hear how it spoke back to me?"

It.

"How terribly shocking," the petite one said, but she didn't look at all shocked. She looked as if she wanted no part in whatever her friend was planning as she went to pick up the handkerchief for her only to be stopped with a hand on her shoulder.

"Let the servant do that. It is the reason they exist."

I looked around me. "I see no servant nearby that could assist you with your problem. How awful it must be to have to pick it up yourself. But don't mind me. I won't tell a soul that you stooped to pick up your own handkerchief from the ground."

One of the guards behind me chuckled but it cut off when the female glared at him.

"Pick it up," she said more firmly and pointed to it.

"No. Do it yourself. I don't answer to you." I folded my arms across my chest, weathering her glare as she turned it on me, refusing to do what she wanted even when that tang of magic filled the air around me.

Kaeleron had warned me to keep my fangs sharp, and now I was beginning to understand the reason why. Not all in his court were as accepting of my presence as him and Neve. This fae looked ready to gut me where I stood, and I felt sure that if I hadn't been Kaeleron's pet, she would have gone through with it.

"Elanaluvyr, let me pick it up for you," the petite one hissed, a little desperate as she glanced from me to her friend and then the guards.

"Let the mutt pick it up. She is here to serve, is she not? Or is it only our king you serve on your knees?" The third one grinned at me as I tensed and my gaze shot to her, hearing her speak to me that way startling me enough that my guard slipped. "Oh, she *is* a little whore. I am surprised he let you leave his bedroom."

"I am not a whore," I snapped at her, my fangs emerging as the way she was looking at me, as if I was filth and disgusting, unworthy of her king, set fire to my blood.

"Then what are you?" Elanaluvyr stepped closer to me, darkness marring the beauty of her fine features as she scowled down at me and almost snarled, "How did you come to be here, sullying the Shadow Court with your presence? Were you a gift to him? A servant? His mistress? I *will* know."

I wasn't sure why she was so desperate to know how I had ended up in her precious Shadow Court, and I didn't really care. All I wanted to do was leave, but I couldn't now. Leaving would show weakness, and I had the feeling that if I showed any weakness around this particular female, that I might find myself in grave danger. She might seek to remove me from the court in a permanent, life-ending way, regardless of how Kaeleron would likely punish her.

Her eyes were wild as she waited for my reply, as if her sanity hinged on me easing her mind and denying I had anything to do with her king.

Especially anything involving the bedroom.

"If you want to know," I countered her, stepping right up to her, almost nose to nose with her as I clenched my fists at my sides and stared her down, "he sullied your precious court when he *bought* me at a black-market auction."

Her dark eyes widened as her head inched back and then she burst out laughing.

"Why in the name of the goddess would our king buy you?" She laughed in my face, and then towards her friends, and the two of them joined in, the sound ringing in my ears, mocking me as fiercely as their words. She swiped a tear from her eyes. "How ridiculous. Our king has no need to buy females."

I was beginning to get that impression, and that this female despised me so much not because I was an interloper and something other than a fae, but because she felt threatened by my presence.

She wanted Kaeleron.

"Ask him." I shrugged and smiled at her, my prettiest smile. "Because I am fairly sure that paying someone a million gold coins for me counts as buying a female."

I turned away from her.

"Such a filthy little mutt. Lying about our king. I shall have your head for that."

"Elanaluvyr," the petite one hissed in warning and I looked back at the trio to find her holding Elanaluvyr's arm, stopping her from coming at me.

Elanaluvyr flexed her fingers, her nails like talons as they raked through the air, her eyes dark as midnight and filled with rage and hunger. My wolf side had me turning my front to her again, every instinct I possessed warning me that this female meant to attack me with more than words, and all because I had spoken the truth about her precious king.

That precious king appeared in view, crossing the twilight-sun-kissed courtyard, his strides long and hurried as if he was trying to escape the males and females who stood as he approached and said things to him, all of them fawning over him.

Elanaluvyr was quick to scurry over to him, her two companions rushing on her heels.

Kaeleron's expression remained as cold as stone as she greeted him. He didn't even slow.

"Poor Elanaluvyr. How she longs for my brother." That gentle and familiar female voice had me spinning on my heel, eyes widening as I came face to face with the beautiful owner of it.

She was tall and striking, her fall of black hair like satin and her silver eyes bright with amusement as she mocked the female who had been threatening me moments ago.

"You shall have to forgive her. She has been chasing his heels for almost a decade now, and I am still not sure whether she wants to claim his heart or is like all the others and simply wants to claim his crown. One is not his to give and the other is something I doubt anyone could claim."

Which was which? Did he not have the right to give his heart or his crown?

I struggled to recall her name, feeling a little flustered as I realised we were alone. There was no sign of the guards. Had they disappeared when this female had approached me? How much had she heard?

"I am Jenavyr." She dipped her head in a short bow.

I fumbled a curtsy, unsure what the correct greeting was for the sister of a king. "Saphira."

Her smile was warm and genuine as she leaned towards me. "Would you like to see a more charming side of this city?"

"Yes." I couldn't say that word fast enough, and not only because I wanted to see more of it.

The thought of escaping all the vicious looks and horrible remarks that had left me feeling I needed to watch my back and couldn't let my guard down had me leaping on the chance. The opportunity to see more of this place was only made all the more appealing by the fact it would be the king's sister acting as my escort.

"I thought you might say yes." Jenavyr cast a fond look at the castle and the gardens, and her brief smile made me look over my shoulder in the direction Kaeleron had been heading.

He stood at the edge of the garden, looking right back at her.

At me.

For a crushing moment, I thought he might come and demand I return to my room, but then he dipped his head, and disappeared from view beyond the castle wall, a trail of nobles following him.

"Come then." She took my arm, draping it over hers, and patted it. "Let us find some peace and quiet away from the court politics and desperate females, and see if perhaps we can discover a place that is more… *us*."

I blinked at her. *More us*.

It hit me that she had seen right through me as we walked down the gentle slope towards the imposing castle gatehouse. I looked at the garden behind me, at the highborn coming and going, and that feeling cemented within me.

I didn't belong here.

These noble fae weren't my world—my people.

My gaze drifted to the larger area of the town, beyond the black and grey stone walls that had no doubt been constructed in part to separate the highborn from the commoners. Those were my people. I tracked the cobbled road that snaked through to the town until there was nothing but open, wild land in my sphere of vision. That was my world.

Jenavyr led me towards the main gate, towering over me and making me feel small, drawing glances and elegant bows from the nobles we passed. I looked from them to her, as curious about her as I was about the town I was finally going to see up close.

She didn't dress like the highborn.

No elegant gowns for this female.

She wore black leather pants and a royal blue long-sleeved blouse that matched mine, but beneath her breasts she wore an onyx leather corset over her blouse. Her outfit was rugged and made for work, not something I had expected the sister of a king to be wearing, certainly not in this world.

She looked far from a beautiful princess.

She was a striking warrioress.

Right down to the sword sheathed at her hip.

She noticed me staring at it and loosed a soft chuckle.

"I'm sorry. I didn't expect the sister of a king to dress as you do... like I am... let alone carry a weapon." I grimaced through my apology, sure it wasn't enough.

"Ah, so I should be wearing hideous dresses and be keeping my hands clean and soft?" She gazed down at me, silver eyes bright with amusement as she half-smiled and I grimaced again, feeling terrible for what I had said as she added, "Many in this court believe the same, though they would not dare to mention it beyond secret whispers between trusted allies. My brother saw to that."

"How?" That question left my lips before I could stop it,

curiosity pulling it from me as I openly stared at her now, the thought of learning more about the king making me want to press her for the answer.

She simply said, "He executed those on his council who were against my being allowed to earn a position within his army."

I halted beneath the arch of the smaller gateway between the highborn and common districts. "He *executed* them?"

For speaking out against his sister and daring to believe they knew what was best for her.

"It was a rather bloody affair, but then court politics often ends that way." She seemed rather blasé about her brother murdering people merely because they hadn't agreed with him.

"What happens if *I* don't agree with him?" My mind raced, filling with gruesome images, and my heart galloped with it.

A sigh rolled from her as she patted my arm where it rested over hers. "My brother can be... *ruthless*. But he only does what he believes is necessary to maintain order within his court, and this court is not as bad as some of the others. Kael can be... I am sure he is often conflicted about the things he must do as king. But there are many things we do not agree on and he has not killed me yet."

She meant the last part as a way of lightening the mood, a joke of sorts, but I couldn't find much to laugh about in what she had said. I had begun to relax and lower my guard in this place, but now as I looked around the highborn houses and the street behind me, and the castle that loomed above it, some of the light this place had gained in the last few days shuttered and died out.

And all I saw was darkness and shadow.

The sneers of the nobles as they looked at me.

The whispered comments passed between the females, and even the males.

The way some openly eyed me as if they wanted to tear me down, while others gazed at me as if I was something they could steal and drag into the shadows to do the gods only knew what with.

I suddenly wanted to return to my room, where I felt safe.

Jenavyr rested her hand on my arm, her touch light but firm, and her voice pitched low, serious at last as she said, "No one will dare harm you, Saphira. It would be their head. My brother would not tolerate it."

He would execute them.

And something buried deep within me whispered that he would enjoy it.

That he would take pleasure from making someone bleed and hurt.

"Why did your brother buy me?" My voice trembled as I tore my gaze from the nobles and forced it back to Jenavyr, attempting to block out the darker side of this world I could only see right now.

There was light in this world.

I had witnessed it.

It wasn't all shadows and blood.

No matter how many times I told myself that, it wouldn't stick, and my imagination was running wild, conjuring terrible things, shadowy monsters that dogged my every step as we began walking again.

"My brother's motivations are his alone to know. It is not my place to speak of them, but I do not condone what he did." Jenavyr's gaze drilled into the side of my face as I looked at the first buildings of the main town, trying to banish those monsters in my mind. "He has been... How is Kael treating you?"

The concern in her voice, and in her eyes as I looked at her, touched me deeply, soothing some of my fears away and helping me chase the monsters out of my head. She had the look of a female who wanted to protect something, who was ready to fight her own flesh and blood if she heard Kaeleron had been mistreating me. That she would face his wrath by arguing with him over my wellbeing reaffirmed that feeling that I had found an ally in her, and maybe one in Neve too.

It bolstered my courage.

"Well." It was the only answer that came to me as I thought about how Kaeleron had been treating me so far. "I've only seen him twice. Once for dinner and once for a swim in the lake."

My cheeks began to heat so I turned my face away from her, pretending to study the buildings that were closest to the gate. The one to my right was a beautiful combination of grey stone for the ground floor and a half-timber upper floor under a black clay tile roof.

"That was a few days ago," I added, wanting to feel her out about why Kaeleron hadn't summoned me since that moment he had held me in his arms and tried to make light of how foolish I had been and how it might have gotten me killed. "I hadn't seen him at all until just now."

"My brother has been busy with court and preparations for Beltane. I have not seen him much beyond our scheduled meetings where I file reports about the regiments."

So he hadn't been avoiding me then?

Some part of me whispered that he had. That moment had shaken him too, and he had retreated, throwing himself into his work to avoid me. And perhaps punish me a little.

"Let us not talk of Kael. He can be so very tiresome." Jenavyr smiled, her whole face lighting up with it, and it was hard to believe she was related to him when she looked like that, as if she was all light and warmth, no trace of darkness and shadow in her. Maybe the two of them were a fractured whole, and he had received all the darkness while she had been graced with all the light. “Come. Let us explore. I might even treat us to a sticky bun at the finest bakery in Falkyr.”

“Falkyr?”

“By the Great Mother, has my brother told you nothing?” She swept her arm out as she turned with me. “Welcome to Falkyr Castle, daughter of wolves.”

This female was definitely the light to Kaeleron’s darkness.

I took it all in—the bustling terraced town of half-timbered buildings around me, the great black wall that rose beyond them, and the onyx castle perched above them, its backdrop the jagged mountains and that twilight-kissed aurora.

Falkyr Castle.

“It’s so... strange compared with my home. I feel like I’ve gone back in time hundreds of years.” I drank in the castle, with its towers and turrets, and many arched windows, a small part of me wondering where Kaeleron held court within that monstrous building, the other trying to spy my balcony.

“I do not know much of your world. My brother forbids me from visiting it, but whenever Oberon visits, he tells me tales of that realm. I suspect they are somewhat embellished.”

Apparently I wasn’t the only female out there who had a controlling family member who didn’t let them do things they wanted to do. Jenavyr looked as if she longed to see my world, just as I had longed to see it.

“You must tell me of it.” She patted my arm again, her look almost conspiratorial. “I will ferret out whether Oberon has been lying about it.”

I swallowed.

She frowned.

“You do not wish to tell me of your world?”

I shook my head. “It isn’t that. I just... I haven’t seen much of it myself. I... um... I wasn’t allowed.”

Her frown deepened, her lips compressing as she studied

me, and then she huffed. "I feel it is time females took more power and autonomy in both of our worlds."

"Amen, sister," I murmured with a smile. "But I'll tell you what I can."

We turned back towards the town and followed the main street that wound downwards through it as I spoke of my world and all the things I could think of that might be of interest to an unseelie fae. But as we ventured further from the imposing castle, I found myself more absorbed in this world, falling silent as I studied it. I forgot all about home and my family, and Kaeleron as I lost myself in taking it all in. The street was growing busier, with many people coming and going, and we had to dodge several carts as they rumbled up the hill towards the castle.

The town had been broken up into more levels, land flattened out in places to allow room for colourful gardens and even animal pens, each level edged with a thick dark stone retaining wall. The houses were set back from that wall, forming roads in front of them where people walked or stopped to talk. There were pathways down from the levels, steep steps that hugged the walls, and the roads sliced into the levels, keeping a steady angle upwards towards the castle.

Several of the great stag-like creatures and two horses grazed in one pen beside a larger building with broad wooden doors that had been opened to reveal the workshop inside. I peeked inside to find a farrier at work, lit by the golden blaze of the furnace as he worked to shape glowing iron into a shoe for a waiting stag.

"What creature is that?" I pointed to the glossy black beast.

"An elkyn. Beautiful creatures, are they not? They are very temperamental though and hard to tame." Jenavyr gestured towards the ones in the pen that were rubbing their sharper front horns against the wooden fence, as if they were irritated and itched. Their antlers were small compared with the one the farrier was working on, barely as long as their pointed horns. "These are young. They will need to be worked for many more years before they are tame enough to pull the carts. But I prefer horses. The black one you see there is mine."

"A beautiful creature." I meant it.

It was large—far larger than I had expected a female to ride—and looked like a very patient beast as it stood stock still in one spot, idly chewing hay, as if it was waiting for its appointment with the farrier and was aware that was the reason it was here. An intelligent beast, one Jenavyr clearly loved as she gazed at it.

We walked onwards, weaving through wooden market stalls that had been set up in a square near a large pond that filled the space below one of the retaining walls, my gaze roaming over the tools and items on sale, and then the bread and vegetables that had been laid out in baskets.

Surrounding the square were more half-timbered buildings, each with a store on the ground floor. Tailors and seamstresses, bakers and butchers, grocers and confectioners. There were even furniture makers, small book shops, and places selling intriguing antiques. I stopped outside a store that had bowls of coloured powders and several moody but beautiful seascapes on display in the bay window. This town had everything, and I wanted to explore every shop one by one.

But Jenavyr pulled me onwards.

We passed a weaponsmith and I slowed, watching the shirtless muscular fae male as he beat the steel with a great hammer, each strike precise as if he had honed his skill for centuries.

Maybe he had.

Unseelie appeared to be very long-lived if the ages of my handmaidens were anything to go by.

"I must speak with Garandil." Jenavyr released my arm and

briefly smiled at me before heading into the forge, where the soot-streaked male set down his tools to greet her.

I paused to take in the town and the people that bustled around me, fascinated by it all, bewitched even.

But the longer I stood there while Jenavyr spoke with the blacksmith, the stronger a feeling within me grew.

There was tension in the air.

My ears twitched, my wolf senses sharpening as I watched the people, looking closer now. Something wasn't quite right about this place.

Few of the people smiled at each other, even when they were deep in conversation or seemed close to one another. I studied the people coming and going, that feeling crystalising into something I could grasp and put a name to.

It was sombreness.

It was the best way I could describe the heaviness in the air and the way people went about their business, but none laughed and few smiled.

My gaze roamed to the castle that loomed over them all.

The people here weren't happy.

Why?

Jenavyr stepped out of the forge and looked from me to the people I was watching. "Perhaps we should head back soon. You must be tired."

"I'm not. I want to see more." I didn't want to return to that room that suddenly felt small and stifling as I thought about being trapped inside it with nothing to do. "What's over in that direction?"

I pointed back the way we had come, to the place where the road had branched into two.

"The docks." Jenavyr took my arm again, glancing once more between me and the people as we turned, her grip more rigid now.

The townspeople weren't the only ones feeling tense. Part of me whispered to return to the castle as she wanted, but the rest of me howled to see more of this town because I wanted to understand why its people were so solemn.

"Docks," I echoed. "I've never seen docks before."

It was enough to have me marching forwards, past all the fascinating stores and the intriguing people. People that only became more intriguing as we entered a broader section of road and a more industrial area of the town. Large warehouses lined the cobbled road, and there were more carts here, rolling up from the docks I caught glimpses of through the buildings. The tall masts of the ships called to me, but they didn't hold my attention for long.

Standing outside one of the wood and stone warehouses were a group of what appeared to be goblins, each of them barely tall enough to reach mid-thigh on me. Their leather caps had been fashioned to accommodate their long, pointed ears, and rugged pants and sleeveless tunics in earth tones made their skin that ranged from light sage to deep forest green only stand out more to me. I tried not to stare, but diverting my gaze from them only had it snaring on something else.

Dwarves.

It was the only word that came to mind for the trio of stout, bearded males dressed in leather and plate armour that were looking over several heavy sacks of minerals that had been leant against the stone lower half of another warehouse.

"Traders, from the mountains and mines of the Shadow Court," Jenavyr said beside me. "The goblins bring foraged goods from the western woods, such as mushrooms and herbs, as well as a fine brew that bears the royal seal. The dwarves are responsible for running the royal mines as well as several quarries. Many of their ancestors worked on the castle. They are great stone masons. Their artistry and skill are second to none, and you can see many of their carvings on the façade of the castle, around the doors and windows."

I turned to tell her how fascinating this world was, and stopped dead.

Two large shirtless males carrying big wooden boxes and loading them onto the back of a cart captured and held my gaze.

They towered at least seven foot tall, with broad muscled bodies, and legs like tree trunks packed into worn thick leather trousers. Rather than feet, they had large black hooves, and instead of having a humanoid head, they resembled bulls, complete with glossy horns. One even had a gold ring through his nose.

Minotaurs!

There were actual minotaurs in this world, walking around and working just like the fae, goblins and dwarves, as if they were nothing out of the ordinary. I was tempted to blink and scrub my eyes to make sure I wasn't imagining them. One of them caught me staring and huffed, his nostrils flaring, and I dragged my eyes away from him, feeling incredibly rude.

Jenavyr chuckled softly beside me. "You look like you just saw your first minotaur."

"I did." I turned on her, my eyes wide. "We don't exactly get many minotaurs in my world. They'd kind of stand out."

Her fine black eyebrows rose. "I suppose. I would imagine you do not see many like them either."

She subtly nodded towards something.

I looked there and every inch of me locked up tight.

"By the gods," I breathed low, "what are those?"

They were the creepiest thing I had ever seen. They dwarfed the minotaurs as they moved in a stilted fashion up the road towards me, tattered black robes writhing like shadows across the cobbles. Thorny vines wrapped around their thin bodies, pinning the layers of their robes in place, and formed into a thick sweeping high collar from their chest to the back of their deer-skull heads. From their antlers, tinkling silver charms and threads of crystals swayed.

"They are—" Jenavyr cut off, going rigid beside me, and I feared these foul creatures had cast some kind of spell on her, my eyes darting to her as the warmth in the atmosphere turned frosty.

She stared beyond them.

I looked there, at the handsome blond male who stepped from what appeared to be a tavern, the muted sunlight catching on the metallic royal blue embroidered edges of his fine black tunic. He said something as he looked back into the tavern, waving his hand in a regal way as he dipped into a bow, and smiled in a way that made me feel someone had been teasing him and that bow had been mocking.

His deep blue eyes swung our way and the easy smile that had been gracing his lips dropped away.

He jogged down the steps and right over to us, passing the deer-skull-headed creatures as if they were nothing at all to be concerned about.

"Jenavyr. What brings you out of the castle?" His accent was muddied, but I thought I detected a hint of Irish among the blend of English and something else. His gaze landed on me. "And who is this? A new recruit?"

"None of your business." Jenavyr's tone had lost all warmth and her expression gained a glacial edge. "I am merely escorting her around town, and that is all you need to know."

I was sorely tempted to inch away from the firing line of whatever bad blood existed between her and this newcomer.

"Come now, Vyr. You leave for days, skulking off to the western reaches, and now you return in an even fouler mood?" He reached a hand out towards her.

She shot it a withering look that had it halting before it could touch her. "What have I said about calling me that, Riordan?"

Riordan shrugged. "Not to call you it. But it's fine for Kaeleron and Oberon to call you it, and hell, even Mal can use it but by the gods... how dare I call you Vyr, right? I've only known you for what... a century?"

"Longer. Believe me. I am aware of every day I have had the displeasure of your company."

His face darkened. There was definitely bad blood here, but as I glanced at Jenavyr, I swore her frostiness had nothing to do with his presence or her dislike of him. Her gaze kept darting to the tavern he had exited.

Riordan folded his arms, causing his tunic to pull tight across honed biceps, and a flicker of red emerged around his pupils.

Every instinct I possessed as a wolf shifter warned me to back away, to bare fangs at this male and keep my distance from him, because he wasn't a fae.

He was a vampire.

One who walked beneath the twilight sun as if it was nothing.

"I don't know what I've done to piss you off this time. Apparently, something. Maybe you should have stayed out by Wraith Wood and let me handle things here. Better yet, step down as second in command and go play princess."

The skin around Jenavyr's eyes darkened as her silver irises brightened, and her shadow grew restless on the ground, growing tendrils that writhed and even snapped at the cobbles.

"The only one who should step down is you. I believe I have proven myself more capable than you on... *all*... occasions." She rested her hand on the hilt of her sword.

"Want to test out that theory in the ring, Vyr?" He reached

for his own weapon and stepped up to her, using the few inches difference in their height to look down on her. "Or are you still too afraid to face me in a fair fight?"

She wrapped her fingers around the grip of her sword and sneered. "I do not need to prove myself to you, vampire. Now step out of my way. You are hindering official castle business."

He scoffed. "How low you have fallen if your official castle duties now include babysitting a wolf."

Jenavyr's shadows snapped at his polished riding boots and he was quick to leap back a step, moving so fast I could barely track him.

He scowled at her.

She scowled right back at him.

I fidgeted with the sleeves of my blouse, doing my best to fade into the background as they silently fought a battle of wills, each second that ticked past cranking the tension in the air higher.

And changing the atmosphere between them.

The sharpness of their glares slowly faded, something akin to heat beginning to flicker in their eyes as their breaths came faster.

And just when I wasn't sure whether they were going to fight or do something far more embarrassing for me, Jenavyr grabbed my hand and dragged me away from him, pulling me at a clip down the road towards the docks.

I looked at the building the vampire had exited as we passed it, peering through the open door at the revellers inside, and the buxom females who sat on the laps of a few of them.

"What is that place?" I craned my neck to see more as she swiftly pulled me away from it and the vampire.

"It is not a place for you." Her voice was as sharp as a sword as she bit those words out, her grip on my arm growing firmer as she scowled at the building and her shadows raced towards it only to halt as she grimaced, her jaw flexing. "It is a tavern that has a reputation with men looking for a good, easy lay."

"Oh." I couldn't drag my eyes away from it, even as my cheeks heated and her grip on my arm became bruising, anger rolling off her in powerful waves that had my instincts warning me away from her. When I lost sight of it, I looked at her, at the fierce lines of her hard expression, no trace of light or warmth in her beautiful face now. Catching the vampire in that place had angered her, and I wasn't sure it was because she didn't like him. "Perhaps he had court business there."

A weak attempt to soften her mood.

I wasn't even sure why I was making excuses for him, but I felt compelled to say something, to ease her mind and her anger. It was probably that part of me that still felt it was my duty to help anyone who was struggling in my pack, seeing what I could do to lessen their load, even if it was just letting them talk and get things off their chest.

She huffed. "Perhaps he did, but I doubt there is any court business that would require him to visit such a place."

"Maybe he was hungry." Another weak excuse, but this one had her grip on my arm loosening a touch, enough that it no longer hurt.

"Perhaps." She glanced back in the direction we had come, a look in her eyes that was far from the hatred she had shown towards the vampire. In fact, it seemed quite the opposite emotion.

"Do you like him?" I whispered that question, sure she would be angry with me for asking it, but I had seen wolves in my pack act in such a manner with each other, always fighting and acting cold towards the other, and more often than not it turned out they liked each other but were battling it for some reason.

"No," she snapped, quick to deny it, and then fell silent for a full minute before she quietly added, "I am to marry some court prince. Which one, I do not know yet, but it will happen."

"Whether you like it or not?" I shifted closer to her, compelled to be nearer her so she would know I was there with her—for her.

She hesitated and it was answer enough for me.

"I know how that feels," I admitted and sorrow welled up in me as I thought about my pack and Lucas, that ache to know my family were safe returning to cloud my mind and my heart. "I was essentially betrothed from the moment I was born. My pack did something terrible. My uncle challenged the alpha of the neighbouring pack, hungry for more power, and was defeated. That pack wanted to retaliate by taking over our pack, but my father convinced their alpha to look among our pack for potential fated mates of his people instead... a way of strengthening the bond between our two packs. Fated mates are... sacred... to wolves. Or at least they should be. The alpha agreed and used witchcraft to seek out mates among the immature wolves in my pack. And one of the mates they found was me... and I was fated to his son. That was enough to halt any trouble between our packs. So I grew up knowing who my mate was, and that I would be his once I matured, and dreaming of that day... but what really awaited me was a nightmare and Lucas—"

I cut myself off as my throat tightened and my eyes burned, my soul crying out for the other half of it as my wolf side loosed a mournful howl within me that made me want to scream in rage and frustration. Would I ever be free of this feeling? I hated Lucas. I wanted nothing to do with him. But my instincts weren't getting the message.

Jenavyr's steady gaze bore into me, reminding me I wasn't alone and who I had just opened myself to, telling the king's sister of all people about my past.

Panic had my muscles clamping down onto my bones.

I snared her arm, gripping it tightly, and struggled to breathe through it as I held her gaze, imploring her to listen to me and do as I was about to ask her.

"Please don't tell your brother what I said. I don't want him to know. It's bad enough that I was sold, but being sold by—" I couldn't bring myself to say it as a thousand blades cut my battered heart to ribbons all over again, the pain stealing my breath and my voice.

Jenavyr's silver eyes widened and then softened as understanding dawned in them.

She nodded.

"I will not tell a soul. Your secret is safe with me, Saphira."

I wished I could believe that.

CHAPTER 13
KAELERON

Jenavyr hadn't stopped sniping at Riordan from the moment the two of them had set foot in my office on the second floor of the castle. Riordan, of course, gave as good as he got, the two of them seeming to bask in the glory of irritating me with their inane remarks and poorly executed retaliations.

I pinched the bridge of my nose, an ache building between my eyes as I closed them. Fatigue rolled up on me the moment they shut, the long day of meetings I had endured wearing away at my strength, together with my two commanders.

"I only asked what you might be doing in such a disreputable tavern. The poor creatures within should not be subjected to your advances." Vyr launched the same salvo she had already used several times, her tone scathing.

Riordan sighed, the sound as weary as I felt. "A man has to feed."

The same response he had given each time my sister had remarked upon his visit to one of the taverns near the docks that sailors regularly frequented while looking for some female company.

Apparently, this was not a good enough answer for my sister, since she would not let it go.

I cleared my throat, gaining their attention as I sat back in my new chair on the other side of the also newly delivered desk to them. Furniture I would rather keep in one piece. To their credit, they both fell silent and straightened, their backs going rigid as they faced me instead, standing almost shoulder to shoulder.

"I did not summon you to hear you bicker." I draped my hands over the arms of my chair and surveyed them. "I wished to hear your reports."

Riordan irritated my sister further by being first to speak. "The second legion has been training in the west fields near the garrison, and the new recruits are coming along nicely. The north-eastern range is quiet and the south-western reaches have reported their latest scouting party found no sign of anyone crossing the mountain passes. Malachi is due back any day now with information from the Summer Court."

I pushed back from my desk and stood, my legs aching as they straightened, a sign I had spent far too long sitting in chairs or on thrones today. Malachi's return might be a problem, but I would deal with it when it happened. The demon would understand.

Vyr's gaze drilled into me, and I knew why she watched me so closely. She believed that when Malachi returned, there would be a reckoning, and she wanted to speak frankly about it with me, as was her way.

I met her gaze, silencing her with a look, and turned from my two commanders, heading for the grand arched window to my left, near one end of my desk, as instead of berating me she filed her report about Wraith Wood and the preparations she had overseen there, together with the trade routes. I lifted the scrolled iron latch and pushed the leaded window that reached almost from floor to ceiling open, relishing the fresh sea-laced breeze that swept into the room.

Movement below seized my attention.

The little wolf.

Riordan said something, his words distant as I watched the slender silver-haired female below me. She stood near the balustrade that edged the patio on the cliff-side of the gardens, fingers toying with the loose platinum strands of her hair as she gazed out to sea. It was a strange pleasure to observe her without her knowledge, watching her fingers combing the unruly strands that caught the rising breeze, and then as she nimbly plaited the long length of her hair, until it hung in a single braid that snaked down her spine.

How soft might her hair feel in my fist if I gripped that braid?

I failed to notice Vyr moving up beside me until she spoke.

"Maybe we should take a break. We have all been working for hours now. Well, two of us have." Another easy shot at the vampire and his tavern activities. "I could use some fresh air. We all could."

I kept my gaze fixed on the little wolf, unsure I could pull it away from her if I tried, and my sister had already caught me watching her, so there was little point in covering what I was doing, and equally little need.

I owned Saphira and could look at her if I wanted.

"You don't have to ask me twice." Riordan was already halfway out of the door.

It snicked shut behind him.

"Beltane is approaching," Vyr murmured, watching me closely. "What will you do?"

"Beltane," I muttered, considering the implications of what

my sister was really asking. She was not interested in what I would do at the great feast and the rites. She wanted to know what I intended to do with Saphira while they were happening.

How would the little wolf cope with it?

If I included her, things would certainly be more interesting than usual, and it would be a pleasure to watch her during the feast and the rites, studying her as she navigated her first Beltane.

But it might be wiser to keep her safely locked in her room that night instead.

"We are also due to visit Ereborne soon." Jenavyr sounded even more cautious now and with good reason.

I glared at the sea, watching the white foam lace the rolling waves and a black wooden galleon that rode them, heading towards the docks.

The thought of leaving Saphira unprotected in my court while I visited with the high king had my shadows growing restless, snaking outwards to climb the stone walls towards the window, as if they wanted to wrap around her as they had that day at the lake.

Shielding her.

Protecting her.

I could put off many things to keep her safe, but Beltane or visiting my high king were not one of them.

Both had to proceed as planned.

"Issue guard duty to two of your finest men." I did not look at Vyr as I issued that order. I kept my gaze locked on the little wolf as she casually strolled in the direction of the lake.

"And who will they be guarding?" Vyr asked.

"You know who."

She leaned into view, angling her body to track Saphira with her gaze as the wolf disappeared behind the wall of my office. "Is that really necessary? Saphira will not like—"

I cut her off with a look. A silent order.

She nodded. "As you wish."

And hesitated.

"What is it?" I moved to one of the windows at the end of the room to my left, beyond my desk, opening it to allow more air in the room, and happened to find Saphira sitting on one of the benches beneath an arbour laced with flowers the colour of her eyes.

"Saphira spoke to me of her pack and things that happened in her past." Each word was carefully measured, spoken slowly and reluctantly.

I held my hand up to silence my sister, even when I wanted to know what the little wolf had told her.

"Did she give you leave to speak of this to others?" I slid a look at her, seeing right away in her eyes that Saphira had not.

"No, but I thought it might be useful information for you to have. You seem to want to understand her better so you can discover the reason Neve told you to take her, and I thought perhaps—"

I stopped her again, denying the part of me that wanted to hear it. "I would rather hear it from the wolf herself."

That surprised me, and my sister too judging by how her eyes widened slightly. There was no logical reason to wait to know the information she had gathered. It made more strategic sense to know it now.

It hit me that I *wanted* the little wolf to open up to me as she had to my sister.

Which made no sense at all. I had no reason to want to hear it from her lips. It made more sense to hear it from my sister now.

And yet, I still desired that Saphira be the one to tell me of her past.

To open up to me.

I could order it, as part of our contract, and offer to knock a handsome sum off her debt, but that did not sit well with me and instead I found myself making plans, forming a route that would lead to the little wolf speaking to me of her past and herself.

"Send the handmaidens for Saphira." I put my back to the window. "She will dine with me within the hour and will tell me of her visit to the town."

Jenavyr bowed and made for the door.

As it closed behind her, I turned back to the little wolf where she perched on the wall now, near the thundering falls.

"I will know what you make of my world."

CHAPTER 14
KAELERON

The little wolf swept into the room right on time. My first test for her had been a choice between two dresses, one more revealing than the other. She had chosen the more traditional gown.

Her gaze lowered to the strapless corseted dress as she noticed me gazing at it. The material faded from light teal at her breasts to deep sea blue at the hem, and had been encrusted with pearls and diamonds around the top of the corset, the mass of them appearing as if it were the crest of a wave. More pearls and diamonds had been stitched over the length of the dress, glittering in the firelight, and gathered more densely near the hem.

"I preferred the colour," she mumbled, "It made me think of the sea."

A sea I had noticed she enjoyed watching.

A dress I had picked for its colour too.

"The other one seemed a bit plain in comparison." She arranged herself in her chair at the other end of the long dining table, wrestling with the heavy skirt and pulling a face at it as she stuffed the layers down the gap between her thighs and the arms of the chair.

A female clearly unused to wearing dresses.

"The other is the colour of my court." I waited, holding back my smile as she stiffened and blanched a little. Would she snap those delicious fangs at me or turn meek? I hoped it was the former.

She did not disappoint.

"Such a boring colour. I thought you would prefer black, or onyx, or obsidian." She gave up trying to arrange her skirts, her look conveying exactly what she thought of the colour of my court.

"Those are all words for black, little lamb. Do remember I am quite intelligent and not at all as stupid as you wish me to be." I poured myself a glass of wine and used magic to fill hers at the same time, earning a little jolt of a gasp from her. She had forgotten a lot since our last meeting apparently. My intelligence and my magic. "Royal blue, silver and black are the colours of my court, and have been since long before I took the throne, and will continue to be long after I am gone."

"Will that be soon?" She sat up straighter, an eager glint in her eyes. She was mocking me again, or teasing me at the very least. "If you die, do I get set free?"

"You are property of this court until you are granted your freedom." I took a long draught of my wine and relaxed into my seat as the potent drink eased the day's tension from my muscles and mind.

Or perhaps it was the little wolf's presence that eased the latter.

"I figured as much," she muttered. "Scratch the dying part then, please. I don't want to find out who I might end up with as my next owner. Oh! Or would it be Jenavyr? I could live with that."

"Jenavyr would not ascend the throne. Females are not heirs in this world, much the same as they are not heirs in yours. Another would claim my crown, and believe me, little one, they would not be offering you contracts and methods of repaying your debt to me. They would want to lay claim to more than my crown. They would want to claim all of you."

Each word that left my lips had Saphira tensing further, her gaze growing wary as she struggled to hold mine and pretend she was unaffected by the prospect of falling into the hands of a male more likely to claim what had been paid for.

"Fine. You can stick around," she mumbled into her wine. "Better the devil you know, and all that."

I swirled my wine in my glass as I studied her, enjoying being able to openly look at her without my sister scrutinising me, watching me for a weakness and a way of making me surrender the wolf back to her pack.

"My sister failed to mention much about your visit to the town. I believe she keeps your secrets well." I smirked when she stiffened, her shoulders hiking upwards as her fingers tightened around the stem of her wine glass. "But I have ways of making you talk."

Her pretty face darkened into a scowl. "If you even think about ordering me to tell you things, I'm going to read it as a suggestion and ignore you."

My smirk became a grin. Such a fierce little thing.

"And what if I used other methods to convince you instead?" I patted my thighs. "If you sit here a while, I am sure we could loosen that tongue of yours."

She rolled her eyes. "I don't think my tongue is the thing you want to loosen. The wine does that enough. I would say it was my panties you want to loosen, but I haven't failed to notice you don't supply them with my pretty dresses when I'm summoned to play doll."

No one had supplied her with undergarments?

I swallowed another mouthful of wine at that revelation, attempting to cool that heat that stirred within me at just the thought of the little wolf sitting opposite me wearing nothing beneath her gown. No barrier between us should I order her to perch upon my knee and slid my hand between her thighs.

How would she react to such a touch?

With the heat and need she had shown flashes of during our swim in the lake?

Or with a cold, scathing look and a threat to remove my hand with her fangs?

Great Mother, I wanted to know.

"Come, little lamb." I patted my knee again, shifting in my seat this time as my trousers grew uncomfortably tight, my cock shooting rock hard at the thought of her claiming a spot across my thighs and pressing close to me, that divine scent of her filling my lungs as her breath skated across my lips.

"Are you always such a pig?" She scooted back in her seat, moving as far away from me as she could get. "Why don't you give up already?"

My grin was pure male satisfaction as she turned her nose up at me but her cheeks coloured a little. She could act unaffected all she wanted, but her delicious scent and that intoxicating reaction gave her away. She enjoyed my attentions.

"The chase only makes the hunt sweeter." I stroked my thigh, drawing her attention there. "Something you should know."

She opened her mouth to retaliate, but snapped it closed when the servants entered with the food. I studied her as her gaze flitted over the dishes as they were set down on the table one by one, her irritation giving way to fascination as servants lifted cloches to reveal food she hadn't seen before.

"I know those!" She pointed to a tiered stand of sweets,

singling out the small sticky buns on the middle plate. "Vyr took me to the bakery that makes them. I've never tasted anything so sweet and perfumed."

"Vyr?" I arched a brow at her.

Her cheeks coloured. "Your sister said it would be all right to call her that. If it's not—"

"What my sister wishes you to call her is her business." Yet I continued to frown at her, at this little wolf who had charmed my sister so swiftly that she had allowed her to call her by the name I had given her when we had been children.

A name she rarely allowed people to use.

The little wolf picked at her soup as a servant set it before her, her gaze downcast, and this would not do. I had not summoned her to dinner so she could hide in her food and shy away from me, as charming as this reaction to me was and as telling of her fear of me.

"Did you enjoy the sweet?" I flicked my fingers towards the tower of treats and gently nudged it towards her with magic. "If you have a sweet fang, little lamb, by all means indulge it. Although it makes me wonder how sweet your lips might taste after you have indulged in the treats."

She halted halfway through reaching for the bun, her wide eyes darting to me as that bewitching hint of colour touched her cheeks, and then in a lightning fast move she seized one of the buns and hurled it at me.

I easily caught it, snatching it out of the air before it could strike me, and held her gaze as I bit into it. The sublime sweetness of it as the syrup oozed from the soft crumb tore a moan from me. It had been so long since I had tasted one of the buns that it caught me off guard.

The little wolf looked ready to hurl another as she bit out, "You're so overdramatic. Moaning to get my attention. If you're trying to make me blush, it won't happen."

It already was, the rose on her cheeks deepening a shade as I stared at her and licked the sugary syrup from my lips.

"I assure you, if I wanted to make you blush, you would stand defenceless against me." I popped the other half of the bun into my mouth, chewed and swallowed it, savouring the taste of it that transported me back in time to my youth, when I had often indulged in such treats with my sister and brother.

My brother.

My mood faltered as I thought of him, of that night he had been taken from us, and the last time I had seen him.

Shadows twined around my legs beneath the table, their presence a comfort as darkness clouded my mind and my heart.

"I saw goblins and dwarves, and minotaurs in town." Saphira's bright voice was a light in that darkness, a great golden spear that cleaved through it and pulled me back to her. Her eyes were as bright as her voice, glittering as she pushed aside the soup and helped herself to several platters of meat. Next time, I would order more so I at least stood a chance of eating some before my little wolf claimed them all. "I can't believe they exist. I've never seen so many stores either. Back home, we have a few general stores in the nearest town, but nothing like the ones here. There had to have been three blacksmiths."

"Four," I corrected, and she took her eyes off her mountain of meat and looked at me, her silver eyebrows raised high on her forehead. "There are four forges. Garandil's is the most famous, but I prefer Fierel's. It is more out of the way, but Fierel is a master swordsmith. His forge is second to none."

"I'll be sure to visit it when I'm next in the town." She carefully cut her meat into nice little squares and then picked them off one by one, working her way through enough protein to feed a small army, all the while talking about the town as if this place was home now.

Which I supposed it was, given that I had no intention of letting her go.

She sighed. "I don't think I've ever seen a tailor before, or a seamstress. Some of the dresses in the window were beautiful. They look softer than the dresses worn at the castle. They flowed so elegantly on the mannequins."

"And you shall have them all." I tipped my wine glass towards her and her eyes lit up. I held back a grin as I added, "I shall add them to your debt."

She scowled at me and then a slow smile wound its way across her wine-stained lips. "You'll buy them for me... because you'll want to see me in them."

I did not bother to deny that.

I listened as she prattled on about her visit to the town, fascinated by how her face lit up as she spoke of the things she had seen. She was my captive—my property—and yet she seemed to be enjoying herself. Making the most of her situation? Or was she truly enjoying her time in my court?

"Enough about me. I must be boring you. What about you? What did you do today? You looked ready to flit away in black smoke this morning." She sipped her wine and attacked another slice of meat.

"This morning?" I frowned over my wine at her.

She set her fork back down, the meat forgotten as she gazed at me. "When I saw you in the garden, crossing towards the castle, trying to outrun a gaggle of rather excited highborn who were dogging your every step."

"I am flattered you watch me wherever I go. Perhaps you fear you might lose my attention to the ladies of my court?" I held her gaze, my fascination only growing as she snorted and rolled her eyes.

This was the candour I craved with her.

This back and forth between us, as if she was not a servant and I was not a king.

No one dared speak to me as she did.

"If you want such vile, horrible women warming your bed then go for it. I have no stake in this game of yours." She took another sip of her wine and then lifted the glass in the air, saluting me with it. "I'm not interested in you."

"Liar." I smirked at her.

She huffed and inspected her wine, some of her warmth fading as she studied it rather than me. "If I was watching you, it was only to see if one of your oh-so-dainty ladies might trip and fall on her face in her hurried pursuit of you. It would have brightened my day no end. Some of them need to be brought down a peg or two."

I frowned now, my wine forgotten and my amusement gone as my shadows stirred in response to her words and the way she withdrew from me, seeming to curl inwards as if to protect herself.

"Do you have reason to desire such a thing?" I asked, voice as cold and dark as my shadows as they inched outwards, eager to scour the castle for the one who had upset the little wolf. "Has someone said something to you?"

She straightened and shrugged, and then cleared her throat, as if that would rid her of whatever was bothering her.

"It's painfully clear I don't belong here... trapped in this stuffy castle surrounded by stuffy fae who think themselves far superior to everyone else." Her voice was too bright—too forced. Someone *had* said something to her, and it had wounded her, the little wolf who was normally so bold and so brave. "I've never met such haughty, entitled and grossly rude people."

I was very much not amused now.

Shadows flowed from me, snuffing out the light of the fire

and surrounding her, even though she did not notice, was too busy staring at her wine and avoiding looking at me.

"You will report any derisive remarks anyone makes about you to either myself or Jenavyr." I dug my emerging claws into the arms of my chair, anchoring myself in place as she lifted bleak eyes to me, that look cleaving something within me. Shadows spilled from it, dark and treacherous, hungry to make whoever had wounded the little wolf pay for their insolence.

"What do you care?" she bit out, anger flashing across her face as she bravely held my gaze, her eyes fixed on me but the way she stiffened telling me she had noticed my shadows and how they blanketed the room, a wall between us and everything else. Everyone else. "You don't seem to give much of a damn about them. You couldn't get away from them quickly enough."

"You are right. I do not care much for them. These lords and ladies belong to my court through their bloodlines. Through tradition. Their place in my court is written in the blood of their forefathers. I merely have to tolerate them, but my indifference towards them has led to some overstepping and believing they have power in my court and a right to do as they please." My shadows closed in around her but her eyes never strayed from me, even as her shoulders tightened further, revealing she was well aware of their movement towards her.

My voice turned colder as anger burned through my veins, stoked by the thought that my failure to control my court might have led to Saphira being exposed to their more vicious side.

I had given them too much free rein, and now some among them believed they had a right to speak to another in my circle in a manner that had obviously wounded her.

"Tell me who offended you and they shall be dealt with." The tips of my fingers blackened as I gripped the arms of my chair, struggling to hold back my wrath as I waited for a name, a direction to aim my fury.

Saphira folded her arms across her chest. "So you can murder them? Jenavyr told me how you deal with those who anger you. I'm not a snitch, and I can fight my own battles."

"So I can punish them as they deserve and put them back in their place," I corrected, and amusement rippled through me, a shimmering band of light that loosened the hold the darkness had on me as I studied the fierce little wolf who glowered at me, her chin tipped up in defiance. "And can you fight your own battles?"

She huffed. "I can."

Sensing she would continue to refuse to name the one who had wounded her and that ordering her to reveal her attacker would only make her more angry, and less likely to speak, I made a mental note to speak with my sister and the guards who had been with Saphira this morning and gain a name that way.

Instead of pressing her, I changed the course of the conversation, circling back to something she had said that had caught my attention.

"You called my castle stuffy."

She prodded at her meat. "It is stuffy."

"Define *stuffy*." I slowly calmed my shadows, reining them back under control, not wanting them to lash at the wolf if she said anything that offended me more than her declaration that my castle was 'stuffy' already had. "You have every comfort you might need. You have one of the largest guest rooms and the only one with a balcony and a view of the entire town. Your every need is catered for. I feel that is rather gracious of me given your position."

She leaned back in her seat and looked around her as my shadows fell away to reveal the room and the roaring fire, and sighed. "It's a nice castle, and my rooms are far better than a cramped cell in a dungeon and I really have no complaints… but I do have a complaint."

Contradictory little female.

"And your complaint is?" I refilled her wine glass for her and she didn't even flinch this time, just picked the glass up and sipped it as if it was perfectly natural it had filled itself before her eyes.

She was growing accustomed to my world. To me. She had not even flinched when my shadows had encompassed her, filling the room.

"I don't know. I just… the view is lovely, but it's not… My pack lands are densely forested, set in a valley deep in the mountains, and my home is a cabin, but I'm rarely in it. I spend so much of my day outside, helping others, doing my work. I guess… I think being inside all day just feels a bit… claustrophobic. It's a pretty cage, but a cage nonetheless."

Interesting.

The place where I had travelled to for the auction had been in such lands, far from any sizable town. It made sense that she might find the castle and the town confining given how open the land I had taken her from had been.

"I shall have to find you work that involves you being outdoors then." I tapped my finger against the table, pretending to contemplate this, and then smirked at her. "Perhaps you can clean out the stables every morning."

She glared at me for that and made an obscene gesture with her hand.

"Did you enjoy your sojourn around the town?" I wanted to hear more about it, to draw out that female who had been filled with light and excitement before she had fallen down a dark path by recalling what had happened to her this morning, before my sister had escorted her down into the town.

"I did. But... something bothered me when I was in the town. Are your people happy?"

"Yes." I did not falter, did not even take a breath before I answered her. "My people are safe and have everything they need."

Her gaze grew distant, her light dimming. "There's a difference between being safe with everything you need and happy."

"Is there?" I had given my people everything, had expended great magic to seal the borders to shield them from danger and did whatever was expected of me in order to keep the lands strong and fertile. They were safe and protected, and had no reason not to be happy.

Yet, the way Saphira looked at me, a wealth of hurt surfacing in her eyes, said at least one person in my court was unhappy.

"I was safe at my pack. I had everything I needed." She toyed with the bottom of her wine glass, nudging it.

"But not everything you wanted," I husked and her shoulders went rigid. I sat back and hardened my tone, determined to shut down this line of conversation, because I was the king of this court and she had not seen enough of it to draw conclusions about how I ran it. "Perhaps you are projecting your own feelings onto my people. I assure you, they have all they need and they want for nothing."

She kept her gaze downcast and gave a subtle nod, and I felt sure she would hide in her wine glass for the rest of the meal, but then she pushed it away from her and lifted her head, her eyes locking with mine.

"It was rude of me. I'm sorry. If you believe your people are happy, then I'm sure they are happy."

A veiled challenge.

"They are happy," I declared, my tone firm. "Now, you were telling me of what you saw in the town. What did you find most fascinating? The market? The minotaurs? Those dresses you will soon receive?"

A flicker of light emerged in her eyes as she silently studied her wine and then she shuddered.

"It is not cold in here, so what did you recall that made you shiver?" I canted my head, curious now. This female had taken everything in her stride so far, had stood up to me countless times and showed little fear of me, but something she had seen today had rattled her. If it was the fae who had been rude to her, I would hunt them down and claim their heads and place them on pikes in the courtyard as a warning to others.

"After I saw the minotaurs, there were these tall, thin creatures dressed in black and they wore deer skulls as masks."

I chuckled at her description, sure she would shiver again as I corrected her, "They do not wear masks."

Her eyes went as round as full moons and just as bright. She blinked at me. "They don't?"

I shook my head. "It is all them, I am afraid, and they would be offended to hear you speak of them in such a manner. Lich are sensitive, a fault born of centuries of persecution by the crueller fae of this world, who treat them as if they are an abomination. When I ascended the throne, I took great pains to win them over, because what many see as monsters, I see as powerful allies. The ones you saw today are the royal necromancers of my court."

"Royal necromancers," she murmured and met my gaze again. "What do they do?"

"They question the dead for me."

Rather than looking horrified as I had expected, she looked fascinated by that, leaning forward a little as if she ached to know more.

Curious little creature.

Just how fearless was this lamb dressed in wolf's clothing? Fearless enough to face me in my true form?

CHAPTER 15

SAPHIRA

I was bored.

After my dinner with the fae king, I had been assigned new guards, and these ones dogged my every step, and refused to let me leave the castle grounds. My one and only attempt to near the main gate when I had wanted to visit the town had ended with them taking hold of one arm each and forcibly turning me around, albeit rather gently. When I had asked whether I was confined to the castle, they had nodded.

It might not have been so bad if my shadows had been talkative, but neither of them had spoken a word in all the times I had tried to strike up a conversation.

Neither of them would tell me where their king had gone.

He wasn't in the castle, I knew that much. The pressure of his presence had disappeared the morning after our dinner, soon after several boxes had appeared on my bed during breakfast, each one containing one of the gowns I had admired in the seamstress's window. He had given me presents I knew he wanted to see me wearing and then he had disappeared on me.

Confusing king.

I strolled around the garden, keeping to myself, studying the beautiful blooms and the wildlife. Every visit to the garden had me finding something new and different. Yesterday, I had wandered to the orchard side of it and had found a stunning tree with white bark and blood-red leaves.

The air cooled as I neared the ponds. Each was more beautiful than the last, but my favourite had a broad lip just high enough to comfortably sit on and a small waterfall that tumbled into it from the higher level of the garden, filling the quiet with its soothing melody. I picked up the path that took me to that wilder area of the garden, where plants grew where they wanted and a brook glittered over crystalline pebbles.

This was my favourite spot in the garden.

This slice of wilderness that felt like a paradise, an oasis of calm and beauty that sank warmth deep into my bones and eased my mind and my body. I could feel nature here, as if her presence was a tangible thing I could reach out and touch in the air, and could draw into me.

A peacock called, the sound echoing around the stunning gardens, so familiar to me. The colourful birds were definitely the same species I had seen back in my world, at a zoo my parents had taken me to when I had been a pup, one of the rare times they had taken me somewhere before they had begun travelling less and had grown determined to keep me close to Harper pack lands.

I smiled fondly as I recalled my visit to that zoo, and how excited I had been to see all the birds and animals. As a child, it had been enthralling. Now? I knew what it was like to be put in a cage and stared at, and to long for freedom and returning to my home where I belonged.

My shadows closed in as I stooped to run my fingers

through the brook, startling the colourful fish that called it home and watching them dart away.

I glanced at the two males, both dressed in fine tunics similar to the one Riordan had worn, with fitted trousers and knee-high boots. Both armed with a sword. Neither looked at me, their eyes fixed straight ahead. My gaze drifted to the woods just a few hundred feet away from me, where the trees grew denser and the shadows thickened, and then back to the guards.

What would they do if I shifted and ran?

Would it surprise them enough that they would lose precious seconds in pursuing me and I could slip their grasp?

The thought I could run for a while made me want to do it, had me itching to shift and feel the wind in my face, but the repercussions of these men losing me kept me firmly in place and in my human form. Kaeleron would punish them if he discovered I had escaped their watchful gazes. It was clear they had been assigned to me to keep me safe, and I only had myself to blame for the increase in security.

If I hadn't told Kaeleron about what had happened in the garden that day with the unseelie females he wouldn't have changed my guards and locked me in the castle grounds.

He also wouldn't have cleared the garden of nobles.

Now I didn't even have the highborn to watch when I was bored. I hadn't seen a single one in all my visits to the garden and I was beginning to suspect they had been banished from the castle, or at the very least they were removed the moment I made it clear I wanted to leave my room and go for a walk. There had been a few milling around when I had been on my balcony this morning, enjoying the warmth of the twilight-sun and the view of the town.

Forgetting my desire to run in the woods in my wolf form, I

followed the path that crossed the brook, soaking up the beauty of this place. The orchard stretched below me, each tree a different colour, some heavy with fruit while others were bright with blooms. The air was sticky and sweet, perfumed in a way that reminded me of the buns.

I shivered, heat coursing through me as I recalled how Kaeleron had taken a bite of the bun I had dared to throw at him, how a deep moan had rumbled from him, steeped with pleasure that roused fire in my veins.

Some wicked part of me wanted to hear him moan like that for another reason.

I shut it down, slamming the lid on it. This cursed heat was only growing stronger, my hungers only growing bolder, and I felt as if a clock were ticking down and soon I wouldn't be able to control these needs that were only getting more and more overwhelming.

I wasn't sure what I would do when the full force of it hit me.

Locking myself in my rooms sounded like a good start, but it wouldn't help, not here in this place where the people could teleport. If Kaeleron summoned me and I refused to go to him, he could simply appear in my room. And then what would I do?

Possibly pounce on him.

I breathed deeper, inhaling the cool, crisp air, struggling to quell this rising beast within me. My wolf side had never felt so unsettled. So wild. I crouched and ran my hands through the grass, feeling the dew coating my fingers, trying to root myself in nature and calm my wolf side and my primal instincts. It was slow, painfully slow, but gradually, little by little, I pulled back on the reins and found calm again, the heat falling away and the hungers fading.

I lingered, my hands still in the grass, savouring that connection between myself and the earth.

And just breathed.

I felt I could breathe here in a way I never could back home.

My gaze lifted from the grass to the mountains and that slice of sea beyond the castle.

And calm flowed into me.

A sensation that all was right in the world.

Strange that I so often felt that way here, in a world that was not my own.

I took my favourite path back to the main formal garden, passing under a series of beautifully carved white wooden arches studded with glittering black jewels that seemed to hold the universe within them. My gaze lingered on them as I passed, catching the stars that sparkled and shifted in their depths, my eyes growing heavy.

I stifled a yawn as I descended the worn steps to the main garden and picked up the wide paved path that led to the elegant circular fountain. The sound of the water trickling from one tier to the next lulled me as I passed, only making me more tired, but I pushed on, determined to make the most of my freedom, heading towards the lake-side edge of the patio. The water glittered in the aurora-kissed light, beckoning me to swim in it. Perhaps I would do that tomorrow. Although I wasn't sure how my shadows would react.

Birds flitted across my path as I banked right, towards the pergola that led back to the castle, and I breathed in the scent of the spears of lilac flowers.

And stifled another yawn.

"I'm tired," I murmured to my shadows as I neared the castle. "I'm returning to my room and if you follow me there, I won't be responsible for what happens to you."

I gave them my best withering look, one I had been practicing in my mirror in my room so I could act as haughty as the highborn should I run into one again.

Neither male looked inclined to leave my side.

So I huffed and stomped towards the side entrance of the castle.

When we neared it, they suddenly peeled away from me, and I twisted to look at them, unsure why they had stopped following me.

They stood with their heads bowed and hand pressed to their chests.

Crushing pressure slammed into me.

The scent of a wild storm swept me up in it.

Kaeleron.

I pivoted in the direction I had been heading, turning slightly more to my left, so I was facing the main gate, and froze right down to my breathing.

The fae king strode towards the castle with purpose, dressed in striking black and gold armour that made him look like a dark knight, his handsome face etched in vicious lines as he tugged his gauntlets off and handed them to Jenavyr where she hurried to keep up with him, wearing her usual leathers.

Here was the true fae king, and he was commanding. *Breathtaking*. The epitome of power as he barked orders at the males on his heels and his sister.

And then he noticed me.

I couldn't breathe.

Every inch of me locked up tight as awareness of him battered me like a storm, his silver eyes holding me immobile, deep under his spell. Heat poured through me, hunger rising rapidly as he strode towards me, the distance between us narrowing until I couldn't bear it, wanted to claw my way out of my skin to reach him.

Something inside me aching in response to the sight of him.

Tugging me towards him.

Before I realised what I was doing, I was standing at the front of the castle, near the main entrance.

I couldn't ignore the gravity of him as he disappeared into the castle, the guards halting at the grand archway, only his sister following him inside. That gravity pulled me towards him, had me following him too, moving swiftly and silently for fear he might hear me and stop me, my lungs still feeling too tight and my belly warmed in an unsettling way.

I tracked his scent into the gloom of his castle, steps light on the black marble floor of the broad entrance corridor. It led me to a cathedral-like room that I had discovered only a day ago was the great hall—Kaeleron's receiving room. The great black arched wooden doors were ajar, but rather than slipping inside the expansive room, I pressed my hands to the beautiful carvings of nature on them and stilled right down to my breathing.

"Do not start on me, Vyr," Kaeleron growled and the pressure of his presence increased, but not enough that I couldn't breathe and felt as if I was about to be squashed into the elegant marble floor.

Either he constantly tempered his power now or I was growing more used to it.

I peeked around the door, gaze seeking him. He stood on the dais near his throne at the far end of the room, the two rows of ornate black columns carved with vines, leaves and stags that supported the ribs of the high vaulted ceiling filling the space between us.

The sight of him struck me hard again, a vision of power and strength, and darkness as he loomed at the top of the steps to his throne. A male ready to do battle, or perhaps one who had already fought one.

He looked weary.

Exhausted almost.

As if his mask had slipped and this was his true appearance, without all the false smirks and fierce shadows designed to disarm or strike fear into others.

He sank onto his throne. "Spare me the lecture."

Jenavyr planted her hands on her hips. "I will not, brother. Had I realised you intended to go to Ereborne dressed for war, I might have stopped you. What a wonderful impression you must have made!"

Kaeleron snarled, "I know my duty. Do you remember yours?"

That verbal barb I didn't understand seemed to hit its mark as Jenavyr fell quiet and lowered her head, but then she rallied and lifted it, looking right at her brother.

"I remember," she bit out. "How could I ever forget? I am constantly reminded of it with every suitor Ereborne sends my way. It does not mean I have to like it."

"And I remember mine, and it does not mean I have to like it either. We both have our burdens to bear, sister. I cannot forget mine, and you should not forget yours." Kaeleron's expression slowly darkened, shadows rising like a collar around his shoulders, snaking from the gaps between the metal plates of his armour. "I did as expected of me. The visit is done and our continued support ensured. Do not think I enjoy this any more than you do."

Jenavyr lingered a moment longer, her back to me so I couldn't read her expression, and then she stormed away, exiting through the side door.

Had they been arguing about Jenavyr's future marriage? It was wrong that she had to wed someone she didn't love, and I wanted to find her and tell her that, to comfort her when she had to feel she was on the verge of losing everything she loved in her life—her freedom, her position, and her brother.

And perhaps a certain vampire she claimed to hate.

Kaeleron sighed and then his gaze slid towards the door where I hid.

His tone was pure amusement as his voice traversed the one-hundred-and-fifty feet between us. "Hiding in shadows from a shadow king was not your brightest idea. What does my little lamb want from me?"

I stepped out from behind the door and huffed. "Nothing like you're thinking, that's for sure. I want my shadows gone."

His smile was feline. "I could lift your shadows for you, blast them away from the corners of your soul and make you forget things for a while."

"That was a poor attempt to seduce me." I rolled my eyes as I approached him. "My guards. I meant my guards."

But his teasing stirred something dangerous within me as I came to stand before him, drowning in his presence as he lounged on his throne, looking every bit the powerful dark king with his hair tousled from his helmet and his armour in place.

Silver eyes slid over me from head to toe and back again, the weariness that had been in them fading, erased by the heat that built there instead.

I stood my ground, refusing to squirm under the weight of his gaze.

"Did you miss me, little lamb?" His grin grew salacious as he canted his head, one of the braids he wore behind his ears falling away from his neck while the other caressed the corded length of it, drawing my gaze there.

"No," I bit out, flat and matter of fact. "I have rather enjoyed the silence."

"But not the confinement."

"So you did order them to keep me locked in the castle." I

glared at him now, the heat of anger rising to almost overshadow that heat of desire his wicked smirk roused in me.

"Are you angry with me, little lamb?"

"Stop calling me that." I was tired of always being compared with a lamb, a creature of innocence and purity, one that was weak and vulnerable. I bared my fangs at him. "I'm a wolf."

"A lamb in wolf's clothing," he muttered, amusement shimmering in his eyes, all the fatigue I had seen hidden back beneath his mask again.

"I'm going to my room." I pivoted on my heel, turning my back on him.

"I have an order for you." That stopped me before I had even taken a step away from him, the coldness in his voice sending a chill tumbling down my spine as my mind raced forwards to imagine what his latest demand might be.

I slowly turned back towards him.

He prowled towards me, all menace and masculinity, his steps echoing with a metallic ring in the suddenly too small room. All the air left my lungs and my heart kicked up a notch, thundering in my ears as he closed the distance between us, each step closer he came ratcheting that unbearable heat within me up another degree.

Until I was on fire.

On dangerous ground that felt ready to burn to ashes beneath me.

My wolf side snarled within me, a growl of pure hunger and domination, threatening and cajoling this male who held a dangerous power over me.

He stopped toe-to-toe with me, forcing me to tip my head back to hold his gaze, his scent and heat enveloping me.

"Remove my armour for me."

Five words spoken in a low voice, barely a whisper, but as

powerful as the tides, as the ocean and the moon. A command I felt right down to my soul as it sent the heat curling through my veins into the stratosphere and scalded my cheeks.

Strip him.

He wanted me to strip him.

CHAPTER 16
KAELERON

"Remove my armour for me."

I issued that command half in jest, half out of a pure animal need to feel her hands on me and watch her reaction to my order. Another delicious blush climbed her cheeks and she struggled to hold my gaze as I stood before her, so close we were almost touching. I waited to see what she would do.

Accept my order, or refuse to carry it out?

If she chose the latter, I would find an amusing way to punish her.

After a moment where she looked as if she might be biting back more than a few choice, harsh words, she reached for the first buckle without complaint.

Her scent maddened me as she leaned in closer, rising onto her tiptoes to reach the black leather strap that held my pauldron in place.

After my visit to Ereborne, Saphira was a breath of fresh air, lifting some of the weight from my shoulders as she silently worked to carry out my order, her focus on her task as she tackled unfamiliar fastenings.

I knew that I shouldn't, that this female was not meant for me, not in this way, but I found myself pressing closer still and lowering my head. She discarded the first pauldron with a harsh clatter of metal on stone, making her irritation clear as she treated my armour with contempt, and then leaned to reach for the second one, exposing her neck.

My lips hovered tantalisingly close to her skin as I leaned in and breathed in her scent, holding it in my lungs. It was enticing, filling every inch of me with warmth, and I frowned as I scented her again, coming close to brushing my nose against her warm skin as I fought to decipher why she smelled so enticing.

"What are you doing?" Her voice trembled and I realised she had stilled, her hands resting on my shoulder as I breathed her in.

"You smell of green pastures and sunshine, of rolling hills and endless blue skies." My voice had never sounded so thick, so strained, as it did as I murmured those words, struggling to convey the scent of her.

She laughed. "You're ridiculous."

She was trying to brush off my words, attempting to let them run off her back and not affect her, but she *was* affected. I could feel it in the air and smell it on her. As she tackled my other pauldron, I lifted my hand and lightly traced a line down the curve of her neck, eliciting another delicious tremble. My fingers drifted lower as I savoured the softness of her skin, tracing the edge of her blouse.

She swatted my hand away. "Stop that. I'm undressing you as ordered. I didn't say you could do the same to me."

She threw my second pauldron and stepped back, stealing her warmth and closeness from me, and my shadows grew restless with a need to pull her back to me, to press her so close that there was no air between us. I reined in that urge as she fumbled with my breastplate, her hands shaking now as they tugged at the straps on my left side.

How would she react when the black plates fell away to reveal my body?

Would she be as bold as she had been at the lake, drinking her fill of me?

"Wolves have sensitive noses," I said as a way of distracting her from what she was doing so she would not stop, and satisfying my own curiosity. "What do I smell like to you?"

She froze halfway through unbuckling the final strap on my left side, her eyes sliding to meet mine, a flicker of banked heat in them.

Bewitching.

"You reek of sweat and leather, a hint of sulphur and the horrible tang of magic."

A laugh rumbled in my chest as she hit me with her crushing description of my scent, far from the more floral and poetic one I had expected.

"It was a long ride from Ereborne." I watched her as she finished with the strap and then I took hold of my breastplate, lifting it up and over my head. I leaned to my left to set it down.

Her gaze leaped to my bare chest and then away the moment I looked at her again.

I straightened and gestured to my lower half. "Continue."

"You know, if you're naked under there too, it won't bother me. You'll be bitterly disappointed when I don't react to this little game of yours." She attacked the straps at my hips with renewed spirit, yanking them so hard she jerked my hip forward.

Another chuckle escaped me, a sound I had almost come to miss in the last few days during my visit to the high king.

"You will react, little lamb," I purred close to her ear,

savouring how she stiffened and her fingers stilled close to my skin, almost touching me. Unbearable. I wanted her hands on my flesh. I lifted my hand and brushed the backs of my fingers down her cheek. "Rose will kiss these cheeks, and fire will light your eyes, and you will fight it as you always do. Why fight against what you want, little lamb?"

"You're quite the egotistical male, my king." She mocked me with a curtsy. "But of course, how could I resist you? I'm sure the ladies at Ereborne, wherever that is, fawned over you, so surely I must too."

"Is my little lamb jealous of the attention I receive?" I feathered my fingers lower, drifting them beneath her chin, and gently took hold of it when she refused to look at me, her gaze pinned to my chest. I pinched her chin between my thumb and forefinger, and lifted it, holding her facing me until she found the courage to meet my gaze.

"No." A simple answer that was part truth, part lie. She did not want to desire my attention, railed against it with all she had, but some secret part of her enjoyed these moments we shared.

Enjoyed being the centre of my attention.

I lowered my head, pressing my cheek close to hers, and whispered into the shell of her ear.

"If you want my company, Saphira, you only need to ask."

She tensed, but she didn't push me away or lash at me with words. She remained where she was, our skin touching, the contact between us electric despite its innocence.

"I lied," she murmured and I was the one who tensed now, sure she was going to admit that she did want me, that she would finally break and beg me to take her. "You don't reek of sweat and all that other stuff."

I leaned back, frowning down at her, half of me dissatisfied by her deception in making me feel she would give in and admit she wanted me, and the rest of me curious about what I smelled like to her. I hadn't been lying about her scent. She smelled like the outdoors, like nature incarnate, a soothing scent that reminded me of lighter days, when I had spent many hours lazing in the sun, watching the world pass me by.

"You smell like a storm… a winter storm. Wild. Snowy. Fierce." She averted her gaze, studying my bare chest.

Was she aware of how her gaze scalded me, made me burn with an inferno and a need to feel her hands on my skin? I doubted it. If she knew the desires she roused in me with only a look, she would flee.

She huffed, a brittle sound. "There. I said it. Now let me work in peace."

She went back to attacking my lower half, removing one plate at a time, and a hint of disappointment coated her scent as the last fell away, revealing supple leather pants rather than bare skin.

"You can remove those too if you would like," I husked, enjoying that bewitching blush that stained her cheeks even as she scowled at me.

"A suggestion. Not an order. So I think I'll turn you down."

"You could turn me on instead," I growled and reached for her.

She pirouetted beyond my grasp and shook her head. "I don't think you need any assistance there. Are we done?"

I nodded. "We are done."

As little as I enjoyed the thought of letting her leave my sight, it was better she went. I needed to focus on recording what I had learned at Ereborne and the ideas about Saphira's purpose I'd had while there, and then I needed to speak with Neve to see if she'd had another vision while I had been gone.

Saphira turned away but immediately came back to face

me. "Do all fae ride horses? Jenavyr's one is beautiful. Was that your horse I saw with hers at the farrier?"

I chuckled again, a little amused when that lingering hint of blush on her cheeks grew stronger in response, as if the sound of my laughter affected her.

"I do not ride a horse. Not if I can help it. I have an elkyn."

Her eyes lit up and she had never looked so curious, or so close to bursting from holding back her desire to know more.

So I took her arm, startling her as I draped it over mine, our bare skin brushing and bodies in danger of colliding, and purred down at her.

"Does the lady wish to meet him?"

CHAPTER 17
SAPHIRA

I didn't resist Kaeleron as he ushered me through the quiet castle, heading down corridors I had never seen before. His presence was a constant pressure against me, his scent and his power buffeting me together with awareness of his half-dressed state.

He looked even more the wild king now, a force of nature with his glistening pale skin stretched taut over honed muscles and his black hair no longer neatly pulled back into a half-ponytail. Strands had fallen down, caressing the silver tips he wore on his pointed ears, luring my gaze to them again. He kept his noble profile to me, his striking silver eyes fixed ahead of us as he guided me towards this creature he had said I could meet.

It was hard to focus on the thought of finally seeing one up close—and the king's personal elkyn out of all of them—when Kaeleron was beside me, his presence consuming my focus, demanding and alluring.

His fingers stroked a steady, teasing rhythm on my arm, as if he wanted to keep me aware of him, keep my eyes on him. Like there was any danger of my focus drifting elsewhere.

"Where is everyone?" I didn't take my eyes from his profile as I asked that, growing increasingly aware that the castle was too quiet.

Too empty.

"All around us." His deep voice rolled over me like a wave, sweeping me up in it, and I looked for the people I couldn't sense.

And gasped.

We weren't travelling along a corridor as I had thought. We were travelling along an avenue of black mist, completely embraced by the shadows. Fear threatened to shake me, but fascination overruled it, my eyes darting around as I struggled to take in that I was travelling through the shadows, cloaked in them and concealed from everyone.

More alone with Kaeleron than I had ever been.

I went to reach my hand out to brush through those shadows.

Kaeleron's grip on my arm tightened, his other hand clamping down over it as he rumbled, "Do not let go."

I leaned closer to him instead, my pulse jacking up as the shadows thinned in places and I peered through them at the ghostly world beyond them. It looked like the castle corridors and rooms, but it was a mere phantom of them, intangible and shimmering like smoke.

I gasped as we passed straight through a wall and into the garden, mouth going dry as my mind raced to imagine what might happen if I let go of Kaeleron when he was performing such a manoeuvre. Would I be stuck in a wall? Doomed to die trapped within the heavy stones of this castle?

Kaeleron chuckled as I pressed closer to him. "Afraid, little lamb?"

"No." A lie. A pathetic one at that.

He saw right through it, the rich timbre of his laugh

warming my bones, and startled me by sliding his arm around my shoulders, tugging me closer still.

"I will not let you go," he husked.

And part of me knew he meant something different by those words. They were a confession rather than a statement. A warning.

A confirmation of the feeling that had been growing within me from the moment I had signed that contract, blindly believing it meant what it said, interpreting it in the way I wanted it.

Kaeleron didn't intend to set me free.

At least, he didn't intend to let me leave his lands.

His version of setting me free was far less innocent.

I felt it as his hand glided down to settle on the curve of my waist, as he pulled me closer still, until our bodies pressed together and I knew only him.

He intended to set me free of the invisible bonds that bound me, from the pain of what Lucas had done, and the shackles my family and my duty had placed on me.

And by the gods, some part of me wanted that.

Wanted him.

I didn't struggle as he held me. No. I leaned closer still, savouring the feel of his muscled body against mine and that bewitching scent of his filling my lungs. Willing to drown in his presence and his power, to bravely shut out the voice that screamed at me about my mate and my duty, about my pack and what was expected of me.

And listened to the instinct that howled at me to embrace this strange new world.

And everything offered by its dark king.

I raised my eyes to his face, on the verge of surrendering in the safety of his shadows, hidden from the world.

But they evaporated, revealing a pasture surrounded by

trees that slowly went from ghostly to solid, and I staggered a little as my boots hit the grass, the sudden change from drifting on air to walking on hard earth jarring me.

Kaeleron chuckled at my terrible landing and didn't stop even as I glared at him.

Being so close to him like this felt too intimate and he seemed too different today. As if he was too tired to keep his mask in place and it kept slipping, revealing enthralling glimpses of the male behind it.

"Perhaps we can work on your dismount. I am willing to give you lessons on dismounting." His throaty chuckle and that sparkle in his silver eyes as he teased me… too much.

I paced away from him, needing some space and some air, some time to get my unruly desires in check.

The stroll through the castle with him had been far too pleasant, far too normal feeling, and how pleased I had been to see him return, it all rolled up on me now I was out of his arms. I shouldn't be feeling any of these things for him, shouldn't find his company enjoyable.

He was my captor. My owner.

I needed to remember that, even when part of me wanted to forget.

To embrace this wildness within me.

To be brave.

I looked over my shoulder at Kaeleron, watching him as he strode towards a wooden fence that surrounded a paddock, unsure I could ever be brave enough to reach out and take what I wanted, not when the consequences seemed so great. If I had a taste of him, I would want more. That part of me that craved a connection with someone was seeking a way of filling that void within me as it mourned the loss of my mate and suffered the stinging pain of my rejection.

Kaeleron could so easily be just that.

A beautiful, dark distraction.

But what happened when he grew bored of me?

When he rejected me too?

I wasn't sure I could bear another male rejecting me, and I certainly wasn't looking for someone to love, not again, so I tore my gaze from him and looked for a better distraction, something safer.

One trotted towards me from the other end of the paddock.

In the twilight-sun, the great silver stag's fur shimmered a lustrous pale blue, and the thicker hair that covered the front of its neck and chest shone with purest silver. His large antlers dripped with fine pale vines and delicate lilac flowers, and threads of white moss, as if he were some powerful ancient spirit of nature given form. Intelligent aquamarine eyes that glowed around their pupils landed on me and he snorted and scratched at the grass with his right hoof.

And then regally lowered his head.

I felt a bit like a fool as I did the same and Kaeleron chuckled.

I glowered at him.

He held his hand up. "I was not mocking. I am merely surprised he is so accepting of your presence. It often takes him time to grow accustomed to others."

"What's his name?" Would it be rude to reach out and pet the nose of such a fine, noble beast, treating him as a pet?

"I do not know."

I frowned at Kaeleron. "How do you not know? You're his owner, aren't you?"

"Because I do not speak his tongue, and I am not his owner." He held his hand out and the stag—elkyn—came to him, and the size of him struck me. He was far larger than the ones I had seen before. His shoulders came close to the height of Kaeleron's head, a beast more than large enough for such a towering male to ride.

"So he doesn't have a name?" I cocked my head, looking at the elkyn as it looked right back at me, as if it was assessing me too. "Have you tried naming him?"

"I feel it would be disrespectful." Kaeleron patted the elkyn's neck, the action filled with the affection that was reflected on his face as he smiled at the beast. Actually smiled. The sight of it was startling, warming me right down to my marrow and rousing a shocking heat in my traitorous body. His long fingers danced through the thicker fur at the elkyn's throat. "I do not wish to disrespect him and become to first unseelie to tame and ride an elkyn and also the first unseelie to lose such a privilege."

I leaned my arms on the top bar of the worn wooden fence. "But I see them pulling carts all the time. Many have been tamed."

Although this one was far larger than the others I had seen in town, standing more than a head taller, and would easily dwarf them if they were stood side by side.

He chuckled again as he lovingly stroked the elkyn's neck, long brushes of his hand that the beast seemed to enjoy as he leaned into them. "No. You see the elkyn he watches over. This beast is different to them. A guardian of their kind."

"Like a god?"

The elkyn was beautiful enough to be one, his fur shining with not just blue as he turned his head towards me but a whole rainbow of colours, as iridescent as a beetle shell. He bobbed his head and snorted, as if agreeing with me.

"He is ancient and steeped with magic." Kaeleron's hand stilled on the elkyn's nape as he gazed at it, fond warmth in his eyes. "I tamed him when I was young, the Great Mother smiling upon me and gracing me with this spirit as my mount.

His kind are rare, spread throughout the lands of Lucia, and never had one submitted to being captured, let alone ridden. Many who have tried have paid with their lives."

"You didn't tame him." That feeling stirred deep within me, powerful and profound as something dawned on me. "He chose you."

The fae king looked at me now, shock dancing across his handsome face before he secured his mask back in place, concealing his true feelings from me. "Perhaps he did. The discovery I had charmed a beast so ancient and powerful was viewed as auspicious. An omen of great power on my part and a deep connection to Lucia and her lands and her creatures."

He looked grateful for that as he resumed petting the beast, as if this creature had submitted to him at a time he had needed others to see his strength and power the most.

"No one else has ridden one?"

"No one. Not even the high king has been able to charm such a mount." Kaeleron couldn't have looked prouder about that, and I wanted to tease him about it, but let it slide this time, because I would hate it if I had something that made me feel so proud and happy and someone teased me about it, making me feel foolish for it.

"You said he was magic." I sneakily tried to pet the elkyn as he passed me, but he turned away before I could touch him, making it clear I hadn't earned his trust yet.

"He is magic. A beast steeped in it."

"What kind of magic?" I leaned forwards and settled my chin on my folded hands, gaze tracking the elkyn as he roamed his paddock, pausing occasionally to nibble at silvery moss nestled among the grass.

"He can run on the wind." Kaeleron closed the distance between us and leaned beside me, not a regal king but just a fae male, that mask he wore so well nowhere in sight as he watched his ancient friend. "You have never seen a creature so swift. I can make the journey to Ereborne in less than a day."

"Why not just teleport there?" I twisted towards him, curious about him rather than the beast now. "Why not use magic to get you there like you do when you're moving around the castle. Don't think I haven't noticed you're the one who teleports those boxes of dresses into my room."

His grin was wicked. "Why allow others to do something which brings me so much pleasure? One day I will time it perfectly to find you bathing."

I smacked his arm. "You disgust me."

"Disgust is a strange way of saying *arouse*."

"Be serious." I was tempted to push him, but denied it, not sure if it would be a push too far.

I was still learning the limits of what I could get away with, but he seemed to enjoy this light banter and my retorts, and part of me found it enjoyable too. I had never spoken with a male in the way I did with him, so frankly and without reserve, without thinking about what others might expect me to say or do and falling back on acting accordingly.

It felt freeing.

"No fae can teleport across the borders of the courts, a measure put in place to protect them. If a king wishes to invade another court, he must do so by crossing the border on foot."

I pursed my lips as I mused that, watching him as he watched the elkyn. "Do you often go to war with each other?"

He picked at a lichen on the fence. "Sometimes. War is not uncommon. Lands are often in dispute and there is bad blood between some of the courts. The Shadow Court is fortunate that it is bordered on three sides by the mountains, and one side by the sea."

"What courts share a border with yours?" I shifted to rest

my chin on my upturned palm, not bothering to hide my curiosity or eagerness to know more about this world.

"Only one."

"It must be large if it borders all your lands."

He shook his head. "The Shadow Court is smaller than others, but the border it shares with the Dusk Court only runs along the southern mountain range. To the west, my court borders the Black Pass, and to the north the Forgotten Wastes."

"They sound delightful." I smiled.

Kaeleron chuckled. "If you wish to know more about the courts and these lands, I can grant you access to the castle library."

Now my curiosity was truly piqued. "I'd like that. You're not going to add a membership fee to my tab are you?"

"Not at all." He turned his cheek to me, a small smile tugging at the corners of his lips. "I will find another way for you to pay it off."

I went to shove him and froze when my instincts whispered I was being watched.

Kaeleron didn't take his eyes off the elkyn. "There are always eyes on me, little lamb, and there will be even more of them tomorrow night."

"Tomorrow night?" The desire to look over my shoulder to see if I could spot who was watching us was forgotten as I latched onto those two words.

He nodded. "Beltane."

"What's Beltane?"

"A feast that will take place at night in the forest, surrounded by the trees and the stars." His silver gaze slid to me, studying me closely as it slowly narrowed.

"It sounds interesting." Part of me wanted to see it, even when I was sure it would be full of those haughty highborn that would spend the whole evening looking down their noses at me. I could put up with them for a few hours if it meant seeing what an unseelie feast looked like.

I did need to see a feast if I were to decide which of the three Fs the unseelie did better than my kind after all.

But I doubted I would be invited. There probably wasn't any room for a wolf shifter at a fae celebration.

"It is a great rite, one all the courts will be celebrating," he said, a flicker of something in his eyes that was part curiosity and part challenge.

He took my hand as his gaze seared me right down to my soul.

His smile feline.

Wicked.

"One you will be attending, little lamb."

CHAPTER 18

SAPHIRA

The night seemed darker than usual, aurora chasing across the starlit heavens above me. A chill hung in the air, skittering over my skin, making me even more aware of the dress my handmaidens had selected for the evening's celebrations.

One of loose blood-red material that bordered on sheer, cinched under my breasts with a band of golden swirls and glittering rubies. The two long slits up each thigh allowed the cold air to invade beneath the flimsy layers of the dress as I walked, my satin slippers silent on the steppingstones I had been told to follow into the forest.

My heart drummed a frantic rhythm I tried to calm as I strode forwards, my step not faltering, following not just the steppingstones but the magic bubbles of light that bobbed in the air along the path, chasing back some of the gloom.

And the music.

It was growing louder, the heavy beat of the drums almost matching my pulse and the violence of the strings flooding me with a strange urge to dance, to surrender to their frantic desperation as they reached crescendo after crescendo before crashing down each time, rising and falling like waves around me.

I wasn't sure what to expect as I edged ever closer to the feast and the sound of merriment that danced through the trees, as if the wine had been flowing for some time now. Nerves threatened to have me turning on my heel and hurrying back to the castle, but curiosity pulled me ever onwards, towards the glow of firelight ahead of me.

The steppingstones ceased at a wall of trees, but between the faintly glowing purple-vein-laced trunks I spied more globes of light beckoning me, calling me towards them.

I moved forwards, steeling myself and seeking calm as I tried to peer through the trees that seemed to move to block my view and deny me a glimpse of the celebration.

Until it was right upon me.

My feet froze upon the threshold of a great glade packed with long wooden tables and far too many people. None of them noticed me as they drank and talked, laughing and smiling at each other, a complete contrast to the people I had seen in the castle gardens all those times. I recognised some of them as highborn I had seen there, sneering at others, but most of them were new to me. Big, muscular males in loose shirts and leather pants caroused with dainty, beautiful females who wore dresses similar to mine, but in pastel hues of lavender, blue and teal, reflections of the aurora that danced above us.

Not a single other female wore a red dress.

I had never felt so aware of myself as I lingered on the threshold of this celebration, afraid that someone might notice me and how different I was to everyone else.

While my hair had been left down, a mass of waves around my shoulders and down my bare back, these females wore theirs up, drawn away from their elegant necks. While they wore pastel hues, I wore the colour of blood.

Like a sacrifice.

My gaze darted to a long stone slab near the bonfire off to my left, one that had been finely carved around the sides but was worn on top, as if it saw regular use.

Maybe I should have asked what kind of things happened at the feast.

Maybe this was the reason Kaeleron had bought me.

A virgin to sacrifice at his great celebration of Beltane.

I stepped back towards the forest and froze again as shadows snared me, wrapping around my ankles and calves.

My eyes leaped across the celebration to my right, clashing with Kaeleron's as he lounged beneath the largest tree, bathed in moonlight.

The light from the orbs of magic glinted off his thorny black circlet as he canted his head, the distance between us seeming to shrink as he studied me too closely, his silver eyes searing me.

I was all too aware of how the cold night air affected my body and how the almost sheer fine fabric of my dress failed to conceal my beaded nipples as his shadows drew me towards him, rising to twine around my wrists like shackles. The hairs on my nape rose as he raked his gaze over me, a slow and leisurely perusal of my curves, and my skin tingled in response, my head going a little hazy as I approached him.

There was a strange tang in the air that felt both natural and unnatural. A scent I couldn't place.

I was sure that scent was to blame for the hot shivers that wracked me and filled me with confidence as my steps went from timid to bold strides that carried me through the parting crowd. Heads turned to track me but it didn't scare me. Rather than shrinking away, I only grew more confident, my eyes never straying from Kaeleron's.

When I neared him, he slowly swept his hand over the empty spot beside him on the black velvet of the chaise longue he occupied. A strange choice for a feast, but there were regular dining chairs near the tables that were slowly being filled with dishes of food and carafes of wine. Perhaps this was where he waited in comfort while the feast was being prepared.

He stroked the velvet again, his eyes never leaving mine, and I felt that touch like a caress down my body, his shadows teasing me with an echo of it.

"Sit, little lamb," he purred.

I glanced at the fae who watched me, suddenly aware of all the eyes on me as whatever spell Kaeleron or that scent had woven on me broke.

"Do not mind them." He stroked the seat beside him again and I shivered as his shadows mimicked him, gliding down my spine. "They simply want what they cannot have."

"Finally, some company for you. Must have been getting pretty lonely being the only one wanting what they can't have," I pushed out, trying to act casual even as my nerves ate away at my confidence now and I couldn't get my mind off that altar near the bonfire.

He chuckled, the warm sound rasping in my ears, heating my blood and making me ache to have him do that close to my ear, so I could feel the warmth of his breath on my neck.

On my nape.

I slammed the lid on that desire.

And gestured to the slab at the other end of the glade.

"Is that for me? Am I wearing the colour of blood for a reason? Wouldn't want to stain a nice dress when you sacrificed me."

He laughed now, the sound shocking me together with how his face lit up with it, and then a split second later it shut off and he locked his gaze onto me, deadly serious again.

"If I were to lay you out on that altar, Saphira, it would be so I could devour you."

I swallowed hard and clenched my fists, trying to stop my hands from trembling as his words pushed that image into my mind, a vision of him nestled between my shaking bare thighs, giving me a pleasure I had never experienced before.

"Wicked little wolf," he husked and pulled on his shadows, tugging me towards him. "You like the thought of it, do you not?"

"No, I do not." I plopped down onto the seat beside him, my posture rigid as I tucked my hands between my thighs.

My first mistake.

His gaze tracked where they had gone, darkening by degrees, and the tip of his tongue poked out to sweep along his lower lip in a far too erotic caress.

"Clearly, you hit the wine early tonight." I glowered at him, maintaining a frosty wall between us that felt as if it would crumble at any moment.

Kaeleron lounged against the raised side of the chaise, a vision of wickedness in black, with his tunic unbuttoned enough to reveal the start of his chest and a hint of glorious hard muscles. His eyes never left me as he signalled for someone, a female who hurried from the shadows to crouch beside him.

"Serve my little lamb. She thirsts."

I glared at him, not missing his innuendo. "I thirst for wine, not you. Anything to make you more tolerable."

He chuckled, his face lighting up with it.

"By the gods, have you drunk a barrel already?" I wasn't sure how much alcohol it took to get a fae drunk, but he had to be close to the limit of his tolerance.

"I am not drunk, little lamb."

I snatched the goblet the female offered me and took a great gulp, needing a little liquid courage if I was going to get through this evening of being watched by so many people and teased by this incorrigible fae king who had just discovered how to laugh and was intent on tormenting me with the delicious timbre of it.

And choked on the drink as my eyes watered and my throat burned.

"And this is not wine," I wheezed, my head already feeling lighter, my thoughts a little fuzzier.

My second mistake.

Heat curled through my veins, pooling low, a wicked sort of feeling that tempted me to give in to it and shed my inhibitions, to let go of everything I clung to so fiercely and embrace the parts of me that wanted to be wild and free.

"Mead. Laced with sweet woodruff. It is traditional for Beltane." He stood in a far-too-sexy fluid motion and went to the table, peered into several of the pitchers and returned with one, pouring it into my glass. "Water, to make it easier on your delicate palate."

"My palate is not delicate." I sipped the drink to prove I could handle it, but didn't feel I was proving much now that he had watered it down. The taste was pleasant, if a little earthy, and it was sweet, leaving a faint lingering taste of honey, vanilla and cinnamon on my tongue.

He chuckled again, almost goading me into tossing my mead in his face. Maybe I would have if we had been alone and not the subject of scrutiny. Too many people were watching us. Watching me. A stranger among them, seated beside their king as if I was his queen.

Or his pet.

He swirled a finger down my bare arm, from my shoulder to my elbow, the laziness of that touch reeking of entitlement. I rolled my shoulder, trying to dislodge him, even when some secret part of me craved more of that leisurely brush of his fingers across my skin.

"I'm sure this is drugged." I peered into my goblet, the scent of it matching that unusual tang in the air. "Or I can't hold my liquor."

I went to stand to set it on the table, but Kaeleron's hand clamped around my wrist, forcing me to remain sitting beside him.

"Drink. It is good for you." He gestured to the glass.

"Apparently, it's good for fae and bad for wolf shifters. This is going to my head too quickly." I tried to stand again.

Kaeleron yanked me back down, his voice a black snarl. "Sit."

"I'm not a dog. You can't order me to sit and expect me to beg for a treat." I ripped my arm free of his grip. "If I had known you'd be like this tonight, I might not have found Beltane so intriguing."

He looked at his own goblet, at the dark liquid that sloshed towards him as he tilted it, and muttered, "Perhaps the brew is stronger this year."

His silver gaze slid to me.

"Or perhaps it is something else intoxicating me."

A shiver tumbled down my spine and through my limbs, heat chasing it, and I blamed the mead rather than that husked admission.

"Plenty of females here." I swept my arm across the entire glade. "You'd probably have your pick if you announced you were in need of a little entertainment."

"I have my entertainment right here, little lamb, and there is no female in this crowd that is a match for you."

"It's the dress or the booze. I can't decide which has transformed you into this... this... whatever this is. Is calling you an asshole grounds for punishment?" I wanted to take back those words as soon as they flew from my lips.

His handsome face darkened but then his lips curved into another toe-curling smile that flashed straight white teeth. "Perhaps. Call me it and see how imaginative I get with my punishment. It may or may not involve that altar."

"Is there someone else I could sit with?" I shot to my feet, blood heating to a dangerous degree, unable to deny now that it was Kaeleron who flustered me and not the mead. "Your sister perhaps?"

His gaze lowered to the seat, a silent order to resume my position beside him. "My sister is absent."

I frowned at that. This was apparently an important celebration. What was more important that Jenavyr was missing it to attend to that business instead? Or maybe his sister had witnessed her brother tipsy on mead too many times in the past and didn't want to suffer the embarrassment anymore.

Kaeleron reached up and pushed his black hair back.

Revealing his pointed ears.

They were bare.

No silver tipped their points, shielding them from view.

I tried not to stare, but my eyes refused to move from their delicately pointed tips as a desire rose within me, one that felt more compelling than any that had come before it.

I itched to reach out and feather my fingers along them.

I sipped my drink instead and took my seat again, this time picking a spot right at the end of the black chaise, as far from this tempting fae king as I could get.

"I've never heard of Beltane before. Is it like a solstice?" A change of subject seemed like a good idea and it might divert his attention away from teasing me.

I took another sip of my mead and this time it tasted better, and that sweet spicy tang in the air swirled with the scent of it, invading my lungs and my mind, easing the tension from my body.

"Of a sort. Millennia ago, when the seelie and the unseelie roamed the human world, the mortals felt a need to ward off my kind and appease us to prevent our wickedness from spoiling their lands and taking their people. On the first day of their May, they lit great bonfires and drank mead spiced with woodruff, and danced long into the night, frolicking to celebrate the rebirth of the world through fire. My kind would grace them with our presence, drawing magic from the rite." He swirled his mead, seemingly lost in it. "They no longer celebrate Beltane as they once did, so my kind celebrate it instead, carrying on the tradition with the fire of rebirth."

Several men jeered and I glanced in their direction, and lingered. By the gods, I had never seen a pig as large as the one they were turning on a spit, its skin glossy and dark. My mouth watered as they basted it with what looked like mead from one of the open barrels, sloshing wooden ladles of it over the animal before they swept a thick brush along the length of it, spreading the mead and making sure every part of it was basted.

"The little wolf hungers. She has an insatiable appetite for meat," Kaeleron purred.

"If you mention your nether regions, I will throw this mead in your face." I slid him a dark look, hoping to silence him with the threat, but he only laughed instead.

"Throw it in my face and I will order you to lick me clean, my lamb."

"Ugh. I'm not a lamb." I had to lock my arm up to stop myself from hurling my drink at him, all too aware he would carry out that threat and make me lick it off him if I did.

Since my threat had failed to make any impact on him, I gave him the cold shoulder instead, enjoying my drink as I took in the celebration.

I frowned as a male stepped up behind a female who was bucking the trend and wearing leather trousers and a loose blouse rather than a dress, sliding his arms around her waist and resting his chin on her shoulder. The larger male she had been speaking to a moment ago, one who had feathered his fingers across her cheek and leaned in for a kiss from her, didn't seem to mind the attention the other male was giving her.

In fact, the two of them shared a smile and struck up a conversation.

Kaeleron shifted in his seat beside me, sitting up and leaning far too close to me for comfort, his scent of wild storm swirling around me, as drugging as the mead. I scowled at him, but he didn't notice, was too busy staring in the direction I was.

"Ah. My little lamb is curious. The brunette female is Kali, a warrior who serves in my legions." He placed his hand on the seat beside me, his little finger brushing the side of my thigh, his look unrepentant when I shot him a glare.

She was pretty, with her braided dark hair and pointed ears, and the way her face lit up with her warm laughter, but she looked as much a warrior as Kaeleron had called her, her body honed for battle, but somehow still feminine.

"Which of the males is with her. I thought it was the larger one, but the tall, slender blond fae seems more intimate with her." I studied them closely, struggling to figure out which was her lover.

"They are both her mates."

My head whipped towards Kaeleron so swiftly I almost headbutted him. "I'm sorry. You mean she's in love with both of them, not that they're both fated to her."

He shook his head. "They are fated. It is unusual, rare even, but it does happen. Ivaron, the blond male, hails from the Dusk Court and she met him during talks between the courts, quickly realising he was her second mate."

I looked at that male, with his burnished bronze leather trousers and gold-studded tunic. He looked as elegant as any fae of this court, but perhaps a little less dark.

"The larger male is Taegen. He is a member of the Shadow Court, though he does not hail from this land but rather the Dark Realm." Kaeleron inched closer, his shoulder brushing mine, sending a jolt through me that had me hyper aware of him again. "You would call that realm Hell."

Hell. Many species of immortals came from that shadowy realm, including demons, and I had heard stories that it was where dragon shifters like Neve lived. Even vampires lived there, acting as mercenaries for the other species, willing to fight in their wars for money. Had Neve and Riordan come from that realm?

"He's fae though," I said, not quite a question and not a statement, because I wasn't sure what he was. He had black hair and pointed ears, and had Kaeleron not mentioned where he had come from, I would have assumed he was from the Shadow Court.

"An elf, rather than an unseelie. Her family disapproved of the match, and then she discovered she has two fated mates and they disowned her. Jenavyr gave her a place in her legion." Kaeleron idly swirled his finger around my shoulder, tracing patterns on my bare skin, and I jerked it. This time he stopped without me glaring at him. "Ivaron was away on business and has only just returned. It is little wonder she is so happy to see him. I am sure she would have missed his presence tonight."

Two fated mates.

"Is it a fae thing?" I said.

Kaeleron arched a brow at me. "Missing your mate?"

"No. Having two of them. I've never heard of it before." And some small part of me willed him to say any immortal who was blessed with a fated mate could have two of them.

Because I desperately wanted it to be true.

I wanted a second fated mate—one who would want me and would love me.

"It is a fae thing. I have not heard of another species having more than one potential fated mate. Perhaps demons, and those with fae blood in their lineage." He moved away to refill his goblet.

Disappointment rolled through me, bitter and dark, dampening my mood. For a glorious moment, I had felt hope, had seen an end to my misery. If I had been able to find a new fated mate, the pain that was my wolf side's constant companion would be soothed and healed. I could be happy again.

Kaeleron pulled out two seats at the table and gestured to one of them.

I hurried to take it, wanting to lose myself in the glorious food that had been laid out on the table and maybe more of the mead. If I drank enough of it, perhaps I would forget my sorrows. I swayed with the music as I loaded up my plate, narrowing my world down to it, hiding in it in a way as Kaeleron spoke to his people, his voice distant to my ears.

My wolf side bayed, making me want to throw my head back and loose a mournful howl as rather than making me forget, the mead stripped me of my barriers, allowing everything to flood into my soul. Why couldn't I have been given a fated mate who loved me? Who wanted me? Why did Kali get two males who looked as if they adored her, while mine had rejected me?

What had I done wrong in life to receive such cruelty from fate?

Kaeleron's gaze drilled into the side of my face, but I didn't have the energy to look at him as I played with my food, my appetite gone. Even the meat from the roast pig that was delivered to my table wasn't tempting, but Kaeleron pushed it my way anyway, his eyes still on me.

He took my goblet from me when I refilled it. "You are not a happy drunk."

He was right about that.

"I don't think I've ever been drunk enough to find out whether I would be a happy one or a morose one." I reached for my goblet, my fingers brushing his, sending an electric jolt coursing up my arm that only increased my awareness of him. "Let's find out which I am."

"I think you already know." He held firm, refusing to release the goblet, even as he signalled to one of the servants. "Bring wine for my little lamb."

The same female hurried to him, curtseyed and then left to carry out his order. Odd. Normally he was served by males. I looked around, noticing that all the servants were female tonight, and that several of the attendees were smiling and chatting to them, some even brushing a hand up their hip, and none of the attention was unwanted. The females smiled and blushed for them, even leaned into their touches.

The female returning with a bottle of dark red wine for me pulled my focus away from the servants and guests, and I watched as Kaeleron found a fresh goblet and filled it for me.

"There." He pushed it towards me and I released the one I had a death grip on, letting him take it away.

I sipped the wine, and it tasted incredibly weak compared with the mead, but it was probably better than getting flat out drunk and making a fool of myself, and possibly Kaeleron.

"Eat. It will help." He pushed the roasted meat my way and growled, "That is an order."

I rolled my eyes at him but tucked into the meat anyway, savouring the juiciness of it and the hint of mead that laced it, together with herbs. Delicious. My wolf side growled in approval, ravenous for more. I'm sure I had never been so hungry. I couldn't seem to get enough of it.

Laughter and conversation rang around me, Kaeleron presiding over it all in silence, and part of me felt I should probably strike up a conversation between us but I couldn't stop placing forkful after forkful of meat into my mouth. No matter how much I ate, I wasn't satisfied.

The night air seemed to be getting warmer as the festivities rolled on, the bonfire blazing at the other end of the glade showering golden sparks up into the sky that twinkled and danced like the stars. I tilted my head back, soaking up the beauty of the sky as aurora chased across the full moon. That tang that laced the air grew stronger, invading my lungs, my pores, clouding my head.

By the gods, it was beautiful here.

I lowered my head to tell Kaeleron that and locked up tight.

By the gods!

CHAPTER 19
SAPHIRA

I blinked and rubbed my eyes, sure the wine had gone to my head and I was imagining the scene playing out before me, that I had gotten lost in my imagination and that flicker of desire Kaeleron had ignited in me.

Because the tables were being moved to the edges of the glade and the music had changed, growing darker as heavy drumbeats pounded in my ears and bows slid over strings in a jarring, tumultuous way.

And in the centre of the glade, the males and the females moved to it in a carnal symphony, stripping each other bare, hands sliding over naked flesh and moans ringing out, blending with the melody.

I stared.

Heat scalding my cheeks.

I couldn't drag my eyes away as two men lifted a female between them and began taking her, their rigid cocks sliding into her as she clung to them, her high moans echoing among the others as she threw her head back in ecstasy. Near them, a man had bent a female over one of the tables, his chest plastered to her back as he thrust into her and the male behind him thrust into him, gripping his backside hard.

Kali had one of her mates on his back on another table, riding him as her second mate pounded into her backside.

The heat scalding my cheeks flooded through the rest of me, as if a dam had burst, and I was burning up, my heart thundering as I struggled to avert my gaze. But they held me firm with their unabashed and uninhibited display of lust, with their brazen taking of what they wanted as males and females exchanged partners, as their pleasure-filled cries and the sounds of their bodies meeting created its own symphony.

Near me, one of the servants was on her knees, her dress torn and hanging around her waist as a male took her from behind, gripping her breasts, and she sucked the cock of a second male, and a third male stroked himself off as he watched.

Shocking.

This whole scene was shocking.

And wildly arousing.

Kaeleron moving beside me shattered the spell they had placed on me and my cheeks couldn't have heated any more as I grabbed my wine and drank a mouthful of it, wishing it was cold so it would cool my overheating body.

"Do all your celebrations end this way?" I hid in my drink, trying to shut out the revelry.

Kaeleron chuckled. "No. Beltane is simply proceeding as planned. This is an important part of the rite."

Now the loose dresses made sense. Not that many of the females had remained dressed. They were designed to tempt the males with a hint of what was to come.

I squirmed in my seat.

"You can join in if you wish," he purred, his grin crooked.

"No, thank you. I'm fine where I am." I highly doubted he would approve if I stood up and decided to join in anyway. The only way he would let me join in would be if I picked him as my partner.

And that felt too dangerous.

I went to sip my wine again, mind racing for an excuse to leave and return to my room, not that I expected Kaeleron to allow it.

He had ordered me to attend the celebration, and the rite wasn't done yet. Beltane wasn't over. By the gods, I wished it was. I looked at my wine as my wolf side and all my primal instincts whispered that I didn't. I wanted to be out there, among the males, parading naked and feeling their eyes on me. Their cocks in me. I wanted to be wild. Free.

I lowered my wine. "There is nothing in the drinks, right?"

Kaeleron leaned towards me, all bewitching smiles, temptation incarnate that had me wanting to move closer to him too, to feel our bodies pressed against one another again.

To touch and stroke him as the female beyond him was touching and stroking one of the males, her fingers dancing down his bare chest to wrap around his rigid shaft.

"There is nothing in the drink, little lamb. Not everyone needs help becoming aroused." Kaeleron gestured to his lap and I swallowed as my mouth dried out.

The outline of his erection was unmistakable against his inner thigh beneath the black fabric of his pants.

I squirmed harder, a war erupting inside me as instinct pushed me to reach out and touch him, to know the feel of a male at last and put an end to my wondering whether it would feel hard and rough, or soft beneath my fingers.

An image flashed into my mind, a vision of a nightmare,

Lucas stood before me, taking that female, being inside her as he should have been inside me, claiming me as his mate that night rather than rejecting me.

I growled, the sound low and desperate, born of pain as I curled forwards, covering my face with my hands, trying to shut out that moment as it replayed, over and over again.

"I can't be here," I whispered, my voice hoarse as my throat tightened. "I just can't. I can't be here. I need to go."

Kaeleron's gaze bore into me, silently demanding I look at him.

When he placed his hand on my bare shoulder, I snarled and shoved him off, flashing fangs in his face.

"I can't be here. Let me go!" I shouted, voice breaking now as pain shredded my insides, as the sounds of what was happening all around me tortured me.

Something terrible and dark flickered across his eyes and he leaned towards me, his voice pitched low as he growled, "Why?"

I shook my head and pressed my lips closed, refusing to answer.

His silver eyes darkened, gaining a trace of what looked like crimson around his pupils as the skin around his eyes seemed to blacken, and I yelped as he grabbed my chair and brutally yanked it towards him, until we were hip to hip.

He held me fast in his gaze.

His snarled words a vow.

"Whatever someone did to you in the past, they will pay for it one day, Saphira. I will see to it… and I will take care of you. No one here will harm you. You have my word on that."

And I believed him.

If I told him what Lucas had done, this dark unseelie king would hunt him down and end him, and he would revel in delivering my wrath.

But it was my wrath to deliver with my own hands.

My vengeance.

"Face it," he growled close to my ear. "Conquer it. Whatever darkness plagues your mind, do not let it win."

I wasn't sure I could face it or conquer it. I couldn't get my eyes off the table, or my mind off Lucas.

Shadows teased my arms, my calves, twining around my waist.

And slowly, those images of him with that female, his rejection ringing in my ears, twisted and morphed, becoming filled with shadows and bellows of terror as those shadows rose up, as they wrenched at Lucas, cleaving flesh open and breaking bones.

And I wasn't sure it was Kaeleron or magic turning my thoughts so dark.

It felt as if it came from somewhere deep inside me, some vengeful and wrathful part of me that had been unsheathed when Lucas had rejected me.

Freed.

I opened my eyes and looked at the crowd again, forcing myself to watch them and see the truth of them, that this moment they shared was born of pleasure and lust, and that all of them were enjoying it, savouring the release of their inhibitions and this wild, untamed rite. No one here was in pain. No one here was being forced or tortured. This was a moment of pure, unadulterated pleasure.

Heat beat through my veins, an inferno that rose with each second, my blood like liquid flame as I sank into the scene, as I let it surround me and sweep me up in it, no longer fighting it, seeking the joy in it rather than wallowing in the pain I had experienced.

I squeezed my thighs together as I watched Kali where she sat on one of the tables, her legs spread and back arched, breasts thrust towards the starlit sky as one of her mates feasted on her, his head bobbing between her thighs, his hands clamped over them and fingers pressing into her flesh, as if he couldn't get enough of her taste.

My mind filled with images of Kaeleron like that, of me spread out on the altar, a sacrifice to his pleasure.

My pleasure.

His gaze seared me, even as a female stopped close to him.

"I am only interested in my current company." Those words leaving his lips had my gaze snapping to him, colliding with his as the female he had turned down moved on, finding another male to satisfy her.

"You usually participate too." My voice trembled as I uttered those words, feeling like a fool for not realising before now, and my cheeks flushed hotter as I imagined him out there, in the midst of all those trysts, tangled with the males and females, roaring his pleasure as he came.

He nodded and casually dismissed another female who braved approaching us.

"Don't let me stop you," I muttered, shocked by the bitter edge to my words and how the thought of him with another stirred something dark within me and had my wolf side growling low.

He slowly smiled. "I would participate... if you do. As I said, I am content with my current company."

A clear declaration that if I wanted to join in he would be my partner.

And that look in his eyes warned me he wouldn't want to share me.

I would be his alone.

A nude female strutted right up to him, her bare hips at eyelevel to him now the tables had been moved and we sat like a king and queen surveying everyone from their thrones.

I glanced at her and then back again, that darkness within me growing stronger, my inner growling becoming louder.

Elanaluvyr smirked at me and then turned a pretty smile on Kaeleron, fluttering her eyelashes at him. "I am untouched, my king. My body is yours to do with what you will."

She dared to leaned towards him, breasts swaying in his direction, and planted one hand against the back of his chair, bringing her face close to his as he looked at her. I couldn't breathe as she took hold of one of his hands and guided it towards her parted thighs.

"I am ready for you," she husked.

Jealousy lanced my chest as Kaeleron didn't dismiss her, as he kept his eyes on hers and didn't resist as she slowly edged his hand towards her thighs.

Before I knew what I was doing, I was leaning in and stroking his ear, feathering my finger along the arch of it, across the silver hoops that adorned it, to the pointed tip.

Kaeleron's head jerked towards me, his silver eyes wide before his lids grew heavy. "Leave us."

For a moment, I thought he was talking to me, but then Elanaluvyr stumbled backwards, as if he had pushed her away.

She scoffed and muttered something as she stalked away from us.

Kaeleron's eyes darkened by degrees as I stroked his ear again, a shiver wracking him as his lips parted and his breaths came quicker.

"Those are sensitive, little wolf," he murmured, his voice drowsy, making me wonder how much pleasure he felt from such an innocent touch. He trembled as I touched the pointed tip again and his teeth sank into his lower lip. They were more than just sensitive. They were *very* sensitive. He groaned, the sound shockingly masculine and divine as I bravely stroked my fingers down towards the lobe again. “I wonder… are your delicate wolf ears sensitive too?”

His eyes opened, locking with mine.

“Would you tremble and quake if I stroked them?” His bewitching gaze slowly caressed the side of my face before sliding back to meet mine as he husked, “If I brushed my lips across them and took that delicate lobe between my teeth?”

I struggled to breathe, my lungs feeling too small, because I didn’t know.

And I wanted to.

I wanted him to stroke my ears.

My nape.

My breasts and the flat of my stomach.

To between my thighs.

I squeezed them together, shocked at how wet I was between them, and how clamping my muscles hard sent a shiver of pleasure dancing through me.

“Does it feel good, little wolf?” he purred, his eyes on my thighs. He patted his. “If you sit here, it will feel even better.”

Gods, I wanted to say yes and climb onto his lap.

Instead, I bit out, “No. No way.”

I cast a pointed look at his still-hard cock.

He sighed, leaned back and reached into his pants, adjusting it, which didn’t help matters at all or make me more inclined to sit on his lap because now I knew he had just touched himself and all I could think about was how easy it would be to straddle his lap and rub myself against his caged erection until I satisfied this unbearable heat within me.

He watched me. So close. So intense. Eyes sharp and focused wholly on me. Solely on me. As if I was everything he needed.

Everything he wanted.

“You definitely added something to the wine,” I muttered,

glaring at it, desperate to blame it for the flames rising within me, an inferno that threatened to burn away my inhibitions just as it had with everyone else.

"I did not." His answering smirk was all amusement as he leaned towards me and touched my flushed cheeks, his gaze growing hooded as I shivered at that brief caress. That drugging feeling of his fingers on my flesh was gone in a flash as he murmured, "You are burning up. Perhaps you are hot with lust, little wolf?"

"Stop mocking me with that name." I knocked his hand away—the hand he had just used to adjust himself—to touch himself—and scowled at him. "It's the mead. I'm not used to such strong alcohol. My family never let me drink."

It hadn't stopped me indulging in it when I had been at Chase's house with my friends though.

He muttered, "Your family never seemed to let you do anything. Your life has been so sheltered, my little lamb."

Ugh. Maybe it was better to let him call me 'little wolf'. It was certainly preferable to being called a lamb all the time and being made to feel right down to my bones how innocent I was in his eyes.

"No, it hasn't. I've experienced plenty." The denial sounded weak even to my own ears.

He turned a darkening look on me and demanded, "Tell me all the things you have *experienced*. I believe I paid for an untouched female."

I hit him with my best scowl. "There's nothing in our contract that says I have to divulge private and very personal information."

"You must do all I ask," he countered.

A brittle scoff burst from my lips. "No, not all you ask, and not this. I'm here at your *celebration* and that's enough for tonight."

He slid a look over me, scalding me from head to toe and back again. "Very well. I will let you keep your secrets—for now—and in exchange you will sit here."

He tapped his lap with a single finger.

I actually debated it this time. Confess that my experience of the world was as limited as he believed it to be and admit I was just as sheltered as he had said, or sit on his lap.

Nestled close to the evidence of his arousal.

As embarrassing as it was, it was an easy choice.

I went to go to him, but he seized my arm and brutally tugged me to him, forcing me onto his lap and caging me with his strong arms. I fought his hold, unwilling to be made to do anything like this or let him think he could do as he pleased with me.

"Still, little wolf," he hissed into my ear, his breath fanning my neck. "There are males watching you. Males I do not trust."

I stiffened, my heart pounding, and then realised he was probably creating an excuse to make me sit on his lap without making a fuss. So I brought my right hand around in a fast arc aimed at his face.

He easily caught my wrist, and his thumb stroked the sensitive skin there as he purred, "Relax. I am only trying to protect you."

"I highly doubt that." The venom left my words as he looked off to his right and then left, and I looked there too.

And got an eyeful of males watching me as they were being sucked off or ridden, their gazes hot on me.

Predatory.

An inferno rather than heat exploded within me, coursing through every inch of me, morphing into arousal as Kaeleron wrapped his arms around my waist and murmured against my skin.

"This way you are safe."

I didn't feel safe as I looked at him, my lips dangerously close to his, his breath caressing my mouth.

I felt as if I was burning up.

On fire with need I couldn't control, that felt as if it was shredding me apart from the inside out, a living thing that wanted to escape the cage of my body.

"I need to go. Now," I breathed as that fire built. I was too hot. Burning up. I writhed on his lap, unable to get comfortable, each shift of my body against his only making things worse as my need grew, as that terrible urge to position myself astride him and rub against him became near overwhelming.

Hijacking control of me.

I looked at all the males, gaze darting from one to the next, the inferno within me building with every one I watched for a heartbeat, with every rigid shaft I set eyes on. I couldn't breathe. I clawed at my chest, at my throat, needing air.

Needing to cool down.

My dress felt too tight.

My skin was on fire.

I clawed at it, desperate to get out of it, my dress or my skin I didn't know.

My short claws sliced through the delicate fabric of my dress, shearing one of the straps. It fell away, cooler air kissing my skin above my right breast, but it wasn't enough.

I stared at the males, aware of the hard body beneath mine, the heady wild storm scent of him filling my nostrils and drawing all of my focus to him. I wriggled on his lap, desperate to rub myself against him, to feel that hard masculine body against mine, a growl slipping from my lips.

A demand to touch me.

My back arched as I kicked my legs and the dress fell between them, exposing my thighs, a moan escaping me as my nipples beaded, the fabric abrading them. Teasing them.

Kaeleron's gaze was like fire on me, branding me, making me burn hotter.

I couldn't take it.

I desperately clawed at my dress, at him, needing to hold him and needing to break free of his arms, torn in so many directions that something within me was threatening to break.

"I can't," I bit out as another wave of desire rolled over me, dark and delicious, pulling me deeper under its spell, and I realised what was happening.

Why I felt sick.

Shaking violently.

So desperate for a release from all this pain.

My bones ached, muscles clamping down onto them as I reached for a hint of pleasure, squeezing my thighs tight together.

My arousal reached fever pitch.

"Saphira?"

My name was a drug on his lips.

I shivered and burned, desperate for him to speak it again.

To free me of these chains that bound me.

The night closed in and I wanted to howl at that full moon, wanted to strip off this dress and dance among the males, tempting this fae king until he submitted to me.

No.

I pushed from his arms, stumbling as I hit the ground, my head foggy and the need pounding in my veins demanding I return to him. He had what I needed. Was what I wanted.

No.

I kicked off my slippers and ran barefoot through the grass, hitching my dress up so I didn't trip as I sprinted as hard as I could, the cool dewy touch of nature beneath my feet soothing some of the heat that had grown unbearable.

I was going to burn up.

Crumble to ashes.

I ran hard. Fast. Until the sounds of the feast disappeared into the night. Until silence surrounded me.

And I didn't stop running until I reached my room.

I threw all the windows open, letting cold night air roll into the room. It wasn't enough. It didn't cool me as I needed. I burned. It didn't stop my thoughts from spinning out of control, all centred around a certain dark fae king and the way he had looked at me.

I *burned* for him.

My primal instincts snarled and demanded I return to the feast.

To him.

I had taken three steps towards the door before I caught myself, steeling myself against my instincts as they pushed me to find Kaeleron, to give in to every wicked need he roused in me. He would gladly pleasure me until I was out of my mind, high on the mating heat and him.

All I had to do was give in and ask him.

I gritted my teeth and curled my hands into tight fists, fighting that urge to find him. To fuck him. It wasn't going to happen. I would probably die of embarrassment if he knew the state I was in, how my sanity was slowly being stripped from me by my primal instincts to mate.

I buried my head in my hands and shook it.

Not going to happen.

I went to the bathroom and splashed water on my face, and when that didn't work, I lifted the bowl and doused myself, spilling water all over the stone floor.

But still the fire within me grew hotter.

I clawed at my sodden dress as it stuck to my skin, frantic and wild, my heart thundering and limbs shaking as need became pain, as that pain threatened to steal my sanity from me.

I was burning up.

A growl pealed from my lips.

And only a male could quell this heat threatening to destroy me.

My wolf side howled for Kaeleron.

CHAPTER 20
SAPHIRA

I groaned and pulled at my dress, my face twisting as misery joined the pain and the need rioting within me, and took to pacing my room, restless with a need to return to the feast and find someone.

Anyone.

I was no longer feeling picky. Kaeleron. Riordan. Any male would do.

I gritted my teeth, fighting that urge.

I didn't really want that. My instincts did. That deep primal instinct that demanded I mate.

Maybe I could sleep it off.

Maybe a few more glasses of wine would make me so tired that this violent need to mate would subside because I wouldn't have the energy. I absently clawed at my dress, not realising I was slowly shredding it until I caught my haggard reflection in the mirror. My pupils were blown, my crimson dress in tatters, and my hair was a damp tangle of silver that looked as if I had been rolling around in the bushes with a male already.

"Someone should have given me explicit details about this,"

I groused, blaming my mother, and the teachers at my pack, and even my ancestors for not deciding this was something maturing female wolves needed a full breakdown about so they knew what to expect.

Because this need to claw my skin off and this pain that twisted inside me, as if it might kill me if I didn't find a release for it, wasn't something I had anticipated.

And, really, I only had myself to blame.

I shouldn't have stopped my mother when she had started to talk about maturity, trying to warn me about what would happen.

But I had given in to embarrassment, hastily withdrawing and shutting her down.

I regretted it now as I doubled over, clutching my stomach as need became agony, and hadn't realised my hands had moved of their own accord until I was palming my breasts, thumbing my nipples, shivering as little jolts of pleasure tripped through me.

"Maybe I can deal with this alone, or at least take the edge off."

I knew it wouldn't help, but refused to listen to sense, because I had to do something. Anything.

I sat on the end of the bed, battling that urge to claw at my skin as I writhed on the spot, unable to keep still. When my hands cupped my breasts, a red haze engulfed my vision and my back arched, some buried instinct within me rising to the fore, trying to wrest control from me. I needed more. I brushed my nipples, exposing the breast where my claws had sliced through the strap, swallowing hard as I fell back on the black covers.

My other hand drifted to between my thighs and I yanked the irritating material away and didn't hesitate. I spread my legs and pressed my hand between them, stroking and teasing my damp cleft, reaching for another hit of pleasure to dampen the pain and satisfy my needs.

Ripples of pleasure were all I felt though, echoes of the satisfaction my body and instincts craved.

A sob broke free of my lips as I tried harder, squeezing my clit, desperately tweaking my nipples.

It wasn't enough.

I cried out in pain as my insides cramped.

As fire scoured me.

Another sob tore from my lips.

I was going to die.

I was going to die in the most embarrassing way.

I felt sure of it as I rolled onto my side and curled up into a ball, my skin burning up, sweat beading on my skin as pain jolted my bones and had my muscles shaking.

Someone knocked on my door.

"Saphira?"

Oh gods no.

I buried my face in the bedclothes as that deep voice rumbled through my door.

Kaeleron.

I had been wrong.

Now I was going to die in the most embarrassing way, expiring from the pain of my first mating heat with a too gorgeous for his own good fae king as my witness.

"Saphira, let me in."

A very polite fae king.

He could have entered if he wanted. The door wasn't locked and even if it had been, he could have teleported inside or just ghosted through the obstruction in his shadows. But instead he was lingering on the other side of it, and he sounded concerned.

"No," I muttered. "Go away."

He sounded less concerned as he bit out, "I will not leave. Something is wrong with you. I can feel it."

"Great." I pressed my face deeper into the covers. "Gods, kill me now."

This couldn't get any worse.

"I am coming in."

Maybe it could.

I twisted upright to tell him no, but he barged into the room, and every instinct currently ruling me growled at the delicious sight of him.

Here was what I needed.

This dark, towering male whose power embraced me as he stalked into the room, his black hair wild as if he had been running his hands through it and his silver eyes hungry.

No, I did *not* need Kaeleron.

"Go away." I scrambled and reached for a pillow, hurling it at him and then grunting as my body cramped again.

The pillow hit him square in the face.

He didn't even try to block it as he prowled towards me and flicked his right hand out. The door behind him slammed shut and the window shutters followed it, like a wave of magic rolling through the room.

"I did this," he growled. "I will take care of it... of you."

Mortified, I shook my head. "No."

My instincts howled 'yes, yes, yes!'.

My inner wolf, my primal side, more animal than human, responded to him—to his arrogance and his dominant nature as he stared down at me, looming at the foot of the four-poster bed.

I tried to crawl away from him, hoping he might leave if I ignored him, biting back another grunt as pain seared me and twisted my insides.

"Saphira." My name was a command on his lips and I

thrilled as he gripped the bedclothes and yanked on them, pulling me back towards him, not letting me escape.

Part of me howled at the display of aggression.

I glared at him.

A king.

Too much like an alpha.

He wielded power. Strength. And by the gods, my body responded to it like a drug, writhing as he looked at me, his gaze hooded and demanding.

He wielded power *over me.*

I shifted on the bed, rubbing my thighs together, unable to stop myself as his gaze seared me, scorching away my reservations, giving my instincts a firmer hold on my mind as well as my body.

"I will only do what you want—what you ask—you are in control." He held his hand out to me. "Let me see to your pleasure."

Those words wreaked havoc on me.

I didn't feel in control.

His scent, his commanding masculine presence had me wanting to climb him.

Claw him.

Fuck him.

It felt as if my wolf side was trying to burst free of my skin to get to him as he looked at me, his gaze heated, as if he wanted me.

My mind swam, my back arching off the bed, breasts thrusting upwards as I clawed at the covers, as I writhed and succumbed to the fire. Too much. I couldn't survive this. I cried out as pain swept through me, and it came out as half human, half wolf, a howl of agony that had Kaeleron's expression shifting from aroused to fearful.

I threw my head back and howled again, sobbing towards

the end of it as I desperately clutched at the sheets, as I twisted them into my fists and every inch of me tensed so fiercely I feared my bones would shatter.

"Saphira," Kaeleron whispered softly and then his hand was on my bent knee.

His touch like a brand.

But not one of fire, but one of blessed ice.

"Touch me," I sobbed, writhing and aching, desperate for more of that sweet coolness.

I all but clawed my dress up, air kissing bare skin, no trace of shame touching me as I exposed myself to him and spread my legs.

"Please, gods… touch me."

"I will take care of you." He pressed a knee into the mattress beside me, his weight rolling me towards him. "Do not fight it. Give yourself over to it. The pleasure will be all the sweeter."

I drew in a sharp breath, a sigh that hitched in my throat as his palm shifted from my knee to my inner thigh.

Need swamped me, wrenching control from me, and I gave myself over to it just as he had instructed, shedding all fear and embarrassment, surrendering to my desire.

To Kaeleron.

His fingers danced along my inner thigh and I moaned as my back arched from the bed, as I tore at my dress, exposing my breasts.

He murmured something that ended with 'little wolf' but I was too far gone to hear him as blood rushed in my ears, as my body trembled beneath his questing fingers.

A gasp shot from my lips as he stroked between my thighs, my body jolting and my hands flying to the pillow above me. I clutched it, twisting it in my hands as he parted me, as his fingers dipped between my petals and teased me.

Sweet mercy.

I rocked my hips, shameless in my pursuit of pleasure as it built within me, his touch easily doing what mine couldn't. He stroked harder, each brush of his fingers taking me higher as his gaze scalded my face. Feeling emboldened, my need to mate flooding me with a desire to goad and dominate him in return, to push him into giving me his cock—his seed—I opened my eyes and met his, staring into them as he touched me. Stroked me.

His fingers dipped lower, his lips parting as his breaths came faster too, and I moaned, not holding back my pleasure as he circled my slick entrance. I dug my claws into the pillow, my eyes rolling back in my head as I raised my hips, silently encouraging—demanding—he press his fingers inside me.

He groaned as he eased them inside, the heat of them scalding me and the thickness of them satisfying some new, wicked part of me. Oh, how his cock would feel inside me, stretching me around him. I opened my eyes again and raked them over him, down to his hips.

His hard length kicked beneath the material of his trousers, as if responding to my gaze, and I groaned as I rode his fingers, imagining it was his shaft inside me instead.

A bomb detonated inside me, the suddenness of it tearing a cry from me as my hips jerked and heat swept through me, fierce and unbridled, and my thighs quivered, shaking so fiercely they couldn't support my weight. I sank into the bed, breathing hard, some of the pain abating as release swept me up in it.

I waited for him to leave, sure he would and that I would be fine now.

Only he didn't.

And I wasn't.

The pain rolled back in on the final pulse of my release,

stealing my breath with its ferocity, and I gasped and rocked my body on his fingers, instinct at the helm. I rode them hard, desperate to find another release, but it didn't come as easily this time. The pleasure of my first one lingered inside me, dampening what I received as he stroked and touched me, as he teased my clit with his thumb.

I gritted my teeth and palmed my breasts, flicking my nipples, trying to push through it and find another release, a stronger one perhaps, that would satisfy me completely.

A growl slipped from my lips as he spread my legs, bracing them apart with his shoulders, and delved between them, his tongue stroking me. I flung my head back and cried out as he sucked and teased, clutching my breasts and pushing my hips up, pressing against his mouth as he turned my fantasy into reality.

I stared down the length of my body, trembling as his dark head moved between my thighs, moaning as he lifted his head enough to lock gazes with me, his tongue stroking me, his eyes darker than I had ever seen them, commanding and holding me under his spell as he pleasured me.

"Oh gods," I muttered, lost in his eyes, in the pleasure of his touch and how wicked it felt to watch him as he took me with his mouth. "Oh gods."

I cried out as another release rushed through me, shaking like a leaf in a hurricane as Kaeleron clamped his hands down over my thighs and held me in place, not letting up. He pushed me through the release, pushed me higher, towards the next crescendo.

It hit me in a blur of light and heat.

But it still wasn't enough.

I groaned as he eased back and kneeled between my thighs, sinking his fingers deep into me again, filling me.

Still not enough.

I writhed and moaned, struggling to keep still as I clawed at the sheets, ripping them to shreds.

I needed more.

My gaze dropped to his caged erection.

I needed that.

"Fuck me," I whispered, half mad with need, too far gone to be embarrassed about demanding that from him.

It was what he wanted after all.

He wanted me to beg him for sex.

And here I was.

Begging him.

"Fuck me, please?" I reached for him, wanting to take what I needed, delirious with need of it.

"No."

That firm refusal lashed at me, making me falter for a heartbeat as my gaze flew to his.

I had never seen him looking so stern. So cold.

His jaw flexed as he stared down at me, his fingers slowly pumping into me, the sting of his rejection and the need to make him leave, to make him stop now and spare myself more hurt and humiliation fading with each stroke that had my instinct to mate rising again, flooding my mind and seizing control of my body.

"Fuck me or find me a male who will," I growled, my voice bordering on inhuman as I gnashed fangs at him.

"No," he snarled right back at me.

Violently flipped me onto my front and pulled my hips up.

I barked out a moan as he licked and laved me with his tongue, his strokes harder now, more demanding. The roughness of his touch thrilled me, rousing that part of me that needed this.

Needed a firm hand. Needed an alpha.

A powerful male to satisfy me.

I shattered under his ministrations. A haze built in my mind with each release he gave me, a strange warmth rolling through my body to slowly quell the pain. His fingers teased and filled me, his tongue tormented me, and his eyes never left me.

His gaze seared me as I came undone again and again, each one leaving me more hazy, more tired, until with a final hoarse cry and trembling thighs, I sank into darkness.

"Rest."

His voice echoed in the inky black.

Soft.

Commanding.

An order.

I obeyed.

CHAPTER 21
KAELERON

I stared down at the slumbering wolf, the tears that dampened her cheeks and the scent of her tormenting me.

The one I had bought her from had done something to her.

He might not have touched her body, but that did not mean he had not messed with her mind—that Saphira had not seen things that had imprinted on her. Her reaction to the rite remained with me, rousing my shadows and my darker nature that whispered at me to hunt.

To kill.

She had been drowning in whatever darkness had closed in on her before I had pulled her back to me.

It had been a mistake to order her to come the celebration. I could see that now. There were things about this wolf I should have known, and not only whatever trauma the male wolf had inflicted upon her.

I touched her flushed cheeks, a buried part of me relieved to feel they were cooler now.

The rite had affected her more deeply than I had imagined it would.

I had no love for it normally, but I had found it interesting purely because she had been there with me and I had been able to watch her reacting to the events as they had unfolded. I had liked watching her walls shatter...

But...

I regretted it all now.

I felt responsible for the pain she had suffered because of it, even though I had not known she would react so strongly to the sight and scent of the rite. She loosed a soft sigh as I stroked my fingers across her cooling cheek and feathered them up to her damp brow to brush her wet silvery hair back from it.

What madness had gripped her tonight?

I had hoped to shake her a little, maybe even loosen her inhibitions, but instead I had inflicted pain upon her.

Guilt gnawed at me as I watched her sleep, this peaceful beauty a stark contrast to the wild, desperate female I had found in this room when I had followed her here, needing to know what was wrong with her.

I knew too little about wolves.

I could see that now.

And I intended to rectify that when she woke. She would tell me what had come over her, and confirm my suspicions for me.

That she was in the grip of a mating heat.

The way she had moved in response to my touch, her sweet cries as pleasure had taken her, and the hungry look in her eyes as she had gazed at me, silently demanding more, swam in my mind, keeping my own need at a steady boil.

Her plea for me to fuck her had almost been my undoing.

Would she have begged any male like that, or was it me in particular she wanted so fervently?

She had demanded I find her a male if I would not take her myself, but had seemed to regret her words the moment they left her lips, and had been all too happy to subject herself to my caress, seeking her pleasure in it instead of issuing another command to find her someone else who would do as she desired.

As if I would let another male touch her.

I growled at the thought of another male laying his hands on her, my teeth sharpening and darkness staining the tips of my fingers as ancient markings tracked down each one towards my palms.

She was *mine.*

Mine alone.

Visions of her moving so sensuously with another male, lost in her hungers and a slave to her desire, had my darker side pushing to the fore, my nails transforming into inch long claws I brushed over her skin in a possessive caress.

If another male had come to her tonight, would she have begged him to take her as she had begged me?

Would she have given herself to him?

Or was it me alone she desired?

I did not allow myself to answer that question.

She was the key to my vengeance, a tool, that was all. This mating heat was a complication, but I would see to it that she was protected from other males who might be less gentle or considerate with her. Once she had fulfilled her role in my revenge, I would return her to her world.

And I would uphold my vow to slaughter the wolf who had sold her.

I dragged my hand away from her soft skin, curling my fingers into a fist as I reined in my darker side, tempering it with the promise of vengeance against the one who had hurt her. Soon.

Patience.

I was not sure I had any where this female was concerned, and that was dangerous. I could not let her distract me from my vengeance, not now that I felt I was close to achieving it and it would soon be within my grasp.

Delivered by a lamb in wolf's clothing.

Although, she had not seemed much like a lamb tonight.

She had been all wolf.

A predator on the hunt.

A wild and sensual female who had taken what she had wanted from me, greedily accepting pleasure and demanding more.

I pondered that as I cast magic on the windows and the door, ensuring they remained locked to anyone but me until the morning. Keeping her safe from other males.

And glanced back at her before I teleported to the garden.

The sound of the feast drifted on the night breeze, summoning me back to it. I should return there to do my part, but the thought was far from appealing. I looked over my shoulder at the castle, in the direction of my slumbering wolf, and then stepped into the dark void again, teleporting not to the feast or my room, but to my private retreat deep in the heart of Noainfir, the mountain that protected the castle like a great shadow.

Magic stirred around me as I strode across the mosaic floor of the giant marble rotunda, glowing in the great crystals that clung to the cragged walls of the cave, each violet shard larger than I was.

My eyes slipped shut and I stilled, feeling the magic as it swirled around me, as it grew stronger in response to the celebrations above.

And what I had done with Saphira.

I walked to one of the seating areas, my steps falling silent as I crossed several ornate rugs and passed tables ladened with books and sheets of my notes and theories on Saphira and her role in my vengeance. The candles on the tables flickered to life as I passed them, adding a warm glow to the air that glittered with golden motes. Rather than sinking into one of the upholstered chairs as I had intended, I continued towards the edge of the circular platform of the rotunda where it fell away into a cliff that dove down to the sliver of sea that entered the cave through the far end of it.

My mind on Saphira.

On the way she had moved for me, responding to my touch so sweetly, and so wickedly, her supple body arching under my caress, silently begging me for more.

My eyes slipped shut and I palmed my cock, rubbing my hand down the aching shaft as I pictured her on her knees, her wild silver hair falling around her shoulders, her breasts swaying as she moved in time with the strokes of my fingers.

I shredded the laces of my leathers with a claw and groaned as cool air kissed my overheating length, wrapped my hand around it and fed it into her slick pussy, savouring her moan as I stretched and filled her, as I sank myself as deep as her sweet sheath could take me.

Possessively deep.

My left hand gripped her hip as my right fisted her hair, twisting the soft strands around my hand, and I planted my right foot against the bed, using it for leverage as I pounded into her, as I gave her everything she had begged me to give her, relishing her cries and the sound of my flesh slapping against her as I thrust my cock deep into her.

Punishing thrusts.

Marking her as mine.

Making her need no other male.

She moaned and clenched me, cries growing louder as I

angled my hips and took her harder, deeper, my rough breaths mingling with hers as we strained for release together, as her scent engulfed me and her heat gripped me.

It hit me in a blinding flash that robbed me of breath in a yell that echoed around the cavern.

My cock throbbed in my hand as my trembling legs buckled beneath me, each jet of seed that burst from me staggering me.

I sank to my knees, struggling to breathe.

"By the Great Mother," I muttered, bracing my free hand on my thigh, my shaft still throbbing with release that ebbed and flowed through me, making my head spin and heart labour.

The magic.

It was just the magic of Beltane in the air.

It had intoxicated me more than I had known and that was the reason I was half blind from an orgasm that had shaken me to my core.

The magic was the reason I had climaxed so hard.

Not the bewitching little wolf who had cried my name when her mating frenzy had shattered.

CHAPTER 22

SAPHIRA

It wasn't the bird song that woke me. It was the warmth that flowed through my limbs, warmth that I floated on, luxuriating in the divine perfection of the feeling of weightlessness and peace. I stretched my arms out, sinking into it, feeling more relaxed than I had ever done and unwilling to question what had caused it.

Until I edged my right leg out further and that calm warmth was joined by a touch of soreness between my thighs.

I bolted upright in bed.

"Oh my gods."

Humiliation and horror combined to have me curling into a ball, burying my face in my knees as I hugged them to my chest.

"Oh my gods," I groaned into the black covers.

The *tattered* black covers.

I groaned again, willing the earth of Lucia to open up and swallow me, because I wasn't sure I could face what I had done.

I certainly couldn't face Kaeleron.

I rolled onto my side, pulling the shredded covers over my head, trying to shut out the still-far-too-hot replay of him holding my gaze as he feasted between my thighs. Oh my gods. What had I done?

What had felt good. Right. That's what I had done.

I had surrendered to my instincts as Kaeleron had told me to, had released the hold I'd had on all my needs and wants, pushing through my inhibitions and unleashing a side of me I had never known existed.

A carnal, wicked side.

A side that wasn't afraid to do what I wanted, to take what I wanted.

And it had felt freeing.

Wonderful, in fact.

But that didn't mean I was going to parade around the castle like a peacock, my chin held high and not a care in the world. I was going to do what old Saphira wanted me to do.

I was going to avoid the heck out of Kaeleron and pretend last night hadn't happened.

That a powerful dark fae king hadn't been the one to give me not only my first orgasm.

But my first *ten*.

All in one night.

I groaned into the covers, "Oh my gods."

Not only that, but I had begged him to take me. I had offered up my body on a platter to him.

And he had turned me down.

Both my wolf and my human side flinched at that, his rejection lodged in the two halves of our shared soul like a dagger. He had paid handsomely for my virginity, and when I had thought he would claim what he had bought, he had looked so hard and so cold, so very distant from me, as if he hadn't really been there with me.

And had told me 'no'.

Not once, but twice.

I cringed as I recalled what I had said to him to earn that second refusal. I had asked him to find me a male who would fuck me.

"Kill me now," I muttered into the covers, burrowing deeper into them. "I'm such a fool."

I should have seen it last night when he had come to me and taken responsibility for my situation, and had told me he would take care of my needs. He had been distant when he had rejected me because he had been going through the motions, pleasuring me to ease the burden of the responsibility he felt, not because he wanted me.

And I was a fool because in that moment I had wanted him.

Still wanted him.

I sank into the maelstrom of my emotions, overwhelmed by them as one after another clues revealed themselves to me, things I had missed last night while lost to lust.

Like the fact he hadn't taken any pleasure for himself, had only focused on me.

And that he hadn't been here when I had awoken, and I couldn't scent him on the pillows, so he hadn't stayed for even a moment.

How badly had he wanted to leave the whole time he was with me?

How quickly had he escaped after ordering me to rest once my fever had broken thanks to his skilful mouth and fingers?

"Oh gods. I'm a blind idiot." I rolled onto my front, tucked into a ball still, wrapped in the blankets like a shifter burrito.

Had he returned to the celebrations after he had dealt with me out of a sense of duty, seeking himself a better, more beautiful female to satisfy his needs? Had he indulged like the other males the moment he hadn't felt a need to watch over me?

I banged my head against the mattress, groaning and

silently beseeching the land to really open up and swallow me, or transport me far away from this castle and its king.

And then I shoved up onto my hands and knees, refusing to let another male break me, to let the pleasure I had felt last night become pain that tormented me. I had done nothing wrong. I had been vulnerable, in pain, desperately in need of a male to break my heat. Many female wolves had been in the same position as I had and they hadn't let it beat them.

I wouldn't either.

Several females at my pack hadn't found their mate yet, and whenever their heat hit them, they had their pick of the single males, all of them more than happy to service their needs and help them through their heat. No feelings were involved in the nights they spent together, sating the demands of the mating frenzy. Sometimes females took a different male each night, and when the heat had broken, things all went back to normal. No messy emotions. No thinking they had a right to the other or were now a couple.

If I had been back at my pack, all of them would have stepped up to help me.

Kaeleron had done just that.

And I could be like any female at my pack and accept that his help had been needed, and I was grateful for it, but now it was done. That moment between us, we had been different people.

Now things would return to normal.

No messy emotions.

I shuffled to the edge of the bed and padded barefoot to the windows, flinging the shutters and then the windows open, letting light and a warm sea breeze into my stuffy room. No messy emotions. Kaeleron had done me a service. That was all.

It didn't mean anything.

"I shall go for a walk," I announced to no one in particular, needing to say it aloud to give myself the courage to do it. "If I run into him, things will be normal and not at all awkward."

I was getting very good at lying to myself these days.

Determined to make the most of the day and not hide away in my room as he probably expected, I bathed and did my best not to think about him as my hands glided over my bare curves. I jumped from the bath earlier than I had wanted when he refused to leave my mind and dried off and then dressed in my leather pants, riding boots and a dark blue blouse, and paired it with an under-bust corset that had been delivered to my room with the new blouse.

I imagined it was a gift from Jenavyr rather than Kaeleron, since I had admired the one she wore.

It laced at the front and I cinched it tightly as I looked at my reflection in the mirror, making sure I could still breathe but that it showed off my curves too.

For no reason in particular.

There was no one in this castle I needed to impress, or wanted to catch their eye.

I braided my silver hair in a long rope that hung down my back and added a little kohl around my eyes, liking the look of it now. I had never been one for make-up, had only bothered with it on special occasions, but now I preferred how my eyes looked with a smudge of darkness around them. It brightened the blue of my eyes.

There.

I looked quite pretty.

And not at all like a female a male might jilt.

I forced my chin up as I stepped from my room and headed downstairs, noting the absence of guards. *Freedom.* It put a spring in my step as I took the sweeping marble stairs two at a time, bounding down them, and broke out into the warmth and light of the garden.

The scent of the blooms blended with the salt of the ocean, a delectable perfume that I breathed deep of as I meandered around the garden, picking paths that no one occupied. Not because I was trying to avoid someone. I just needed a little me time. That was the reason I kept my gaze on the flowers and insects too, tracked a bird that flitted across my path and up into one of the trees. I wanted to be alone today.

A perfectly reasonable thing to want.

All perfectly normal.

My senses reached around me, charting the position of all the fae, from the highborn that lingered in the shadows of heavily foliaged arbours, whispering among themselves, to the gardeners that worked hard to deadhead the flowers and keep them looking beautiful. Not to avoid them.

Well, maybe a little to avoid them because I didn't want to run into Elanaluvyr and her clique.

My step faltered.

Had she sought out Kaeleron again when he had return to the feast alone?

Had he accepted her advances?

I shook my head. I didn't care. It meant nothing to me if he had sought her out and they had been together. What we had done had been purely physical, a release I had needed, and an end to my suffering. I could be practical about this, just like any other wolf female of mating age.

Yet I found myself sneaking down unoccupied paths and steering clear of everyone else in the garden and not really enjoying my walk as my mood slowly darkened, my thoughts returning to how Kaeleron had looked when he had rejected me.

"Maybe I should head back," I murmured.

My ears twitched.

"Did you hear about the king's unplanned absence from court today?" a female whispered and I peered through the bush of bright violet flowers to my left, trying to see her.

Her male companion chuckled. "No doubt he is sleeping off the festivities. The rite was rather energetic this year."

"I barely had the strength to leave bed this morning. Had I not been sharing it with a common guard, I might have lingered." The distaste in her tone made me wonder why she had slept with a guard at all if she was going to hate what she had done afterwards.

Forbidden fruit, I supposed.

What happened at the rite, stayed at the rite.

I had seen many males and females I had recognised as highborn there, cavorting with servants and guards, seeming to enjoy having a taste of them. Slumming it apparently had appeal in the fae world as well as my one.

"Normally the king is present for court the next day though," she said, her tone thoughtful.

They drifted off together, leaving me standing there, an answer for his unusual absence ringing in my mind.

He was avoiding me.

Embarrassment crept up on me, slipping past my rigid defences, and I barely leashed the desire to bury my head in my hands and hide. Instead of running back to my room with my tail tucked between my legs, I forced myself to walk to my second favourite spot in the garden—a beautiful white wooden circular gazebo that had blood red vines growing up the ornately carved posts, their white blossoms hanging like grapes across the arches.

It had a seat beneath it that faced the edge of the garden

and the stunning view of the sea and the mountains, and from it I could watch the boats coming and going from the sheltered harbour of the town below. That would occupy my mind for a while, might even shift my thoughts away from Kaeleron.

Only when I reached it, a male was sitting there.

CHAPTER 23
SAPHIRA

I backed away a step, intending to leave before the male noticed me, but he stood and pivoted to face me in one fluid motion, his silver eyes clashing with mine.

Silver eyes that were familiar and foreign at the same time.

The stranger bowed gracefully, bending at the waist as his right arm came across his stomach and his left extended out at his side with a flourish. He straightened, his wild short black hair kissing his pale forehead as his eyes locked with mine again and a smile curved lips only a shade darker than his skin.

"My lady," he murmured as a way of greeting, and I frowned at him, studying him closely, watching his every move as something buried deep within me said to keep my distance from him.

This male was dangerous.

He smoothed his fine black tunic, his eyes remaining fixed on mine, and I tried to place him, searching my memories to figure out whether I had met him before. Given his mocking greeting, I suspected he knew of me at least, and maybe that meant he was part of the court but a member I hadn't run into on any of my walks.

"You may greet me with 'my prince'." He rolled his hand in my direction, gesturing for me to follow his instructions.

"A prince?" I continued to frown at him. "No one here has ever mentioned there's a prince at this court."

His smile was feline, and it reached his eyes, making them shine as he said, "I am not of this court. Merely a visitor. Perhaps considered a friend by some."

"By the king?" Kaeleron was the only one I could imagine as this male's friend. They both walked a fine line between light and terrifying darkness, and both held a power that was so potent it was a tangible thing around me, snaking and twining around my limbs and crawling over my skin.

"And his sister, and perhaps some others at this court too." He gestured to the bench between us. "Shall we sit?"

"No thanks." I remained where I was, keeping a healthy distance between us.

He chuckled again. "So blunt. Are all your breed so forthright? Your kind certainly seem to be gaining a foothold in fae lands. Almost seven centuries on this earth and not once had I seen a wolf in Lucia, and suddenly there are two. First a male, and now a female."

I stiffened. "A male?"

There was another wolf shifter in Lucia?

My pulse picked up, heart racing as I considered who it might be, and fear washed through my veins as my mind locked onto Lucas. Odd that I instantly leaped to fear, even my wolf side afraid that he might have come to find me, that he might take me from this world before I was ready to leave.

Before I was strong enough to face him.

The fae prince held his hands out before him, the gesture

calming, and I realised I had been growling and flexing my fingers, my fangs on show as my lips peeled back off them.

"The wolf I met was a Scottish alpha and had his mate with him. I safely escorted them from the lands of the Nightmare Court."

Not Lucas then, or anyone I knew.

Nightmare Court?

I shuddered at the name alone, images springing into my mind of what that court would be like. If the one of shadows was dark and frightening enough, I never wanted to see the Nightmare Court.

"Are you from there?" I said, suppressing another shiver and the urge to step back to increase the distance between us.

The male shook his head. "No. I am not from anywhere. Not anymore. I am a wanderer." He gestured to the seat again, his lips curling in a warm smile that again reached his eyes. "Come. I do not bite. Let us sit a while and conspire. I am sure there are a great many things you wish to know about the ruler of this court. I know many of his secrets."

His grin was all mischief.

He liked the idea of spilling all Kaeleron's secrets to me, and I wasn't sure he wanted to do it to arm me with information about my master. He looked as if he wanted to do it to irritate Kaeleron more than anything. A male unafraid of Kaeleron's wrath? How powerful was he if he didn't fear the shadow king?

"I am Oberon." He extended his hand to me, his expression warm and open.

"Oberon," I echoed, my eyebrows rising high on my forehead. "I know that name. Vyr mentioned you. She said you told her tales of my world... and something about wanting me to verify what you had said about it."

His face brightened. "Vyr. She is well? I admit, I wanted to see her too, but she is absent from the castle. Away on some business apparently."

"She's well. I think. I haven't known her long enough to tell whether she's well or not really. But she seemed fine the last time I saw her." I cringed as I recalled our trip into town and run in with Riordan. "Although, I feel her *business* is an excuse to get away from a certain vampire."

Oberon arched a fine black eyebrow and I felt I had said too much.

Before I could ask him to forget what I had said, he chuckled.

"Riordan has been annoying her again?" He shook his head, flashing straight white teeth in a broad smile. "The fool will never win her that way."

I leaned towards him, wanting to 'conspire' just as he had offered, the words on the tip of my tongue.

Oh my gods, you see it too?

I held them inside instead, feeling I had already said too much and it really wasn't my place to gossip with a relative-stranger about the princess of this court. I was trying to earn Vyr's trust and maybe win her friendship, and I wouldn't achieve either of those things if she heard I had been debating her possible feelings for the vampire.

"Sit with me, wolf. Anything you say will not leave my lips." He took a seat, turning his back to me, and patted the spot beside him. "I am a great master of secrets."

Rather than taking it, I walked past him to the wall and leaned against it, enjoying the breeze now I was out of the shade of the gazebo, and that strange twilight sky that shifted with colourful, bewitching aurora.

I sighed as I studied it, planting my hands beside my hips to steady myself as I tipped my head back further.

Oberon watched me, his gaze a caress of power that hummed along my skin.

I lowered my eyes to him. "I'm Saphira by the way."

I extended my hand to him, and he rose and slipped his into it, his skin cool against mine but thrumming with power that echoed in my bones as he gently gripped my hand and lifted it.

And brushed his lips across the back of it.

My eyes widened, eyebrows shooting high on my forehead.

He chuckled as he released it and eased back a step, his handsome face filled with genuine warmth and light that was at odds with everyone else I had met in this world.

"Are you always this charming?" I said, a ripple of shock rolling through me at my blunt question. Oberon was really going to end up thinking all wolves were rather forward.

His smile held. "Not often. But charming you comes so very easily. I find it is not a chore with you."

I frowned and pursed my lips as I puzzled over his words, and then smiled. "I'm going to take that as a compliment, I think."

He came to stand beside me, his hands tucked behind his back, stretching his black tunic tight across his chest, and sighed as he gazed out at the sea, his eyes fixed on a distant point. I twisted and looked there, enjoying the strangely comfortable silence that fell over us, wanting to see what he was looking at with such an odd expression. As if he longed for whatever he was looking for, but despised it at the same time.

"Where is home for you?" Those words rose unbidden to my lips, born of some part of me that knew the source of his look, because that same feeling existed in my heart too.

I loved my home, but hated it at times. The confinement. The inability to do the things I wanted to do.

To be who I wanted to be.

"King's Water. In the Stygian Isles. Far from here." He didn't take his eyes off the horizon as he pointed towards it.

No matter how hard I looked, I couldn't see the islands he spoke of, but I imagined he could, even if he was only seeing them in his mind.

"And how long has it been since you were last there?" I said brightly, a little teasingly.

He smiled and slid me a look. "Many lunar cycles. I am a wanderer, after all."

"Of course. A wanderer. The perfect excuse to roam far from home for long periods." My smile was wicked now and he returned it, that light in his eyes brightening. "I like that term. Wanderer. Maybe I'll call myself a wanderer one day. When I can leave here."

I scanned the horizon, a smile playing on my lips, warmth curling through me as I thought of all the adventures that awaited me out there.

"Wandering is dangerous. Holding allegiance to no court, even more so. Better you remain here, Saphira, where you are protected."

I levelled a black look on him. "You sound like my father. Always telling me to stay with the pack where it's safe. Well, look where that got me. Sold to a fae king."

It was his turn to frown at me, his eyes darkening like a violent storm and the thrum of his power growing stronger against my skin. "Sold to a fae king? To Kaeleron?"

His black eyebrows pitched low and the very air around him darkened. Not the air around him. I raised my eyes to the sky. Clouds were gathering, heavy grey and ominous, blotting out the beautiful aurora-kissed heavens.

Oberon growled, "I came here because I had business with Kaeleron, and saw you and grew curious as to what a wolf was doing in Lucia... and now I discover it is because Kaeleron owns you."

I nodded. "Isn't it like him? It certainly feels like it is. He's an overbearing asshole who issues me orders and makes me follow them or I will never earn my freedom from this place. I can't stand him."

My mood faltered again, all the light that had been building inside me while talking to Oberon flowing out of me. Kaeleron's rejection rang in my mind, together with how distant he had been. He hadn't really wanted to be there with me. He had only been helping me out of a sense of duty and responsibility, and maybe even guilt.

Oh gods, I had been a pity fuck of sorts.

Everything he had done, it had been done to ease his own mind.

And now it was all hitting me again in front of a man I barely knew and I couldn't hide the hurt, couldn't seem to school my features to pretend there wasn't a part of me that was breaking.

"No, he is not like that," Oberon murmured, some of the clouds breaking apart as he drew down a slow, deep breath, his shoulders heaving with the action, his gaze intense on me. Crimson ringed his pupils as he looked at me, his expression dark, and then he forced his gaze to above my head, towards the distant mountains, and snarled, "There will be a reckoning."

I didn't get a chance to ask what he meant by that.

One moment I could see him, and the next all I could see was darkness.

All I could feel was the cold press of shadows against my limbs.

"Now, now," Oberon said, his tone all amusement, "it would appear you have little right to be angry with me, old friend. I should be the one angry with you. What were you thinking?"

I pushed against the cage of shadows wrapped around me, battering them with my fists, my struggles useless as my hands passed straight through them but I couldn't escape them. I stumbled around in them, blind and beginning to panic.

And walked right into something very hard.

Very masculine.

That scent of wild storm hit me, rousing heat within me that quickly turned to horror as I backed away.

Kaeleron's hand wrapped around my wrist, his grip so hard it hurt as he spun me around so my back was to his chest. His hand wrapped around the front of my throat, keeping me in place against him, his hold sheer possession that roused something startling within me. The feel of his claws poised so close to my skin, and all his strength against my back, stirred wicked need in my veins that had me trembling and breathless even when I knew I shouldn't enjoy it.

I angled my head back, peering into the shadows, wanting to see his face.

The shadows dissipated as if I could command them, revealing him.

I stilled.

Oberon was wrong. Kaeleron wasn't angry.

He was livid.

Darkness branched from his bright silver eyes, a corona of crimson encircling his pupils as he stared down at me, his lips set in a thin line and jaw flexing.

"Return to your room," he growled and reluctantly loosened his grip.

"Is that a suggestion or an order?" I sniped back at him and wrenched free. I sashayed away from him, turning my chin up and squaring my shoulders. "Either way, the answer is no. I'm not done with my walk."

"You. Are. Done." He stepped towards me in time with each hard word he bit out, punctuating them. "I order you to return to your room."

"No." I walked a little faster, heart pounding as adrenaline rushed through me, and sense screamed at me not to antagonise him.

"What were you doing talking to Oberon?" he snarled, right on my heels.

I quickened my pace, storming through a flower-laced pergola, heading for the castle. "*Talking*. You might want to try it sometime rather than just ordering people around like they're your property."

"You *are* my property."

I stopped so quickly that he walked right into my back.

I whirled on him, the horror I felt on my face for him to see, unable to mask it as shock swept through me, surprise that he had just gone there. "I belong to no one."

"You belong to me," he growled and reached for my arm, but I shoved it behind my back, evading his touch. "You do not speak to Oberon. *Ever*."

Darkness flashed in his eyes and shadows writhed from his shoulders like onyx wings.

"You don't get to say who I can speak to." I held my ground, even as the part of me that wasn't all riled up and furious with him whispered that he did because he did in fact own me.

I was his property, whether I liked it or not.

And part of me had forgotten that.

I blamed the mating heat and his far-too-skilled tongue.

"You're in a shitty mood," I snapped at him. "I don't want to talk to you until you're in a better one. Barging into my conversation, ruining my walk, threatening your friends. What is wrong with you?"

"What is wrong with *you*?" he shot back. "I saw how you were looking at him, how wounded you looked. What did he say to you that has put you in such a terrible mood?"

Oh my gods. He had stepped in and protected me with his shadows because he had seen my horror over what had happened last night and had interpreted it as horror over something Oberon had said to me.

I looked up at him, seeing that wrath simmering in his eyes as he looked back in Oberon's direction, a dark and terrible hunger to harm a male who had been nothing but kind to me, and had even managed to lift my spirits for a moment.

I wasn't going to stand by and let Kaeleron blame Oberon for my bleak mood.

"*You*," I barked, gaining his attention and a confused look. I planted my hands on my hips and glared at him, heart labouring, mind spinning. Was I really going to do this? Yes. Yes, I was. "You're the reason I'm in a shitty mood. I get it. I know you didn't want to be there last night and just felt obligated to help, and I appreciate that, but you could have put on a better performance and not looked so disgusted—"

"Disgusted?" He cut me off, earning himself a growl.

I gave him another one when he crowded me, menacing and far-too-sexy as he backed me up against one of the ornately carved wooden posts of the pergola, leaving me with nowhere to go.

Making my wolf side want to wrap itself around him.

"I wanted to be there." His voice pitched low, a purr that held my attention and had my eyes falling to his lips and watching them as they moved in a tempting symphony. He planted one hand against the post above my head, and gently wrapped the other around my throat before sliding it over my skin to my neck and settling it on my nape. A shiver bolted down my spine, heat rising as his skin grazed my nape, drawing all my focus there, to that spot a male would mark during a mating. His hooded gaze lowered to my lips and they tingled, the traitorous things wanting to feel his lips on them. "I wanted to be there, Saphira. I enjoyed last night as much as you did. Maybe more so."

His smouldering gaze lifted to lock with mine, searing me, making it impossible to breathe.

"Watching you," he husked and I trembled as he palmed my nape, my legs weakening as I stared into his eyes, lost in them. "Feeling you come on my fingers... your tight little body quivering from my touch as you sobbed my name." He flashed sharp teeth, crimson flaring in his eyes. "I will never forget how good that felt."

I gripped the post behind me in an effort to remain upright as my world narrowed to only him, to the heat of his body so achingly close to mine, to the scent of him in my lungs and fogging my mind, and that searing, claiming look in his eyes that branded me with his name.

"But you wouldn't—" I blushed. Hard. Unable to bring myself to say it, too embarrassed to bring up the fact I had begged him to take me like that.

"Fuck you?" he husked, sexy and deep, apparently not at all ashamed to bring it up. He stepped closer, his body brushing mine, and angled his head as he held my gaze. "Do you know how hard it was not to fuck you like you were begging me to, little wolf? How much I wanted to sink my cock into you and satisfy both of us? I wanted it, but I could not. You needed relief—a gentle hand—and I most certainly would not have been gentle with you. You would not have allowed it."

He swept his hand around to the front of my neck and pushed my chin up with his thumb, keeping my eyes on his as I tried to look at anything but him, shame, embarrassment and need spiralling together within me to create a maelstrom of emotions I wasn't sure I could survive.

He lowered his mouth closer to mine, his breath bathing my lips as he murmured, "If I had fucked you, it would have been as hard as your heat demanded. I would not have been gentle. I would not have been able to. I was too worked up by you—the way you moved, your little body slicked with sweat, the scent of you maddening me—and this regret you feel would have been a thousand times worse. So I took care of you... and then I went somewhere private and I thought of you as I stroked myself off."

I shivered, wicked images flooding my mind, rousing heat in my veins and a need to tiptoe and press my mouth to his to goad him into touching me again.

"You are not ready for me," he whispered close to my lips, "for the things I want to do to you."

Another shiver wracked me, this one hot and needy. As hot and needy as that look in his eyes.

"When you are ready though," he lowered his hand from my throat and grazed the front of my hips, making me jump and tense as a flash of pleasure bolted through me from just that muted touch, and growled, "I am going to fill you up and fuck you so hard—so thoroughly—that you will only ever want me. Are you prepared for that?"

I trembled at the thought of him branding me like that, making me crave only him. My wolf side wanted it, had me on the verge of pressing closer to him as I angled my head back, aching more than ever for him to kiss me—something he hadn't done yet.

I wasn't prepared for any of it. He was right about that, but

I didn't want to admit it. What he was talking about was more than satisfying a mating heat or scratching an itch.

It was possession.

Pure possession.

Something flickered in his eyes.

Something that made him look vulnerable for a heartbeat before he covered it so masterfully, slipping his mask back into place. I knew that feeling he was hiding so well, hadn't wanted to admit it to myself either, and had been just as horrified when I had realised it existed within me. He felt he was on dangerous ground with me, and that flicker of vulnerability stemmed from the thought I might actually want him—that I desired him as he desired me—and he was unwilling to let himself believe that.

I had shut it down out of fear of rejection.

What had made him pull away?

I didn't get a chance to discover the answer to that question, because while I shut things down by withdrawing and pulling up my barriers, he did it in a way that punched my fear button hard enough to leave a bruise.

"What we did was only natural, and it was nothing to be ashamed of, little lamb. It meant nothing. I felt obligated to service your needs. Not that I did not enjoy it. Any time you need me to scratch your itches for you, you only have to ask."

I glared at him for saying that, turning what we had done into nothing and plunging that blade through my chest.

"You're such an asshole," I barked.

And turned on my heel and stormed away from him, anger shortening my breaths and lengthening my strides. I couldn't get away from him fast enough, but while I could escape his physical presence, I couldn't banish him from my mind. His taunts echoed in it, conjuring images of him taking me hard, over and over again, a different position each time.

I wasn't sure whether there was something wrong with me for still wanting the bastard, or with him for turning what we had shared into something cold and clinical in order to protect himself from whatever this thing was growing between us.

But I knew one thing.

The heat he had awakened inside of me wasn't done.

CHAPTER 24

SAPHIRA

Eight days had passed since I had called Kaeleron an asshole and I hadn't seen him once. I wandered the gardens, not really paying attention to the pretty blooms and dazzling birds today, my thoughts firmly stuck on the annoying fae king who was giving me the cold shoulder. It certainly felt as if he was anyway. That first night, I had been content to entertain myself, watching the lights in the town below and listening to the chatter of the people coming and going. Even late in the night, the streets had people moving around them, and when they had all eventually retired, I had too.

The next morning, I had eaten breakfast, bathed and decided to walk the garden, following my usual route. No sign of my guards. Either Kaeleron was beginning to trust me or he no longer cared whether I made a break for it. I had settled on it being the former when I had walked too close to the gates to the city and had been scowled at by guards who had crossed long spears over the exit. Hint taken. No leaving the castle grounds.

I had thought Kaeleron would summon me that evening,

brushing off our argument and taking his doll out to play. But he hadn't.

He hadn't summoned me the following night, or the one after that and the one after that, or last night either.

Every night I waited.

And every night I went ignored.

I chalked it up to calling him an asshole, the part of me that had cooled down quickest in the aftermath of our verbal boxing match latching onto it and how at Beltane he had threatened to get imaginative with his punishment if I went ahead and called him that name.

"Not very imaginative after all," I muttered, holding back a huff. "Cold shoulder is so old school."

I had thought myself a master of it but it turned out Kaeleron excelled at the cold shoulder treatment. I wasn't sure I could have done it better myself.

A familiar scent swirled around me, but it was only faintly laced with wild storm, mingled in with layers of vanilla and blooms whose names I was yet to discover.

Jenavyr.

I lifted my head in time to catch sight of her crossing the grounds at a pace, heading towards the gatehouse, and hurried to intercept her. She noticed me as I neared, her bright silver eyes swinging my way and the clouds in them lifting as she smiled.

"Saphira, it is good to see you. Have you been well?" Vyr stopped and turned towards me.

I lost my nerve as I neared her, asking if Kaeleron was around twisting into something else.

"His royal pain in my ass hasn't been making me do stupid tasks for the last few days, so I'm great." I forced a smile, hiding how much her brother had hurt me as it all rolled up on me and I realised that his silent treatment had worked, blending with what he had said to shatter my confidence. "I was wondering whether maybe we could walk around town again?"

Jenavyr's fine eyebrows pinched together. "I would not let him hear you speak of him like that."

"Too late for that." I shrugged.

She sighed and shook her head. "At least hold your tongue a little in the coming days. Kaeleron is due to return tonight, and I expect him to come up with some foolish demand for you, but he will be in a terrible mood. He always is when he comes back from Belkarthen."

"Belkarthen?"

Vyr pointed to the south, beyond the castle gates. "A port city near the southern border. We grew up there, and moved here shortly after Kael ascended the throne. It is the most beautiful city... but not to Kael. He avoids it now and only goes there when it is absolutely necessary, or completely unavoidable."

She stared off in its direction, her gaze warm and filled with unmistakable love for the city Kaeleron seemingly hated.

"The city council expects him to visit after each rite, to ensure everything ran smoothly and the rite succeeded. Kael has already been to the towns bordering Wraith Wood to check the Beltane celebrations were successful there too."

My cheeks heated at the mention of Beltane and I slammed my mental barriers shut on any memories of that night that involved Kaeleron. "About Beltane... Is that usually how you celebrate?"

Vyr laughed, but her voice was serious as she said, "I will be having words with my brother about taking you. I warned him against it. We probably looked like heathens to you, but it is tradition, and both unseelie and seelie require the rites in order to generate magic, and magic in our lands is fed by blood and sex. So there are sacrifices made, and pleasure had. I am sure it all sounds very primal to you."

It did, but it wasn't the primal side of it I was hung up on as I looked at Vyr.

Had Kaeleron missed out on topping up his magic because he hadn't slept with anyone?

Presuming he had been telling me the truth and hadn't returned to the celebration to join in with the festivities.

I schooled my features in an unreadable mask when Jenavyr studied me a little too closely, plastering on a pretty look of interest rather than revealing how mortified I still was about what had happened and how angry I was with Kaeleron for what he had said.

And how frustratingly hot her brother made me with just a look.

Or a few wicked words whispered against my lips.

"The feast was rather lavish, but where does all the leftover food go? It seems like such a waste when it was hardly touched." Terrible subject change. I grimaced at it.

Jenavyr looked at the gates behind me. "Nothing is wasted. The food is distributed to the less fortunate in the city."

That was good. I fidgeted with the ties of my corset, trying to think of something else to say and beginning to squirm under Vyr's scrutiny as she narrowed sharp silver eyes on me.

"You know," she said, slowly, thoughtfully, "my brother grew bored of the celebrations more than a decade ago and now he just attends them rather than participating."

I recalled how many females he had turned down at the rite. "I'm surprised to hear that. I was sure your brother would have liked having his ego petted so thoroughly."

She laughed, the sound bright and real. Not forced. At least one of them knew how to laugh. I shut out the sound of Kaeleron laughing at Beltane, banishing it from my mind and pretending it had never happened. There was no warmer side to Kaeleron. Nope.

"Perhaps." She gave one last chuckle. "But believe it or not, my brother spends all his time thinking about the business of running the kingdom and very little about his own wellbeing. He could probably use a little time spent seeking pleasure."

I toyed with my hair, trying to conceal my blush as his deep voice rolled through my mind, telling me how he had stroked himself off while thinking of me. Had he really done that or had he said it to get a rise out of me?

Jenavyr stepped closer and glanced around us before settling her gaze on me and whispering, "Do not think it went unnoticed that he left shortly after you did. Several guards saw him crossing the green to the castle. I hope he did not overstep, Saphira."

I shook my head, letting my own mask fall away so she would see that her brother hadn't done anything I hadn't wanted, because as angry as I was with him, I didn't want her thinking badly of him. He hadn't done anything against my will. In fact, he had waited for me to ask him. He could have taken me right then, taking advantage of my mating frenzy, but he hadn't.

And I was beginning to think he had told me the truth and he had held back for my sake, knowing I would regret what we had done in the cold light of morning, when the heat no longer gripped me. He had been chivalrous. Kind. And a bit of an asshole.

But many males would have taken everything I wanted to give during my frenzy, using my delirium to get what they wanted.

"I didn't see you there." Another poor attempt at changing the subject.

Vyr was kind enough to go along with it. "I was busy elsewhere. Not everyone gets to enjoy the celebrations. I had work to do."

"You weren't the only one absent. I didn't see Riordan either." I was pushing it. I knew it when she tensed, her shoulders going rigid, and the warmth left her eyes. I wasn't mentioning the vampire to upset her. I wanted her to know he hadn't been there, enjoying the rite, in case she had avoided it so she didn't have to see him with other females. "Kaeleron seemed surprised by his absence."

Vyr's shrug was stiff. "Oh, really? Well, I do not know what the vampire was doing. Perhaps he was celebrating elsewhere. He is not fae so he does not need to join in with the festivities in order to regenerate magic for the lands."

"I'm not fae either, but I was there. Other non-fae were there too, joining in." I mentally cursed when I blushed, wishing I could master them and stop them from happening whenever I thought about what I had seen that night or someone brought up sex. "Doesn't everything we do that night help with the magic?"

Had Kaeleron been better off finding a fae female to pleasure?

"It only takes one of the partners to be fae for it to work, and the stronger the connection between them, the deeper the lust runs, the more potent the magic they generate will be." Jenavyr sidled closer still and murmured, her eyes on mine, "Do not think people failed to notice their king did not return."

So he hadn't gone back then. I blushed harder. Godsdammit. Giving myself away judging by the little smile on Vyr's lips.

"Tell me you were in control at all times, that the magic in the air—"

"I was in control," I interjected, unable to bear the thought of her mentioning what I had done with her own brother. It was too embarrassing.

"Good. Then we shall leave it at that and a warning to not

provoke him when he returns. He was in a foul mood when he left." She waved as she walked away, heading for the gates, and I cringed as she added, "It might have had something to do with someone righteously calling him an asshole."

She smiled over her shoulder at me and disappeared from view.

I groaned.

How many people in the castle knew what I had said to him in the garden? Worse, how many people were aware that he had come after me that night, and hadn't returned to the rite?

What rumours were circulating about me?

About us?

I stiffened as the air around me chilled and a female voice growled behind me.

"Did you spread your legs for him, you filthy mutt?"

CHAPTER 25
SAPHIRA

I spun on my heel, whirling to face the female. Elanaluvyr. Behind the dark-haired beauty stood the rest of her clique, one looking at anything but me, and the other looking ready to pummel me into the dirt. I breathed hard, my eyes darting back to the fae who stood closest to me, a female who looked like she didn't just want to beat me into the ground.

She wanted to kill me.

Her pointed ears flared back as she bared her teeth at me on a snarl. "Answer me, mutt."

I had two choices. Lie through my teeth about what I had done with Kaeleron or prepare to fight. While this fae was stronger than me, she was slim and her hands didn't show any sign that she had done manual labour a day in her life. The fae didn't seem so different to my breed. They kept their females docile and genteel too. No fighting for them, unless their name was Jenavyr or Kali.

So I could maybe take Elanaluvyr in a fight, using what little training I had received before my parents had discovered what was happening and had disciplined both Chase and

Morden. Training I could barely remember, but hoped came back to me in the heat of the moment.

Elanaluvyr scoffed. "Even if the magic of Beltane made my king make a poor decision, he will make the right one when the time comes. He would never choose a mutt for his queen. When the time comes for him to wed, you will be displaced as his favourite and relegated to his whore where you belong."

My claws punched out of my fingertips, my wolf side growling and baring fangs at the female.

A female who wanted him.

Who had offered herself to him at Beltane and had almost tempted him when Vyr said he hadn't participated in the last decade.

"When I am warming his bed, satisfying his needs night after night, I will ensure you find yourself in the dungeon, and that any male who wishes to slake his lusts will find you there, collared and chained like the dog you are."

Broken images of cages, of chains and steel collars, of Lucas and that female, of Kaeleron and this one, stuttered across my eyes.

Elanaluvyr leaned towards me, just as she had leaned towards Kaeleron, her body bared to him, tempting him, and whispered, "You are nothing but a disposable whore to my king."

I saw red.

Before I knew what was happening, I had the female's throat in my hands and I was choking her as I snarled, as I bared my fangs for all to see.

"You're nothing but a spineless bitch," I snapped, shaking her hard with all my strength, anger at the helm, a fury born of the thought of this female with Kaeleron, with the power she might wield and how she would use it to have her revenge on me. It wasn't going to happen. I wouldn't let it.

"Desperate for a male who doesn't want you. Pathetic whore!"

Elanaluvyr loosed an unholy sound and launched at me, ripping my hands from her throat. Her fist slammed into my gut, lifting my feet off the ground. Pain spiralled along my limbs as my breath left me in a grunt.

"You are the whore." She fisted my hair and yanked my head back, and struck me hard across my face.

I staggered, stars winking across my vision as I tripped across the flagstones, fighting to remain on my feet as the world spun around me and I tasted blood. Not good. I had been wrong. This female did know how to fight.

Or she was being fuelled by pure, unadulterated rage like I was.

I twisted, keeping low as Chase had taught me, and unleashed a fast uppercut that caught her under her jaw, snapping her head back in a far too satisfying way. Before she could recover, I slammed my fist into her gut, my blow clumsy as adrenaline stole control of me, the high of the fight swiftly claiming command of all my faculties. I growled and struck again, swinging my left fist this time, a follow up blow Morden had drilled into me in the limited time he had been able to train me.

The fae easily blocked it as she recovered and hit me with a punch of her own, one that sent my head reeling again and fiery lightning spiderwebbing over my skull as I staggered away from her, seeking space to recover my wits before I attacked again.

She caught me by the front of my blouse and hauled me back to her, and held me aloft before her, my feet dangling and toes scuffing the ground as I wriggled in her grip. I flinched as she yelled at me, spittle splattering my face as hers reddened with each word she hurled.

"The whole castle is speaking of how you lured him away

from the rites, endangering our strength—the strength of this court—and making it vulnerable. Maybe it is better I eliminate the threat of you right now before you destroy this court!"

She hurled me.

Fucking hurled me through the air like I weighed nothing.

I cried out as I hit the wall of the castle, sure I heard the sickening crunch of bone near my shoulder as it took the brunt of the impact, and screamed as I dropped to the ground, whatever bone had broken jarring with the secondary impact and sending fire shooting down my arm and over my skull.

My breaths shortened, pain stealing the air from my lungs together with my courage as Elanaluvyr ignored her friends' pleas to stop and launched at me again.

Nailing my hip with a fierce kick that vibrated along my bones.

I curled inwards, protecting my vital organs and covering my head with my forearms, panic and fear melding to have fur rippling over my skin as my wolf side charged to the fore. I was stronger in that form, but changing would leave me vulnerable for several seconds in which this bitch could easily deal a killing blow. I couldn't risk it.

The way she kept up her barrage of kicks, hands against the wall above me for support now as she hemmed me in, said I wasn't getting out of this alive either way.

I gritted my teeth, struggling to bear the pain building inside me with each hard blow against my shins or forearms, and when she began stomping on me, slamming her heel down against my hips and sides, I made my decision.

Better to die as a wolf than endure this shit like a little lamb.

I growled low, urging the shift, forcing it as the pain clouded my mind, threatening to strip consciousness from me.

But the pain was too much.

Shifters couldn't hold their animal form when they were in pain.

A lesson my parents had taught me the moment I had been old enough to manage my first shift and one of the most important ever bestowed upon me.

I had made the ultimate mistake—I had left it too late to fight back.

"Die," Elanaluvyr growled.

"Fuck that," I muttered and when she went to kick me again, I moved with all the speed I had left in me, my shoulder screaming in agony, and went to grab her foot to shove her off balance.

Only that kick never came.

I reached out with my senses but felt nothing through the pain. It eclipsed everything. And the scent of blood—my blood—masked all the smells around me.

Dreadful silence surrounded me and I blinked open gritty, burning eyes, lowering my hands a fraction, enough to see past them but not enough that I couldn't bring them up to defend myself if this was a feint designed by Elanaluvyr to leave me vulnerable to a head attack.

Not only silence enshrouded me.

Shadows did too.

But it wasn't Kaeleron who snarled.

"What in the Great Mother's name are you doing?" Jenavyr. She sounded a lot like her brother when she was angry—commanding, intimidating, and just a little terrifying. "Have you lost your mind? Both of you?"

The shadows parted and Jenavyr's eyes widened as they landed on me. I grimaced as I tried to uncurl, my arm screaming and every place Elanaluvyr had landed a blow aching and burning.

Maybe I had lost my mind, because I had been fighting over

Kaeleron because I wanted him, and I wanted him to want me. To pick me.

"By the Great Mother." Jenavyr crouched beside me, worry flashing across her eyes and her face as she reached for me and I flinched, anticipating how much it was going to hurt when she touched me. Her hand halted a short distance from my skin, her power caressing it, so much like Kaeleron's when she was furious. "How badly are you injured?"

I shuffled up into a sitting position, trying not to give away that I felt as if I was falling apart, and failing when my shoulder burned and my hand flew to it, gripping it hard as pain throbbed down my arm and up my neck. Behind Jenavyr, Elanaluvyr smirked, sick pleasure glittering in her eyes.

All that adrenaline I had felt during the opening moments of the fight returned, narrowing my focus down to my opponent as I sought an opening, a way to take her down.

Jenavyr's face darkened, wrath incarnate as she turned hard silver eyes on Elanaluvyr. "Guards. Take her away."

Elanaluvyr's eyes widened and she shook her head, her panicked gaze darting over her hands as if she had just come to her senses and wasn't sure how my blood had gotten on them and her pretty silk slippers.

"No. Wait. I did not start this," the fae female shrieked as two male guards grabbed her and began hauling her away. Her voice rose towards hysteria. "She started it. She is a rabid beast that needs to be put down!"

Vyr swept to her feet, every bit the commander as her cold gaze speared Elanaluvyr, silencing her.

Or maybe it was what she said.

"The fate of both of you is King Kaeleron's to decide."

Elanaluvyr blanched, as if she knew what her fate would be.

Death.

Some primal part of me snarled at that, at the injustice of it. This fae's death was mine to deal. This fight was mine, not his. I tamped down that feral bloodthirsty part of me, trying to tame it, so startled by the force of the desire that I almost missed the look Vyr levelled on me.

I wasn't sure my fate would be much better judging by that look that warned she was going to tell Kaeleron what had happened, and he would know the fight had been over him, and where did that leave me? Far too vulnerable, that was for sure.

Vyr helped me onto my feet and I gritted my teeth as I hobbled towards my room. She growled and pulled me against her, and darkness swirled around us, and then we were before my door. I sagged against her, silently thanking her for helping me by teleporting me here as some of the adrenaline waned to leave me tired and aching, and a little envious of that particular skill. If I had been in possession of it, I could have teleported away from the fae bitch before she had been able to attempt to puncture every organ in my body with her foot.

Which revealed a glaring hole in my plot to win that fight. Any moment I had come close to dealing a fatal blow, the fae could have teleported out of my reach. Not only that, but she had magic at her disposal and I still wasn't sure what kind of things the unseelie highborn could do with that power. I needed to learn to pick my fights, and do my research before them if I stood any chance of winning and surviving life at this court. I had the feeling that now word was out about what had happened during the rite, that Elanaluvyr wouldn't be the only one coming for me.

I needed to practice fighting and learn more about this world and its people.

Starting tomorrow.

Tonight, I just wanted to sleep.

Or maybe pace a little to work off the adrenaline and post-battle energy and then sleep.

Jenavyr pushed my door open and helped me inside.

"I will send a medic up to you," she said and released me.

I grabbed hold of her arm to stop her. "Please don't tell Kaeleron."

She hesitated, her expression softening, and I thought I had won and would be spared the agony of him discovering why I had been caught up in a fight against one of his court, but then she glanced away and sighed. "I cannot do that. My loyalty is to my brother first and foremost. It is my duty to inform him of everything that happens within the court. Even this."

I wanted to argue with her, but what was the point? I understood where she was coming from and I didn't want her to endanger her position or even twist her loyalties a little for my sake. So I nodded, letting her know I understood, and watched as she exited my room and closed the door behind her.

All I could do now was hope she had been wrong and that business in Belkarthen would keep Kaeleron away for a few more days, long enough for me to heal.

Unsure how long it would take for the medics to arrive, I unlaced my corset, thankful for the extra protection it had given me. Flashes of the fight replayed across my mind and fur danced over my skin, my wolf side agitated by it all. My hands shook as I removed the corset, my claws still out as I twisted what had happened in the fight in my head, so it was Elanaluvyr on the ground, cowering and desperate to live. Pathetic. Weak.

I cast my corset away from me, growling as I began to pace, as adrenaline drowned out the fear and the pain, replacing it with rage and a fight instinct that had me wanting to find where the guards had taken the fae female and have my revenge. This fight wasn't over. I wasn't done.

I was going to do my research, and I was going to practice my limited fighting skills, and then I was going to have a rematch with the bitch.

My fingers flexed and curled, claws pressing into my palms as I paced, mind whirling with a need to lash out and make the female pay for what she had done. My shoulder ached, throbbing deep in my clavicle that I was sure was broken. I would break her bone in return. I touched my split lip. I would make her bleed.

The fae would likely utterly destroy me, but I didn't care. Here in this rage-fuelled high, I didn't care.

I wanted to destroy her too.

I stalked to the end of the room and back again, and caught my haggard reflection in the full length mirror near the blood-red dressing table. Split lip. Bruised cheek. A huge spreading blotch over my collarbone. And those were the wounds I could see. The ones I could feel were too numerous. Bruises mostly. I gingerly prodded my side and gasped as pain lanced it, fire licking through my blood.

The door blasted open.

Inky night exploded into the room.

CHAPTER 26
SAPHIRA

A shriek tore from my lips as I whirled in the thick, chilling shadows threaded with glittering flecks of silver and gold, my eyes flying wide as the darkness parted to reveal him.

Wrath incarnate.

Shadows streamed outwards behind Kaeleron, forming great wings that clung to the shoulders of his tunic, blending perfectly with the inky fabric. Silver eyes stained with crimson darted around the room, his eyebrows pitched low above them.

I stiffened as his searching gaze landed on me, fresh embarrassment rolling through me. I couldn't believe how violently I had reacted to the thought of Elanaluvyr in his bed—at his side. Where some reckless, foolish part of me wanted to be. But as his eyes narrowed on me, raking over my body, lingering on every exposed injury, my traitorous body warmed and my heart fluttered, a timid thing in my chest, beating unsteadily in his presence.

So irritatingly uncertain.

So filled with hope.

Because he was here, with me. Not in the dungeon. Not with the fae bitch.

He was here, and he was looking at me as if he had stolen that seed of rage that burned within me still, demanding I find her and end her, that she pay for what she had done to me and the things she had called me.

Kaeleron strode towards me, darkness pouring off him, streaming behind him to blot out the rest of my room, narrowing the world down to only us as he wrapped that glittering night around me in a soft, almost tender embrace.

Shielding me with it.

His gaze darted between my injuries again, leaping the most between my collarbone and my lip, and darkness branched from his eyes in jagged tendrils as they became more crimson than silver, his expression so fierce that I couldn't look away. The menace he radiated had my wolf side shrinking back in submission and a touch of fear as he closed the distance between us down to nothing, coming to tower before me.

Shock rolled through me as he tenderly brushed my hand away from my split lip and ran his thumb over it, inspecting the cut, his eyebrows knitting hard as he stared at it. Those shadows bracketing his eyes spread further, and his skin paled towards white, the transformation startling me.

His canines and the incisors closest to them were jagged fangs as he snarled.

"Who did this to you?"

His sister hadn't told him about what had happened. He didn't know. Had he come to my room for another reason only to scent my blood and find me looking like I had been run over by a truck?

Maybe he had wanted to see me as badly as I had wanted to see him.

"Answer me," he gruffly commanded, his voice a low growl

that rumbled like thunder, a rising storm that would wipe clean this world, all because someone had hurt me. "Who did this to you? I will see to it they are punished. I will see to it they can never lift a finger to harm you again."

"Why?" That question tumbled from my lips, my heart stuttering as I stared up at him, strangely unafraid of that wrath and dark hunger for violence that shone in his eyes.

He had never been so dark, so terrifying as his shadow wings shifted and tendrils of night snapped at items in my room, restless with a need to kill. But he didn't scare me, because I knew he wouldn't hurt me. This rage in him was born of the fact I had been hurt, and he hadn't been there to stop it.

And gods, it was delicious.

He paused, seemingly caught off guard by my question. "Why?"

"Why do you care?" I fought to keep my voice steady and confident, afraid he might see how much hinged on his answer, how desperate I was to hear him tell me that what we had shared had meant something to him. So much for no messy emotions. My stupid heart was getting caught up in him, wanting something from him I knew he couldn't give me and that it wasn't wise to want. But I couldn't stop myself from speaking and putting it out there. "Why would you punish this person? Why protect me?"

Kaeleron was all glorious darkness as he crowded me, as he backed me towards the wall. When my back met the cool stone, his hand fell to my neck and his thumb grazed my throat as his fingers claimed my nape.

He snarled, "Because you are mine, Saphira."

Shock swept through me again, and I had to fight against the urge to find the meaning I wanted to hear in those words. He owned me. He wasn't speaking of me as a possession in a way a man who desired a woman did—the way a mate would. He was speaking of me as a possession because he owned me.

He was only protecting his interests.

I knocked his hand away from my throat and turned from him, a heavy feeling pressing down on me, one that threatened to break me when Elanaluvyr hadn't been able to. Tears pricked my eyes and I hated them, hated this world, hated him, feeling like such a fool for thinking Kaeleron might want me the way I wanted him.

Neve had told him 'to tread this path, you must not tread it alone'. And Kaeleron hadn't been happy about that. He needed me for a purpose he hadn't revealed yet, one I was beginning to suspect had nothing to do with my body. My time would be better spent trying to learn from Neve why he had bought me rather than pining after a male who had stated in that dungeon that he was tired of me.

Elanaluvyr was right. Kaeleron was only interested in me because I was new and he owned me and had apparently decided that spending time in my company was fine as long as it ended with him getting what he wanted. I was entertaining. Summoned whenever he was bored. Sooner or later, I was going to end up as nothing more than someone he summoned to fuck when he was tired of his queen. Or whatever my purpose was would be revealed and I would no longer be 'necessary'.

Did he even intend to let me leave once I had paid off my debt?

I was starting to doubt that too.

Doubt was a bitch.

A real mood-killer.

I headed towards my bed.

Kaeleron caught my wrist and pulled me back to him, not letting me get far. I was too tired and sore, hurting both physically and emotionally to see him right now. I just wanted to curl up on my bed and drift in my pain, and maybe while I brooded, I would figure out why I was here.

"I'm not in the mood for your games today," I muttered and twisted free of his grip. "Find someone else to entertain you."

He scowled as I pivoted away from him, handsome face darkening again.

And swept me up into his arms, ripping a gasp from me.

"Put me down." I pushed at his broad shoulders. His firm shoulders. Gods. I shut down that flicker of heat that licked through my veins. I was not going there again. Desiring Kaeleron had been a mistake. Letting my heat get the better of me had been a mistake. I was going to master both and learn to resist them. "Put me down."

Kaeleron didn't pay me any heed.

Rather than stride towards the bed as I expected, he carried me like a princess towards the bathroom.

The door opened before he could reach it, and the lamps on the walls flickered to life as he entered, that familiar tang of magic lacing the air, and the sound of running water had me tearing my gaze from his face to settle it on the large copper clawfoot tub that stood in the centre of the room. The water steamed as it rapidly filled the bathtub, and that steam shimmered with something unnatural.

Or at least unnatural in my world.

The ease with which Kaeleron opened doors, lit lamps, and filled a bath all using magic was astounding.

I added a little envy of his ability to use magic to my ever-growing list of reasons I felt so inadequate in this world. I wasn't sure how Riordan coped with being surrounded by so many powerful beings, all with abilities beyond his reach. Although, he hadn't been lacking in confidence when I had met him. He was probably comfortable in his own skin, and with his abilities and power. Confident he could hold his own even against these unseelie. Unlike me.

Kaeleron set me down on the soft bathmat.

"What are you doing?" I glanced at the bath and then tensed and swatted his hands away when he tugged my blouse out of the waist of my pants. "What are you doing?!"

I caught his wrists when he reached for my blouse again, stopping him.

The harsh lines of his face softened just a touch as his silver gaze lifted to meet mine, enough to have me relenting. There was need in that look. Need I could define, even if I didn't understand why it was directed at me. My thoughts whirled as he gently stripped me and lifted me in his arms again, and slowly, almost reverently, lowered me into the warm water. The first touch of it was bliss, a heat and lightness that rolled through my body to loosen my tight muscles and soothe my bruises.

I let go of my fears, of all the doubts that clouded my mind, and sank into the water, letting it carry them all away.

I had wanted to fight tonight. To draw blood. Maybe even kill. I wanted to learn to fight better, so I could hold my own. I wanted to know more about this world that was beginning to feel like home. I hadn't thought about my pack in days. I hadn't thought about Lucas. I had lost myself in enjoying my time here, enjoying the company of a certain fae king.

I wasn't sure who I was anymore.

I wasn't sure who this Kaeleron was either as he picked up a sponge and began gently cleaning my skin, taking his time around any of my injuries, all soft and very careful with me.

But I wanted to know this me who felt true and real, as if I was emerging from some kind of cocoon, finally discovering myself.

And I wanted to know this Kaeleron.

This tender, attentive male.

He growled, "I will find out who did this and they will pay for it."

This tender, attentive and slightly homicidal male.

His gaze tracked his hand as he brushed the sponge over my skin, and I watched his face, watched the storm building in his eyes together with a war he waged between a dark hunger and a soft sort of worry, and his shadows as they grew sharp at times before softening to mist.

"Why were you fighting?" His gaze darted to meet mine, no silent command to answer him in it, just a softness that made my breath catch in my throat together with my hammering heart.

I clammed up, refusing to answer that question, because I wasn't ready to admit that I wanted him. Not to him, anyway. I was feeling bold enough to admit it to myself.

I wanted him. I had missed him.

I had always known I was fated to Lucas, so I had never even entertained the idea I could fall in love with someone else, that I didn't need to be fated to someone to be happy with them.

But here I was, in a freefall that was both terrifying and a little exhilarating.

I waited for him to push me to answer him, the demanding and bossy king, but he didn't, even though that storm in his eyes built faster, the darkness bleeding across his skin around his eyes again.

He dipped the sponge into the water and squeezed it out above my shoulder, sending water running down my chest, and then lowered his hand and gently brushed the sponge over my uninjured collarbone, drifting down towards a bruise on my chest.

My hand whipped out of the water, fingers clamping down

around his wrist, and I grimaced as I accidentally sprayed droplets over his fine black tunic and his neck.

"You don't have to bathe me." I held him firm when he tried to move and twist free of my grip. "I can take care of myself. I'll be healed in a few days, good as new. I'm fine, really."

I was babbling and far from fine, but being taken care of was new to me—I had always been the one taking care of others —and the fact it was Kaeleron tending to me so carefully, so dutifully, was tilting my world on its axis faster than ever. Half of me screamed at me to release him and just enjoy it, savour his attention and how good it felt to have someone take care of me for a change, and the rest wanted to run for the hills before I slipped from falling to fallen in the space of a night.

When Kaeleron had turned down my request that he take me, that had been humiliating and painful enough. I wasn't sure I would survive the blow to my heart if I let myself fall for him and he rejected me. I couldn't do this.

I pulled up my walls, building them brick by brick, coating them with steel, trying to defend my heart against him.

Kaeleron tore down that wall with nothing more than a soft, aching look and a handful of words.

"Let me do this," he snapped, shadows writhing viciously, striking at the stone walls—at anything but me—but that soft, almost wounded look in his eyes remained. "You could have been killed, Saphira."

And it had shaken him.

It had shaken him so much that he now needed to take care of me. No. This was more than taking care of me. This wasn't about cleaning my wounds. This was about confirming I was whole and alive, and would recover.

"Please, let me do this," he whispered, the flash of vulnerability in his eyes as he gazed at me stealing my breath.

And a piece of my heart.

I released him, that piece of my heart close to breaking for him as he carefully tended to me, as he swirled his fingers through the bathwater to heat it again for me and do something to it that sank warmth into my skin, making my body feel lighter again, chasing away the pain. Magic. He was expending magic for my sake. To heal me.

To keep me whole.

Alive.

What terrible thing had happened in his past to trigger this response in him, this near-desperate need to ensure I would recover and reassure himself that I was alive, safe, and protected now that he was back with me?

I wanted to know, but I didn't have the heart to ask, to dredge up whatever pain he was reliving as he took care of me.

I melted under his careful attention, under each soft caress of his hands across my skin and the way his gaze lingered on my bruises. His left hand came to rest on my clavicle, and my skin and bones heated, but I felt no pain as he applied pressure, setting the fractured bone back in place. My skin tingled, that light feeling gathering beneath his palm, and sweat dotted his brow, his gaze growing intense on my shoulder.

"I cannot fully heal broken bones, but I can help them mend." He glanced at me, gaze meeting mine for a heartbeat, revealing his regret and maybe a touch of frustration.

I placed my hand over his, holding it to my shoulder, and felt it tense beneath my touch, as if he hadn't expected me to hold it. Or maybe he had felt that electric thrill that chased up my arm upon contact too.

"Thank you," I whispered, letting him hear in my voice how much I meant that and how grateful I was, and part of me needed to alleviate his worry, so I added, "Wolves heal quickly. I'll be fine in a few days."

He swallowed and glanced at his hand, and nodded.

I released his hand and rather than withdrawing it, he lifted it to my face, cupping my cheek and turning my head towards him. His gaze lowered to my mouth, growing hooded, and his thumb played maddeningly across my bottom lip, the touch so light it almost tickled.

I couldn't tell what he was thinking when he looked at me like that, with such ferocity and intensity, as if I was the only other person in this world, making it impossible to breathe.

But I wanted to know.

Even when I was a little afraid of what the answer might be.

CHAPTER 27
KAELERON

My fingers still tingled from the soft feel of Saphira's skin beneath them, my darkness tempered by the softness of her eyes as she had gazed at me, but as the distance between myself and the slumbering wolf grew, her hold over me faded.

Shadows swept behind me like a midnight cloak, tendrils writhing across the flagstones as I crossed the courtyard to the entrance to the dungeon. Rich aurora chased across the sky above me, stars blanketing the inky canvas beyond the shimmering veil, and the night whispered to me.

Beckoned me.

Stilted, broken images of Saphira's injuries flashed across my vision, gaining pace as I neared the stone arch in the side wall of the castle. Her clavicle, bruised and broken. Her lip, split open. Her delicate cheekbone, bearing a black mark that wrenched at my soul.

No more than scratches in the grand scheme of things, injuries that could have been so much worse, but each wound cleaved at my control like a sword, cutting slices of it away.

Claw-tipped fingers curled into fists at my side, trembling as I thought of how afraid she had been, that acrid tang of fear I had scented upon entering the castle grounds still singeing my lungs. Together with blood. Her blood.

I had lost all reason the moment I had scented it.

Had been outside her room in a flash, breaking the door down, my shadows pouring into the air around me.

And there she had been.

Wounded.

Bleeding.

Broken.

Shadows ripped at the flagstones around me, shattering some and hurling others clear across the courtyard. They threatened to tear the stones from the arch as I passed under it and I barely leashed them, pulling them hard back under my control. They seethed with me as I stalked down the slick stone steps to the dungeon, as I scented my prey ahead of me.

Her fear. Her blood.

I would savour both.

The dark-haired fae female flashed fearful eyes at me as I strode into view, shuffling backwards in her cell, until her back hit the far wall and she could go no further.

"My king," she whispered, gaze imploring me, even when she knew I had no mercy to give her.

She had tried to take something from me.

All who dared such a thing faced the same punishment.

Death.

"Kaeleron," Neve warned, the dragon female evidently aware of where this was going. She approached the bars, no love in her eyes as she glanced at the cowering fae female. "At least do it outside. Blood is so very hard to remove from these old stones and I prefer not to have to endure the irritating sound of hours of scrubbing from your servants."

The hope that had been building in the fae female's eyes turned to horror or perhaps betrayal. Had she honestly believed Neve would care about her fate? My seer could be as ruthless as any of us when she felt her precious treasure trove was threatened, and the kind of death I wanted to give this fae would end with her entire hoard splattered with blood.

I wrenched the barred door of the cell before me open with magic, the sound of iron striking iron singing around me, together with the startled gasp of my prey.

The fae female huddled and shook her head, pulling her filthy fine dress towards her as she gripped her knees. "Please, my king. It was a moment of madness. It will not happen again."

"It will not," I agreed, darkness pouring through my veins as I considered what her moment of madness might had stolen from me.

How I had failed to protect the little wolf.

I sneered down at the female and snared her with my shadows, hauling her towards me, the inky vines burrowing deep into her flesh and tearing a pained scream from her.

I would protect Saphira now.

I would ensure no one dared harm her and would remove this danger from her path.

My fangs lengthened, the world sharpening around me as I sank into the darkness, as I gathered it to me and wrapped myself in it. Images of Saphira continued to flutter across my mind, fuelling the rage that consumed me, swept me up in it and shattered my control.

She had been wounded. Had bled.

She might have died.

The images of her distorted as my breaths shortened, as my past surged up on me, twisting her face into that of another, older female who bore the same dark hair and silver eyes as my own. Her terrified screams rang in my ears and my chest heaved with each laboured breath I pulled down into my lungs as my throat closed and I wanted to throw my hands over my ears to shut out the sound.

Wanted to tear my gaze from that sliver of her as she fought her attackers, desperate to live even as her life leached from her in thick almost black rivulets that spilled down her nightdress.

Rage and darkness purred within me as that memory twisted again, the female taking the form of the one I dragged from the cell with my shadows, hauling her up the stone steps as she wailed and begged for mercy.

No mercy.

Whatever shred of that quality I had possessed had been killed in that moment all those centuries ago.

When night air kissed my skin again, I hurled the female forwards, sending her tumbling across the courtyard, and fought the hold the darkness had on me, the part of me that wanted answers refusing to let it kill the female before I had them.

"Why did you attack my little wolf?" I snarled and advanced on her.

She scrambled onto her knees and shuffled away from me. "She started it."

I scoffed at that. I knew Saphira well enough now to know that she wasn't the sort to attack unprovoked. Only when she had been pushed to her limit had she turned on me rather than seeking to excuse herself and leave my presence, choosing the more noble and peaceful way out.

"I ask again. Why did you attack my little wolf?" I stalked towards her, shadows snapping at the flagstones near her, keeping her hemmed in as the spell I had woven kept her magic from her, ensuring she couldn't escape me.

She tossed fearful glances at each sharp black blade that

slashed at the ground, her arms coming up to shield her chest as she curled inwards, trying to make herself a smaller target.

As if that would help her.

I had impeccable aim.

She swallowed and turned those deliciously fearful eyes on me, and then showed her fangs. "Little wolf? She is a mutt. A filthy fleabag who taints this noble court with her presence."

One of my shadows lashed at her leg, drawing blood and a satisfying shriek of pain.

"You dare call her a mutt?" I stalked closer, canting my head as I studied her, cataloguing all the places I would slice her open before I was through. For every bruise she had inflicted on Saphira, I would inflict a cut upon her.

She would bleed for what she had done, and then she would beg, and then I would kill her.

"She is a mutt," she snapped as she uncurled, planting her hands on her knees and facing me now, her courage rising as fire filled her eyes. "She is undeserving of a place in your bed, let alone one at your side. You are no better than your father, choosing a common whore as—"

Shadows slammed into her, a thousand sharp needles that shot straight through her, punching from the flagstones behind her and straight out of her front as they lifted her from the ground, crucifying her.

She screamed, the sound garbled as blood filled her lungs, as it drenched her dress.

My chest heaved, rage so hot it threatened to burn away my sanity blazing in my veins as her words rang in my ears. My vision swam, the world wobbling and distorting around me, my head spinning as I replayed that blood-soaked night all those years ago, and then my memories unravelled, rolling backwards through my youth, through tender smiles and loving looks.

The images of my parents became clouded with blood.

With screams. With a sickening replay of their final moments in this world.

And then Saphira.

Afraid.

Bleeding.

Broken.

The fae female's screams rose in volume, pain-drenched as I tore into her with my shadows, as I hurled her to the ground with them and pinned her to the flagstones. An unholy snarl ripped from my lips as I launched at her, darkness descending upon the world, blotting out the night.

I ripped through flesh and bone with my claws, drenching my black-tipped fingers with her blood, the scent of it and her delicious cries fuelling me.

The ground beneath us quaked, the walls of the castle shaking as I unleashed my wrath upon her. The flagstones vibrated, several exploding into dust under the pressure as cracks branched out from beneath my boots, snaking across the courtyard and leaking shadows. The forest groaned, the sound of splintering wood echoing through the night as the stars winked out and the moon hid.

But still I was not satisfied.

Something dark and brutal within me howled for more, howled at me to protect Saphira, to remove all threats to her from this world.

The very air trembled around me, vibrating with the malice filling my heart, demanding satisfaction.

I would hunt all threats in this world down, and then I would travel to her world and end all threats to her there too. I would ensure no one dared harm her again.

The scent of Saphira filled my lungs, my mind, my raging heart. Green pastures. Sunshine. Endless blue skies. Everything I had loved once, long ago.

The world stilled.

I stilled.

And then there was silence.

And only the sound of my rough breaths as I loomed over the dead fae female, panting as my muscles burned from the exertion and the blood on my hands grew cold.

Someone whistled low.

I turned on the intruder on a savage snarl.

Riordan.

The blond vampire stood a short distance away, at the edge of the carnage, still dressed in his uniform, as if he had heard the commotion and come running from his office in the barracks.

And he wasn't alone.

Oberon stood beside him, wearing only hastily fastened black pants that had the button undone, his bare feet close to the ring of blood splatters that surrounded me and the dead female.

His silver gaze was grave as he stared at the corpse at my feet and then at me, silently demanding an explanation.

I had none to give as I struggled to claw back control and calm myself, my breathing rough and uneven, my fingertips stained black beneath the blood on them and my teeth as sharp as daggers.

"You were right to summon me," Oberon said quietly as he glanced at Riordan. "I suggest you leave now."

The vampire nodded and made a fast exit.

"What is this all about, Kael?" Oberon eyed the broken body again. "The wolf? Is she something to you?"

When his searching gaze landed on me, I snarled, "She is my revenge."

My old friend didn't look convinced by that declaration.

"What happened to warrant such a merciless response from you?"

That moment I had burst into her room and had seen her bleeding, her fear swirling around me, and that pain and rage glazing her eyes, rolled over me like a surging wave, but when it swept back again, it was another female before me, bleeding and afraid, fighting for her life. An older female who haunted my sleep. Lost many centuries ago.

"She attacked Saphira," I growled.

Darkness closed in, the air vibrating with *my* pain and rage as my shadows grew restless, snaking towards the dead female at my feet as if she was responsible for the death of that older female, when she wasn't even the same species as the ones who had taken my mother, father and brother from me.

Those shadows rose, stealing the light from the world as grief rolled up on me, threatening to break me all over again.

Oberon casually swept his hand through my shadows, gathering them all from the air, and stared at them as they writhed and tightened, clamping down on his pale flesh.

"The wolf female is not them," he murmured thoughtfully, softly, as if he feared pushing me too hard and knew I was liable to break, and then the Great Mother help this world. "She lives still. You need to remember that. You need to breathe... Perhaps some tea might do you good?"

I shot him a dark look. "*Tea.* You always talk of tea at times like this."

Oberon shrugged. "Tea seems to be the one weapon I have in my arsenal when you are in a black mood."

I stared at the shadows he had tamed so easily with a simple wave of his hand as they snaked around his arm in a loving caress, as if he commanded them now rather than me. There was something about Oberon, something I had felt for a long time now. Something he was hiding.

Just as I had a nagging feeling in my gut that Saphira was hiding something.

I had always been attuned to others in a way that allowed me to see more than they showed to others, but I had never been blessed with the gift to penetrate the hazy veil and discover the truth beyond as my mother could. Perhaps if she had lived longer, I might have learned to control the power in the way she had been able. Instinct served me well though, and I listened to it. Trusted it.

Oberon was hiding something. So was Saphira.

And in time, I would discover their secrets.

The shadows dissipated as my shoulders loosened and I half grimaced and shook my head as I looked at the broken body resting at my feet. "I do not think tea will fix this."

Oberon looked at her too, uncaring of the blood that stained his bare feet, and then at me. "Perhaps I shall offer tea to Saphira instead, to calm her after her ordeal."

The thought of Oberon anywhere near her had my rage rising again, my shadows returning as they found a new target. Oberon was a threat to be eliminated. He charmed others too easily, knew how to smile at the right time or just the right thing to say. He was a danger. There were other ways to take Saphira from me, ones not involving death.

Ones Oberon excelled at.

I pinned him with a black look, my body coiled tightly, the urge to strike him down running strong in my veins, but I somehow managed to hold my shadows back, to deny the need to end him and the potential threat to Saphira.

Oberon sighed at my lack of a reaction and drawled, "Disappointing."

He wanted me to react. He wanted me to reveal that I desired the wolf, that part of me needed her, and that part of me grew ruthless and dark whenever I thought about her.

He wanted me to confess I would destroy this world in order to keep her safe.

I hadn't survived centuries on the throne of the Shadow Court by revealing my weaknesses, and Saphira was just that.

A weakness.

Not only within me, but within my court.

Where this female had sought to eradicate her and failed, others might follow her example and succeed if I wasn't careful, if I didn't put an end to it now before it began and maintained order within my court.

"What will you do with this?" Oberon jerked his chin towards the dead female.

I smiled darkly.

"Send a warning."

CHAPTER 28

SAPHIRA

Heavy black clouds swirled across the sky outside my window as I sat on the padded seat in the tower area of my room, rain pelting the glass as I hugged one of the pillows to my chest and watched the sea, losing myself in how dark and lethal it looked today, as if it was responding to my mood, or perhaps that of the owner of this castle.

The ruler of this unseelie court.

I compared the sea today to how it had appeared yesterday, fascinated by how dramatically it could change. One day, it was smooth and blue, barely a ripple on the surface, and the next it was rough and steel grey, battering the rocky shore with great waves that hurled white foam into the air.

Rain travelled like mist across the land, slowly devouring the mountains and hills that struggled to free themselves of its hold, peeking through at times.

Everything seemed darker today, a little more grim. Almost sombre.

I shook my head at that, aware it was just my mood

colouring my perception of the world around me, and glanced at the door.

"I should leave my room," I murmured as I set aside the pillow, as if saying it aloud would give me the courage to step over the threshold when I feared what I would find out there.

Feared how people might react to my presence now.

My wolf side pushed for freedom, all of me wanting to run free, run until I was exhausted and could sleep without replaying that fight in my dreams.

A fight that always ended in my death.

No matter how fiercely I fought, how cunning I was, the unseelie female always bested me.

I wrapped my arms around myself, trying to keep the sudden chill at bay, and huddled down into the comforting thick robe I wore over my clothes, lifting one side of it so I could bury my nose in the soft, warm fabric.

The rain that battered the leaded window grew heavier as my mood darkened.

In an attempt to distract myself from what awaited me beyond my door, and how weak I felt, I stared towards the mountains that embraced the castle like great jagged black wings. What kind of creatures lived in those mountains? Or the forests I had glimpsed from my balcony? What would I find if I bravely ventured beyond the protective walls of this castle city?

Death probably.

This wouldn't do.

Hiding in my room wasn't going to solve anything.

Kaeleron had mentioned a library once and I wanted to see it. I wanted to see if I could read the records it contained, and if I couldn't, I would ask him to cast a spell on me that would allow me to read them. I would learn about this world and its dangers, and grow stronger.

And one day, I would be strong enough to face Elanaluvyr and win.

I stood and crossed the room, casting off my robe and tossing it onto the bed. I smoothed my appearance, running my hands over my dark blue blouse and black leather pants. I could do this. I would find Kaeleron and ask him to give me directions to his library. Or better yet, I would find Jenavyr and ask her, avoiding the awkwardness of seeing the fae king after he had tended to me. I still wasn't sure what to make of that, but the part of me that had been softened by his careful attention had yet to harden again, leaving me rather defenceless where he was concerned.

Better to not face him just yet.

Where would Jenavyr be?

I had spied guards coming and going from a squat, fortified building in the grounds of the castle, and had spotted Riordan among a group of soldiers gathered outside it once. Maybe it acted as a garrison of sorts, where the soldiers assigned to protecting the castle had their living quarters. I could start there.

I eased the door of my room open, half expecting to find guards stationed outside it. There was no one in the elegant hallway, but voices drifted along it, distant and muted. Several of them. I headed in the opposite direction, closing my door behind me and hurrying left then banking right, my pace quickening as I strode towards the end of the corridor, where it met the gallery.

I had discovered the gallery a few days ago during one of my adventures, avoiding Kaeleron although I hadn't been aware he was away from the castle at the time. The paintings hanging on the wall to my right, facing a bank of arched windows that overlooked a broad green and the building I suspected was the garrison, were beautifully done. Each portrait was a blend of darkness and light, a masterful rendering of the figure it contained.

Jenavyr appeared very noble in hers, her head held high as she stood with a regal sword point down before her and a pale gold crown atop her black hair.

Kaeleron was far too handsome in his, and I avoided looking at it, partly because I found myself stood before it staring at it for long minutes, losing track of time whenever I looked at it, and partly because he had been painted seated on a spiked black throne before a night time lake.

The same lake he had swum naked in with me.

The next painting was the most intriguing.

A beautiful couple stood in the arched entrance of a half-timber building, eyes filled with love as they stood arm in arm, pressed close together, and gazed at each other. They radiated warmth and light. Love in its deepest, truest form, captured for everyone to see. I envied them. Even my parents had never looked as happy as this couple did, and all without either of them smiling. I didn't know who they were, but their black hair and the female's silver eyes made me suspect they had been Kaeleron and Jenavyr's parents.

But the portrait that always stole my breath, that roused a deep feeling of sorrow in my heart, was the one at the end of the gallery.

It was smaller than the others.

Set away from them.

As if someone had wanted to hide it, or had been reluctant to put it on display.

It was a study of three children, each with black hair and silver eyes. A young girl who appeared barely six in human years, her silver-blue dress pooled around her legs as she sat on the ground before a seated rangy teenage boy with unkempt hair, dressed in a fine tunic. My gaze shifted to the boy who stood to his right, head held high, shoulders squared. A boy who looked no older than ten.

A boy who was smiling with all his heart.

Kaeleron.

I knew it in my soul.

He stood so proudly, reflecting the man he had become, but there was such warmth and light in his eyes, a softness to him I couldn't see in the male he was now. What had happened to this smiling boy?

Did it have something to do with the reason he had needed to take care of me last night, had felt compelled to reassure himself that I was alive by being the one to tend to my wounds?

I glanced back at the portrait I felt sure were his parents, and then the boy seated between Jenavyr and Kaeleron.

Did it have something to do with them?

The seated boy was older than Kaeleron. The clear heir to the throne of the Shadow Court. But he wasn't the one on the throne now. Meaning he was dead. I wanted to know what had happened to them, but I didn't want to pry or reopen old wounds. Maybe in the library, I would find the answer to those questions too.

I dragged myself away from the portrait of happy siblings, trying to find one of them and hoping it would be Jenavyr.

But when I stepped through the door at the end of the gallery, one that led onto a broad balcony that overlooked a courtyard of sorts, I found the owners of the voices I had heard. I glanced back at the door behind me, debating slipping back through it before I was noticed, but their low murmurs drew my focus back to them. They were all looking at something below them.

I edged forwards, using all the stealth I could muster, sneaking to the edge of the stone balustrade to peer into the courtyard, curious about what they were looking at.

And froze.

Shock iced my limbs and stilled my heart as I stared unblinking into the crowded courtyard.

At Elanaluvyr where she hung from her wrists on a curved crossbeam of a black Y-shaped pillar that mimicked her pose.

Brutally clawed and bloodied.

Dead.

Sickness rolled through me as I reeled backwards, tensing as my back met the stone wall, and I struggled to breathe as a maelstrom of emotions rioted within me. I wanted to feel bad, I wanted to feel responsible, and I knew I should be horrified.

But as I stared at her broken body, a strange, dark sense of satisfaction rippled through me.

And then there was the feeling that shocked me most of all.

Rage.

Anger that I had been denied a chance to defeat the female myself in a rematch.

That someone else had taken that moment—my revenge—from me.

On a vicious growl, I pushed away from the wall, pivoting towards the cluster of fae gathered at the far end of the balcony who were all watching me now. I bared my fangs at them as I prowled towards them, on the hunt for the king.

Aware he was the one who had stolen my kill from me.

My wolf side snarled and snapped fangs at that, battering the cage of my human form, wild with a need to put him in his place, to punish him for daring to steal what had been my kill to make. The strength of my rage was overwhelming, startling even as it swept me up in it, as it stole control of me and had me stalking past the gawping fae, heading for the staircase in the vestibule.

I lifted my head and scented the air, trying to catch a trace of Kaeleron's in it.

The smell of wild storm hit me hard.

The fae on the balcony were quick to disappear, leaving us alone as their king emerged from the doorway ahead of me.

"How dare you!" I snarled, curling my hands into tight fists at my side as my fury reached boiling point, my wolf blood running hot. "I wanted a rematch!"

"So bloodthirsty today, little lamb." Kaeleron arched an eyebrow at me as he teased me, evidently unbothered by the threatening growl that tore from me as I stormed towards him.

I mentally rolled the sleeves of my blouse up, preparing to clobber him for mocking me with that nickname of his. I was not a lamb. I was a wolf, and I would show him just how sharp my fangs were.

"You will have plenty of opportunities to get your fangs bloody in my court. I am sure of that." He remained where he was, shoulders relaxed, utterly calm in the face of my fury. "This will not be the last challenge you will face—or the biggest."

A veiled warning to watch my back.

That knocked a little of the wind out of my sails and I slowed my steps, the ominous feeling that accompanied his words making me reconsider striking him and potentially making an enemy of him too.

I glanced at the dead female, hung on grim display for all to see.

"You didn't have to kill her," I muttered, unsure whether I would have shown her any mercy had I been able to fight her again. Even now, I wanted blood. Her blood. I wanted to taste it on my fangs.

Kaeleron stepped closer, halting mere inches from me, his power pressing down on me, dark and malevolent as he growled, "I did. Her death is a message."

That disturbing ripple of satisfaction swept through me

again, but I held my ground, refusing to let him see that some part of me was pleased he had killed her. I jerked my head towards the mutilated body. "It was a little extreme."

He crowded me, glowering and dark as he looked down at me, silver eyes ringed with crimson, and murmured, "Extreme would be using her entrails as bunting. I was restrained."

If that was restrained, I didn't want to see what he was capable of when he let loose. Gods, it wasn't healthy for me to find what he had done alluring, or condone it, but he had never been so hot as he towered over me, all darkness and death embodied, and growled.

His words pure possession.

"Her death is a message. No one touches what is mine."

CHAPTER 29

SAPHIRA

A cryptic message accompanied my breakfast the next morning.

Wear your most comfortable clothes and meet me at the glade near my brother's elkyn.

I folded the note and set it down beside the plate on the table before me, tucking it slightly beneath so it didn't blow away in the warm salty breeze as it swirled around me. As I considered what might be waiting for me in that glade and what Jenavyr might have planned for me, I picked at the mound of bacon, sausages and eggs, and nibbled on buttered toast. I doubted I was about to receive a riding lesson, but I couldn't come up with another answer.

My shoulder ached as I reached for my tea, a subtle reminder that I wasn't completely healed yet.

But I was healing faster than expected.

Because of Kaeleron's magic?

My bruises were already gone. My lip healed. The only injury that remained was my shoulder, and even then it was only tender. I pressed my fingers against my clavicle, probing the bone, marvelling at the lack of pain and how quickly it had mended. Who needed the medics when you had a powerful fae king at your disposal? I doubted the healers could have fixed me as quickly as he had, not if what he had said about the hierarchy of power in Lucia was true.

I pushed the almost empty plate away from me and stood.

As I turned from the table, movement below snared my attention. I canted my head as I watched Oberon and Kaeleron crossing the garden, heading for the main gate, deep in conversation. Thick as thieves. There was a strong friendship there, one that made me pine for Everlee. Maybe when I next crossed paths with Kaeleron, I would ask him about my pack and whether he had heard from them.

My gaze lifted to the town and the rolling landscape beyond the walls of Falkyr.

"Everlee would lose her mind if she saw this place. A castle. Princesses. Kings. Magic and mayhem." I sighed. It was right up her street, the sort of thing she would die to see as a deep lover of all things fairy tale.

I strode into my room and glanced at the wardrobe, and shrugged. I didn't have anything more comfortable than what I was already wearing—leather pants and a blouse. It wasn't as if I had a nice, loose pair of sweats or some yoga pants at my disposal. Hopefully, my current attire would be suitable for whatever Jenavyr had planned for me.

I plaited my silver-white hair into a long braid as I strode through the castle, heading for the main vestibule and descending the elegant staircase, and let it fall against my back as I crossed the garden, keeping my gaze away from the grisly display of power still hanging in the courtyard.

My wolf side snarled and bared fangs in that direction anyway, glad the bitch was dead even if I hadn't been the one to make the kill.

Maybe Kaeleron had spared me by taking it out of my hands.

I wasn't sure I wanted to discover how far I was willing to go to avenge myself. I wasn't ready to face the harsh truth of it, not yet. I didn't want to admit that buried within me, deep beneath the layers of love and affection, of care and kindness, lurked a monster as wrathful and dark as any unseelie.

One that craved violence and bloodshed.

My boots chewed up the path, my strides longer now as I picked up the pace, as if I could escape that part of me and leave it in the courtyard with Elanaluvyr's body.

It didn't take me long to reach the paddock where the majestic elkyn grazed. He lifted his head as I approached and snorted as he dipped it again, as if in greeting. I nodded back at him and hurried onwards, heading for the glade.

As I neared it, it dawned on me that it was the same glade where the Beltane feast had been held, a broad scorch mark on the grass where the bonfire had been and that dreadful stone altar still standing off to the left side of it.

Jenavyr was sitting on it, her sword belt resting beside her and the sleeves of her navy blouse rolled up as she nimbly wove several blades of grass into a thin rope threaded with small flowers. Her silver gaze lifted as I approached, her hands stopping their work and lowering to her lap. She set the grass braid down beside her sword and hopped off the altar.

"Good, you are here."

"And why am I here?" I looked around the glade, but Jenavyr and that altar were the only things in it. I had no clue about why she had summoned me to this place.

Her fine eyebrows knitted, a puzzled look in her eyes. "To train, of course."

"Train?" I spluttered, sure I had misheard her. "As in... learn to fight?"

"Why else would I ask you to meet me here, where we could be alone?" Her frown deepened and then relaxed and her eyebrows rose, a hint of a smile curling her lips as she said, "Or did you think I brought you here to gossip about my brother?"

"Ew, no. I don't want to talk about him." Lies. Terrible lies. I desperately wanted to talk about him, starting with asking where he had been going with Oberon, both of them looking as if they were up to no good.

Oh gods, were they going to that tavern near the docks?

My face must have given me away, because Vyr sighed and said, "I presume you saw him on his way to the blacksmith? Oberon has been bothering him about a new blade for years and he finally relented."

"No, not at all. Well... yes... I saw them... but I don't care what they're doing." I had to get better at lying.

Mostly because Vyr's smile had turned wicked and knowing, as if she could see right through me.

"It is no business what feelings you have for my brother—"

"None. Zero. You said something about training?" Even I flinched at the desperate subject change that screamed I was trying to cover up something.

But Vyr was graceful enough to play along with it.

"Very well. No one will see us here, so we are free to train as much as we like." She gestured to the centre of the glade and I walked there, nerves rising as I realised this was meant to be a secret. It was Chase and Morden all over again, and I feared if her brother discovered what she was doing that he would stop her before I could learn to fight and protect myself, just as they had when my parents had found out about it. "Let us start with taking the measure of your current skill. How much training have you had?"

"Not much." I flexed my fingers as she gave me a look that

said she was well aware of that and I hated how weak I felt as I remembered the way she had found me, curled into a ball, only able to defend myself. "You missed the bit where I got in a few hits."

"I saw enough to know you would have been killed had I not been there to intervene, and this court would probably be a far different place." The wistful look in her eyes as she scanned the glade and the mountains that loomed over it had me looking there too and remembering something from last night, something that had happened after Kaeleron had dried me off, tucked me into bed and ordered me to rest like an overbearing mother.

Or a very sweet male.

I remembered the castle shaking, as if an earthquake had hit it, but I had been too tired to open my eyes let alone move. The air had felt thick and heavy, the tang of magic stronger than ever, and there had been pain.

Not within me.

Within the very fabric of this world.

"King's possess much power. They draw deeply from the lands of Lucia, their connection to it giving them the power to shape it, and that magic can both create and destroy. Everyone felt it last night, Saphira. How close he was to losing control. No part of these lands remained unaffected." She looked off towards the castle, her gaze bleak but soft, laced with worry. "My brother has fought hard to be strong enough to protect this court, and while his methods of keeping those within it safe are not of my choosing, it has been a peaceful place for centuries now. The land has been calm. But when you were hurt, when he failed to protect you... I have not felt him that angry in a long time."

How close had Kaeleron been to losing control? What would have happened if he had lost it? I shuddered, not wanting to know the answer to that question, because the grim look on Vyr's face said it would have been catastrophic.

The power he possessed.

Power far beyond my reach.

If I were in his position, I wasn't sure I would be strong enough to contain it as he did. What had he gone through to make himself strong enough physically and mentally to endure the weight of all that magic running in his veins? Enough that it had cost him that beautiful, bright smile he wore in that portrait of him and his siblings.

"His need to protect," I started and faltered, my courage failing me as Jenavyr looked at me, pain surfacing in her eyes. So much pain. I couldn't bring myself to ask and hurt her more by dredging up bad memories.

She swallowed and turned her cheek to me, and sighed as she gazed at the castle. "It was born the night we lost our parents and brother in an attack on the castle in Belkarthen."

Now his hatred of that city made sense, and so did the way he had reacted to me being hurt, his need to tend to me. I had triggered terrible memories for him, had shattered the floodgates on the pain that still clearly lived within his heart, and in turn, his pain had reopened Vyr's wounds too.

"Teach me to fight," I said as I tipped my chin up and squared my shoulders. "Please. Teach me to fight. I want to be stronger. I want to be able to protect myself. I don't want that to happen again."

Vyr nodded several times, her expression thoughtful but a little lost, as if the memories still had her in their grip, haunting her even as she moved to face me. "You said you had some training."

"Only a little." My heart hurt as I remembered Chase and Morden arguing over my lessons and where they should start. They never had been able to agree on what was necessary for me to know and what wasn't. "Chase and a friend tried to train me once. We only managed a few basic attacking and blocking techniques before we were discovered and my parents spoke to them. They fell in with pack tradition. At our fourth meeting in the woods, they told me I didn't need to know how to fight because they were there to protect me, as were the other males in the pack."

If they hadn't been discovered, or if I had been treated like the males of the pack and given the same rights as they had, I might have known how to defend myself when Lucas had set upon me and I might have escaped before he could put me in that cage.

Or it might have done nothing to help me.

Lucas was an alpha, a strong one. All the training in the world probably wouldn't have helped me.

I clenched my fists and refused to think like that, because one day, at the end of this training, I would be strong enough to face him and he would pay for what he had done to me.

"Your world sounds far too much like mine," Vyr grumbled and then tipped her shoulders back, her expression going steely as she looked down at me. "Few females here can fight. It falls to the males of this world. It is time we changed that."

"Hell yeah." I could get onboard with that. Females everywhere needed to know how to defend and protect themselves. They needed to realise they were strong, just as I was realising how strong I was. How brave I could be. "Did you learn to fight when you joined the guards?"

"No. It was before then. My brother trained me in secret." She smiled slightly, that wistful look returning as she gazed beyond me, towards the castle. Those looked like fond memories to me, but there was an edge of sadness to them. "When he was old enough, Kael put me through my paces for lunar cycle after lunar cycle... until I was finally too exhausted for our secret morning weapon training sessions. He let me have a break… by swapping to training with my magic."

Her brother had taken great care of her, ensuring she could defend herself and even hold her own against the males of this world, and her earlier words made me think it had something to do with how they had lost their parents and brother. Kaeleron had wanted to know she could protect herself if he wasn't there to do it for her.

He had needed to know she could survive in this ruthless, brutal world of unseelie.

"Let us put you through your paces." Vyr motioned for me to move back. "Begin by showing me what you learned at your pack."

I went through the moves, trying to remember every punch and kick Chase and Morden had taught me, but not doing them justice judging by how disappointed Jenavyr looked.

"My form sucks. It's been a while and I'm a little rusty." I didn't want her thinking that my friends had done a bad job of training me. They had done their best and it wasn't really their fault I had forgotten it in the years since they had taught me the basic moves. I could have continued practicing in secret alone out in the woods instead of running in my wolf form, but I hadn't. When my parents had shut them down, I had shut down my own practice too. I had given up on learning to fight.

"Your form does indeed *suck*," Jenavyr said and I had to smile at how she used my vernacular, her tone so regal that it almost made me laugh.

She came to stand beside me, a few feet of grass between us, facing the same direction as I was.

"Copy my moves." She assumed a fighting stance, her feet braced slightly apart for balance.

I did the same and followed every move she made at a deliberately slow pace, her technique different to the teaching method Chase and Morden had employed with me. Her fists gently cut through the air, allowing me to see every shift of her body and mimic it.

My shoulder twinged but I ignored it, continuing to repeat the swings and uppercuts, and short punches she showed me, working through them one by one even as she came to stand before me to simply watch my technique.

And continuously correct me.

"Tuck your hips." She shifted them for me, her hands firm, and then nudged my elbow. "Keep this in. You are swinging too wide and losing power."

I lost track of time as she drilled me, over and over again, but I was sweaty and aching by the time she rubbed her chin and nodded thoughtfully.

"I think that is enough for today. You have done well. A far better student than others in my legion." She patted my shoulder and I grimaced, causing her to snatch her hand back. "Does it still hurt?"

I shook my head but she saw right through that lie too, so I gripped my shoulder and rolled it slightly, easing the tight muscles. "A little. The bone is mending surprisingly quickly."

"Kaeleron healed you." The surprise that coloured her silver irises said she hadn't been aware of what her brother had done that night.

"I think so. He did something to the bathwater." My cheeks scalded as her eyebrows shot up and I waved my hands in front of me, horrified I had just announced her brother had been there, bathing me, seeing me naked. "It was all very innocent."

"I bet it was," she muttered.

"He seemed... not himself."

Those words stole the thunder that had been building in her eyes, replacing it with concern, and she sighed as she glanced off at the castle again. I thought she might say something about him, about why he had been so different that night, revealing the answers I wanted, but she went to her sword instead, gathering it up and fastening it around her waist.

"We shall meet here at the same time tomorrow and I will run you through footwork, and then we will spar, and I will not go easy on you. Do not be late."

"I won't be."

I kept my promise.

And Vyr kept hers, leaving me aching and bruised in places.

But feeling stronger.

One step closer to my ultimate goal.

To make Lucas pay.

CHAPTER 30

KAELERON

The knock on my door was far too gentle and patient to be anyone but my sister. She eased it open before I could bid her to enter, striding into my office with purpose, pulling a pair of supple black leather gloves off and tucking them into her sword belt.

A belt that held two swords.

"You are training her with weapons?" I growled those words, the thought of Saphira handling a sword stirring something dark and dangerous in my blood.

My sister's look was unapologetic, and a little irritated.

It had been close to two weeks since she had started training Saphira, and her regular reports were the only contact I'd had with the little wolf in that time. I wanted to growl at the stacks of papers on my desk—a blend of reports and requests—and the endless meetings that kept me from her, together with the training that left her so tired that by the time I was done for the day and ready to dine, she was sound asleep.

A crueller male might have woken her and demanded she join him for dinner.

It had crossed my mind.

But I knew from first-hand experience how taxing on the body and mind training could be, so instead of demanding her presence, I dined alone with thoughts of her, mulling over everything I had learned and seeking her purpose. I had taken to visiting Neve too, passing time with her discussing Saphira and hoping it might trigger another vision in the dragon.

So far, I had failed in that department.

Saphira's role in my vengeance remained a mystery.

"She is doing well, brother. An exceptional learner and a very quick study. I thought it provident to teach her how to use weapons too, given she might often be within reach of a blade in this castle, even if she must disarm someone to get her hands on it." Vyr settled her left hand on the hilt of her own sword, one that looked far too long for the petite wolf to wield.

I would need to see about getting Saphira a short sword.

Or perhaps a dagger, given Vyr's last report about her impressive speed and agility.

Plus, a dagger could be easily concealed about her person and even if it were seen, few in my court would find the sight of it on her threatening. They would believe she was playing at being a warrior, foolishly believing such a small weapon could protect her from them.

A dagger it was.

"Of course, it might have something to do with her past training."

I raised my eyebrows at her. "Past training?"

This was my first-time hearing about it.

"I have been trying to learn more about it. So far, all I have learned is that Chase trained her when she was at her pack, before her parents discovered them and put an end to it. So like our world. Females left defenceless," she grumbled, her words and mood darkening as she spoke.

Before she could go off on her usual tirade, I held my hand up, halting her and regaining her attention, my own mood darkening as I got hung up on the name she had uttered.

"Who is Chase?" Shadows stirred at my feet on the black marble floor, restless as I considered the likely gender of the person Vyr had mentioned, given her complaint about wolf packs refusing to teach females to fight. The only conclusion I could draw was that Chase was a male. A male had taught Saphira to fight, or had at the very least tried. "Someone close to her?"

Images of this faceless male training her flashed across my mind, his hands on her curves as he guided her movements.

The growl had pealed from my lips before I could stop it.

Vyr's smile was all mischief and delight. "This subject seems strangely important to you."

I shut her down with nothing more than a glare. "Discover who Chase is."

"Intelligence is not my forte, brother. You have a spymaster for that." She arched a brow at me when I snarled again, not the least bit satisfied with that answer.

"This is an order, Vyr. I want to know who Chase is and I expect the information by the end of your next session."

She had the audacity to roll her eyes at me, a trait she had surely picked up from the little wolf. "You could ask her yourself."

I brushed that suggestion off with a wave of my hand, because I was not sure what I might do if this male turned out to mean something to her. There were ways to be intimate without claiming the flower of a female. I had no way of telling whether Saphira had been touched by another in the way I had touched her, and she had responded so sweetly to my caress, a wild little thing as she had sought her pleasure. What if this male had been the one to teach her how to writhe like that, how to move her body in that bewitching way?

Darkness blanketed the room, my claws emerging to dig into the arms of my chair as I growled through my fangs.

Saphira was mine.

Jenavyr cleared her throat from somewhere within my shadows. "There is one thing I wanted to mention."

I pulled back on the shadows, drawing them to me, clawing back control as the reckless part of me that wanted to claim Saphira as my own demanded I hear what my sister had to say, in case it was vital to securing Saphira as more than my possession.

I shut that unruly side of me down as I stared at my sister, waiting to hear what she had to say, because this information might be vital for another reason—it might reveal Saphira's purpose to me. I had gone through half the books in the library, had pored over ancient tomes, and had visited Neve hoping she would have had another vision, all to no avail. If the dragon did not experience a vision soon, I would force one out of her.

The longer Saphira was in my court, the more dangerous her presence became.

To me.

I would not lose sight of my vengeance now.

Blinded by a female.

"Saphira is strong." Jenavyr pursed her lips, her gaze thoughtful as she considered something.

"Wolf females can be strong, and I was told she is born of alpha blood." Although I had my doubts that the wretched thug who had sold her had been telling the truth about that.

My sister still looked confused, her brow crinkled as she continued to stare at me.

"What is it?" I studied her, almost able to see the cogs

turning in her mind as she worked through whatever was bothering her.

But then she shrugged. "I know wolves can be strong, but I think this is different. I do not know how... her strength and speed just feels... unnatural."

"You have never trained a wolf before. It is likely that you are expecting her to feel like a fae, to respond like one, and that is the reason you are confused." But as I looked at her, I had the feeling it was more than that.

My sister was clever, astute, and often noticed small things about people. Years of being allowed to do nothing more than watch others as a child had taught her to look hard at them to divulge their secrets to entertain herself.

What secret was Saphira hiding?

CHAPTER 31
SAPHIRA

My legs ached as I sank into the black velvet upholstered wooden armchair, the latest round of training Jenavyr had put me through wreaking havoc on my tired body. Vyr was nothing if not persistent, and had apparently adopted her brother's methods of training—no breaks until I broke.

But I was getting stronger every day, learning new ways to attack and defend, and Vyr had even complimented me this morning after our session.

And then she had announced Kaeleron had requested my presence this evening in the drawing room.

I was starting to suspect the compliment had been her way of softening me up before she had issued that order to me, and before I had discovered the low-cut silver-grey blouse that had been left on my bed with a corset and a pair of dark brown pants. I had planned to spend most of the evening in my bath, lazing in the warm and soothing water, letting it erase my aches and pains so I would be ready to get up tomorrow morning and go through the paces of training again.

It was swordplay day tomorrow.

Vyr never went easy on me when we trained with weapons.

But there was a part of me that was glad he had finally summoned me, that had been missing our time together while we had been apart because of his work and the demands of running a court. I just hoped he didn't ask why I had been so tired lately, retiring to bed early each night, and just assumed it was because I was still healing. If he grew suspicious, I would have to lie in order to protect Jenavyr and my training. If he discovered the truth of what was happening, he was bound to take my training away from me and punish his sister.

My traitorous gaze drifted to Kaeleron where he sat in a large black wingback armchair in front of a roaring fire in the onyx-walled drawing room, the warm light flickering across his handsome face, adding to his brooding air.

Although, I was starting to wonder why he had summoned me.

He had barely looked at me, even though I had worn the clothes he had selected for me, ones that revealed a hint of cleavage, and hadn't uttered a single syllable in the last twenty minutes. I felt invisible as I sat in the matching armchair opposite him, an empty expanse of crimson rug the only thing separating us, and I didn't like it. But if he was content to brood and glower at the fire, it was fine with me. We weren't the only two people in the room after all.

Vyr flowed with grace around the large room, dressed in soft black cotton pants that hugged her long legs and a loose black blouse, her onyx hair braided down both sides of her head behind her ears, the plaits thicker than the ones Kaeleron wore in his own hair. Hers formed a soft net made of four long braids that weighed down the rest of her hair.

The room Kaeleron had chosen for this evening was a study in gothic, with its black walls and blood-red furniture that matched the furniture in my own room. The cherry-coloured wood shimmered in the firelight, an almost metallic quality to the grain. It framed the armchairs and the matching couch to my right that faced the fireplace, and made the side cupboards and tables stand out against the stone walls.

"We used to have all this furniture in what is now your room, but it seemed so crowded in that smaller space," Jenavyr said as she ran a hand over the side table where servants had set out silver trays of glasses and a crystal decanter of amber liquid that Kaeleron was slowly working his way through in moody silence. "Now half of it is here, in our private drawing room."

"Do you not bring guests here?" I looked at the room, at the beautiful vases that stood on the side tables and on plinths in the corners of the room, and the elegant chandelier that hung in the centre of the ceiling, formed of globes of golden light that danced and moved around the gilt arms that resembled branches of an upside down tree.

That ceiling had been painted as beautifully as the one in the dining room, the artist having perfectly captured the stunning aurora-kissed starlit sky of this court, and was framed with gilded cornicing too.

"No," Kaeleron muttered.

Jenavyr rolled her eyes at him. "The furniture was our mother's. A wedding present from our father. Although I am not sure why blood-coloured furniture could be considered romantic. It was expensive though. The finest craftsmen in the court worked on the pieces."

"I've never seen wood like it." I stood and went to the side table, running my fingers over the smooth surface and watching the grain shift colours as the fire flickered.

"It comes from the Forest of Blood," Kaeleron stated, all matter of fact.

I pulled a face as I withdrew my hand. "It does look a bit

like blood. But a forest of blood? Like… is that rivers running red through the trees or corpses spread around feeding them?"

The thought this beautiful wood might be created by trees sucking up the blood of the dead turned my stomach and made it a bit less fascinating.

But only a bit.

Vyr chuckled. "No. Nothing like that."

Kaeleron swirled the amber liquid in his glass, his eyes on it. "It is a beautiful place. The leaves are deep scarlet and the bark of the trees is almost black, and the ground beneath their roots is as blood-red as the canopy above. It is a strange, ethereal sort of place, and befitting of the Twilight Court whose castle is nestled in the beating heart of that wood."

"I don't want to think about why something called the Forest of Blood suits the Twilight Court." I curled my lip. "It makes them sound barbaric, as if that red carpet beneath the trees is in fact made of the blood of those they have slaughtered."

"Who says it is not?" Kaeleron arched an eyebrow at me.

I shuddered.

Vyr sighed, came to me and placed her hand on my arm. "Ignore him. He is in an overdramatic mood because court did not go well."

Kaeleron huffed and knocked his drink back, and then glared at the glass as if he could shatter it with his mind. Which he probably could. I still didn't know the full extent of his powers or how strong they were. I had only been given hints about them, and that he could level this kingdom if he wanted to.

His gaze slid to me, catching me staring at him, and his fine black eyebrows rose as he tilted his empty glass towards me. "I could take you there one day."

"No thank you," I blurted, despite how tempting that offer and the thought of seeing more of Lucia was.

He kept holding the glass out towards me.

I huffed as I took the hint and grabbed the decanter from the silver tray on the side table and pulled the stopper out. The pungent heat and sharpness of the alcohol hit my nostrils, singeing them, and I wrinkled my nose.

"It smells like paint stripper," I muttered.

His eyebrows rose higher on his forehead. "Paint stripper?"

"Something the king doesn't know about. Colour me amused." I grinned at him as I crossed the room to him, weathering his scowl that made him look far too handsome and alluring. I had missed our moments like these, this back and forth we often shared that seemed to lighten something inside me and made me forget my aches and pains. "If you can't figure it out for yourself, I'm not going to baby you by telling you the answer."

His expression hardened further.

I tilted the decanter towards his glass.

In a lightning-fast move, he snared my wrist and twisted me, pulling me down onto his thighs and spilling the alcohol all over my low-cut blouse.

"Godsdammit," I growled and shoved his arm back, only spilling more of the pungent liquor on myself when he resisted. "Let me up."

His grip was iron and his husky chuckle wickedly warming as he held me firm.

His silver gaze fell to my chest, the intensity of it sending heat spiralling through me, ripping awareness of the world from me as I stilled, breathing hard as I waited to see what he would do. The metal coverings on the tips of his pointed ears and the rings he wore in his piercings glinted in the firelight as he slowly leaned towards me, the braids he wore tucked behind his ears falling forwards as he angled his head.

A shiver wracked me as his breath skated across my throat, waves of tingles chasing over my skin as my nipples beaded against the corset I wore beneath my blouse. Awareness of how close his lips were to my skin ratcheted up my temperature, shortening my breaths as anticipation swirled through me, the wicked part of me he had unleashed urging him to do it.

Touch me.

Caress me.

I burned with the heat of a thousand suns as I waited, desperate to feel his lips, his tongue, on my flesh again.

And fought it.

Fought that fire that blazed in my veins as his tongue laved a path across my damp chest, chasing the drops of amber liquid trembling on my skin.

I squeezed my eyes shut, desperately trying not to be affected by him, trying not to melt into him and give away how good it felt as he slowly stroked his tongue across my overheating flesh, his breath teasing me as he inched downwards.

Towards my breasts.

Heat pooled between my thighs despite my fight and I squeezed my legs together, clamping down on a shiver as his free hand grazed my waist.

Drifted lower to my thigh.

As if he could sense the heat and need building there.

Jenavyr cleared her throat.

Kaeleron growled against my skin at the interruption, snarling softly against the mounds of my cleavage, the rumble of it vibrating through my body.

I stiffened as awareness of the world slammed back into me, panic lancing me, and clumsily shoved against him, pushing him back and tumbling from his grip to land on all fours on the rug at his feet.

I unleashed a growl of my own as I came to my feet and snapped fangs at him, barely resisting the urge to shift into my wolf form—my stronger form.

He merely lifted a single eyebrow at my threatening behaviour, a challenge in his eyes that dared me to deny I had liked what he had been doing and that I had wanted him to go further.

My heart thundered as I held his wicked gaze that felt as if it was stripping me bare, exposing the truth of me.

I wanted him.

I still wanted him.

Right here. Right now. Regardless of our audience.

But I wasn't going to give in to that want.

"I think I will retire for the night, and I suggest you do the same, Saphira. My brother is clearly drunk." Vyr held her hand out to me.

I looked at it and then at Kaeleron, heart pounding, limbs trembling. I should take her hand and the out she was offering, I knew that. It was dangerous to remain here with Kaeleron when he had fired me up, had me wanting things I shouldn't, but I didn't want to leave. Not yet.

"I'll head up soon," I said and didn't miss the concern in her eyes as she looked from me to her brother. "I just need to ask him a few things and then I'll head to bed. Alone."

Not that I expected Kaeleron to join me. Or wanted it.

I just didn't want Vyr thinking that her brother was the sort of male who might force me to do something I didn't want. He wasn't like that. For all his darkness, I had never once felt as if I was in any danger with him. He teased and tempted, but never did anything I didn't want.

Vyr nodded and shot her brother a warning look before she exited the room, leaving us alone.

I picked up the decanter that had fallen on the floor, rescuing it before all of the vile contents stained the rug, and when Kaeleron offered his still-empty glass, I shot him down with a glare.

"I'm cutting you off." I took the decanter to the side table instead, stoppering it and leaving it there as I returned to him. "I wanted to ask you something."

"How did I get to be so very handsome? Genetics, I am afraid," he drawled with a wicked smile.

I rolled my eyes. "Not that. Something else."

"But you admit I am handsome." He was fishing, and there was an edge to his eyes that left me feeling he needed to know what I thought of him, as if it was important to him.

"You're stupidly beautiful. Now let me ask my questions."

He regally waved his hand, earning another eye roll from me.

"Did you contact my pack?" I hadn't realised how much hinged on the answer to that question, or how desperate I was to know it, until I uttered it aloud.

"I sent word to them that you are safe, together with a warning to keep their distance from the male wolf and his companions."

My shoulders sagged as all the tension knotting them loosened and a sigh escaped me, but then I considered what he had said, and grimaced. "I should have mentioned the one who sold me was the alpha of the neighbouring pack."

"I described the insidious prick rather well." Kaeleron eyed what little liquid had made it into his glass and downed it in one.

"Insidious prick certainly suits him," I muttered and then hesitated.

He looked up at me, a frown marring his brow. "Another question?"

"At Beltane..." I swallowed and forced myself to continue when my nerve wavered. "When that bitch approached you and you let her guide your hand towards her thighs... did you want to sleep with her?"

His right eyebrow arched and then lowered into a smouldering, mischievous sort of look that heated my blood as he purred, "No. I wanted to provoke you, little wolf. I wanted to see if you would bare your fangs and drive away any female I showed interest in."

My jaw clenched as it hit me and I had to hold myself back so I didn't box his ears.

He had wanted to make me jealous so I would reveal I wanted him, and I had done just that, stepping in to steal back his attention, exposing the truth of me to him—I desired him. I wanted him. And I wanted him to be all mine.

"Prick," I muttered and he smirked at me. "For that, you owe me. I want access to your library. I want to learn more about this world and the courts, and the powers you all have."

"Why?" He canted his head, his gaze piercing.

"Because I just do. I figure I need to know what I'm up against if I'm to remain here, and then that thing Neve said has been bothering me. That I'm necessary to you and something about treading a path and not being able to do it alone. She had a vision and I was in it, didn't she?" I had been so focused on surviving in the Shadow Court and nursing my own wounds that I had forgotten all about that moment in the cells until a few days ago, and since then I had been trying to figure out a way to bring it up when I next saw Kaeleron.

He nodded. "It is vital that you are here, but we do not yet know the reason why. I am working to uncover it."

"You didn't buy me for my virginity." My heart thundered as I put that out there.

He smirked.

Bastard.

"I'm going to bed." I pivoted on my heel, but shadows snaked around me, holding me in place as they twisted me back around to face him. I fought them, but my hands passed straight through them, the black threads of them dissipating like smoke only to reform the second my hand had passed them.

"Not yet," Kaeleron growled.

I huffed. "I cut you off, remember? No more liquor. Why did you summon me here this evening anyway? You've been moody all night, perfecting the silent brooding type, barely even looking at me. Was it just that you've forgotten how to pour your own drinks?"

His expression turned deadly serious as he pulled me towards him with his shadows, so serious my nerves returned, rising swiftly as he stared at me.

"Kneel," he commanded.

I swallowed as I obeyed, easing to my knees before him on the crimson rug as he sat up, no trace of warmth in his features now, and trembled as he placed his hand on the left side of my chest, the weight and warmth of his palm rekindling my arousal.

Was he checking my collarbone was healed?

How sweet of him.

I relaxed a little, my nerves washing away as he stared at his hand, at my chest, his look so fierce and intense.

And then screamed as pain flared where his palm touched me.

I instinctively jerked backwards, trying to escape his touch as the scent of burning flesh singed my nostrils, but he seized my other arm in a bruising grip, his expression grim and dark as he held me in place.

My lungs tightened, head swimming as the pain grew stronger, as the fire licked hotter across my skin, chasing in circles beneath his palm, and the edges of my vision grew dark as unconsciousness loomed.

And then he released me.

My teeth ached from clamping them against the pain as I fought to breathe through them, my vision spinning, twisting the world around me.

"That is why I summoned you," Kaeleron growled.

I looked down, blinking back tears, and frowned at the trail of golden embers that chased over my skin, finishing forming a black circular mark on my flesh. A stag that had a crown suspended between its antlers and five stars above it, surrounded by a ring of symbols.

Confused and struggling against the pain that continued to thrum in that spot, I lifted my unsteady hand towards it.

Kaeleron captured my trembling hand and tensed, something like regret flashing across his eyes before they hardened again. "It was necessary."

"Necessary?" I wrenched free of his grip and staggered to my feet, my mind clearing in an instant as the reality of what he had just done hit me. "What was necessary? Marking me like livestock?"

Rage like I had never felt it blasted through me, incinerating any trace of the desire I had felt when he had held me on his lap. I snarled at him, flashing fangs, hating him for what he had done.

He had marked me.

BRANDED ME.

Like I was a fucking cow.

Or a slave.

Declaring me his property.

"You will be safe now." He sounded too calm, too unaffected by the anger I levelled on him as I stared him down, as my chest heaved and lungs burned, as I fought to hold back the shift and the urge to sink my fangs into him. He picked up his glass and held it out to me. "Now, I command you to pour me a drink."

I stormed to the decanter, hurled the stopper from it, and marched it back to him.

And poured the contents all over his head.

"I'm tired," I snapped, unsure whether I meant I physically needed sleep or was tired of his games and him being an overbearing asshole. Probably both.

I didn't stick around as he lifted his hand and wiped the amber liquid from his eyes.

I stalked right out of the door and slammed it behind me.

And broke into a run that had me back in my room and slamming that door behind me in under a minute.

I pressed my back to the finely decorated wood, breathing hard and trembling, silently cursing his name as heat scorched my veins and his scent filled my lungs, and the memory of the soft rasp of his tongue against my skin maddened me.

I shut it all down.

To hell with him.

I touched the mark he had placed on me, a beautiful brand but a brand all the same, and tears filled my eyes, hurt welling up as everything I had begun to believe about him crumbled before my eyes, revealing what a fool I had been.

I was property to him, a tool he apparently needed for some reason, and a fool he enjoyed amusing himself with.

Nothing more.

I had been blind, but now I could see the truth of it all in this mark, this one act.

And I was done with his shit.

CHAPTER 32
SAPHIRA

I stomped to the training ground the next morning, the heavy clouds that blotted out the twilight-kissed sky echoing my mood as I plotted all the ways I would use my training to punish Kaeleron once I was strong enough and skilled enough.

The clock was ticking for the fae king.

The brand the bastard had placed on my chest flared with a tendril of heat that chased around the ring, keeping me constantly aware of it. It had been doing it all morning, had ruined my breakfast and my old favourite hobby of watching the people coming and going from the castle, had ruined my nice warm bath, and was threatening to ruin my new favourite hobby of getting strong enough to kick his ass.

Jenavyr glanced up from setting her sword belt down on the stone altar, took one look at my face and was crossing the glade to meet me. "What is wrong?"

Furious, and more than a little hurt, I yanked my navy blouse to one side, revealing the mark near my left shoulder.

Jenavyr's beautiful face grew darker than the thunderclouds gathering above us, ribbons of shadows rising from her shoulders as she stared at the mark, a myriad of emotions crossing her eyes. Mostly anger, but there was a touch of relief too, relief I couldn't understand.

She lightly brushed her fingers over the brand. "It was wrong of him to do this."

"He said it was to keep me safe." I looked at the mark, hating how beautiful it was, hating him, and tears pricked my eyes. I sniffed them back, because I was not going to get all weepy over this. I was going to get even. "I want to fight with swords today. You said we would train with swords."

"I did, but that was before I saw this and your mood." She shifted her hand to my shoulder. "Do not despise him for it. Do not punish him."

I knocked her hand away with the back of my forearm and took a step backwards, away from her, as I scowled at her. "He fucking branded me, Vyr! Like property. Like a fucking animal."

"No!" Vyr seized my arms in a tight grip, her gaze wild as she shook her head. Her hard tone softened as she added, "No, it is not like that. This mark is not that. It will keep you safe."

I struggled for air as I wrestled to break free of her grip, my throat closing and my mind shutting down, refusing to listen to her, because she was lying to protect her brother.

"Listen to me, Saphira," she murmured, keeping hold of me, her fingers flexing against my arms as she lowered her head so she was eye-level with me. "It is not like that. This mark is a bond. Something only kings are capable of and something which few offer to others. It is a power that binds you to him."

"Like a slave," I spat.

"No." She looked close to rattling me as I refused to listen to her. "Like a promise. It is a vow, Saphira. An unbreakable vow. A promise to keep you safe and to protect you. It was wrong of him to do it without your permission, but I cannot fault his methods, not really."

I snorted. "I can."

I looked at the mark as it pulsed with heat, gaze tracing the intricate lines of it and the animal I now recognised as an elkyn rather than a stag. It was a pretty brand, but a brand nonetheless. I had a hard time believing it was a promise. Kaeleron had placed this on me to protect me, and I wasn't fool enough to think its position on my chest, somewhere so obvious to other fae, hadn't been selected for a reason. He wanted others to see it. He wanted them to know I fell under his protection.

How was that any different to being branded like an animal was, to show they were owned by someone?

"I prefer your methods of keeping me safe," I muttered to Vyr as I covered the brand again and then lifted my gaze to meet hers. "What would Kaeleron think of you training me?"

She straightened and blinked, and threatened to push my world of its axis when I had just found my balance again.

"Kael was the one who ordered me to do it."

I blinked back at her, struggling to comprehend what she had said as that wall I had meticulously constructed last night, a barrier designed to keep the fae king out of my heart, cracked.

"I'm sorry. It sounded a lot like you just said your brother asked you to train me." I stared at her, sure I had heard her wrong.

But she nodded.

"It was his idea." Her brows furrowed as she glanced at my chest, at the spot on my blouse the hid the mark he had put on me. "He needs to know you are safe, Saphira, even when he is not here. This training and that brand will ensure that."

Kaeleron had ordered Jenavyr to train me in secret, just as he had trained her, ensuring she could defend herself and could fight if necessary. With this one act alone, he had shown me how differently he viewed me compared with my pack, treating me as if I was an equal.

Not inferior to him because I was female.

Not something to shelter because I was weak.

He sought to make me strong. To make a warrior out of me. To give me the courage to raise myself up and stand tall beside any male.

Damn him.

I scratched at the brand through the thick fabric of my blouse, still hating it and how it burned at times. Jenavyr was right and it had been wrong of him to do it without asking me. If he had asked me, if he had explained what this brand was, would I have accepted it? Yes. Because I would have known it was born of an act of kindness, a desire to know I would be safe, and a need to ensure no one dared harm me again.

But instead, he had forced it upon me.

And for that, he could stew for a while.

And then when I was done letting him stew...

He could grovel.

CHAPTER 33
KAELERON

When Saphira had filed a request—*in writing*—that she be allowed to learn more about the people of my court because she was curious about how so many different species had come to serve me, I had been pleased that the little wolf desired to know more about my world.

Now, I realised it was some twisted form of punishment.

I barely leashed the growl as I looked up from the three-dimensional map that took up the central space in the castle war room to find her smiling at Riordan.

"Fascinating!" she said, sounding and looking brighter than I had ever seen her, her blue eyes positively aglow with curiosity as the vampire regaled her with stories of his time in the Dark Realm. "I can't believe you ran across him in Hell of all places. And Oberon calls himself a wanderer. I'm surprised the Shadow Court runs as smoothly as it does given how often its ruler is absent."

Riordan flicked me a nervous glance.

I had no need to make Saphira a dagger for her to plunge

one in my chest. Repeatedly. Her verbal blows were fatal enough.

"What were you doing in Hell?" She beamed at the vampire, only having eyes for him today.

Riordan awkwardly preened his blond hair back. At least one of them was aware of my devolving mood and how dangerous the path they were treading was, although I suspected that Saphira knew too and that was part of her game.

No doubt she enjoyed tormenting me together with my sister.

Jenavyr had refused to speak to me yesterday and had buried herself in her work today, reviewing the rosters and the progress the newest soldiers were making with their training.

"I was with the Preux Chevaliers." Riordan twisted the signet ring he wore on his little finger, spinning it around the digit with his thumb, not a sign of his nerves but of his regret. That item was the only thing he had left of his family, and since leaving Hell, he had lived without knowing their fate. Whenever I had offered to escort him to the human world, where they resided, he had made his excuses. The vampire's hand slipped to the back of his neck and he scrubbed it. "They're a mercenary corps. An army for hire, I suppose."

"And now you work for the Shadow Court."

I was painfully aware of how Saphira avoided mentioning my name.

She idly rubbed at her chest, at the spot where I had branded her, a motion she had subconsciously made several times now. Was the mark irritating her? It would settle in a few days and she would no longer be aware of its presence, at least not as she was now.

"And now I work for the Shadow Court." Riordan gave her an easy smile that brightened his sapphire eyes, and made me want to gouge them out with my claws.

I glared at the map and the mountains that separated my court from the Black Pass instead, and then beyond it, to the lands of the seelie and the Summer Court. So close, yet so far from me, beyond my reach right now. Soon.

Patience.

That patience frayed as Saphira continued.

"Why don't you work for the Preux... whatever... now? Did he poach you?"

Riordan laughed, so easily, as if he didn't have a care in the world. "Not exactly. I was... ah... kicked out of the Preux Chevaliers."

A less observant person might miss the way the vampire spun that ring on his finger, or how that brightness in his eyes and that easy smile dimmed a little as he admitted that.

"Oh. Were you a *bad* boy?" Saphira smiled teasingly.

I could not hold back the low growl that rumbled up my throat or stop the tips of my fingers turning inky as I dug emerging claws into the map before me.

"I fucked around and found out." Riordan's tone was all business, not a trace of warmth or amusement in it.

Wise male. He was in danger of fucking around and finding out again, and I would not be as kind as his last commander had been. There would be no banishment. Only death.

"Western reaches," I grumbled and held my left hand out towards Riordan. "Last year and this year."

"Apparently, stealing your commander's woman from him is a career-ending mistake." Riordan shrugged as he went to one of the bookcases set into the black stone walls and gathered several leather binders.

Saphira looked a lot less enamoured with him, her pale eyebrows knitting as her gaze tracked him as he crossed the room to me. "Who'd have thought seducing someone else's lover would be a terrible idea? Are all men ruled by their dick?"

Riordan's eyes widened as he took that dagger to the chest.

I chuckled under my breath as I took the binders from him and set them down on the edge of the map, my gaze fixed on the area around Wraith Wood and the markers positioned there.

Saphira hurled one at me too. "What are you laughing at? I distinctly recall you sporting a hard-on for the whole of Beltane just because I was sitting beside you."

"Not just because you were sitting beside me," I purred as I lifted my gaze to lock with hers. "Because you were sitting *on* me."

She huffed, her eyes widening slightly as she folded her arms.

"And who made me sit on you?" She shook her head. "You know what. You don't get to talk until you're on your knees, grovelling for my forgiveness for branding me like I'm a cow."

I smiled wickedly, gaze narrowing on her. "If you want me on my knees before you, you know our deal, little lamb. You only need to beg."

Colour climbed her cheeks but then her eyes became nothing more than thin slits. "That is not going to happen."

I gave her a sly look as my grin stretched wider, and she glared at me, her lips thinning as she silently dared me to mention what had happened between us.

I would not.

Because some darkly possessive part of me did not want anyone else to know. I wanted to keep her all to myself.

"Aaaand now the air in here makes sense," Riordan said, and we both hit him with a glare. He held his hands up. "If you need the room, I am more than happy to exit it and leave you two alone to... uh... work things out."

"There will be no working things out," she muttered and turned her cheek to me, fixing her attention back on the vampire as she haughtily tipped her chin up.

"Until I beg forgiveness, apparently," I muttered right back at her. "Which is not going to happen."

She huffed again. "You're dead to me."

I chuckled at that, because we both knew it was a lie. She might be mad at me, but I had not missed the secret glances she stole whenever she thought I was not paying attention, lingering looks that had spoken of yearning more than once. She still wanted me, desired me as much as ever, and in time, she would surrender to me again.

Although she seemed rather intent on shutting me out and pretending I did not exist.

"How is it you can walk in this world without burning to ash? Does the light not affect you here, like it doesn't in Hell?" Saphira angled her head, her focus fixed solely on the vampire, but I knew she was aware of me, of how my mood had been darkening drop by drop from the moment she had begun talking with Riordan.

Flirting with him.

"The same reason you just bit his head off. He branded me." Riordan unbuttoned his black tunic, revealing a dark undershirt, and tugged it off his right shoulder, so it slipped down his muscled arm. He pulled the sleeve of his undershirt up, exposing toned pale skin that flexed beneath his brand as he moved. "My brand lets me walk in the sun."

"It does?" Her eyebrows shot up. "I didn't realise they could do things. I just thought—"

She looked at me, her gaze colliding with mine as I watched her closely, watched the vampire closely too now that he was flashing his body at my little wolf. A step too far.

"What does mine do?" Her eyes searched mine.

"It allows you to summon me if you are in danger." I held her gaze, letting her see the truth in it, that the mark wasn't a brand in the way she thought it, it wasn't a sign of possession, it was a link between us, a bond that would carry me to her should she ever need me.

"Oh. Well. That's... sort of nice." She hit me with a hard look. "But I'm still not forgiving you."

"Not until I grovel. Yes, yes. I received that message loud and clear." My gaze flicked to Riordan and I was about to tell him to get dressed again when Saphira turned back to the vampire and set fire to my fury.

By stroking her fingers over the mark on his arm.

"It is sort of pretty, I suppose," she whispered.

Shadows exploded between them, a wall of darkness that hurled the vampire away from her and gently knocked her backwards. Riordan hit the wall between two bookcases with a grunt. Saphira gasped as her backside met the hard marble floor.

"Enough!" I snarled as I pulled my shadows back under control, fighting to calm myself before I had to pick up the scattered pieces of Riordan from my war room and begin looking for a new third in command. I levelled a black look on the little wolf as she planted her hands behind her, wide eyes fixed on me and her breathing unsteady. "Find another to question. You and the vampire are done."

"What's Riordan done now?" Jenavyr strolled into the room and stopped as she spotted Riordan picking himself up off the floor and dusting off his tunic and Saphira pushing to her feet. My sister glared at Riordan as he buttoned his tunic, covering his body, her eyes darker than I had ever seen them as she moved between him and Saphira. "What in the Great Mother's name are you up to?"

"Nothing." Riordan closed the final button, his motions

jerky and filled with the anger reflected in his crimson eyes. "You always leap to the worst conclusion, don't you?"

"Well, you do have a track record of seducing females," she snapped and planted her hands on her black-leather-clad hips. "Old habits die the hardest, do they not?"

"This again?" Riordan squared up to her, his jaw flexing as he gritted, "I was feeding. *Feeding.* A guy needs to eat. That male I was... that isn't me anymore. I changed the moment I realised what a fucking idiot I was. But Kaeleron tells you my sordid history and it sticks. I could be a fucking nun and you'd still think I was sleeping my way through Falkyr."

Vyr refused to back down. "Because your reputation precedes you, vampire. More than one or two pretty females have tales to tell of your charms."

Saphira wisely edged out of the line of fire, inching closer to the map and me.

Riordan threw his hands up in the air, looking at the vaulted ceiling as if he might find some help there. "Oh, forgive me for needing to blow off some steam from time to time. You're one to talk, Vyr. Had a nice Beltane, did we?"

"Do. Not. Call. Me. Vyr," she growled and then pivoted on her heel, storming towards me. "And I did not attend Beltane."

Riordan stared after her, blue eyes wide, mouth agape.

The first time I had seen him speechless.

I looked between the two of them as Vyr scowled at the map, angrily shuffling the legion markers around the Shadow Court and muttering under her breath, and Riordan stared at her back, looking far too stunned.

Far too pleased.

"And you," Vyr snarled at me and it seemed my neck was next on the chopping block. "It was wrong of you to brand Saphi without her consent."

Saphi?

How close were my sister and the little wolf growing? It didn't seem like a good thing, given one day her usefulness would end. But Jenavyr had never had many friends, despite her attempts to befriend various females throughout the years. The servants had kindly played along with her out of obligation, and the highborn had been more interested in courting my attention, only using her to get closer to me.

She was close to Neve, despised Riordan with a passion, and truly enjoyed Malachi's company whenever he was at the castle. It was good for her to have another female for company, even if it would not be a permanent situation.

I shrugged at her and said the one thing I knew would distract her from her anger at Riordan. "Oberon brands people without consent all the time."

"That is *not* a valid reason to do as you please with someone." Vyr firmly shook her head, shifting her long black hair across the shoulders of her blue blouse. "Oberon does a lot of things civilised people should not."

Saphira whispered, "I like Oberon. He seems nice."

Everyone looked at her.

I arched an eyebrow at her, adding another male to the list of ones I needed to watch more closely around the little wolf.

Riordan howled with laughter.

She shot him a confused look, a mulish twist to her lips as she found herself under scrutiny, and then glared at me, as if I had been the one to laugh at her.

"Oberon is not *nice*," I said as I rounded the map to her side, closing the distance between us so the vampire would stop stealing her attention. "Only the side of him you have seen is nice. The other side... I would not cross him."

She shuddered and wrapped her arms around herself. "He seemed so charming."

"Charming, eh?" I looked at her, watching the colour climb her cheeks. "More charming than I am?"

She laughed this time. "Good gods. No. When have you ever been charming? It goes Oberon, Riordan, and then you're somewhere down here."

She held her hand at head height for Oberon, lowered it to level with her breasts for Riordan, and then bent over and waved her hand close to her ankles for me.

Vyr stifled a snicker.

I silenced her with a look.

"Most charming male in the Shadow Court. I'll take that." Riordan grinned.

"I have met lich with more charm than you," my sister shot back.

And the two of them were in each other's faces again, exchanging verbal salvos.

I tuned them out as I returned to studying the latest troop movements in the other courts, comparing their positions to the reports I had received from the people I had concealed within them and shifting the markers if they had been moved to another location. Saphira watched my every move, but I had the feeling her attention was elsewhere and she was only pretending to be interested in what I was doing.

Jenavyr stormed out of the room, Riordan hot on her heels, and Saphira watched them go, her gaze lingering on the door long after they had exited through it.

I studied the closed door and then glanced down at her, seeking any trace of desire in her eyes or in her scent, the darkness that prowled in my veins whispering that she wanted the vampire and that was the reason she was gazing after him.

And growled at her.

"What is wrong?"

CHAPTER 34
KAELERON

Saphira angled her head towards me, the globes of magic light that bobbed in the air above the map in the war room casting a warm glow over her beautiful face. "Have they ever... I mean... I can't help but wonder if they have a thing for each other."

I scoffed at the very idea of my sister with Riordan. "Great Mother, no. I have spent most of my years trying to keep them from killing each other. There is no love there, little lamb."

She shrugged. "Vyr denies it too, but the way they act around each other. I'm not buying the hate. I've seen enough wolves cover their feelings with aggression."

My gaze strayed to the fortified wooden door again, Saphira's words echoing in my mind as I thought about my sister and the vampire, about how they had acted around each other from the moment Riordan had joined us, and unease grew within me.

They did hate each other, did they not? Things had not changed.

Saphira's words were so quiet I barely heard her as she whispered, "She said she's to marry."

My focus darted down to her, shock rippling through me. How close were Saphira and my sister? Vyr never spoke of her impending nuptials to anyone, and only brought them up rarely around me. Neither of us wanted to contemplate what fate awaited her.

"Tradition dictates that she must marry. Relations between the courts depend upon the females in the ruling line marrying into another to strengthen the bonds between them. It is not something I wish upon her, so do not give me that look, little wolf." The anger and disappointment that shone in her eyes was immeasurable, and vicious. I stared after my sister, a heaviness growing within me as I thought about her and the choices we faced. "I will do all in my power to ensure it never happens. This is my burden to bear."

Saphira's look softened, warmth blooming in her eyes as she gazed at me, as if I was some gentle, worthy male. I looked away from her, pinning my gaze to the map, because she did not know me. She did not know the things I was capable of or how cruel I could be, or the lengths I would go to in order to protect my sister.

I moved one of the pieces, placing it near the southern border close to Belkarthen.

Saphira reached over and picked it up, toying with the carved piece of black wood. "What are all these?"

Her gaze lifted to mine, curiosity brightening it now.

I took the piece from her, a shiver bolting up my arm as our fingers touched, and carefully set it back where it had been. "The black ones are markers for the Shadow Court forces. Shields for the legions. Swords for the undercover operatives I have in other courts."

"And this one?" She picked up a winged wraith from the mountains bordering the Summer Court.

"My spymaster." I took it from her, weighing the piece in my hand and staring at it.

It had never felt so heavy.

It was only a matter of time before Malachi returned to the Shadow Court, and each day closer we grew to that fateful moment, the heavier this piece felt in my palm.

"It all sounds very intriguing." Her gaze darted over the map, studying each kingdom, and settling on the Twilight Court. "I'm glad there's a whole sea between here and there."

I almost smiled at her fear and dislike of that court, all based on what I had told her about the source of the wood she so admired.

"Do you station your legions along the borders in case someone dares to march into your lands?" She toyed with one of the Nightmare Court legions that had recently been posted close to the Dusk Court.

"We do."

"And these legions?" She touched two shields close to the border between the Nightmare Court and the Dream Court, one of which was white and the other inky blue.

"The white belongs to the Dream Court, a seelie kingdom. The Nightmare Court keep a legion permanently posted there to keep the peace between the two sides of Lucia." I swept my hand out across the left hand side of the map, where few pieces had been placed. "I rely on an exchange of intelligence from other unseelie courts to know the whereabouts of the legions within the seelie courts, and even then it is rare to discover the locations or sizes of their armies. It is dangerous to insert operatives into those courts, but not entirely impossible. I have managed to embed several non-fae operatives in various courts."

I pointed to the most westerly island of Lucia—the Aurelian Court, close to the seelie high king's island home of Aurien—and then the mainland south of there, to the densely forested Spring Court, and its neighbouring court in the centre of the seelie lands, next to the Black Pass and just north of the Dream Court—the Golden Court.

I had not dared risk attempting to embed an operative into the Summer Court in the north of the mainland. I left that task to my spymaster, since he couldn't be easily traced to my court if he was captured.

"Do the two sides of this world ever go to war?" Her gaze lifted to mine again.

"Rarely since the accord between the two high kings was written in blood and signed. It is an offence to march into another court, and one punishable by death if that court belongs to the other side of this land. No unseelie can march into a seelie court without breaking the accord and the peace between our peoples. So as long as no court marches into another, whether that is seelie or unseelie, and no king crosses a border without permission, the accord stands and peace reigns... at least on the surface. We are all civility and smiles as we plot each other's downfalls." I grinned at her.

She rolled her eyes. "It doesn't sound too different to wolf packs."

I lowered my gaze to the Black Pass that separated the Shadow Court from the Summer Court, my shadows growing restless as hunger to cross that broad strip of land and the mountains beyond it stirred within me. I curled my fingers into tight fists and drew down a steadying breath, clinging to my control and my calm.

Malachi would return soon with news of the Summer Court. This time he might bring me the information I needed to take down that court once and for all.

Saphira followed my gaze to the Summer Court, a crease forming between her brows. "You don't like the seelie, do you?"

"No unseelie likes the seelie. No seelie likes the unseelie. We are two sides of a coin, sharing many traits, but we could not be more different, or hate each other more violently. The seelie are treacherous, wretched beings, and if I had the power, I would wipe every single one of them from the face of this map," I growled, shadows twining around the sturdy legs of the table, snaking tighter and tighter as I thought of the seelie, of the lies they spread and the false airs they used to deceive and ingratiate themselves to other breeds, making themselves appear the noble and gentle beings of Lucia while they painted my breed in shades of darkness and horror.

As monsters.

The room closed in on me, the shadows turning inwards, pouring through my veins to stifle what little light existed within me.

I would show them a true monster.

One day.

"Where does your high king live?" Her tone was soft, distracting me from my dark thoughts and pulling me back to the room as light seemed to pour into it again.

Her focus shifted to me again, eyes tracking my hand as I placed Malachi's piece back where she had found it.

"Ereborne." I pointed to the island nestled in the heart of several courts south-west of here, a castle city like no other in the unseelie realm.

"The most powerful unseelie male in this world lives there?" She leaned over the map to study it more closely. "It's so small compared with the other courts."

I smiled wickedly and took hold of her arm, done with my work and determined to make the most of the fine day. "A title is not the only measure of power. How many alphas in your world are taken down by a more rabid wolf?"

She walked beside me, her arm looped around mine, a thoughtful expression on her face as we exited the room and strolled along the corridor on the ground floor of the castle.

As if it was the most natural thing in the world for us to be doing.

As if she was my queen.

"You do realise you liken yourself to a rabid wolf," she said as we stepped out into the afternoon light and she released my arm. She tilted her head back, her face to the sky, and drew down a long, deep breath as her eyes fluttered closed, so much pleasure in that small action, as if the war room had been a cage and now she was free.

"Not myself. I am neither rabid nor a wolf." I held my hand out to my right, gesturing towards the spot in the garden I had noticed she favoured. The same spot where I had found her conversing with Oberon as if he were as nice as she believed him to be. I prayed she never found out just how cruel and violent Oberon could be.

One of us deserved not to be judged a monster by her.

"You know what I meant. If you could seize that power and become high king, would you?" She ambled ahead of me, her shoulders shifting in a sigh as her blue eyes flitted about the flowers that lined the path towards the wall and the waterfall overlook.

"Perhaps. Perhaps not. I believe I would prefer to remain here, at my court. Power is not everything." I slowly raked my gaze down the line of her spine, taking in her tempting curves, images of her spread out before me on her bed flashing across my mind. Such a wild, unfettered thing she had been once she had let go and embraced her passion in pursuit of her pleasure rather than being ashamed of it.

"Quit staring," she muttered as she scowled over her shoulder at me, a touch of red on her cheeks.

The flicker of heat in her gaze said she did not mind me staring.

Not really.

She was just clinging to her sense of right and wrong again, closing herself off to the pleasures of this world and the flesh because someone had told her it was the right thing to do.

I lengthened my stride to keep up with her, closing the distance between us. "You were the one who insisted I beg forgiveness on my knees. If anyone is responsible for the mental images I now have of us, it is you. I merely indulge them, taking pleasure where I can."

Her eyes flicked to me and back to the path, and the colour on her cheeks deepened, a delightful blush that made me want to trail the backs of my fingers down her soft skin to feel the heat of it.

"I'm still waiting for that apology." She touched the spot on her chest where I had given her my brand, drawing my gaze there and then lower as her hand fell to her breast.

"And I will gladly give it one day, in a form that might please you." I licked my lips, gaze fixed on her breasts.

She rolled her eyes and folded her arms over them. "Nothing you do pleases me."

I chuckled, the sound slipping out before I could stop it, and she gaped at me.

So I scowled at her and swept my left hand forwards, summoning shadows to sweep her along. They twined around her limbs and cupped her backside, the sensations relayed to me as if it were my own hands touching her. She fought them every step of the way to the gazebo, hands slapping at the tendrils of night, her beautiful face set in a black snarl as she bared fangs.

When we reached the gazebo, I released her and she was quick to hurry away from my shadows as I withdrew them, pulling them to me. She strode to the wall that embraced the garden and leaned against it, staring first at the waterfalls that thundered into the bay below and then out to sea.

Ships bobbed on the gentle waves, slowly making their way towards the port, while others anchored out at sea.

"Why don't they enter the port?" She frowned at them, her lips pursed. "The only vessels I ever see in the harbour fly your flag."

She absently touched the brand on her chest again, one that also bore my court's seal.

"Because no outside ship is allowed to dock here. Any goods they bring to my shores must be handed over at sea, beyond the boundary of the Shadow Court." I watched as one of my ships met one from the Night Court at sea, the two boats bobbing in unison as they were lashed together so the goods could be transported between the two.

"Why?"

"Such a curious little lamb." I smirked at her.

She huffed. "*Wolf*. And you said I could ask any questions I wanted. You gave me permission to question people of this court about things that happened here and how they came to be here, remember?"

"I did not expect you to be interrogating me, but I will answer your questions. They must meet at sea to trade goods because the Shadow Court borders are closed and have been for many years now. No one from outside my court is allowed to enter it, whether that is on foot or by sea." I charted the course of another two ships, neither of which looked as if they were making their way towards Falkyr. One bore the dragon flag of the Stygian Isles and had been built for war. The other was a small merchant vessel bearing the flag of the Forsaken

Court, most likely heading back from a trading mission with the Winter Court to the north.

"You make this place sound like a cage," Saphira murmured, her focus fixed on the two boats trading goods just beyond the border of my court.

"Not a cage. Merely protected, and with good reason."

She leaned further forward, folded her arms across the top of the wall and rested her chin on them. "As someone who spent a great deal of her life 'protected', I can say with good authority that's a cage."

I turned my back to the sea and studied her instead, watching the subtle changes in her expression as dark clouds gathered in her eyes. "I do not expect you to understand my reasons, but this is my court to rule, and I shall rule it as I see fit."

"Until a more rabid wolf comes along." Her blue eyes darted up to me and then back to the ocean, a sombre edge to them as she sighed. "I don't have first-hand experience of a lot of things. I'm first to admit my life has been sheltered... but rabid wolves, as you put it, aren't the only ones who differ in strength. Alphas do too, and sometimes one is foolish enough to let that power go to his head."

I frowned down at her, my hands coming to rest against the stones on either side of my hips as she watched the sea with a sorrowful edge to her expression. "You speak of someone you know?"

She shook her head, her silver-white hair brushing her shoulders, the soft strands loosening from her braid to catch on her blouse. "I never knew him. I only know of him. My uncle. He challenged the alpha of the neighbouring pack in an attempt to take control of it and seize more power."

"Sounds much like court politics to me," I murmured, my mind on the way several courts had ended up with a new king in the last few decades, usurped from within by another member of their family or from without by another bloodline with royal ties. But internal battles were not the only way courts changed hands. "It is not uncommon for one king to challenge another in this world. What happened to him?"

"He paid the price for his actions." Her gaze lowered. "He was executed and my cousin, Chase, was left without a father, and Morden lost his father and brother, and my pack ended up without an alpha. The mantle passed to my father."

I mulled over what she had said, filing away the information about the one called Chase and marking down this new name, Morden, in my mental roster of people I wanted to know more about. I would task Vyr with discovering more about this new male.

Saphira stared at the sea, a trace of fascination in her expression, layered with sorrow and a hint of hurt that had me closing ranks with her, edging nearer against my will, some powerful part of me demanding I be closer to her.

"I think our worlds are more alike than I could have imagined." The hurt gained a foothold in her eyes, beginning to overpower the fascination directed at the ocean and the sorrow for her uncle and family. "You have courts. We have packs. You play at civility while plotting murder. We employ deception and outright lies to get what we want."

I grew increasingly still as she spoke, each word that left her lips cranking the tension within my body higher and higher, and not because she talked of the unseelie as if we were dark and cruel things.

"Who in your court—your pack—acted in such a manner?" My voice had never sounded so cold, so dark, as I stared down at her, heart pounding like a war drum that demanded blood and vengeance, because she might not have said the words, but she had said enough for me to know someone had gravely wounded her with deception and lies, and they had taken what they had wanted with them.

That little crease between her fine eyebrows formed again as she twisted towards me, her gaze lifting to lock with mine, no trace of fear in it as she faced me even when I knew my wrath, my dark desire to harm the one who had harmed her, was written all over my face.

"Not my pack. He was never my pack, and I was never to be part of his, apparently." Though she kept her voice steady and full of malice, it came dangerously close to breaking as pain surfaced in her eyes.

Pain I recognised.

I had seen it in her eyes when she had been in that cage.

When she had been in my dungeon.

Only in the last few weeks had that pain disappeared.

And now it had returned.

And I growled low as I realised why.

"You speak of the wolf who sold you."

She swallowed hard and averted her gaze, that pain so fierce in it that tears lined her lashes and she angled her face away from me, as if she was ashamed I had seen them, and perhaps angry too—but not at me. At herself. Because she was letting this pain rule her.

As I had let my pain rule me all those years ago.

"What did he do?" My voice pitched low, a vicious snarl as I took hold of her arms and twisted her towards me, needing to see her face as I asked that because I knew she would try to evade the question if I let her withdraw and I wanted answers.

I wanted to see the truth in her eyes.

They leaped to mine, the tears in them ripping at my soul, shredding my control so rapidly I did not have a chance to hold my shadows at bay. They whipped from me, but rather than lashing at the world in a fit of rage, they swirled around her in an embrace some buried part of me hoped gave her comfort.

Because those eyes, so haunted and distant, revealed how much this male had wounded her, and how that pain continued to fester within her. Even now, far beyond his reach, the wolf still had influence over her.

Invisible bonds I could not shatter.

"Saphira," I whispered, urging her to answer me, and silently demanding she grant me permission to hunt this wolf for her, to end him as I should have the night he had dared to sell such a spirited, beautiful female.

"I believed the lies… that his parents had been killed in an accident in the mountains. I grieved for him. My heart broke for him. But that accident that placed him in power as alpha was no accident at all and I learned it that night… Lucas killed them while their backs were turned." Tears slipped down her pale cheeks as she turned her profile to me, her voice whisper-soft as she stared out to sea and gripped the wall, as if she needed to anchor herself. "I wasn't the first he betrayed."

My claws dug into my palms and I squeezed my fists, relishing the pain as I drew blood.

The sharp edge to her voice, the twist of her expression as she spoke of betrayal, and the pain that glittered in her eyes spoke to me, revealing something new about her that felt vital, a warning I needed to heed and in a way had failed to already.

She abhorred betrayal.

This Lucas had broken some kind of cardinal rule by betraying her. Not by betraying his parents, but by betraying her. Loyal and gentle little wolf. But a fool to trust so easily. Not a fool perhaps, but too innocent to know better, sheltered by kind and loving people and led to believe all were like them.

The male's betrayal must have been a great shock to her.

A blow that had cut deeply enough to leave a scar.

"Using wit to defeat another, playing such games, has a place and a purpose, but a battle between kings or a fight to overthrow a current king and take their throne, should be a battle carried out with honour. Face to face. The wolf is spineless. Weak. He will find his end sooner rather than later." A vow. I made those words a vow, a veiled one but a vow nonetheless. When my vengeance was done, I would find this Lucas and I would end him.

For Saphira.

She snorted. "He might be a bastard with no morals, but he has a strength that serves him well. He's good at manipulating those around him into doing what he wants and as long as that gift continues, he will be safe, protected, and a force no sane wolf would dare face."

"I am not a wolf, and there is no place where this male can hide that I will not find him." I lifted my hands to her face, framing it in my palms, and stared down into her wide, bewitching blue eyes as everything dark within me writhed and snarled, baying for blood and death. "Say the word, Saphira, and the wolf is as good as dead."

Those bewitching eyes widened.

A trace of excitement in them.

For a heartbeat, I could see a shadow of darkness within her, a tendril of night that echoed the hungers within me, a vicious and cold need for vengeance. For destruction. For death.

And then it was gone.

She tore her gaze from mine and stepped back, slipping from my grip, and wrapped her arms around herself as she looked at the castle, a flicker of regret crossing her features.

Shadows writhed at my feet, hungry to find the wolf and kill him, to tear him apart piece by piece and gift her with them, but I tamped down that urge, aware that Saphira would not appreciate it. She was no killer. She was kind and gentle, or at least believed herself only capable of light and warmth, but twice now I had seen her darker side, had seen the wolf beneath her innocent exterior.

A vicious and violent beast that wanted blood.

I had stolen her revenge on Elanaluvyr from her and she had looked ready to fight me.

How badly did she crave vengeance against Lucas?

How deeply had the wolf harmed her?

I would find out the answer to the latter, and would mould her into a weapon fit to carry out the former. Now she had tasted what it was like to lose your revenge to another, she would only crave it more.

Just as I did.

"You still haven't taken me to your library," she murmured, voice distant, as if she was afraid to bring up my failure to carry out my promise to let her use it, or perhaps she was just lost in her thoughts and looking for a distraction from them.

I ushered her towards the castle, letting her walk in brooding silence beside me, aware she needed the quiet and the space to think. So like me in many ways. Whenever I craved silence and peace so I could plot my revenge, I went to my sanctuary.

Saphira had no such place, so I would grant her one.

The library.

I led her up to the fourth floor, to a corner of the castle few visited and one of the largest rooms on the floor, and watched her closely as I leaned past her and twisted the knob, my back to the wall and my shoulder against the wooden panels of the door. I eased it open, savouring how her eyes slowly widened as the library was revealed to her and I cast a simple spell, one that had the lamps in the spacious room lighting one by one.

She slowly stepped into the room, eyes dancing over the

three levels of black wooden shelves packed with books and accented with brass fittings that encircled a main sitting area, up to the glass dome above that open area that allowed light to flood the room during the day and revealed the endless stars at night.

I leaned against the doorframe, gaze tracking her as she moved deeper into the room, the fascination painted across her face a beautiful thing to behold.

Until she turned a confused look on me.

"What?" My eyebrows dipped low, because I knew that look, that teasing edge to her eyes.

"Do you have a brother I don't know about?"

I locked up tight, heart seizing as I thought about my brother, and her expression softened as she noticed my reaction, her hands coming up and an apology dancing in her eyes, but I shook my head, dislodging the pain and subduing the shadows that twined around my legs and my shoulders, because I knew she had not meant to wound me.

"I'm sorry," she whispered, her brow furrowing as she inched a step closer to me. "I was going to make this whole joke about the library and I forgot… I can't believe I forgot."

Vyr had told her.

I stared at her as that sank in, as she held my gaze, hers softer than I had ever seen it, all of that tenderness directed at me.

"My brother is not dead," I said, voice hollow and distant to my own ears.

"But Vyr said—"

"My sister believes he is gone. I know he is not. Seelie took him. I am sure of it." I shifted my gaze to the stone fireplace behind her, at the other end of the open area, and summoned a little magic, enough to spark a flame that rapidly, hungrily engulfed the dry wood in the hearth. I forced a smile and purged the darkness from my heart just as that fire purged it from the room, not wanting this moment marred by it all. "That is a conversation for another time. I believe you were making a joke?"

She didn't look sure if she should continue, so I waved her on, my smile gaining genuine warmth as I waited.

"You asked if I had a brother." I willed her to take the bait, needing the moment of lightness to illuminate the darker reaches of my heart as I looked at her standing in a library my brother would have loved. He had always been the more bookish of the two of us. "I answer 'no'."

Not right now, at least. I would have a brother again soon.

"Um." She tripped over the words. "Then... perhaps your... sister... loves to read?"

I frowned. "Also no. She despises books. What are you playing at?"

A little smile was my reward for playing along, acting the role of the gruff king she had assigned me in this little farce of hers.

"I'm trying to figure out why there are so many books. A family collection perhaps? Or a public library?"

I genuinely frowned at her now, as I realised where she was going with her teasing. "A private collection."

"Whose?"

"Mine," I snarled.

"But there's so many books." She took them all in, surprise colouring her eyes and her mouth gaping open, and then sized me up.

I folded my arms across my chest. "You make me sound like some kind of heathen."

"You're not?" Her eyebrows shot up and then she smirked. "I thought you were."

"I have read most of them." I smirked right back at her

when she gawped at the numerous shelves and the thousands of books they held.

"How old are you?" She blinked at me.

I sighed.

I knew exactly where this was going.

"I'm just saying, as a king you must be very busy, yet you've read all these books! Or you're not a very good king and neglect your duties in favour of reading." Her smile grew teasing and a little wicked.

As did mine as I closed in on her.

"I am a *very* good king," I purred. "Exceptionally skilled. Very attentive. Able to anticipate what my people need. Willing to give it to them. But then I thought you were aware of that, since you had first-hand experience."

A blush climbed her cheeks as she backed away from me, and her eyes widened as her back met one of the bookcases.

I leaned in close, bringing my lips down to her ear as I caged her with my body.

"Perhaps you have forgotten how skilled and attentive I am," I murmured against her skin, eliciting a shiver that I felt and savoured as her breath caught. "I am more than happy to remind you. You only have to ask, little wolf."

"Kaeleron," she whispered, my name a balm on her sweet lips but a shock that leaped along my bones too, sizzling like lightning through my veins, and angled her face towards me, bringing her lips closer to mine.

My breath caught.

The world narrowed down to her.

To those lips.

So close to mine.

I shifted my head slightly, a fraction closer, aching to know the taste of her lips.

"Kaeleron," she murmured again, setting fire to my blood.

No female had ever uttered my name with such need.

"Yes, Saphira?" I traced my lips across her cheek, heading for her mouth.

"I want..." She placed her hands on my chest, over my thundering heart, "...to read now."

She shoved me backwards.

I growled and she smirked.

"Wicked little thing," I rumbled, watching her cheeks catch aflame to betray her true desire as I stared down into her eyes.

The one she had been too afraid to voice.

I bowed mockingly and lifted my gaze to lock with hers as I straightened, snaring her.

"Very well. Read all you like. I have business to attend to anyway. Unlike some believe, I am rather busy." Not busy enough that I would not have blown it all off had she wanted me here, in the library. No, I would have indulged her just to see her shatter, to see her come apart in my arms, breaking for only me. "But as payment for your wickedness, I order you to join me for dinner..."

I faded into the shadows, relishing how she shivered as I disappeared from view, that flicker of heat still in her eyes.

"Where you will sit on my lap and tell me all you learned."

CHAPTER 35
SAPHIRA

Kaeleron had failed to join me at dinner.

I had sat there staring at the empty chair at the far end of the table, mind filled with all the things I had noted in the books I had flicked through, a blend of interesting facts about elkyn, the history of the lich, and a history of mining in the Shadow Court. I had no clue how I had ended up falling into that book. Maybe it had been the mention of Falkyr that had caught my eye when I had been flicking through the pages, followed by something about dwarves that had roused my curiosity. Before I had known what was happening, I was devouring all the facts about mine shafts that dated back centuries, the dwarven clans who worked them, and the prized metals found in the heart of the mountains.

I had wanted to ask Kaeleron whether his black armour was crafted from such a fine metal.

Jenavyr had confirmed during our training session that her sword had been forged from it, a gift to her from her brother when she had gained enough skill with a blade that he had decided she was worthy of something a little finer than the swords the regular guards used.

She had also been the one to apologise for her brother's absence last night.

Apparently, he had been summoned to the legion posted near Wraith Wood after there had been a report of people being spotted in the mountains that bordered the western fringes of the vast forest and hadn't returned until this morning.

A reasonable excuse for his absence, but still it prickled. He had taken the time to tell Vyr where he was going, but hadn't come to tell me, instead letting me dress in that ridiculous shimmering navy silk gown he had delivered to my room, a bias-cut one that hung from one shoulder and was so light it clung to parts of my body, revealing them, and sit in that dining room unsure where the hell he was.

Well, if he summoned me to dinner again, I was going to refuse to go and see how he liked it.

Still, his unplanned absence had given me one thing, a rare gift that I was determined to treasure and make the most of in case it never happened again.

Vyr had told me I could wander the city without an escort.

At first, I had been sure she was joking so she could see the castle guards slam their spears across my path like they always did whenever I approached the main gate, but she had taken me there and the men had remained at their posts on either side of the heavily fortified stone archway, gazes fixed straight ahead.

I had hurried through the gate in case my chance at freedom was snatched from me, grabbing it while I could, and then I had locked up tight and looked back at Vyr, and had asked her to come with me. I had no reason to be afraid. I knew that as I traversed the main street of the city, listening to the low chatter of the people coming and going along it, and gazing in the windows of every store. No one even looked at me. Not a single one of the common folk knew who I was and the finely dressed highborn I did come across didn't seem to care.

In fact, they all avoided me if they noticed me.

Yet, I had still panicked, that night Elanaluvyr had attacked me flashing across my mind to make my heart race and limbs tremble, and asked Vyr to come with me.

Her words had stayed with me during my walk.

I was stronger now. I didn't need her protection.

I *was* stronger, she was right about that, but my visits to the town had been so few that I still felt out of place, as if everyone was watching me and knew I didn't belong here, in this place where I felt I belonged the most.

I looked back at the castle that loomed at the top of the hill, above the terraces of half-timbered buildings.

Or perhaps not the most.

I was beginning to feel I belonged there more now, high up in that castle, in that stunning garden or those lush woods, surrounded by all that nature and beauty. The feeling was indescribable and hard to pin down, but it beat within me, a vivid and vibrant thing that drew me back towards the castle. I continued onwards instead, sure it was just fear of being alone in the city and noticed by someone that had me wanting to return to the safety of the castle.

The window of the bakery caught my gaze and held it, the sweet confections laid out in baskets and lacquered wooden boxes luring me towards the store. I stood there in front of the bowed glass window, eyes flitting over the colourful treats nestled like jewels in black paper. What would they taste like? Would Kaeleron like them? I imagined he had probably had them before, but what if he hadn't? What if I could give him something he had never tried? Would his face light up, some of the storm clouds lifting from it? He liked sweet things. He might like these.

A pang hit my chest and my shoulders slumped a little as I patted the empty pockets of my black leathers.

Not that I had gold to buy them with. I didn't have a single coin in my possession, and I doubted the shop owner would believe me if I said they were for the king and asked them to charge the castle, and what sort of present would that be anyway if I had Kaeleron pay for them?

And why the heck did I want to give him a present?

I jammed my hands into my pockets. I suppose he had spared me from a terrible fate, and offered to let me work off my debt, and then he had decided to train me so I was stronger and knew how to fight, and to top off all that he had given me free rein in his own personal library.

I was beginning to feel dangerously like a guest rather than a captive.

"Saphira." A deep masculine voice startled me from my thoughts and I looked off to my left, towards the source of it.

"Riordan." I smiled as I spotted him across the broad cobbled avenue, heading up the hill towards me.

He looked harried as always, his blond hair tousled, as if he had been running his hands through it, and several guards trailed after him. Not guards, I realised as he said something to them and they bowed their heads, acknowledging an order. Soldiers. Part of his regiment?

The vampire jogged over to me, leaving the dozen men to continue the march up the hill to the castle, and looked me over and then all around me.

"No guard today?" He looked as surprised as I had felt upon discovering I was allowed to head into the city without an escort.

"I'm considering it part of an apology from Kaeleron for

being branded or maybe because he ditched me at dinner last night." I shrugged when he arched an eyebrow at me. "Vyr says he was called away to Wraith Wood and was gone all night."

"I met with him this morning. He is not in a good mood after that visit, but I can't blame him given the potential threat to his people. Sightings of seelie are a good reason to be a touch furious."

"Seelie?" My eyes widened and pulse picked up. "There were seelie within the Shadow Court?"

"Rumours at least. Several sightings close to the borders of Wraith Wood. The whole area is on high alert. Kaeleron hunted them all night, and returned furious that he couldn't find them." Riordan scratched his stubbled chin, his lips quirking. "Although, maybe I shouldn't be telling you everything. If Vyr didn't—"

"I won't tell anyone," I interjected, eager to know more, because I could only imagine how unsettled the people of Wraith Wood must be with seelie potentially in their midst, as well as just how furious Kaeleron must be. He had closed his borders to protect his people, but the enemy had infiltrated them. "Do you know where Kaeleron is?"

"I do." He glanced over his shoulder, as if checking no one was listening in, but as he continued, I realised he was looking in the direction of something. "Listen... if you really want to risk your neck by seeking him out when he's like this... I won't stop you. I'll just warn you to be careful. Be really careful."

"Where is he?" I gazed beyond him, in the direction he had been looking, towards the bend in the main avenue before it swept downwards towards the docks, sure Kaeleron was somewhere in that direction and wanting to know why.

Riordan's expression shifted back and forth as he debated telling me.

"Either you tell me where I can find him, or I wander off in that direction without a clue and try to find him myself. Who knows what might happen to me in those dark alleyways?" I smiled up at him as he scowled at me.

"Manipulative little creature, aren't we?" He huffed. "Head over to Fierel's, the blacksmiths. It's north-west of here. Take the passage over there and follow the right branch that takes you towards the outer wall. You'll find him there... and do not tell him I sent you. I like my head where it is."

Was Kaeleron in such a bad mood that he would kill one of his own inner circle?

I shivered at the thought he might be, and what I might be getting myself into by seeking him out, but then steeled my nerves and straightened my spine, because my primal instincts demanded I find him and see that he was fine, that this seelie incursion hadn't shaken him.

"Thank you," I said as I hurried towards the alleyway, determined to find Kaeleron before I lost my nerve.

"Your funeral," Riordan muttered as he walked away. "I'll pick you out a nice casket."

I flipped him off over my shoulder, earning a husky chuckle from the vampire, and then the passageway swallowed me and I focused on my hunt, my wolf instincts coming to the fore as I scented the air, seeking a trace of Kaeleron.

No doubt he was at the blacksmith to order weapons for his men, arming his legion with the finest swords available.

I caught the scent of ash, steel and wild storm, and tracked it through the narrow alleys between old buildings, heading deep into the outskirts of the city. When the scent grew fainter, I backtracked and took another path, banking right.

And came out into a small, cobbled square in front of a half-timber forge with a crooked tiled roof and a beautifully crafted metal sign above the open doors, and several barrels of water stood outside it.

I stepped forwards, looking for the blacksmith in the heart of the building, where a great stone forge blazed red-hot, casting warm light over the tools that hung on the walls and the stacks of raw materials, and several anvils.

Two bare chested males worked at the forge, bathed in fierce light as one stoked the coals while the other turned a long strip of metal, pushing it deep into their fiery hearts before withdrawing it to check the temperature.

One male I didn't recognise.

The other I did.

Kaeleron wiped sweat from his brow with the back of one hand as he gripped the strip of metal with tongs in his other and carried it to an anvil. He picked up what looked like a hammer and began striking the metal, his movements precise and practiced, mesmerising to watch as firelight chased over his glistening chest and arms.

I stared, lost in the sight of him as he worked the metal, the rhythmic sound of his strikes echoing my heartbeat. My wolf side howled at the glorious sight of him, his honed muscles streaked with soot and ash from his work, slick with sweat from the heat of the forge and the exertion of working the metal.

By the gods.

A low growl rumbled in my chest, something primal within me rising to the fore as I studied him, as I drank my fill of him. I had never seen anything so masculine.

So utterly male.

Every muscle of his torso and arms moved in a delicious symphony as he worked the metal, his handsome face set in hard lines of concentration, gaze focused on his work with an intensity that would have robbed me of my breath if he had looked at me that way.

It dawned on me that Riordan had asked me not to reveal he had been the one to tell me where to find Kaeleron because this was meant to be a sort of secret—a place Kaeleron came whenever he needed to work off some steam or distract himself from something.

I suddenly felt as if I was imposing, interrupting something where I wasn't welcome or wanted, something private.

But before I could turn to leave, Kaeleron inspected his work and rose to his full height, saying something to the other male as he went to turn towards the forge.

His silver gaze landed on me.

Rather than scurrying away like I wanted to, I planted my boots to the cobbles and remained where I was, facing him and holding his gaze.

Seeing him.

Really seeing him.

It wasn't a king standing before me. It was just a male. There were no adornments on his ears, no fine clothing or a crown to denote his rank. It was as if he had been stripped of those things to reveal the man beneath the kingly veneer—a man with the flame of joy born of passion in his eyes—a flicker of the boy in the painting.

He said something to the other male as he handed the worked strip of metal to him, barely paying him any attention, his striking silver eyes remaining fixed on me. He tugged the leather gauntlets he wore off and set them down on the anvil.

And then he was striding towards me.

My pulse picked up and I swallowed to wet my suddenly dry throat as Kaeleron prowled towards me, honed body streaked with soot and sweat, flooding my imagination with visions of him labouring over the fire, working up that sweat as he skilfully crafted weapons.

Damn.

If he had been born a blacksmith, I still would have found him irresistible. A crown hadn't given him power. He had been born with it, with an allure that snared me and had me aching for him to come to me.

"I'm surprised to see you like getting your hands dirty with such manual labour." My words wobbled, betraying my nerves, or perhaps that fluttering of desire that made me tremble as he continued to hold me immobile with nothing more than a look so intense it did indeed steal my breath.

He chuckled, the warmth of that sound heating my bones, my heart.

Another glimmer of the boy in that painting, one who had known how to smile, how to laugh.

Kaeleron didn't help the flush of desire turning my blood to fire. Instead of giving me a moment to quell it, he stoked the flames by bending over one of the large wooden barrels outside the blacksmiths and splashing water over his face to wipe the soot and sweat away.

Water that dripped and rolled down his chest, cutting through the dirt as he straightened again and turned towards me.

My gaze tracked one of the droplets, mouth going drier as it rolled over the square slabs of his pecs, snaked towards his impressive abs and cascaded down the valley between them, heading for his navel.

And lower.

To that trail of dark hair that led my gaze to the low waist of his leathers.

That fire in my blood became an inferno.

His husky chuckle had my eyes leaping up to his face, my cheeks scalding as his lips curled into a wicked, knowing smile.

"Some manual labour is more than enjoyable. It is a pleasure, Saphira," he purred, the way my name rolled off his tongue sending a shiver down my spine and making my eyes drift closed.

I snapped them open before they could shut fully, but the damage was done. His smile widened. He knew the power he had over me, how close I was to tackling him right here in this courtyard, where anyone could see, because I hungered.

And I couldn't blame my mating heat this time.

This need growing inside me, it was all because of him. He stoked the flames of my passion as expertly as he had stoked the flames of the forge, making me burn hot enough that I was in danger of melting, of begging him to mould me into that wild, wanton beast he had turned me into that night of Beltane—a woman who knew what she wanted and pursued it without reserve, without shame, taking the pleasure she needed and demanding more.

Uncaring of the consequences.

"Dinner was lovely, by the way," I said, trying to cool my desire by driving a wedge between us.

Kaeleron's dark eyebrows pitched low and he sighed, the hunger in his eyes replaced by what looked a lot like guilt. "I apologise for that. I was called away and barely had time to inform my sister. I asked her to explain my absence to you."

"She did. This morning." The bite to my words surprised me, and I fell silent as I contemplated the burning within me, the anger he had sparked by not telling me he had to leave, by letting me sit there like a fool at dinner, alone and forgotten.

Unimportant.

Because in the grand scheme of things, that's what I was. Unimportant. A diversion. Entertainment.

And gods, I was a fool, but it hurt.

"You know what. It's fine. I don't care. I live to serve, like others in your castle. I'm sure the cooks and the servants who brought dinner to the table aren't complaining, so I have no reason to either. I'm just like them. A servant. And you're a king. You get to do what you want. I'm just the entertainment."

I turned to leave, my throat closing and chest tightening, and I hated myself for saying all that, for putting it all out there, because now I felt cold and vulnerable, open to attack.

And desperate to hear him correct me—to tell me I was something more than that to him.

Kaeleron captured my wrist, holding me in place, but I kept my face turned away from him, not wanting him to see the turmoil in my eyes, the tumultuous emotions that I couldn't tame, that were too powerful to be crushed and cast aside. I hadn't realised how much his absence had hurt me, or how much the fact he hadn't taken a second to inform me had wounded me.

His fingers flexed around my wrist, warm and strong, and I gritted my teeth, despising how that touch soothed me, stirring a need to look at him, together with tears that stung my eyes.

"You are not just entertainment, Saphira."

I wanted to believe that, I really did, because some reckless part of me had started to feel at home here, had started to see Vyr, Riordan and Neve as friends, and Kaeleron as something more than that. I had lowered my guard, and now I felt I was paying the price for it.

Suddenly tired and longing for quiet, to be alone with my thoughts, I tugged on my arm, but he only tightened his grip.

"You are right. I should have told you. I thought Vyr would let you know right away, and that is on me. Do not blame her."

"I don't. I blame you." I kept my back to him, my arm stretched behind me, locked in his fierce grip.

"That is fine." He sighed. "But perhaps this might make it better."

I frowned as he slipped something cool onto my middle finger and looked back at my hand, wanting to see what it was.

A ring.

He released my wrist and I drew my hand up before me,

studying the beautiful intricate silver ring. Miniscule markings lined the band, a language I had seen in the books and tapestries in the castle but couldn't understand. My handmaidens had told me it was ancient fae.

"It is called a moon ring," he murmured as his fingers traced the band and the circular opalescent stone set in the heart of two crescent moons. "I thought it might suit you."

My eyebrows knitted harder as I noticed he wore a matching ring.

"It will protect you." He stroked the ring again, grazing his thumb over it, his fingers against my palm as he stared down at it. "It took me longer than expected to finish them. I had wanted them ready before my trip to Ereborne."

I was too hung up on what he had admitted to hear the rest of what he said.

I stared at the ring, my eyebrows rising high on my forehead as I took in how intricate it was, how delicate, and how beautiful and fine. "You made this? I thought you had bought it."

His smile was small, almost awkward, as if my discovering he had made something so incredible had left him as vulnerable as I had felt just moments ago.

"It's beautiful," I admitted and the air of vulnerability he wore faded a little. "Thank you."

His thumb swept over the band on my finger again, his gaze distant now. "If I had not been born royalty, I believe I would have been a blacksmith or a jeweller."

And he was back to looking vulnerable.

Because whatever gates guarded his heart, he had just opened them a little to me, letting me see some secret inner part of him he preferred to keep hidden.

"I didn't really think you had the fine motor control to make something so delicate," I teased, my smile bright, trying to ease the tension building in him.

And he was too delicious as he purred, "You know how skilled my fingers are."

I shivered, barely suppressing the urge to bite my lower lip as I recalled just how skilled they were, as my body hummed with echoes of that pleasure he had given me and my nipples beaded.

"I can't really dispute that." I eased a little closer to him, growing aware that he was still holding my hand, his thumb grazing my fingers as his gaze remained locked on me.

The corners of his lips quirked into another dangerously seductive smile.

I glanced down at the ring again, avoiding falling under its wicked spell. "It really is beautiful. I can't imagine making something so intricate. I wouldn't even know where to begin and whatever I made would probably look like a gnarled piece of metal at the end of it. How did you even inscribe such tiny lettering? Or make those little vines that are holding the moons?"

"Centuries of practice, little wolf." He turned my hand, making the pale stone catch the light. Colours like the aurora above us chased across the heart of the stone.

"Centuries?" My gaze darted up to lock with his and I feigned shock. "How old are you?"

"Five hundred and sixty years old." He sounded proud about that.

"My gods, you're old." I gaped at him and he scowled at me, and I couldn't stop the smile from blooming on my lips. "I read about you in the library."

"Do not believe everything you read in the books there. Some are a rather... abridged... history of this land and its people."

"Well, it didn't mention your blacksmithing hobby, so I believe that." I looked at the ring again. It truly was beautiful.

Probably the most beautiful gift I had been given and one that spoke to me on some deep level. A moon ring. A present fit for a wolf shifter. "What's your favourite thing you've made?"

He pursed his lips, expression growing thoughtful and pensive.

And then he said, "I have made many things in my life, but the most important to me is my sword. I spent months crafting it and imbued it with power through ancient spells."

"The same language that's on here?" I lifted my hand and he nodded. "Ancient fae. I can't read it."

"It is a language few know, and one we do not share with others. It is almost... sacred to my kind. Wait here a moment." He pivoted and walked away before I could stop him, heading back inside the forge, where he retrieved something from the blacksmith.

I frowned at the bundle of worn brown leather he held in his hands as he returned to me.

He held it out to me. "My apology, for branding you without your consent."

"Another gift?" I took the supple bundle of leather from him and unwound the thin strap that had been wrapped around it, and then unrolled it.

Revealing a beautiful dagger that was as long as my forearm.

The silver metal gleamed in the low light as I closed my hand around the black leather wrapped hilt and lifted it before me.

"I admit, it took me longer than I had expected. I began working on it when Vyr started your training." The lightness in his deep voice stole my focus from the dagger, the warmth in his eyes as he looked at it stirring an echo of that warmth and lightness within me. "I had considered a sword, but my sister mentioned your speed and agility, and I thought perhaps a dagger might be more suitable, especially given your slight frame. It is a weapon you could easily wield and would not slow you down. So I set about crafting you one that would complement your skills and work with you, rather than against you."

So much passion.

This male before me was so different to the fierce, hard king I knew him to be.

He was passionate, warm, and animated as he talked openly about the weapon he had made with me in mind, his love of blacksmithing on show for me to see.

I wanted to keep him like this, even when I knew it was impossible. A court needed a king, and the mask would fall back into place before I knew it and I would lose this warm, bright male. I had read enough about the courts now to know how they ran, and about the kings of the other courts, each more brutal and ruthless than the last.

But a few of them were warm and kind.

Like the king of the frigid Winter Court, who had loved and lost his seelie fated mate.

I stared at the dagger, at the delicately carved wolf head that acted as the pommel and the cross guard beautifully inscribed with ancient fae. At the reflection of Kael in the blade, his handsome face warm and beautiful, alight with his passion as he spoke so openly with me.

"I read about your court," I murmured, unsure whether I wanted to go there, wanted to bring up what I had read and what I had seen with my own eyes. I was overstepping, I knew it, and if Vyr were here, she would warn me not to do this, but I wanted this male before me to remain. I wanted his people to see this side of him. "You said you closed the borders, but what you didn't say is that you did it when your parents died. I didn't realise just what that meant until I read about it and then some of the things I've been feeling during my visits to the city began to make sense."

His expression gradually darkened, a slow death of the warm male reflected in a dagger crafted of his passion and a need to protect.

He remained deathly still and quiet, the power he radiated growing darker as our shadows on the cobbles grew restless, pooling in the cracks between the stones.

Nerves threatened to silence me, but I squared my shoulders and lifted my eyes to meet his, because someone needed to say it. I needed to say it.

"Are your people happy?" I echoed the question I had asked him before.

And just like before, he was quick to say, "Yes."

"Are they though?" I looked around us, that feeling that they weren't growing stronger within me as I looked at the blacksmith where he stood at the doors of his forge, watching us with a cautious air, with a touch of fear in his eyes. I shifted my gaze back to meet Kaeleron's. "Because I can't see it, Kaeleron. Everywhere I look in this town, I see my own reflection. I see people who are smiling on the surface, to hide their pain. Their fear. Their resentment."

He growled and I stiffened, but I wouldn't back down. Not this time. I knew what I was seeing, because I had lived it. I had been the one who felt trapped in their home, unable to come and go as they please, who had been cut off from the world.

"You closed the borders, Kaeleron. What does that mean for the people of your court? What does it mean for those who had come to work here from other places? Some of the people here aren't from Lucia." My breath hitched as the ground beneath my feet trembled and the blacksmith behind Kaeleron stepped back into the shelter of his home, slowly shaking his head. I couldn't do as he wanted. I couldn't stop now. "Are they trapped here?"

"They are protected. They have everything they need." The same bullshit he had told me before.

"And what price are they paying for that protection? How many of them have families outside the walls of the Shadow Court? How many of them don't know what has happened to those people? How many people come to your borders, wanting to find their family, and are turned away?" I felt like a bitch as I asked those questions, as I ruined the moment we had been sharing, driving that warm male further from me.

In the hopes I could draw him back again, that I could open his eyes to what he had done so he would loosen his hold on his court and free his people.

He growled as he stepped up to me, darkness branching from his eyes, staining his skin as his irises gained a crimson corona.

I wouldn't be silenced.

"Can you see how afraid your people are of you or are you truly blind to it?" I looked beyond him to the blacksmith.

Kaeleron looked over his shoulder at him too, some of the tension in his body fading in an instant when he saw the older male cowering in the shadows of his home, watching us as if he feared for his life.

"You might believe you are keeping your people safe, you might even truly believe they are happy, but there is a difference between keeping your subjects safe and keeping them caged. This kingdom is beautiful, Kaeleron, but to many it's a gilded cage."

He snarled in my face, his canines and the incisors beside them as sharp as the dagger I gripped in my trembling hand.

Gods, I was being an ungrateful bitch by doing this to him

when he had just been so kind to me and had let me see the warmer side of him, but someone needed to say it.

And deep in my heart I knew it had to be me.

He knew my history, he knew how caged I had been, and he might listen to me because of it. He might show his people the side of him I had met today—the warmer, kinder male.

"You closed the borders to your kingdom, for the same reason you closed off your heart—to protect it and avoid pain—but in doing so you condemned your people and yourself to living half a life. You built a cage—no, a magically reinforced steel wall—around everyone and cut them off from the world… from their kin… from their families." My heart pounded against my chest, an unsteady and rapid rhythm that had me shaking as I faced him, as I braced myself for his wrath.

Shadows swept around me, buffeting me and chilling my skin.

And then they were gone.

And so was Kaeleron.

CHAPTER 36
SAPHIRA

Training would take my mind off the things I had said to Kaeleron and the fact he hadn't summoned me to dinner.

I had dined alone in my rooms, staring out at the city as the lights had slowly come on to drive back the darkness, mulling over what I had done. I hadn't been able to hold back the words, not when they had beat within me so fiercely, all the years I had spent at my pack, enduring my gilded cage, rolling into one furious roiling beast within me that had demanded freedom.

I regretted them now, even when I knew I had spoken true, that this court was suffering as I had back at my pack, the walls Kaeleron had constructed around it to keep it safe chafing at them.

Alphas had a right to protect their pack as they saw fit, to decide who had what freedom and what those within it did or didn't do. A king had the same right, and gods, maybe I was just taking out my frustration over my own silence during the years at my pack on Kaeleron.

But I wasn't projecting my own feelings on his people, not as he had believed the first time I had confronted him about it.

I would try to find him later and, not apologise for what I had said, but at least try to heal this breach between us.

Before I found myself living in a dungeon again.

I jogged into the clearing, eager to blow off some steam with Jenavyr.

And found Kaeleron standing in the centre of it, his hands in the pockets of his soft cotton trousers and his head tipped back, silver gaze on the sky.

I slowed to a walk, nerves rising as I realised I was about to face him right now, before I had time to prepare a pretty speech that would soothe his temper and maybe spare me from a downgrade to a prison cell.

"Was Jenavyr called away?" I tried to sound bright and not at all nervous as I approached him, and he continued to stare at the sky, as if I didn't exist. My gut said the reason he was here wasn't because his sister had been called away. This was my punishment. He knew how much I enjoyed these sessions, and he was taking them away from me. "Is my training cancelled?"

His head slowly lowered, his gaze cold and unreadable as it landed on me, and his voice devoid of emotion as he said, "You will be sparring with me today. I want to see what you have learned."

So this was my punishment for speaking out of turn with him.

Not a prison cell.

Not even a fight.

He was going to show me how weak I was, how I couldn't compare with him and how I had merely been playing at being a warrior. He was going to show me how strong he was and how easily he could crush me—the strength and power of a king.

"Come, little wolf." He unbuttoned his black tunic and

shrugged it off, cast it aside on the grass and then tugged one boot off and then the other, leaving himself barefoot and bare chested, distracting me with all that honed muscle. "Show me your fangs."

I remained where I was, heart pounding too fast, adrenaline surging in a way it never had before when I had sparred with Vyr. Because I knew Vyr went easy on me. I knew she pulled her punches.

And I knew Kaeleron wouldn't.

"Why did you have me trained?" I asked, a tremble in my voice as I tried to buy myself time to mentally prepare myself for what was about to happen here in the glade, running through all the moves that Vyr had taught me in my mind and formulating a plan my gut said would fail dramatically.

I didn't know how Kaeleron moved, which foot he led with, what his style was—whether he preferred to press the advantage and focus on attacking, or bided his time to wait for openings in which to punish his opponent.

I had no way of winning this, and that cold look in his eyes said he knew it.

He knew he was walking away from this glade the victor.

"Was it because I was attacked?" I didn't want to think about that night, or the cold rage that had stolen over me the following day when I had discovered this male had taken my vengeance from me.

He shook his head as he tied his black hair back. "No. I had you trained because you believe yourself weaker than a lowly alpha wolf and I needed to open your eyes."

"Open my eyes?" I blinked at him, at the answer I hadn't expected.

"Everything I have done has been training, Saphira. A way of making you realise just how strong you really are and to shake off your doubts." He twisted to face me and rolled his shoulders. "You do not need an alpha, because you are one yourself. You care about your pack. You are willing to fight for them. I saw it in you the first time I set eyes on you. You are strong. Brave."

And he had been luring that strength and courage out in me.

"Every teasing word... every temptation... it was all to make me see how strong I am. It was to free me." I stared at him, unable to believe it, that someone in this world had seen something in me long before I had and that a male would go to such lengths to make me see it, to build up my courage and my strength, and mould me into the female he believed I could be.

"A dangerous thing to do, but one that I found enjoyable." He smirked. "Drawing out your strength I could see flashing in your eyes whenever you fired back at me, whenever I pushed you and you were brave enough to push back, I was well aware how dramatically it could backfire on me, but I could not help myself. However you view me, Saphira, I am not your oppressor. I am not an alpha seeking to hold you back or pin you down into a life of misery—a half life. You wanted freedom, and I gave you the power to take it. Just as I did with my sister. I believe a female can be as strong—even stronger—than any male."

And I believed it too, but I hadn't before I had come to this place. I had always believed males were stronger, that their strength was the reason they were raised to fight, to take the most powerful positions within the wolf packs and lead them.

But now, now my eyes had been opened, and I could see clearly. I could see that Kaeleron was right. A female could be as powerful as a male, as fearsome and brave, and could lead her people and protect them.

And Kaeleron had seen that strength in me, long before I

even knew it existed, and he had drawn it into the light so I could see it.

"Begin," he said and when I reached for the dagger sheathed at my hip, he shook his head. "No weapons. I would not want to scar that pretty face of yours."

I shrugged and removed the belt that held my dagger in place, discarding it on the grass as I held his gaze and smiled sweetly. "You're right. I wouldn't want to scar that pretty face of yours."

He smirked, but his silver eyes smouldered, the heat in them cranking up the fire that simmered in my veins whenever I was near him. "I did not realise you found me so handsome."

"Liar," I muttered and his smirk became a wide smile filled with pure male satisfaction and pride. "I didn't realise you found me so beautiful."

"Liar," he shot back. "There is no wolf more beautiful in my court."

I huffed and unlaced my boots, evening things out between us. "I'm fully aware I'm the only wolf in your court, you know. You need a lot of training in the compliments department."

I kicked my boots away from me. The dewy grass was cold against my bare soles, but it felt good as I scrunched my toes in it, feeling that direct connection between my body and nature that spoke to my inner wolf, drawing it to the fore.

"Then allow me to try again." He mock bowed, his forearm grazing his stomach as he lowered his head, and then lifted it to look right at me, a wicked light in his eyes as he purred, "I have never met a wolf more fuckable than you, my little lamb."

I scowled at him even as I blushed, my entire body flushing with heat. "Fuckable and beautiful are not interchangeable. And might I remind you, you turned down the chance to fuck me, so I can't be that fuckable."

Oh my gods, had I really said that?

His sly grin scorched my blood. "Oh, Saphira, I am going to fuck you. There is no doubt about that. I am going to fuck you so hard, so thoroughly, you will be irrevocably marked as mine."

"Because you paid for me." I needed to shut up, but some pathetic, needy part of me needed to hear him say this combustible heat between us was real.

He prowled towards me, gaze dark and hungry. "Because I want you."

My breath lodged in my throat together with my heart, and I struggled for air as I lost myself in his eyes, in that look that devoured me and awakened me at the same time, rousing heat in my veins that demanded we forget the fighting and just jump straight to the other thing.

"Begin," he purred and my wolf howled in agreement, jumping right to the other thing as my blood caught aflame.

I was so caught up in the hunger swirling inside me that I almost missed the fact his fist was flying towards my face. I barely dodged the blow, ducking to my right, my mind racing to catch up with what was happening.

Fighting. Not fucking. Fighting.

Heart pounding, I drew on all my training, every routine that Vyr had drilled into me coming to the fore. I stepped into him, closing the distance between us, my left fist flying for his kidneys. Only I hit nothing but air. I blinked. He was gone.

Not gone, I realised as he kicked me in the back of my leg and it crumpled, sending me into a very ungainly sprawl on the damp grass.

Just too fast for me to track.

I shoved to my feet and whirled towards him, bringing my fist around with me, using momentum to my advantage in a blow aimed at his chest. He dodged back a step and smacked my arm with the flat of his hand, knocking my blow off course.

"I had thought Vyr would have done a better job than this,"

he muttered as he easily blocked another fumbled attempt to hit him, bracing his forearm against mine as he sidestepped and then shoved me in the chest, knocking me back.

I growled, frustration beginning to get the better of me.

And hurled myself into a pattern of attack that Vyr had declared suited my speed and agility, keeping low to make myself a smaller target as I put on a burst of speed to pass Kaeleron and come around behind him. He twisted with me, denying me his back, and caught my fist as it flew at him.

I screamed as he twisted my arm and then shoved, releasing me as I stumbled backwards.

"Try harder," he snarled.

Anger flashing in his eyes.

Or was it disappointment?

That feeling rolled through me as I launched another attack out of nowhere, a swift barrage of punches without a trace of my intent, a move that had caught Vyr off guard more than once.

Kaeleron huffed and blocked each one as he moved back step by step, keeping the distance between us steady, his hands as swift as mine were, allowing not a single blow to touch him.

"This isn't fair," I snapped, glaring at him as he resumed a relaxed pose, waiting for me to try again.

Acting as if I wasn't a threat to him.

Bastard.

I breathed hard, anger spiking as frustration coiled tightly within me.

"Life is not fair, little wolf. It is brutal. It is cold. It is pain. Anyone who believes otherwise is a blind fool." Kaeleron extended his arm towards me, turned his hand palm upwards and rolled his fingers, gesturing for me to come at him again.

"You have centuries of experience," I bit out. "You've been

trained for war. Have fought *in* wars. I don't stand a chance and you know it."

"Not with that attitude, you do not," he growled and narrowed his eyes on me as his jaw flexed. "Land one blow on me, little wolf. That is all I am asking."

One blow.

He said it as if it was easy. Possible.

He might as well have asked me to pluck the moon from the sky.

The difference between our skill was vast and undeniable, and infuriating.

But I wasn't going to give up.

I curled my hands into tight fists and drew down a slow breath to steady my heart, to calm my nerves, and sharpen my focus. One blow. I could do this. Just one hit. That was all I had to land. My wolf side growled and bared fangs at him as he shifted his left foot behind him, a move he had done more than once, revealing he favoured his right side. My gaze darted over him, calculating, studying my prey. He would try to come around me again, using his speed to gain the upper hand.

This time, I would be ready for him.

I wasn't.

I let out a bark of frustration as pain splintered across my lower spine, his blow no harder than Jenavyr's had been during training, but infinitely more frustrating.

"Stop leaving yourself open," he purred into my ear, his breath caressing my skin.

I whirled, my right fist flying at where his head should have been.

Should. Have. Been.

Instead, he was behind me again, hands clamping down onto the curve of my waist as he chuckled in my ear.

"Fuck. You," I snarled and stomped with my left foot, aiming it at his ankle.

Hitting nothing but grass.

He was in front of me before I noticed, his fist stopping just short of slamming into my stomach. The control he had. The skill. It stole my breath and roused my primal instincts, stirring my wolf side into a frenzy within me as he launched into a barrage of punches I struggled to block. I admired his masculine strength and warrior skill, the way he turned this fight into a deadly dance, even as I grew more and more frustrated.

That frustration got the better of me when I missed blocking one of his punches and it struck my right shoulder, knocking it back, and I followed up with a right hook of my own while he was distracted by what he had done.

And he blocked my forearm with his, knocking it away with more force this time.

I stumbled and fell, hitting the grass hard, humiliated by how easily he could predict my moves and block them, by how weak I was.

That dreadful, cold feeling of self-loathing became a burning whirlwind of anger and rage as he loomed over me and sneered.

"Is that all you have?"

That question rang in my ears, mocking me, flooding me with doubt. Was it all I had? Where was that strength he had seen in me?

Did he think I was weak now?

The thought that he might was like fuel on the fire blazing within me, and a desperate, wild need to prove I wasn't was the catalyst that sparked something within me to life.

Something fierce.

Something untamed.

Before I knew what I was doing, I was launching from the

ground, sailing through the air towards him and shifting as I went. The sound of ripping material accompanied the screaming pain of my bones elongating and shrinking, the kiss of cool air fading under the insulating warmth of the white fur that swept down my body. All of my senses sharpened, the scent of Kaeleron swirling around me as he stood there.

Shocked.

Open.

My paws slammed against his body.

My fangs sank into his shoulder.

My claws raked down his chest.

Blood coated my tongue, the metallic tang of it bringing me to my senses.

Oh gods.

I shoved off him, panting hard, springing away to a safe distance as I stared at him, at the blood trickling down his chest as he slowly lowered his surprised gaze to it.

What had I done?

He slowly canted his head and arched an eyebrow at the bleeding gashes on his chest.

And then he blinked and when his eyes opened, he was looking right at me.

"Oh," he murmured, voice low and eerily calm. "I did not realise we were letting our beasts out."

My ability to breathe left me as his skin paled to moon white, as inky shadows branched from his eyes and his lips darkened towards black, and the sculpted planes of his face grew more angular, feral. His lips split in a wide vicious grin that revealed jagged sharp teeth and his fingers flexed, the upper thirds of them stained black like the skin around his eyes as his nails transformed into inch long onyx claws. The pointed tips of his ears grew sharper as he inhaled, his chest straining with the hard breath he took, luring my gaze down to it.

Beautiful lines of ancient fae markings appeared on his alabaster skin, sweeping from his armpits along the line of his square pectorals to trail around their forms to his throat and over his collarbones where they faded to nothing.

But it was his eyes that bewitched me the most, had me frozen in place as I stared into them.

Crimson bled into the silver, like ink swirling in water, leaving only a jagged band of that familiar colour around his elliptical pupils.

I had never seen anything like him as shadows gathered around him.

Knew I should fear him.

Everything in me knew it, like some buried instinct that warned this male before me was dangerous, deadly, and whispered at me to run. Run fast. Run far. Before he could kill me.

Something dark glittered in his eyes, something vicious and dangerous.

I denied the instinct to run from him, shutting it down with great effort, because the only way to stop this from escalating was to do the opposite. It was to face him and apologise for what I had done.

I let the shift come over me, shaking off my wolf form.

He disappeared in a blur of night. The hairs on my nape rose, my skin prickling as awareness shot down my spine as I finished the shift.

As he slammed into me, his full body pressing against mine, startling me.

A gasp tore from my lips as he grasped my nape in a bruising grip.

And sank sharp teeth into my shoulder.

Before the pain could even register, he pulled his fangs from my flesh and swiped his tongue over the puncture wounds, the slowness of that caress sending pleasure rippling through me. I trembled with it as he eased back, staring at the marks he had placed on me, a crinkle forming between the dark slashes of his eyebrows. His hand lowered to my neck, his fingers teasing the over-sensitive skin around his bite mark, his expression unreadable.

His strange eyes lifted to meet mine, something flaring in them as they widened.

And then he was gone.

And I was alone.

I looked down at myself.

And very naked.

My ruined clothes lay a few feet from me, utterly unusable now. I could shift and trot back to the castle, but I didn't want to let my wolf out when others might see it. I still couldn't believe I had shown it to Kaeleron so easily, sharing that part of myself with him.

All because I had lost my temper.

I huffed and stilled as his scent teased me, my gaze drifting to the source of it.

His clothes.

I shrugged and padded across the grass to them, picked up his tunic and slipped it on. It smelled strongly of him, all wild winter storm and masculine strength, and I drew down a deep breath as I bought the material to my nose, savouring his scent. I hooked his boots over my forearm and buttoned the tunic that reached my knees, covering me nicely. I strolled back to my own boots and weapon belt, adding them to the bundle in my arms, and headed for the trees.

I paused at the edge of the glade, glancing back at it, seeing a replay of Kaeleron's transformation and how quickly he had moved.

I brushed my fingers over the marks on my throat and shivered again, my nape tingling and need pooling low in my belly.

I shut down that hunger born of my primal instincts to mate, to feel my fated one's fangs in my nape, marking me as his. It would never happen, and while Lucas's rejection had deeply wounded me, part of me was glad he had done it now.

I was glad I hadn't found myself bound to such a ruthless, despicable and unworthy male.

I turned back towards the castle, feeling as if I was turning my back on my past, on that make-believe love I had felt for Lucas, shutting a door on a fantasy that I should have known was just that—a fantasy. Real life wasn't all white picket fences, an adoring and faultless mate, a blissful bond and two point four pups. Kaeleron was right about that. And I had been a blind fool. Believing life was fair, that my mate was faultless, that everything my parents had done had been right.

But now my eyes were open.

I strode towards the looming castle, tightly hugging my boots and Kaeleron's to my chest, breathing in his scent and replaying our fight, picking out all the places I had made mistakes or could have done something different to turn the tides in my favour.

Studying it so next time I would beat him.

Without needing to let my wolf out.

I saw a flash of him transformed into darkness and fear made flesh, a male most would have found terrifying and would have run from.

Something was very wrong with me.

Because rather than finding that new, darker appearance disturbing and frightening.

I had wanted him.

And rather than wanting to run from him.

I had wanted to run *to* him.

CHAPTER 37

KAELERON

Letting my darker side steal control of me had been a mistake, but surrendering to my urge to sink my fangs into her delicate flesh had been unforgivable.

I paced across the sitting area of my quarters, still barefoot and unclothed from the waist up, my steps silent on the black marble floor and ornate rug as I moved between the door to the bathroom and my armoury, passing the gold-framed black couches that glimmered in the combination of candlelight from the low wooden table and firelight. My mind churned with disconnected thoughts. Flashes of Saphira fighting, of her laughing, of her looking at me with heat in her eyes.

With something more than lust.

That look in her eyes when I had realised what I had done, when I had found the strength to drag my gaze from my marks on her throat, denying that primal howl of victory within me, had branded me as completely as I had marked her. Such hunger. Such ferocity.

The taste of her...

I closed my eyes and drew down a steadying breath,

attempting to calm the raging need to find her, to pierce her delicate flesh with my fangs again and draw her essence into me, mingling it with mine to keep a piece of her with me.

Dangerous.

I exhaled hard, purging that need. Saphira was a tool. A weapon I would wield. Nothing more.

Yet I found myself glancing at the arched windows that punctuated the black stone walls on either side of my canopied bed, at the fading light, and worry gnawed at my insides, hollowing me out. Had she returned safely from the glade? I drifted to the sheer blue gold-edged fabric that hung from the ceiling above my bed, sweeping through heavy rings affixed to the wooden beams towards gilded columns and draped around them to leave my bed visible to me, and frowned at the world outside the window as I rested my hand on one of those columns.

I should not have left her there.

I should not have let my shock get the better of me like that, leaving her unprotected.

I bit out a curse and stormed to the wardrobes that lined the wall near the door and pulled the doors open, gaze scanning the contents as I hastily formed a plan. I grabbed a loose black shirt and tugged it on over my head, and teleported to the corridor outside her room. I pressed my hand to the wooden door, my eyes slipping shut as I focused my senses, narrowing them to the room on the other side.

And relief swept through me as I sensed her there.

I turned to leave but the door before me opened, stopping me in my tracks, and her soft gasp teased my ears.

"Kaeleron," she whispered, blinking startled blue eyes up at me, and fidgeted with something she held to her chest. "I was... I was just coming to return these."

She looked down at the bundle of black blending with her robe.

My tunic and boots, I realised.

She shoved them at me, catching me off guard as her scent stole my focus. It grew stronger as I took the tunic and boots from her, and I frowned as I lifted the black jacket to my nose and inhaled.

Smelling her on it.

"This smells like you," I purred, savouring the rose that climbed her cheeks and how she averted her gaze. "You wore this."

She nodded. "It seemed better than parading naked through the castle."

I barely leashed the growl that rumbled up my throat at the thought of her walking through my castle naked, for all to see. Her curves were mine alone to admire.

I caught myself breathing in her scent on my tunic again and frowned as I forced myself to lower it. Still, some part of me growled low, possessively this time, enjoying the thought of her wearing my clothes, rubbing my scent all over her supple body.

"I'm sorry I lost my temper." She loosed a long sigh and shook her head. "I don't know what came over me."

"I do," I countered. "You did not like feeling weak. You did not like that I was faster than you."

"Fine, I do know what came over me," she muttered. "I hate being weak."

"You are not weak." I shook my head when she lifted her eyes to meet mine and I could see the denial forming in them, on her lips. "You are strong, Saphira. Stronger than you believe—than your pack let you believe. That lack of belief in your strength is the reason I beat you."

Her expression softened and warmed, a pretty little blush not born of desire but of gratitude touching her cheeks.

"That and you need to work on controlling your emotions. You are too easy to provoke. Your body is strong, but your mind is weak."

Her face scrunched up and she smacked me on the chest.

"You are only proving my point." I arched a brow at her.

"You're lucky I don't bite you again," she shot back, looking ready to carry out that threat.

"Ah, little wolf." I leaned closer to her as I lowered my voice to a purr. "If you bite me again, I shall bite you again."

I trailed my fingers over the spot I had bitten, feeling her tremble beneath them.

"Did you like it?" I skimmed my fingers higher, grazing her fluttering pulse in her throat.

"No," she bit out.

The heat of her cheeks as I feathered my fingers across their scarlet surface betrayed her.

"This pretty blush says otherwise," I murmured.

She slapped my hand away from her face. "It's anger making them flushed."

I chuckled, watching that colour deepen in response to it. "I will freely admit that I rather enjoyed you claiming my neck with your fangs."

"I wasn't claiming anything," she snapped, heat darkening her eyes as she turned her cheek to me.

I caught her other one and turned her face back towards me, my gaze clashing with hers. "You were not? You bit and clawed me—marked me—and then you wore my clothing, mingling our scents on your tight little body."

She hit me with a murderous glare.

"Stop twisting what happened." Her anger and frustration

deflated as she glanced at my shoulder. "How is it? I'm sorry I did that."

I feathered my fingers down to her throat, to the bite mark she was hiding beneath her dark robe. "I am not."

"Gods, you're annoying," she muttered, planted her hands against my chest and shoved me backwards, over the threshold of her room. "Go away."

She did not mean it. I knew it the moment she lingered, her palms searing my chest through my shirt, her heart thundering in my ears as she stared at her hands. And swallowed.

Her fingers flexed the tiniest amount, but I noticed.

Just as I had noticed how she had stood her ground when faced with my other side, my true nature, rather than fleeing. The strength she denied having had shone so brightly in that moment that I could not comprehend how she still did not see it. I had seen it the moment I set eyes on her in that cage, and I had been convinced that strength would be crushed under the weight of her new situation once she had awakened in my world, sold into service.

But instead, she had risen to every challenge.

She was bold.

Brave.

Even when faced with people far stronger, and infinitely more dangerous, than she was.

I lingered with her, a war brewing within me as I breathed in her scent and gazed at her, drinking in her beauty. I should not be here. I knew it. This obsession with her was dangerous, and this path I was treading was deadly. I had a plan, and I had to stick to it, no matter the cost.

Vengeance was everything.

Something I doubted such a beautiful, tender soul could understand.

I went to step back but her fingers tightened in my shirt,

clutching the material and holding me in place. I could have teleported if I had wanted, leaving her empty handed, but I found myself lingering again, filled with a profound need to remain here with her.

Doubts clouded her blue eyes, the soft lines of her face hardening as she struggled with something, making me realise I was not the only one who waged an internal battle this night.

When she grew increasingly tense, her war becoming more intense under the oppressing silence, I could not hold my tongue. I broke the silence for her, shattering its hold on her.

"When you shifted, you caught me off guard. Something no one has managed in a long time." I kept my voice even, steady even as nerves rose within me, stripping me of my strength. A foolish response. I had no reason to be nervous. I had only confessed the truth. Yet I felt oddly vulnerable as I stood before her, enduring her scrutiny as she studied me. I saw her wolf before me, her pure white fur as bright as the full moon, her eyes as blue as the ones peering into my soul now. "Your wolf is beautiful."

Those soft words left my lips unbidden.

A confession that stripped me bare.

And the blush that darkened her cheeks was the most bewitching one yet.

I wanted to touch it and feel the heat of it as she struggled to hold my gaze, as a need to look at anything but me filled her, as if she could avoid what I had said by simply looking away. Or maybe she did not know how to react, maybe no one had ever told her she was beautiful.

Or if they had, they had not really meant it.

So I held her gaze, framed her face with my palms to keep it locked on me, and stared deep into her soul to ensure she heard me.

"You are beautiful, Saphira, and I find your beauty is not

only on the surface. Your inner beauty outshines the external. I am not sure how it is possible, but it is true. You are a rare, and wonderful thing to behold, and to know."

"Shut up," she muttered and lowered her gaze.

"Tell me you believe me and I will shut up," I husked.

She sighed and her features shifted, that war erupting again, born of my request and my words this time.

And then she mumbled, "I believe you."

"Good..." I released her, took hold of the hand I had gifted with a band of moonlight, and pressed a kiss to the back of it, making her jump, "...night."

She gripped my hand when I went to leave and I glanced at her, waiting to see if she had finally found her voice.

"Do all unseelie have it?" she whispered.

And there it was.

"Have it?" I said, knowing exactly what she was talking about but wanting to hear her say it.

She was almost shy as she said, "The beast."

I smirked. "It is not really a beast, and you need not fear me when I am like that. I am fully in control, just as you are when you are in your wolf form. It merely makes me stronger, faster—"

"More dangerous," she put in.

I shrugged that off. "As does your wolf."

She toyed with my hand, pressing the tips of her fingers against mine. "So is everyone here capable of what you did?"

I nodded. "All unseelie have another side, as do all seelie. Whose side is more dangerous is a matter of perspective. The seelie are as dangerous—as dark—as we are... but more devious, employing lies to cover the vicious truth of them."

She frowned up at me. "You really don't like the seelie."

I shook my head, seeing no reason to conceal my hatred of them.

"Because they're sworn enemies of the unseelie?" She was probing, her look curious as she studied me, seeking the deeper truth of my feelings for the other half of this world.

I hiked my shoulders again. "Among other reasons. None of which I particularly feel like talking about right now."

"Hint taken." She smiled and dropped my hand. "Good night, Kaeleron."

It was my turn to stop her.

"Your wolf shares your hair colour. Is that normal?" I was not sure what I had expected her to look like as a wolf, but I had been shocked by the sight of her, so white as snow. As the moon.

So ethereal and beautiful, as if she had been made to walk in my world.

She shrugged her slender shoulders. "It's pretty common. My mother is almost as blonde as I am, but her wolf is more of a tan colour. And Dad has mousy hair like Riordan, but his wolf is brown. But Everlee... my best friend... she's a redhead in human and wolf form."

She came and leaned against the doorframe close to me, her eyes brightening as she thought about her pack, radiating bewitching warmth that had me leaning opposite her, closer still.

"Chase... now he's blond with blue eyes, but his wolf is tan with golden eyes. And Morden has dark brown hair and grey eyes, but his wolf is black... and huge." Her eyes widened as she said those last two words. "He's probably the biggest wolf in our pack."

"Is Morden another of your cousins?" I growled, not liking how her demeanour had changed abruptly as she had shifted between the two males. Chase had elicited warmth, but this Morden, he seemed to elicit something else.

"Good gods, no." She laughed those words. "No. He's my

friend. I've known him my whole life and he serves as one of the pack protectors."

"A warrior?"

She nodded.

I did not like the sound of that, or how she looked when I asked, "Were you close?"

"We *are* close." She frowned at me, easing back a few inches, hurt flashing in her eyes. "You speak of Morden like I'm never going to see him again."

If I had my way, she would not.

"Did you really send word to my pack?" she said, watching me closely, as if I would lie to her about such a thing. I nodded. Relief washed across her delicate features and some of the tension in her shoulders faded. "Have you heard back from them yet?"

I shook my head this time. "I have not heard from my messenger yet."

"Doesn't that worry you?" She inched closer to me again, a desperate kind of look in her eyes, swirled with concern.

"Not at all. Navigating the mortal world can be difficult for fae at times. It is likely the messenger is on his way home, travelling between the waygates that act as portals between our worlds, and will bring word of your pack soon."

She sighed and sagged against the doorframe. "I miss them. I miss Everlee, and Morden and Chase. I miss my mother and father. I miss them all."

Each word was a blade in my heart, one that twisted deep and leaked poison, but I refused to feel bad about what I had done. I had spared her from a life of torment and torture, had given her freedom and had even gone as far as training her, helping her hone her skills and her strength.

And yet she still wanted to return to her pack.

That I could not understand.

"You still long for home, to return to a place where you felt caged? To people who allowed you to be captured and sold?" I frowned down at her, trying to understand why she would want such a thing, when she had railed at me about keeping my people caged to protect them. "You despise how the wolf who sold you had caged you... despised how I did the same thing at first... yet you would willingly subject yourself to a cage by returning to your pack?"

She glared at me, anger flaring in her eyes as her lips flattened. "That is my home!"

Those words lacked conviction.

Her gaze wandered to the windows behind her. To the world beyond them. To my court.

My home.

Sensing she would lash out if I pushed her on this subject, and slowly growing aware of her reasons for wanting to return to her pack—a desire born out of a sense of duty and loyalty more than love—I retreated into the hall behind me, giving her space.

"I am taking over your training."

Her gaze whipped to me.

"But there will be no training tomorrow. You are free to do as you please, but know that Jenavyr and Riordan will be overseeing new recruits coming in from the lowlands and Belkarthen, so my sister will not be available to escort you into town. Meaning you will be adventuring alone if you choose to go down into the city. I do recommend you remain within the city walls."

"So you're ordering me to not leave Falkyr. Got it." She looked pleased by that as she wrapped her arms around herself as she stepped back into the room, as if it was more freedom than she had expected, and then she canted her head, her gaze raking over me. "What will you be doing?"

"Oh, you will be spending time with me. No need to fret about that. But alas... I have meetings all day, so you will have to survive without my company until evening." I summoned my shadows, drawing them to me as my focus shifted to my rooms and I prepared to teleport there. "You will dine with me and tell me of your day... so do make it interesting."

As I disappeared into the inky darkness swirled with golden starlight, she muttered sarcastically.

"Yes, my king."

Her king.

I growled at that, hunger ripping through me at the thought of her being mine, a wild need to possess her flooding me and demanding I return to her.

And finish what we had started in the glade.

Claiming what was mine.

CHAPTER 38
SAPHIRA

So many books. I was never sure where to begin whenever I stepped into the library each afternoon. The pile of books accumulating on one of the tables was testament to my indecision, or perhaps I just had so many that I wanted to read, more than was possible really. Unless I remained here in the Shadow Court for a very long time.

I set the book about the collected history of the unseelie down on my lap and leaned back in the huge plush black velvet covered armchair near the beautifully carved stone fireplace and chimney, sighing as I tilted my head right back to gaze up at the twilight-kissed aurora dancing above the ornate glass dome.

I couldn't stop thinking about what Kaeleron had said to me last night about my pack.

Or that I was beginning to feel at home here.

And so free.

It was strange. Kaeleron had bought me, I had been sold into a life of service, and he could be a demanding prick at times, but I didn't feel caged here. Even when I knew I should.

I sank deeper into the comfortable seat, my entire body relaxing as I watched the sky shifting and dancing.

My parents had raised me to serve others, and to place the needs of the pack above my own. My whole life had been about taking care of others rather than myself. I had accepted that life as normal, just the way of things, and had tried so hard to set aside my own desires, striving to please my parents and my pack.

But looking back, my life hadn't been mine.

It had belonged to the pack.

I hadn't noticed how oppressed I truly was until Kaeleron had come along, giving me a gift I never imagined possible or knew I wanted. He had bought me, taken my freedom from me, and yet I had never felt so free.

I had never had days like I had here, where I was in charge of what I did. Where I had complete autonomy to decide about things that affected me and was able to do as I pleased. If I wanted to lie in bed all day, I could. Or I could explore the town some more, without a guard in sight. I hadn't failed to notice that since Kaeleron had branded me, I had lost my shadows. The guards were gone, and I had gained the freedom to walk where I pleased within the protective walls of Falkyr.

And maybe it wasn't just because he had branded me.

But because he had come to trust me.

I had proven I had little desire to escape him. I hadn't once attempted it. And it wasn't because I didn't want to see the world beyond the walls, or even see my pack again.

It was because this castle felt like home.

And some part of me didn't want to leave it.

Didn't want to leave him.

Another long sigh escaped me as I pondered that dangerous desire. I had fallen once for a male who had flattered me, who had showered me with gifts and with affection, and it hadn't turned out well for me. It would be dangerous to fall for Kaeleron when he concealed so much from me, things that had been beginning to bother me in recent days.

I sat up and looked at the smaller stack of books I had set aside on the ornate oak coffee table in front of me and made a decision.

It was time I learned more about my purpose here.

Because I knew without a doubt now that Kaeleron hadn't purchased me for my virginity.

I set down the book I had been skimming through, seeking something that might amuse Kaeleron at dinner, and grabbed the four books I had found and already devoured. Books filled with fables and fairy tales.

I tucked them to my chest as I strode from the library, nerves rising a little as I made my way down through the castle to the courtyard and then hurried across it, fearing Kaeleron might see me and might stop me.

The arched entrance to the dungeon was gloomy, little light making it down into the stairwell, and I had to use all of my senses to find my way down without slipping and falling on the damp stone steps.

When I neared the bottom, flickering torches chased back the darkness, revealing the cell where I had spent my first few days in the Shadow Court. I glanced off to the right, to the place I had discarded the blanket when I had cast it aside upon discovering it had been the one to cover my cage at the auction, my throat tightening and dark moments from that night flickering across my mind to still my steps and seize control of my body. My breathing grew laboured as my heart thundered, panic rising to the fore as I stared at the spot where it had been and was now gone.

"Saphira." Neve's soft voice shattered the spell that blanket had cast on me and I started, whirling towards her.

The pretty dragon shifter stood by the bars of her home, dressed in a stunning green gown today and her braided hair like spun gold. Her bright amber eyes tracked me as I approached her cell and she didn't move as I reached for the lock on her door and froze.

"It's not locked." I looked at her, sure she wasn't aware of the fact she could have left this place whenever she wanted.

"Of course it isn't." She went to the door and slid the bolt back, her tone questioning my intelligence. "I am not a prisoner."

The door eased open and power lashed at me, buffeting me and making my limbs tremble, as if she had opened the floodgates and a great torrent had burst free.

"Hurry now," she murmured.

I slipped inside, sensing her urgency, and she quickly closed the door behind me.

"It is better it remains closed." She shuffled over to her armchair and pulled it across the flagstones, closer to the bars of her cell, and I frowned as I noticed her hands were shaking as she grabbed the footstool and positioned it a few feet from the chair. She noticed me staring and smiled, but there was sorrow in it, and a trace of fear that shocked me. Neve had seemed so fearless, but opening her cell door for only a second had rattled her. "I do not wish to speak of it."

I nodded. "I'd never make you talk about it, but if you ever need someone to speak to, you can ask for me, Neve."

Because I had been that terrified once, only I had been shut inside an inescapable cage at the time. Neve feared the opposite. She feared leaving hers.

"Now, what can I do for you?" She patted the footstool and settled in her armchair, her smile brighter now.

"I brought you these. I noticed you were reading what looked like a fairy tale when we met and I thought you might like them." I offered her the books and her golden eyebrows rose high on her forehead as she looked between the books and me.

"Kaeleron has allowed you in his library." She sounded surprised by that.

I shrugged. "He's also been training me, and I can wander around the city as I please."

"There is hope for the boy yet." Neve tugged the books from my grip as I pondered just how old she was if she was calling a male of over five hundred years a boy. The dragon studied their spines, her eyes brightening with flecks of blazing gold as she inspected each book and murmured to herself, "How delightful you all are. You are lucky the little wolf found you. You shall have a good home here."

I realised it was fortunate I had already read the books, because they were more than books to Neve. They were treasure. I glanced beyond her, to the corner of her room that had been hidden from view in my cell.

To the piles of books and trinkets stacked here.

Neve growled.

My gaze shot to her and I tensed as she stared me down, her eyes flaming gold, her teeth dangerously sharp.

"Mine," she snarled.

I held my hands up in front of me. "Of course. I wouldn't dream of touching anything. I was just admiring it. Such a beautiful collection. You must be very proud of it."

My smile wobbled as she continued to bare fangs at me, but the fire in her eyes dimmed and then she beamed at me, her expression bright and carefree again.

"Is it not? I have been working on it for decades now. I am still collecting of course, looking for those finer pieces that will add to the beauty of it." Her gaze landed on me as I stared at the haphazard pile, noticing the worn and dented pewter mug on top of one of the books, a few copper coins scattered here and there, and a ruby-red stick that looked as if it might have come from the Forest of Blood. Her hoard was eclectic to say the least.

I realised she was still staring at me.

Or more precisely my hand.

I covered the ring on my finger with my other hand, and her face darkened, her lips flattening and the corners turning downwards as I stole it from view.

"You can't have it," I said, the words flying from my lips and my hackles rising at the thought she might try to take the ring from me. It was mine, and I had grown terribly fond of it in the short time I had been wearing it. "Kaeleron made it for me and he wouldn't be happy if I lost it."

She huffed. "Unfair. I want a ring. He makes you pretty things. Makes himself pretty things he will not give me. I want something."

"What pretty thing of his do you want?" I tilted my head and studied her as she muttered things in a language I didn't know under her breath.

"His sword," she said bluntly in a tongue I could understand.

I chuckled. "Well, I don't think he will surrender that easily. He worked for a long time on it and according to him, it's his crowning achievement."

"Then he can make me a sword... or a ring... or a bracelet, yes, I should like a bracelet. I do not have a bracelet." She glanced at her treasure trove, gaze quickly scanning it. "Yes, yes. I do not have a bracelet."

"I will tell him you want one." I leaned over and touched her hand, trying to get her to focus back on me rather than her treasure.

Her gaze shot down to my ring and lodged on it, and as I moved my hand, her gaze tracked it, eyes wide and glassy.

"Shiny," she murmured. "White for Lucia."

I was losing her again, so I folded my hands together, stealing the ring from view, and she frowned at them, a little pout to her lips.

"I'll let you see it again if you answer a few questions." I wasn't above bargaining to get what I wanted.

She eagerly nodded. "Yes, yes. Very well. Ask your questions about Kaeleron and the path you walk together, but know I have been bidden to remain silent on the subject so there are things I cannot say… and things I can say."

"Why did Kaeleron buy me?" I leaned towards her, resting my elbows on my thighs, desperate to know the answer to that question. Even if she couldn't tell me anything else, perhaps she could confirm my suspicions about this.

"Vengeance tastes delicious, and Kaeleron is starving. Each day that passes without feeding, he only grows more hungry, more reckless."

"You said I was necessary. That he can't walk this path alone. You mean I'm vital to his vengeance."

She nodded.

I exhaled hard, shock sweeping through me even though I had suspected as much. "He needed me strong. That's what he said to me here in this dungeon. He made me eat because he needed me strong. Why?"

"Because you were in danger of breaking, and you are no good to him broken."

"Is that the reason he let me leave the cell, too? Because I was breaking." I had been. I had been in a vicious downwards spiral, letting my grief and my pain slowly devour my will to live. And then I had been moved to my current rooms and shown this incredible world, and little by little, my grief and pain faded and were forgotten.

Replaced by a hunger for vengeance.

"What is my purpose?" My breath lodged in my throat as I waited to hear the answer to that question, as if everything hinged on it.

But Neve shook her head. "That I do not know. The visions are fickle. They refuse to come, and I fear if they do not come soon..."

"What? What will happen to you? Will Kaeleron hurt you?" My hackles rose again at the thought of him harming Neve.

"How ill you still think of him, despite all he has done." Pity shone in Neve's amber eyes as she looked at me.

Guilt churned my stomach.

"I never know what to think. I never know what he's capable of," I admitted, hating myself a little for jumping to the conclusion that he might harm Neve, when he had shown me how protective he was of those he cared about.

"He is not a monster, not to those he loves. He only becomes a monster when those he loves are threatened... as you well know."

Flashes of Elanaluvyr's battered body hanging in the courtyard crossed my eyes.

A violent death Kaeleron had wrought because the fae female had hurt me.

Had become a threat to me.

"Kaeleron would never hurt me," she said with utter confidence and opened one of the books, her gaze scanning the first page. "He would ask me to force a vision, and in doing so I would hurt myself."

That sounded a lot like Kaeleron would be the one responsible for hurting her if he forced her to have a vision.

"He seems content to attempt to decipher your role in his vengeance without my assistance though." Neve flicked the page, a small smile teasing her lips as she glanced at my hands, at that hidden ring. "In fact, he seems to be rather enjoying it."

Her head lifted and she sniffed the air.

And then waved me towards the door.

"Run along. A storm is coming."

A storm?

I scented the air too, and smelled nothing but the musty dampness that clung to the stones surrounding us.

"Visit me again soon," Neve said, her eyes glittering with gold as she stroked the books on her lap. "Bring me my present."

I nodded as I pushed to my feet and went to the door of her cell, opening it only enough to squeeze through it, which seemed to please the dragon as she smiled fondly at the book on her lap and began humming softly.

The steps up from the dungeon seemed even darker as I climbed them, and I frowned at the heavy clouds that roiled in the sky as I exited the arched entrance, stepping out into the courtyard. Maybe Neve was right and there was a storm coming.

Not wanting to get caught out in it, I hurried to the castle and had barely made it inside before the skies opened. Thunder shook the building. I yelped as my shoulders hiked up, ducking my head as the vicious growl of it rolled over the land. I glanced back out at the courtyard, but the other side of the castle obscured my view as another great rumble of thunder made the ground beneath my feet quake and stole my breath.

I had never heard such a violent storm.

Wanting to see it, I hurried up the stairs to the first floor, to the bank of windows that rattled as another great boom shook them.

Lightning flashed across the mountains, forking wildly as it lashed at the jagged black peaks.

Crimson lightning.

It was both terrifying and beautiful as it struck at the world, illuminating it with bursts of blood red. Rain hammered the lands in thick sheets that obscured the mountains and devoured the sea beyond them, and wind whipped through the garden, battering the castle with such force I feared the windows might shatter.

My eyes widened as the storm raged, ravaging the world, driving sheets of water across the garden paths and tearing at the cloth hangings in the gazebo and arbours, and I realised something.

People were out in it, servants who rushed to gather the wooden chairs that were being pushed around in the gale.

And they weren't alone.

Kaeleron battled the wind, shielding his face with his forearm as he helped the servants chase down the unruly furniture and directed those without something to do towards the banners and hangings. Mad fools!

Thunder echoed around the black mountains. Waves crashed against the cliffs and the tower I could barely see beyond the docks, spraying white foam high into the air. Wind howled through the garden, battering the trees and making the water on the patios ripple violently before it slammed into the castle and rattled the glass before me.

I had never seen anything like this storm.

It was raw fury, pure power that made me feel small and vulnerable but bewitched by it.

Kaeleron almost lost his footing as wind ripped through the garden and sent one of the hangings from an arbour flying at him. It slapped against his side, plastered to him, and his face twisted as he struggled to peel it off him and fought to bundle it up.

I hurried down the steps, considering adding myself to the list of fools out in the rain, but when I reached the entrance to the garden, I almost ran into Kaeleron as he jogged inside.

Looking more like a drowned rat than a noble king.

He smirked at me, water rolling down his face from his soaked black hair, his tunic and trousers stuck to his skin. "Did I provide adequate entertainment?"

I looked beyond him to the almost empty garden. All the furniture and hangings were gone, and even some of the planters had been moved to more sheltered positions.

"I'm surprised you didn't just teleport straight inside and let the servants deal with it alone." I looked from the storm battered garden, watching the wind catch the rain as thunder boomed overhead, closer now, and I did my best not to shrink into a small ball as it shook the ground beneath my feet, refusing to let Kaeleron see how easily it shook me.

His silver gaze narrowed on me as he canted his head and ran long fingers through his hair, tousling it further. "Would you, if you had already been out there?"

I had been about to go out to help, even though I had been dry, and he knew it.

I shrugged. "I'm not a king. I'm just a wolf."

"Just a wolf," he echoed, sounding as if he didn't believe that for some reason, and then he beckoned me to move closer, a wicked light in his eyes. "You had your entertainment and now I shall have mine."

My lips flattened as I glared at him, aware where this was heading.

"I will give you a choice. Stand out in the storm for a full fifteen minutes, or help me out of my wet clothes while you run me a bath."

I huffed. “That’s an easy decision to make.”

I went to pass him, heading for the garden, but he snagged my arm and his skin was so cold my entire body locked up tight as goosebumps broke out across my skin. He was freezing, his skin paler than usual, and I looked him over and then beyond him to the storm that continued to rage, sheets of rain dancing across the garden as thunder rolled.

“Do I get a bath to warm up afterwards?” I asked as I looked from the storm to him.

“No.” His smile was feline. “Not even a handsome king to remove your wet clothes, unless you ask me nicely.”

I weighed it up. Freeze my ass off in a storm that was getting worse because I was feeling stubborn, or undress him.

I had done worse things and I had already seen him nude, so it was an easy choice to make after all.

“Fine.”

Darkness devoured us both.

And Kaeleron’s husky chuckle as I quickly clung to him caressed my cheek and teased my neck.

Rousing a dangerous, needy heat in my veins.

CHAPTER 39
KAELERON

It might have been a mistake to blurt that rash set of choices to Saphira.

I struggled for control as we stood in the luxurious bathroom of my quarters on the third floor, her small hands working each button of my wet tunic loose, her body maddeningly close to mine. Her heat seeped through my damp clothes, her pensive face bewitching me as she undid the final button, and her hot hands branding my chilled flesh as she brushed them across my chest, pushing the tunic off my shoulders.

Her scent swirled around me, faintly laced with the sweet tang of desire as she tiptoed and leaned closer, reaching to push the tunic off me. I shrugged out of it and her hands came down on my shoulders, her expression growing more pensive as her eyebrows pitched low and knitted hard, her gaze fixed on the spot where she had bitten me.

She traced her fingers over my skin, the bare caress unbearable as I clenched my fists, fighting the urge to take her in my arms, to trace my own fingers over her supple curves and chart every peak and valley of her body. Slowly. Leisurely. With my lips.

Sense told me to stop her now, to send her away, but I couldn't bring myself to obey it. I wanted more. Craved more.

The thunder of the water into the gold clawfoot tub next to us was as loud as the weather beyond the arched window as it filled the thick silence, as I battled to keep my hands to myself and resist the needs pounding within me, ones that demanded I carry her into my bedroom, spread her out on my bed and take her.

"It's healing nicely." Her voice warbled, betraying the rising nerves I could sense in her.

Not nerves born of fear.

I proved that by stroking my fingers across the exposed marks on her throat. My marks. She shivered, that heady scent of need growing thicker in the air between us, and her eyes slipped shut as she arched into my touch.

Her nerves were born of a need she couldn't control.

"Saphira—" I started but she stole my wits by tugging at my breeches, fingers nimbly loosening the ties.

She shoved them over my hips, hands grazing my backside, and tugged them down my legs and off me.

Leaving me naked.

And her on her knees before me.

It took all my considerable iron will to resist teasing her to discover whether she liked what she saw.

She stared openly at me, hunger darkening her eyes as her breaths came quicker, and her fingers twitched against her thighs.

"Saphira." I stepped back and she growled at me.

Growled.

I had heard her growl like that before, when she had been

lost to her mating heat and I had dared to deny her what she wanted.

This wasn't good.

I crossed the room in a handful of strides and grabbed my robe, my bath forgotten as Saphira continued to breathe faster and faster, her eyes growing wider and darker as she remained kneeling on the tiles, short claws pressing into her thighs now.

"I need to run," she muttered and shot to her feet.

"No, you need a male." I reached for her and she leaped backwards, shaking her head.

"Just a run. I just have so much energy to burn." She pulled at her blouse, seemingly unaware of the action as her face twisted. "I just... I need to run. I can burn off this energy."

Thunder rattled the windows and she twisted towards them, eyes flying wide as her breath hitched.

"You want to run in that?" I jerked my chin towards the storm. "Running will not help you with this. You cannot run from it."

"I can't be here." She clawed her silver hair back, pulling it tight. "I can't. Oh gods... not again."

Her face crumpled and she doubled over, grunting as she folded in on herself.

Any moment now, she was going to demand I find her a male, and I was going to lose my temper.

So I swept her into my arms, weathering her angry growls and half-hearted blows as I carried her tucked close to my chest.

And teleported.

I set her down in the small single room in the timber and stone cottage at the edge of the woods, halfway up the mountain. A retreat that I had built soon after my parents had died, close to the place I used to sit to admire the view when they had been alive. A place only I could go.

"You will be safe here. When the storm clears, you can run. But do not run far. Remain near the cottage. The woods here are wild. Dangerous. Do you understand?" I leaned over, bringing my face level with hers, needing to see that she did understand as she nodded. "I am going to lock the door and when the storm clears, I will unlock it. I will return soon to check on you and bring you some things to make you more comfortable."

She nodded again, shoulders trembling as her pupils dilated and she gripped her trousers, as if trying to stop herself from seizing hold of me.

I teleported away from her, to her rooms this time, unsure what I was doing. Keeping her in the castle when she was maddened by her mating frenzy would be a dangerously bad idea, the thought of her demanding I bring her males or seeking ones out enough to have my claws coming out. But locking her in a cottage?

She was safe from other males, but I wasn't sure it was going to help her.

She needed a male.

She needed pleasure and a release.

But she seemed set on denying that need.

And I wouldn't force her.

Despite how fiercely I wanted her.

Wanted to take care of her needs again, finding satisfaction in watching her break apart, in hearing her cry my name as pleasure overtook her.

Maybe she was better off in the cottage.

Far away from me.

I gathered a few things she might need—her robe and slippers, some books she had on her nightstand, and her blanket and pillow—and then teleported back to her.

She paced the room, strides swift as she clawed at her

blouse, shredding it as she stared straight ahead of her, muttering beneath her breath. Her face contorted and she grunted as she gritted her teeth, stifling a cry that still broke free of her lips.

"Walk it off. Walk it off," she mumbled, tearing at her blouse each time she said it as she resumed pacing, her eyes holding a world of pain.

"This is ridiculous. You know walking it off will not fix this. It will not make the pain go away." I set everything down on the double bed at one end of the cottage and turned back to face her. "You need pleasure, Saphira. Pleasure I want to give you."

She looked at me as if she hadn't noticed I was there, eyebrows pinned high on her forehead, blue eyes wide. Delirious. Maybe she hadn't noticed. Her gaze dropped to my chest, and the tip of her tongue swept across her lower lip.

"Considering devouring me, little wolf?" I smirked at her when she caught herself. "You know what you need."

She wrapped her arms around her waist and doubled over, screaming in pain.

Sweat dotted her brow as she fought for air.

"Do something," she sobbed. "Maybe magic could—"

"No amount of magic can help you with this. You need release. More than we did before." Something within me fractured when she lifted her head, her blue eyes imploring me, silently begging me to help her. I had never seen her looking so defeated.

She opened her mouth and I teleported to her and pressed a finger to it, silencing her, aware of what words would leave her lips. Ones I had thought would please me when she had signed that contract, when I had decided I would tease her until she was on her knees, desperate for me to take her.

My voice was low, rougher than I had ever heard it, as I

held her gaze and said, “Never beg. You never have to beg me. You only need to tell me what you need.”

“You,” she whispered and her face crumpled. “But I can’t ask that of you. I can’t use you like that... like a whore.”

I chuckled at her foolish belief that any part of what we were about to do amounted to using me.

I swept her back up into my arms and carried her towards the bed as I stared down into her eyes.

“We both want this. We both need this. Let me take care of you now, my little wolf.”

CHAPTER 40

KAELERON

Saphira was sleeping soundly by the time the storm broke and the rain ceased, but I still placed my palm against her damp forehead and closed my eyes. I muttered the words of a spell, one that would help her slumber and find the rest she needed. Her heat had been harder to break this time without giving her what she truly needed.

Something I still felt she was not ready for.

No matter how fiercely she begged for my cock.

By the Great Mother, it had been hard to deny her. I rubbed my palm down my still aching shaft, shuddering as pleasure tripped through my limbs. I wanted her. I wanted her so fiercely that I ached to lift my spell, to nestle between her soft thighs and wake her with my tongue, and then rise above her, feeding her my cock, watching her shatter as I fucked her.

I drew down a slow, steadying breath, finding the strength to deny that need I knew would ride me throughout the day, constantly simmering in my veins, demanding I return to her and give her what she wanted.

I gazed down at her as she curled up on her side, tears

dampening her cheeks, and feathered my fingers across them. When she could face her desires without feeling embarrassed about them, when I knew she would not regret what we did, then I would keep my promise.

I would ruin her to all other males.

Shadows swirled around me and I sank into them, reappearing in my rooms. I dressed quickly, tugging on a fresh black tunic and trousers, and shoving my feet into my boots. I laced them using magic as I teleported again, this time landing in the middle of the dungeon.

"Neve," I barked.

The dragon huffed as she rolled over in her small bed and yawned, blinking bleary eyes at me.

"You smell like Saphira," she muttered and burrowed into the blankets. "If you hurt her, I will kill you."

"So possessive. Saphira is not treasure to place on your pile." I smirked when she scowled at me.

"Saphira is more than mere treasure." Her eyes drifted closed and I thought I would lose her to sleep again, but then they snapped open and she shot up into a sitting position. "Bracelet!"

I arched a brow at her.

She threw the covers aside, revealing a plain white nightgown, and was across the cell in the blink of an eye, her slender hand peeking through the bars at me.

"Give bracelet." She scowled at me and then her expression morphed into one of possible disbelief. "The wolf did not tell you. I knew she would forget little Neve."

"Saphira came to you?" I frowned down at her as she pouted at her empty hand. I sighed. "Saphira promised you a bracelet."

"No. She promised she would ask you to make me a bracelet. You made her a shiny ring. I want a shiny bracelet."

So the little wolf had bargained with her in order to keep hold of the ring I had given her. It meant something to her. I ignored the way that warmed me, pretending not to notice it, and focused on the dragon.

"I will make you a bracelet. The most beautiful you have seen. But I need to know—"

"The storm brought another vision," she interjected and I stilled right down to my breathing as I waited, anticipation swirling through me. "You must find something shadowed that wishes to remain hidden. You must find An'sidwain."

"An'sidwain?" In the old language, it meant 'the heart', but it was also a stone—an ancient crystal of great power that was not from this world. "It was lost."

"What was lost can be found," Neve muttered. "I have seen it. It is a little blurry so I do not have specifics to give, but I have seen it. Saphira can lead you to it and you must take her to it. Only then will you have the future you desire."

"An'sidwain," I murmured as I gazed down at the bars that separated us. "There are only rumours about it. I have read accounts that mention the high king and two other unseelie courts, the Winter Court and the Dark Court."

Neither of which I wanted to take Saphira to. The Winter Court because Rhyn would likely charm her out of my grasp, and the Dark Court because I had my doubts it was there and the place was filled with fanatics thanks to the Obsidian Tower and the great shard of sapphire crystal it contained, a source of immense magical power.

"Tell me what you did see." I resisted the urge to order her to seek another vision, one that might give her a clearer picture of the location of An'sidwain. I had to be delicate about this, teasing the information out of her, because if I pushed, she would push back and refuse to give me anything. "The smallest things will do. Was there snow? Sand? Sapphire crystals?"

She frowned at my chest, her face pinching, and shook her head. "I told you. It was blurry. I saw Saphira. I saw you. I saw... I saw *it*."

An'sidwain.

"Could you see where it is if you tried again?" I studied Neve as she shrank back from the bars of her cell, subtly shaking her head as fear flickered in her amber eyes.

"Do not make me look," she whispered and I regretted pressing her as she retreated and pain flashed across her eyes as she grew breathless. "I cannot see it."

She was not talking about the location now. She was talking about An'sidwain.

Her greatest treasure.

And her greatest fear.

A dragon stone from ancient times.

CHAPTER 41

SAPHIRA

Inky night erupted across the door of the cottage I sat outside of on a bench set against the grey stone that formed the lower half of the wall. I kept my gaze on the forest that stretched below me, watching birds flitting between the trees, breathing deep of the clean air and savouring the silence.

"You are awake," Kaeleron said.

"You are so observant," I muttered, not in the mood for him.

He was ruining my peace.

It was hard to enjoy the warm glow of a morning after when the male who had been your bedroom partner the night before had done a disappearing act and once again taken no pleasure for himself. I had just about forgotten that he had rejected me again and here he was, reminding me.

"I have a task for you." He came to stand beside me.

I kept looking at the forest. "Bother someone else."

"I could order you to do it."

I slid him a black look. "I'm not in the mood."

"Because I refused to fuck you." He was observant and

astute. Bully for him. He huffed. "You are still not ready, little lamb."

I narrowed my eyes on him. "Stop calling me that."

"Fine. If you are ready, if you can honestly say you will not blame your heat or regret it, then get up on your feet and I shall fuck you right here against this wall." He slapped his hand against the timber and cream plaster near the door. "Come along then."

My lips flattened as nerves rose, as I saw in his eyes he was serious and that if I wanted it, he would do it. But the bastard was right. Every time I had asked him to take me, I had been wild and delirious, lost in the mating frenzy, and I would have regretted it in the morning, even more than I regretted asking him and having him turn me down.

"Come along, little wolf," he purred, silver eyes growing hooded. "I promised I would fuck you one day, and I mean to keep that promise. Is a wall not good enough for you?"

He petted the damned thing, and the vision of him taking me against it, slamming my back into it and shaking the plaster loose, was wickedly hot, but I managed to school my expression into a deadly glare.

"Some other time then." He smirked down at me.

I rolled my eyes. "What's this task you want me to carry out? And if it involves your manhood and some pun about meat, I *will* bite it off. This cottage is beautiful, but the room service sucks. I'm starving."

"I should have considered you would be hungry after such energetic activities." His smirk widened as he held his hand out to me. I eyed it suspiciously, earning an irritated huff from him. "I have no nefarious plans, little wolf. I simply intend to return you to the castle. Unless you wish to run the gauntlet of the forest and see whether luck is with you today or not. Hunters have reported the harpy numbers are rising again. Just yesterday one of them was injured during an encounter with them. No deaths so far this year, but it is not even summer yet."

I slapped my hand down onto his because I had read about the feathered half-female half-bird beings who stalked the woods of Lucia, and their taste for eating humanoid prey, and I didn't want to test my luck today. I was fast as a wolf, but I was tired too. It would be just my shitty luck to run into a group of harpies and get eaten.

He curled his fingers around mine, his grip gentle. Teasing. Warm. He pulled me up onto my feet so quickly I stumbled into him, my body pressing against the hard length of his.

I shoved him back a few inches.

"So feisty. Are you always like this the morning after?" His husky chuckle sent a shiver tumbling down my spine, a trickle of pleasure that had me wanting to lean into him, to feel all his strength pressing against me. "Perhaps we were not energetic enough."

"Since the only morning afters I've experienced have been here and I've had my reasons to be in a bad mood, then yes, I'm always grouchy."

His fingers settled under my jaw and he tilted my head up, forcing my gaze up to his face as he towered over me, so close his breath skated across my lips as he stood there staring down at me.

What was that war in his eyes?

It looked like the one that echoed within me, tearing me between wanting all this male had to offer and wanting to run for the hills.

"Why don't you take any pleasure for yourself?" My cheeks heated as I let that question fall from my lips, wishing I hadn't put it out there but needing to know why he chose to always pleasure me, to take care of my needs, and deny himself. "Afterwards... did you... did you go and—"

I couldn't bring myself to say it.

"Pleasure myself?" he offered.

I forced myself to nod, even as I silently wanted to die of embarrassment.

"Not this time."

"Why not?" My voice trembled. "Because there was no magic in the air making you horny?"

Oh my gods. I needed to shut up. But the part of me that needed to know why he did the things he did was stronger, louder, demanding I keep going.

"I found pleasure enough in breaking you, Saphira."

"You're kidding me." I pulled back, refusing to believe that.

He shook his head, his handsome face solemn and serious. "I have found there is great pleasure to be had in tending to your needs, in feeling your tight little body trembling from my touch, and in hearing you crying my name when you—"

I slapped a hand over his mouth, muffling his words. "That's enough."

He was grinning when he took hold of my hand and lowered it from his lips, and then pressed a kiss to it, his silver gaze hot and wicked as he said, "If you are so concerned about my pleasure, next time I will give you free rein. Whatever you desire, it will be yours."

He pulled me against him, the feel of his hard body rousing dangerous heat in my veins as his words rang in my ears, evoking visions of us tangled together, bare limbs entwined as we both sought our pleasure.

Kaeleron lowered his mouth to my ear and teleported with me as he husked, "Might I suggest indulging your love of the taste of meat."

My cheeks blazed, the vision of us tangled together transforming into one of me on my knees, his fist in my hair, my mouth on his cock as he worked his hips and grunted in pleasure.

"With your breakfast, of course." He chuckled as the shadows parted to reveal my room and he released me, sweeping his hand out towards the table near the door to the balcony and the plate stacked with bacon and eggs.

"You bastard," I muttered and shoved him away from me, that image still scorching my mind and heating my blood, flooding me with a need to make him pay for playing me like that.

Unfortunately, the only punishment I could come up with was one involving kneeling and untying his breeches, and that didn't seem much like punishment.

I should have asked my mother how long a mating heat lasted.

I was sure it was to blame for my overactive mind and my perma-horny state.

It had nothing to do with any kind of attraction to Kaeleron.

"Just tell me what my stupid task is and leave me in peace." I carried my breakfast tray out onto the balcony and yanked my chair out.

"I need you to scour the books in the library for any mention of An'sidwain. A stone."

A stone?

What was so important about a stone?

I looked back at him to ask that, but he was already gone.

I devoured my breakfast, trying not to think about what Kaeleron had said about meat, and then bathed and dressed as quickly as I could manage, but I was tired, my head a little foggy and my movements sluggish. Kaeleron had been surprised to find me awake. I pondered that as I splashed water on my face and debated the merits of drinking another cup of tea. Had he done something to me last night to help me sleep?

"I should have asked him to put me to sleep before I threw myself at him." But I had asked him if magic could help me, and he had denied it, and I knew in my heart being put under by a spell wouldn't have solved anything. I would have woken up in a worse condition than I had been in before I had been put to sleep, and I didn't want to think about how out of control I could possibly get.

I might not regret Kaeleron being with me, helping me through the frenzy, but I certainly would regret sleeping with some random male.

Or worse, with several random males.

Maybe Kaeleron was doing me a favour by keeping me so close whenever the heat struck me, by shutting me away in that cabin so far from anyone else and refusing to bring me a male to scratch my deepest carnal needs.

And maybe he would come good on his offer to give me what I really craved when the heat hit me next time.

I knew there would be a next time.

The pleasure he gave me was intense, satisfying, and broke my heat eventually, but it wasn't enough to make it go away permanently. Sooner or later, he was going to have to either find me a male or step up to the plate.

Something told me he would step up to the plate and slaughter any male who even looked at me when I was wild with a need for a male.

I had the sneaking suspicion Kaeleron was a possessive kind of male, and that was the reason he had taken me to that cottage, away from any eligible males.

He wanted to keep me to himself.

And by the gods, some part of me liked that.

"Nope. Nope. Not good." I shut down the warmth that

stirred inside me over possessive Kaeleron, denying it before it got out of hand.

I didn't need someone to fall in love with. Didn't want to find myself in that position again, vulnerable and in danger of a broken heart. I knew the perils of love now, and I was going to steer well clear of it. Scratching biological itches was fine. The other thing was a huge no go.

"I'll help him out with this vengeance of his, repay my debt and then it's back to my pack." Why did the thought of returning home to Canada fill me with a heavy feeling rather than one of joy?

I didn't want to contemplate that either. I needed a distraction, and Kaeleron had given me the perfect one. Research!

It was hardly a chore to leave my room and head to the library, a place that was rapidly becoming my favourite one inside the castle. I followed the maze of black-walled corridors and stairs up into the western wing of the castle, where it was wonderfully quiet and no one ever bothered me, determined to find as many mentions of this An'sidwain as I could before dinner.

I glanced at the windows to my left.

Which didn't look like it was far off.

But I had only just had breakfast.

I paused and peered out of the windows at the city and the darkening sky. The hour was definitely growing late. I hadn't really paid attention to how long I had been sitting outside the cottage, trying not to think about Kaeleron. Hours must have passed. And Kaeleron must have summoned me a very late breakfast once I had revealed I was starving.

Fine, I would find at least one mention of An'sidwain before dinner.

I pushed the heavy library door open and pulled up short

on the threshold at the sight of an enormous black-haired male taking up my favourite chair in front of the fire.

He lifted his onyx gaze from his book, looking as startled to see me as I was to see him.

"Um... hello," I said and shuffled into the room, keeping my distance from him as I catalogued as much about him as I could, trying to figure out who he was and how I had never met him before.

Not an unseelie.

The black horns that curled from behind his pointed ears, decorated with gold tips inscribed with fae markings were a dead giveaway that he wasn't one of that breed.

He was ruggedly handsome, his eyes as black as night but sharp as they took me in, raking over me from head to toe and back again, a little rough looking with the scar that bisected his eyebrow and his overlong onyx hair trying to break free of the tie that held it back, curling around to brush his thick neck. A heavy band of black metal with a purple sheen to it inlaid with gold decorations encircled his neck, not quite meeting in front of his throat. And he was as large as a house, consuming all of the space in the chair that had dwarfed me, his black shirt and leather pants, and heavy boots making him blend into it.

A chair I was beginning to feel had been built for him.

"You're new." His voice was as deep as a chasm, as rolling thunder.

I fidgeted. "I've been here a few weeks... months... actually. I've not seen you around before. So one might say you're new... to me, at least."

The corner of his broad, firm mouth quirked.

I shuffled back a step as he rose from the chair, a monstrous male that had to stand over seven foot tall, but it wasn't his size that startled me.

It was the great, black leathery wings that unfurled from his back.

He stretched the bat-like wings and then snapped them closed, and I gawped at him. Utterly gawped. Rude of me, but I couldn't seem to help myself.

"What corner of Hell did he pick you up from?" he said as he looked me over again and I struggled to rouse myself from my stupor.

A demon. He was a demon. From Hell.

I frowned.

One who had just made me sound like some kind of rescue puppy.

"He didn't pick me up from anywhere. He *bought* me," I snapped. I wasn't sure if that sounded better or worse than being some kind of stray. Definitely worse.

The demon seemed to think so.

His onyx eyes gained a deep reddish-purple corona in their depths as they slid from me to something behind me.

Someone behind me.

"It is true, Malachi."

I tensed as that rich, deep voice rolled over me, heating my blood, and turned to see Kaeleron leaning against the door-frame, his eyes not on me but on the one called Malachi. Watching. Guarded.

An unholy growl rumbled through the room, more frightening than the storm yesterday had been, rattling my bones and making me take a step back, towards Kaeleron.

Darkness clung to Malachi's features as he stared the fae king down, his eyes burning with that purple fire now, but glacial at the same time.

"Saphira is not a slave though," Kaeleron continued, as calm as anything in the face of this male's wrath, anger I felt sure would detonate at any moment as I inched a little further out of the line of fire.

I recalled the conversation I had listened into that first day in my cell. Jenavyr had mentioned a male who had been conveniently sent away on business by Kaeleron, one who would never forgive him for buying me. This male. I looked from the demon to the fae king. His wary gaze that remained fixed on the demon told me he had known exactly what would happen when this male learned how I had come to be here and he was prepared for it.

Kaeleron's pose remained relaxed, but I knew better, could spot the tells now as he subtly braced for impact. "What I did could be considered a kindness."

I snorted, even though it was true. "I suppose you did save me from a far worse fate."

Kaeleron inclined his head. "So you see, there is no reason for this to get out of hand."

The demon wasn't listening. He flexed his clawed fingers and stretched his wings, as if warming up for a fight. His horns grew, curling forwards, the gold shifting with them as if it was part of them and just as organic and fluid, able to grow and contract.

"You bought her?" Malachi snarled.

Kaeleron nodded and held his right hand up. "I saved her."

"You *bought* her." The reddish-purple in Malachi's eyes began to devour the onyx of his irises and I figured that was a bad sign because Kaeleron stopped leaning casually against the doorframe and straightened to his full height. "What did you *buy*, Kaeleron?"

"My virginity," I said brightly, still in a bit of a mood with Kaeleron after last night and kind of wanting to see him get his ass kicked by a demon who stood at least six inches taller and had a couple hundred pounds on him.

If anyone could beat him in a fight, it might be the demon.

"Not helping." Kaeleron scowled at me.

I shrugged.

Turned to tell the demon I was only joking as I saw how tense Kaeleron was now, as I realised that this *would* come down to a fight, and that he might just lose it, something that didn't sound so appealing after all as my wolf side snarled and gnashed fangs at the demon.

And shrieked as I was sent flying.

Malachi exploded in a riot of wings, horns and fangs at Kaeleron, passing me in the blink of an eye and catching me hard with the trailing edge of his left wing. It wasn't that blow that sent me shooting backwards into a chaise longue though, my ass hitting it so hard that I rolled backwards and had to fumble to grab the edge of the seat to stop myself rolling heels over head right off it.

It was a wall of shadows that blasted up from the floor to wrap around me.

Cocooning me.

"Kaeleron," I breathed as he clashed hard with the demon, taking a fierce blow to the face as he reached for me, directing his shadows to shield me.

He had left himself wide open, placing protecting me above protecting himself.

The demon snarled, baring huge fangs, and whipped his head forwards, cracking his forehead off Kaeleron's in a blow that drew blood and made me flinch, and unleashed an ear-splitting roar that sent pure terror shooting down my spine.

And then shadows whirled around them.

And they were both gone.

CHAPTER 42
SAPHIRA

I sat on the chaise longue, gripping the edge of it as everything whirled around me, struggling to catch up with what had just happened.

Malachi had discovered Kaeleron had bought me. Had attacked him for it. And rather than defending himself with his shadows, Kaeleron had protected me, taking a vicious blow to the head.

Oh my gods.

The demon was going to kill him.

I shot to my feet and was out of the door in a flash, unsure where they might have gone and praying it wasn't far. My boots were loud on the marble floor as I thundered down the corridor, as I growled at the thought of Kaeleron fighting that demon—a demon I had stupidly provoked.

Everything passed me in a blur as I hit the circular vestibule at a dead sprint and ran down three flights of stairs before I leaped, clearing the balustrade and hurling myself into the centre of the room. I dropped hard, landing on the ground floor in a crouch with a grunt, and exploded forwards, heading for the exit to the garden as my ears pricked.

As the scent of blood hit me.

I bolted into the open, squinting as the sudden change in brightness blinded me for a heartbeat.

Someone grunted, the sound of flesh striking flesh sending fear shooting down my spine.

My head whipped to my left, towards the courtyard where people had gathered, forming a wall around it. Watching their king and Malachi fighting. Why wasn't anyone stopping them? I hit the wall of bodies at a run and growled as I grabbed and shoved them, wriggling my way through. None of the males and females, a mixture of highborn and servants, looked inclined to leap into the makeshift ring to stop the fight.

As if this kind of thing happened often.

Or Kaeleron had ordered them not to intervene.

A swift glance at a few of the guards revealed that had to be the case. They stood on the side lines, fingers flexing around the shafts of their spears or the hilts of their swords, their gazes worried as they followed the two brawling males.

I looked there too, my knees almost buckling beneath me as Malachi slammed a meaty fist into Kaeleron's face and he staggered, barely keeping his footing as he shook off the blow and wiped the back of his hand across his bloodied lips, smearing crimson across his cheek. The bigger male didn't give him a chance to fully recover, caught him with both hands and brought his knee up, smashing it into Kaeleron's stomach and forcing a grunt from his lips.

"Stop this," I snapped and lunged forwards.

Firm hands snared my wrists and held me back and I turned on them with a snarl, baring my fangs.

At Jenavyr.

Her silver eyes were worried as she looked at her brother, as she held me back and let Malachi beat him to a bloody pulp rather than intervening. "Kaeleron knew this would happen the moment you met Mal, and he is prepared to take his punishment."

"For what? For buying me? For saving me from the twisted attentions of males who had wanted to abuse me?" I wrestled against her hold, a red haze beginning to fill my vision as the sounds of the fight rang in my ears and the scent of blood filled my nostrils. Something dawned on me, something that stilled my rage for a moment, and I whispered, "Because Malachi was a slave."

Vyr nodded slowly, her gaze solemn. "Mal went through hell. He lost everything."

But I hadn't.

I hadn't been put through hell. I hadn't lost anything of worth. I had gained something. I had gained a freedom I had never tasted before. I had been granted my wish to see a world beyond the walls of my pack lands.

"That's no reason to let him do this," I snapped, my blood thundering, heart pounding as I stared her down. "Kaeleron has taken nothing from me… and he has given me so much."

And he was paying for it with his own blood.

I looked back at Kaeleron and tears pricked my eyes as Malachi landed on top of him, as the bastard gripped his face and bashed the back of his head against the flagstones, staining them crimson. When Malachi pulled his head up for another blow, I snarled low and white fur rippled over my skin.

I had been made stronger, braver, trained so I could fight.

Fury blazed in the demon's eyes, a rage every instinct I possessed screamed wouldn't be sated by anything other than death.

Kaeleron must have seen it too, because he rallied and shoved the demon off him, his movements sluggish as he rolled onto his front and stumbled onto his feet as Malachi landed on his backside a short distance away.

"Stop this," I snarled.

Neither male paid me any heed.

They clashed again, a brutal collision of claws and clumsy blows that spoke of their exhaustion. Fresh blood rolled from a gash on Kaeleron's neck, so close to where I had bitten him, as Malachi clawed him, cleaving long tears in his black tunic. Kaeleron repaid him by striking him hard in the gut, but something wasn't right.

He was pulling his punches.

Malachi wasn't.

His fist careened into the side of Kaeleron's face, whipping his head to his left, and Kaeleron staggered in that direction, stumbled and dropped to his knees, breathing hard.

"Stop this," I whispered, unable to tear my gaze from him, willing him to put an end to this fight before it went too far.

Malachi lumbered towards him, flexing his claws, pure malice in his eyes.

And when he drew back his fist and looked as if he might deal a killing blow rather than stop, something inside me snapped.

It snapped at the sight of Kaeleron on his knees, vulnerable and accepting of whatever punishment the demon wanted to deal, too exhausted to defend himself.

So I did it for him.

I snarled as I leaped into the ring, breaking free of Vyr's hold as I shifted, leaving nothing more than a shredded blouse in her grip. I didn't feel the pain of my bones reforming. I felt only cold rage, a violent need to kill the demon who dared harm my male.

Instinct roared to the fore, stealing control of my body, blurring my thoughts as my wolf side took the helm, as I launched between Kaeleron and Malachi, a furious wall of white fur and gnashing fangs. I snapped them at Malachi, the scent of Kaeleron's blood driving me deep into my primal instincts that demanded I protect him at any cost.

I lunged at a startled Malachi, clawing his chest and his stomach as I scrabbled for purchase and sinking my fangs into his shoulder as I snarled. I shook my head, shaking him too, the taste of his blood strong on my tongue. But not enough. He grappled with me and I bit his arm, his biceps, sinking my fangs deep into his flesh and trying to tear at him.

The demon would die.

A grunt burst from my lips as he managed to fling me off him and I was on my paws in a heartbeat, head low as I snarled at him, as I snarled at the wall of people who surrounded me, all of them a threat to Kaeleron.

I backed towards him, keeping my head low and hackles raised, my posture stiff as I threatened them all, as I snapped fangs at anyone who dared to move, lunging towards them a few inches to drive them away again before I moved back into position.

Protecting him.

"Saphira." A familiar voice curled around me, warming my chest.

Malachi dared to move.

I skidded forwards a few steps, snarling and snapping my fangs at him, driving him back, and then growled low as I eased back towards the owner of that voice, my gaze darting between everyone, watching for the slightest movement.

"Saphira." The voice again, softer this time, almost coaxing.

I stiffened as someone touched me, fingers plunging into the thicker fur at my nape.

Massaging that spot.

"I am fine," he murmured. "You can back down now, little wolf."

I lifted my snout and looked at him, at the blood that covered him, and the wounds that littered his skin.

And snarled even as some part of me despaired, some distant part that was yelling at me to do as he wanted, to back down because I had already hurt enough people.

It wasn't only Malachi's blood on my tongue.

I looked at Jenavyr where she stood off to one side, my torn blouse wrapped around her arm, and regret swamped me when I realised it hadn't been the shift that had broken me free of her hold. I had bitten her. I had been so frantic to protect Kaeleron that I had hurt her and I hadn't even realised I had done it.

Malachi moved.

Instinct roared back to the fore, howling at me to protect Kaeleron.

I launched at the demon on a savage snarl.

CHAPTER 43
KAELERON

"Saphira." I slowly picked myself up off the courtyard flagstones, a deep ache throbbing in my bones wherever Malachi had struck me and my head pounding. But my pain did not matter. All that mattered was the furious bundle of white fur and sharp fangs that had thrown herself into the fray, risking injury.

To protect me.

Malachi dared to move.

The big white wolf between me and him skidded forwards a few steps, snarling and snapping fangs at him, driving him back, and then she growled low as she slowly crept backwards towards me, her head jerking with her rapid movements as she catalogued the crowd gathered around us.

Watching all of them in case they dared to attack me as the demon had.

"Saphira," I coaxed, gentling my voice and gathering shadows to me, in case she needed protecting from Malachi.

The demon did not look inclined to attack her as he warily watched her, the reddish-purple fire in his irises fading as she bared fangs at him, threatening him. Blood tracked down Malachi's chest from the claw and bite marks she had placed on him, wounds he did not seem to notice as he kept his focus fixed on the wolf before him. In fact, Malachi looked fascinated by her. Because she was defending me, acting nothing like a slave might, or a female who had been purchased for her body.

I eased forwards towards Saphira as the thicker fur at her nape shook and she snarled, gnashing fangs and licking her lips.

Some hollow thing inside my chest warmed at the sight of her, at the fact she was defending me, shielding me from the one she perceived as my enemy. She was no match for the demon warrior if he put any effort into attacking her, but she stood her ground on trembling paws regardless.

To protect me.

Someone unworthy of such kindness, *her* kindness and warmth.

I reached for her ruff and she stiffened as my fingertips brushed her fur and went to turn on me, but I plunged my hand deep into the thick fur at her nape and gripped it hard. Massaging that spot.

"I am fine," I murmured. "You can back down now, little wolf."

She lifted her snout and looked at me.

And snarled.

Raw rage blazed in her eyes as she took me in, and I knew how bad it looked, how wounds littered my body and blood soaked my tattered clothing, but these wounds would heal, and Malachi had pulled his punches, which had been more than I deserved for what I had done by breaking our unspoken covenant that this court would never own a slave.

The wolf looked at Jenavyr where she stood off to one side, the remains of Saphira's blouse wrapped around her arm to stanch the bleeding from wounds my little wolf had inflicted when she had shifted, so desperate to reach me she had fought my sister. Panic emerged in Saphira's clear blue eyes, fury directed at herself now, blending with the rage she felt towards Malachi and her instinct to protect, holding her within its power.

"Calm, Saphira," I murmured, massaging her nape, trying to reach her even as I began to feel it was impossible.

The hold of her instincts were too strong, and the panic in her eyes was a blade that pierced my heart and made me try harder to reach her, to shatter their grip on her and free her from them when she could not do it herself, when she desperately wanted to be free.

Malachi moved.

Damn him.

Saphira snarled and lunged for him, but I gripped her fur and nape hard, barely managing to hold her in place. I drove her down against the flagstones, pinning her, staining her fur with the blood spilled by my fight with Malachi.

I glared at the demon, silently ordering him to remain where he was, to keep still so he did not provoke her again. Whenever the need to protect me rose, she lost whatever progress she made with calming her instincts and returning to me, I was sure of it as I massaged the tension from her nape, as she slowly began to relax beneath my touch again.

"Calm, little wolf," I whispered, the feel of her fur soft against my palm warm and strangely comforting.

The tightness in her trembling body slowly subsided despite her growls directed at Malachi.

I knew the moment her wolf instincts loosened their hold on her, as if some deep part of us was threaded together and entwined, speaking to me, and I knew before I broke my hold what she would do.

She shot off.

"Let her pass," I shouted to the members of my court blocking her path.

They were quick to part, but she leaped over them regardless, sailing high in the air as if she could not wait even a second longer to escape what she had done.

Vyr stepped forwards and looked at me and then in the direction Saphira had run, waiting for me to order her to go after the little wolf to keep an eye on her.

I shook my head, denying her, because Saphira needed time. Her actions had shocked her and she was likely questioning the reaction now, and embarrassed about her public show of force and how she had leaped in to protect me in front of so many people. I had to admit, I was a little confused about it too, and the more I replayed what she had done, the more that feeling I was on dangerous ground grew stronger.

"I like her," Malachi grunted. "She has some balls."

I levelled a black look on my spymaster as I pushed to my feet, gritting my teeth to hide my grimace as pain ricocheted through me.

Malachi looked me over, regret tainting his eyes, and I waved him away, not wanting him to feel bad about what he had done because I had deserved his wrath.

"I told you what would happen," Vyr muttered as she came to me and frowned at the cuts that littered my chest, a concerned crinkle to her brow. "You need to see the court physicians."

I shot her a black look too and then sighed as I looked off in the direction Saphira had fled, my gaze tracking over the endless trees and then up, to a little speck on the mountainside. The cottage. Every instinct I possessed told me she would run there, where she had shelter and was away from the world, could be alone to mull over what she had done and no doubt be angry with herself.

I would give her time to find her calm and her balance again, and then I would surrender to this growing demand within me and would go to her, reassuring myself that she was safe and that today's reports from the woods were thorough and true and the harpies had moved north-west, away from the castle. I glanced at the ring I wore on my finger, one that matched the band on hers, the metal enchanted so it would shift with her. The white stone in the centre of the crescent moons twinkled softly in hues of the aurora.

White for Lucia.

I focused on that small crystal, willing it to reveal more. Needing it to reveal more.

The colour of it shifted, swirling with the rainbow hues of the aurora before it settled on a pure, clear amethyst.

Telling me its twin, the one Saphira wore, was still within the Lucia shadows.

Still close to me then. Still within my reach.

It was all the reassurance I could have right now.

Soon, I would see with my own eyes that she was all right.

"You were not meant to return until tomorrow," I grumbled at Malachi as I pressed my left hand to my shoulder and rolled it, feeling the bone grate in the socket.

Mal lifted a black eyebrow and then understanding dawned in his onyx eyes. "You wanted to prepare her."

I huffed. "I at least wanted to tell her who you are and what to expect, and it might not have hurt to try to teach her to hold her tongue."

"She is a fiery one." Mal looked over his shoulder in the direction she had run.

"You have no idea," I muttered as I scowled at the gathered crowd, the silent threat enough to have them breaking apart and disappearing from sight, leaving me alone in the courtyard with Malachi and my sister.

"I like her." Mal nodded as his horns slowly shrank back to their usual size, the golden tips I had made for him when he had joined the Shadow Court barely reaching his earlobes now.

It had taken several attempts and a lot of research to forge them, enchanting them so they moved and grew with his horns just as the end third of them would have before the seelie had chopped them off to shame him. I had tried to make him whole again. I glanced at the thick metal torc he wore around his neck, another gift I had made him, an item all demon males wore when they lost their fated mate. Or I had tried to make him as whole as possible.

I grunted as I limped towards the castle.

My words a vicious, possessive snarl.

"She is not for you."

CHAPTER 44
KAELERON

Hours passed without Saphira returning to the castle, and I found myself landing outside the remote cottage in a swirl of shadows and starlight, the noise of the castle falling away into silence that normally felt comforting whenever I came to this place. Only this time, I found myself straining to hear movement on the other side of the worn wooden door before me, a sign that Saphira had not run from my court and was still within the safety of the castle walls.

Light footsteps sounded inside the cottage and I breathed a little easier as I stepped back and summoned my shadows, intending to return to the castle now I knew she was safe and had not run from me.

Only the door opened, as if she had sensed my presence, and she peered around it, an awkward edge to her beautiful face as she avoided my gaze.

"Are you okay?" she whispered as she looked at anything but me.

"Malachi would not have killed me." I tilted my head and

frowned. "I do not think so anyway. You did not need to intervene."

The darkness that crossed her delicate features told me she had needed to intervene and the way her air of awkwardness grew said she had not been able to stop herself and was still shocked by the violence of her reaction.

Her gaze slid to the left, beyond my boots. "Is Vyr okay?"

Her brow furrowed as she asked that, and I would have to have been blind to miss how she felt about what she had done to my sister, and how she feared what it might mean for their relationship.

"My sister is well and bears you no ill will, little wolf. She understands why you reacted as you did and you are already forgiven. No harm has been done."

My words did not seem to offer her the relief I had hoped they would, because she frowned and glared at the grass beyond me, a sombre darkness to her expression that I found I did not like. I did not want the little wolf to feel ashamed of what she had done, to feel she had ruined her relationship with my sister, but I was at a loss as to what I could say to her to make her believe that Jenavyr really did not bear her any kind of ill will and their friendship remained unchanged, as strong as ever.

"Did what you do really warrant such a brutal response from the demon?" She looked at my boots, still avoiding my face, but it was progress.

"Malachi has his reasons, and I knew what would happen the moment I handed over coin in exchange for you. I was prepared for it." I checked her over as I answered her, ensuring she was unharmed, but unable to see much of her body. The robe swamped her, concealing her curves and rousing my curiosity and a need to slowly strip it from her.

She lifted her head, but the anger that sparked in her blue

eyes and her scent faded the instant her gaze landed on me, washed away by horror. "Didn't you go to see the court physicians?"

I inspected my torn tunic with a shrug. "I will heal without their help. Nothing here requires their intervention. I was going to bathe after I checked on you."

"To make sure I hadn't run away." Her tone was accusing and sharp.

I shook my head. "No. I knew you would not be so foolish."

But some part of me hadn't been sure and I had been compelled to check she was safe.

She stepped back, holding the door open, and I frowned at her actions, the silent invite, and she huffed at me for it. "I'll bathe them and tend to them. Consider it repayment for the kindness you showed me... but I also want a nice hefty sum taken off my debt."

It was said teasingly, as if she no longer thought there was a debt between us.

I was not sure that there was.

I nodded and stepped into the cottage, and did not fail to notice that she had made the space more to her liking. The double bed had been moved against the wall facing the fireplace, and she had shifted the fur rug to the space between the foot of it and the fire, and had set the two armchairs facing each other on either side of it. The room felt cosier this way, despite the fact the head of the bed was now near the door.

She picked at the edge of the door as she caught me taking in the room. "I like my feet warm in bed. My bed back at my pack was positioned like this, and during the colder months, I always loved how the fire kept the chill off my feet."

I noticed how she had said back at her pack.

Not back home.

Was she beginning to consider my court her home now?

I was not sure how that made me feel. I was not sure how I *should* feel. My eyebrows pitched low as she hurried past me and filled a large washbowl with water. Pleased. I felt pleased that she thought of my court as her home, that she had plans to remain here, close to me.

"I trained as a healer, like my mother. She's taught me everything she knows and I've worked for years taking care of minor wounds for members of my pack." She went to the fire and set the bowl down on the stone hearth, placing a cloth into the water, and then looked at me. "I'd love to study how to help fae with ailments and wounds. I'm sure it's a little different to treating a wolf."

Some deeply rooted part of me warmed, more than pleased as Saphira shared this side of herself so easily with me, allowing me to learn more about her, and strengthening that feeling that she did not want to leave the Shadow Court.

She did not wish to return to her pack.

She wanted to remain here.

With me.

And gods, there was a part of me that wanted that.

I obeyed her silent order when she pointed to the space before her, closing the door behind me and crossing the room to her as she pushed the armchair back slightly to make room for me to stand on the stone floor. She stood and faced me, her hands coming up, her fine eyebrows pinching as she studied my ruined clothes. Her fingers made light work of undoing my tunic and her expression only darkened as she pushed it off my shoulders, leaning close to me as she worked it down my arms, her breath bathing my skin.

Maddening.

While she bent and rung the cloth out, I tugged off my boots and set them aside. The first touch of the cold cloth against my chest pulled a hiss from me, and her look was chiding, teasing.

"Baby," she whispered.

"Shall we find out how you would take it if I placed a cold wet cloth against your skin, little wolf?" I lowered my gaze to her black robe. The neck of it had gaped open slightly from her bending over, revealing creamy skin that I wanted to lick and taste.

A pleasant distraction as she bathed my wounds, carefully cleaning them one by one. Each time she bent to clean the cloth and wring it out, her robe parted a little more. Great Mother. My pulse picked up as I gazed at the hint of cleavage she had unwittingly exposed, my cock growing hard as I imagined lowering my head to stroke my tongue up the valley between her pert breasts.

She huffed as she tracked the path of my gaze and fixed her robe, stealing the beauty of her body from me.

And slapped the wet cloth against my chest.

I shuddered as the water rolled down my stomach and soaked into the waist of my pants.

"You're healing fast," she murmured as she inspected the worst of the cuts, a gash that started at my right shoulder and darted across it. "A fae thing? Or a king thing?"

"My innate magic takes care of most wounds for me." I prodded the area around the gash, pleased at the progress it had made in such a short amount of time. What had been gushing blood when Malachi had given me the wound just a few short hours ago was now little more than a pink streak of irritated skin. "The proximity to Beltane is partly responsible. I have not expended much magic in the short time between then and now."

Her cheeks slowly pinkened as she stared at my chest, her lips parting slightly as her gaze grew hooded.

Thinking about what we had done that night?

She stroked her fingertips across my chest, her blue eyes distant as they tracked her fingers, tracing the shape of my left pectoral.

"What do the fae markings you have mean?" Her fingers followed the line of where they would have been had my true nature been at the fore, and I suppressed a shiver as she stroked them over my pebbled nipple.

"Words of protection and strength, and our bond to the Great Mother, the goddess Lucia."

"They were beautiful." She stiffened and her gaze leaped to clash with mine, and then she cleared her throat and went to the bowl, picking it up and carrying it to the sink to avoid me.

To avoid what she had said.

The temptation to tease her about the fact she believed me beautiful was strong, but I suppressed it and watched her instead, watched how that blush deepened and the scent of desire on her grew stronger, rousing my own aching need of her.

When she looked over her shoulder at me through her fall of silver hair, a shyness to her that was at odds with the heat in her eyes—a need I could name—I had never felt more aware of being alone with her.

So far from everyone.

I had never felt less aware of my role as a king, or even my relentless need for vengeance.

When I was with her, and she was looking at me like that, I forgot a lot of things.

She consumed my focus.

She slowly came back to me, and rather than telling me to leave, or hiding from her desire, she laid her hand on my chest and ghosted her fingers across it in a maddening caress.

I did not stop her as she stroked my chest, as she skimmed

her fingers up my neck to my ear and traced up the outside of it to the silver clasp that concealed its pointed tip.

My gaze grew hooded as she gently removed it, as she watched her fingers while she drove me wild with a soft caress along the top of my ear, to the sensitive tip of it. A shudder wracked me, my breath hitching as my blood burned, as need for her transformed into a hunger that made me feel I was starving and only she could save me.

"Are they really so sensitive?" she whispered, her gaze bold on my face, watching as I crumpled from that light touch, as she pulled down my walls and brought me to my knees with it. Her smile when I nodded warmed the darkest reaches of my soul, so teasing but so pleased. "Do you let your lovers do this?"

I frowned and caught her wrist when I realised where this was heading. "I do not have time for lovers."

"You don't?" Her eyebrows rose. "I'm new to this... but that seems like a terrible shame. I don't think I'd want to be without this now that I've experienced it. I couldn't imagine going weeks let alone years without pleasure."

She stroked her other hand down my chest, down my stomach, and my fingers tensed around her wrist as she flattened her palm against it, her fingers pointed downwards, and advanced lower.

"What are you doing?" I whispered, sounding far too breathless.

Her expression was matter of fact as she looked up at me and inched her hand lower, and I sucked my stomach in at the pleasure and need that bolted through me at the thought she might touch me.

"Showing you how good it feels when you touch me. Taking care of you for once." She edged her hand into my pants and I groaned as her skin met mine, her palm pressing against my aching erection.

I held her gaze as she touched me for the first time, finding no trace of hesitation or fear in her eyes. Not even a hint of nerves. She was bold as she easily broke my hold, as she wrapped her fingers around my cock and used her other hand to tackle the laces of my pants.

My breaths shortened as she palmed me, stripping me of all defences with that touch.

And when she slowly kneeled before me on the rug and eased my aching shaft free of my leathers, her gaze scalding it, I was undone.

"I've never done this before." Her gaze lifted to meet mine as she quietly confessed that.

And then her mouth was on me, her wet heat embracing my cock that went harder still at the feel of her, and I buried my hand in her hair, my breath abandoning me. Great Mother.

She stroked me with her tongue, tasting the length of me, her low hum of pleasure vibrating down my shaft.

I groaned as she took me back into her mouth, as she sucked and rolled her tongue, pressing it to the ridge along my cock as she withdrew again. My fingers tightened in her hair and need spiralled within me, threatening to steal control as she explored me, tentatively stroking her tongue over the broad head, licking the slit, her need perfuming the air stronger with each second that ticked past.

She moaned as I eased back into her mouth, deeper this time, fighting for restraint, and sucked as I withdrew. When I plunged forwards again, holding her head in place, she gripped my hips, short claws pressing into my flesh as another low moan of pleasure twined with mine. I groaned as I lost myself in taking her mouth, as she laved and sucked me and began moving her head on me, countering my movements, making my heart race faster and blood surge hotter.

Great Mother.

I squeezed my eyes shut as my control shattered and she moaned as I plunged into her mouth, as I imagined it was her sweet pussy gripping me so hot and hard, so greedily. I grunted and tightened my grip on her hair, holding her on me as my other hand shot out to brace against the mantelpiece, keeping me upright as my legs weakened beneath me.

My balls tightened. Seed boiled up my shaft.

I bellowed her name as I unleashed it, as my cock throbbed and jerked, jetting seed into her mouth. Pleasure rocked me, blinding me as my legs threatened to give out, as Saphira sucked me still, swallowing around me, a hungry growl ripping from her as she devoured what I had given her.

And when she drew back, her gaze was hot, needy and demanding.

I knew what she wanted.

What she needed.

And this time, I was not going to hold back.

CHAPTER 45
SAPHIRA

The hunger spiralling through me was stronger than it had ever been, blazing in my veins like an inferno that would burn me to ashes if I didn't quell it. I stared up at Kaeleron, my breaths coming faster as I still tasted him on my tongue, as he gazed down at me, his silver eyes dark with need and wicked promises.

I tugged at the sides of my robe at my chest. The need to pounce on him, to bring him to his knees and dominate him flooded me, and my skin felt too tight. Too hot. I was going to die if I didn't get what I needed, if I didn't push him into surrendering this time and giving me what I wanted.

I was sure of it.

But I was no longer embarrassed about this hunger burning within me, threatening to rip control from me at any moment. I was no longer afraid to reach out and take what I wanted, and my growl was demanding as I came to my feet, loud in the quiet cottage.

Kael seemed to know what I needed, and that I needed more this time, that our moments together hadn't been enough to break my heat. The taste of his seed had only cranked up the hunger, revealing what I needed, and now I felt as if I was treading a fine line, in danger of losing control entirely if I didn't get it.

The feel of his hard length throbbing in my mouth had rendered me near mindless with an ache to feel it between my thighs, filling me.

I needed more from him.

All of him.

The moment his hands came down on my arms, I was lost, my control shredded. The hunt for pleasure overwhelmed me faster this time, owning me, making me wild with a need to chase it, to release the insane pressure that had been building inside me the last few weeks.

I clawed at my robe, desperate to escape my burning body.

And then I was on my back on the rug, my hands pinned above my head, the weight of Kaeleron between my hips delicious and maddening. He was so close. Within reach. Body pressing mine into the sable fur. Breath mingling with mine. The heat in his silver eyes scorched me, melting the chains holding me back.

I craned my neck to kiss him.

He moved his head back, just beyond my reach.

When the back of my skull hit the furs again, he moved back to where he had been, hovering tantalisingly within reach. So I tried again, and again he evaded me.

I growled at him.

His eyes shimmered with amusement that touched his lips as he husked in a whiskey-rich voice, "So demanding."

Heat flashed across my cheeks, because my growl *had* been a demand. An order to take me, to fuck me hard and make me feel every inch of him, just as my heat and my wolf side craved.

I wanted him to dominate me, to show me his strength, to use all of it on me.

I wanted him to break me.

He hovered above me, weight braced on his knees and his hands where he gripped my wrists, pinning me in place. Delicious. But I needed more.

I lifted my hips and shamelessly rubbed against him. Needy. A little afraid he might reject me again. That dark thought was quick to come and go, burned away as he shifted his weight and gripped my wrists in one big hand, and slipped the other between us.

Delving between my aching thighs.

I practically howled as he stroked his fingers across my mound.

"Tell me what you need, little lamb." He chuckled when I growled at him for using that mocking name and murmured, "Little wolf."

I arched my hips into his hand.

His gaze grew hooded as he held me in place and parted my thighs with his knees, bracing them apart as his fingers delved between my petals. I didn't hold back my moan as he stroked and teased my clit, as he feathered his fingers lower to caress my slick opening, the look on his face one of pure pleasure as he found me wet.

So wet. So ready for him.

I groaned as he eased two fingers into me, filling me and stroking me deep. He rubbed my clit with his thumb as he worked me to a frenzy with his fingers, my pulse shooting higher as pleasure built within me, as I strained for release.

"Make me come," I whispered, my brow furrowing as I tilted my head back, as I held his gaze, not embarrassed by the intense way he watched my face as he pleasured me. I sank my teeth into my lower lip and arched my back, thrusting my breasts towards him. "Please."

"Never have to beg me, little wolf," he murmured and plunged deeper, taking me harder with his fingers, a frantic rhythm that pushed me closer to the edge.

I reached for it, each thrust of his fingers and stroke of his thumb ripping a moan from me that grew louder and louder as my body tightened like a bow string, in danger of breaking.

I threw my head back and screamed as release hit me, as pleasure rocked me and my thighs trembled against him, my breaths scouring my lungs as warmth spread through me.

And as I came down from it, sinking slowly into the fur, Kaeleron continued to stare into my eyes.

He pulled his fingers free of me, brought them up to his face and held my gaze as he wrapped his lips around them, as he sucked my essence from them.

"Oh gods," I breathed, unsure I had ever seen anything as hot as that, my arousal soaring again as he licked every drop of my juices from them, his gaze dark and hooded, pleasure shining in it as he tasted me.

"Delicious. Always so delicious," he husked. "Tell me what you want, Saphira."

I swallowed my nerves. "You know what I want. What I need. *You*."

He didn't take his eyes from mine as he lowered his hand, bracing it against the fur between my ribs and my arm, holding his weight off me. "Your mating heat means you want just any male."

And I realised that wasn't true.

It might have been the first time the frenzy had hit me, and maybe even the second, but this time, I had wanted him the moment he had appeared on my doorstep. That want had only increased when I had tended to his wounds, and was the reason I had ended up on my knees before him, his cock in my mouth.

Before I could tell him any of that, he growled, flashing wicked fangs, the skin around his eyes as black as night.

"I will not find you another male," he snarled with a possessive light in his eyes, one that made him look as mad as I felt, but drew me to him, making me want to fold him in my arms and kiss him to show him that I wanted only him. "I am the only one who gets to touch you—to see you like this. If anyone else touches you, I will carve them to pieces... slowly... because you are *mine*."

That was incredibly hot. Incredibly possessive.

My primal instincts responded strongly to how demanding he was as he hovered above me, his thighs nestled between mine, his expression dark and commanding. I wanted to cajole him and push him into showing me just how possessive he was and just how fierce he could be. It was the heat speaking, my wolf side wanting to be dominated right now and have the strongest male mate with me.

But maybe it wasn't.

Maybe all of me liked the idea of him taking me hard, staking a claim on me.

I wasn't scared to say the words that fell from my lips.

"You're the only one I want to touch me—to see me like this."

His mouth was on mine before I knew what had hit me and I moaned as he plundered it with his tongue, his kiss fierce and demanding, a potent drug that I was immediately addicted to as I clawed at his shoulders, pulling him closer, unable to get enough of him.

He groaned in response and angled his head, taking me deeper, harder, our tongues clashing as his taste flooded me, mingled with my own. His hands found my robe and he tore it open, ripping a gasp from me as cool air washed over my bare breasts, and then he covered one with his hand and one with his mouth.

I groaned and arched into him, shooting stars of pleasure cascading from the points he teased as I rolled my hips into his stomach.

My hands came down on his head, fingers threading into his hair, and I gripped it hard, yanking him back up to me and kissing him this time.

He seized my wrists and shoved my arms above my head again, and I howled in response to his strength as he pinned me, as he wrenched command from me. He joined my wrists beneath his right hand and delved his left between my thighs again, stroking me, his gaze like pure fire as his cock kicked against my thigh, making me aware of it.

Deeply aware.

I wanted that inside me.

"So wet," he purred. "Thinking of my cock?"

I nodded and licked my lips.

He pulled my robe open all the way and I looked between us, groaning as I stared at his shaft, so thick and long. I needed that. I couldn't stop my hips from rolling, from riding his fingers as he teased me towards another climax, one I wanted to feel around his shaft rather than his fingers.

I growled at it.

He chuckled and shoved his fingers deeper, ripping a gasp from me as he stretched me on the way out, and then repeated the process. Readying me, I realised, and grew even more restless as it hit me we were really going to do this. My body writhed beneath his touch, his gaze, my focus rooted on the object of my desire—my need.

I growled again, demanding he go faster, take me now.

I was ready.

So ready.

In a flash, he was above me, gaze colliding with mine, his weight pressing me into the fur and containing me.

I stilled, obeying that command in his eyes, submitting to his strength as he shoved my thighs apart, as he pushed at his leathers. I lifted my feet and caught them with my toes, shoving them down for him, too eager to wait.

A gasp burst from my lips as his blunt head met my clit and he teased me with it, as he stroked himself lower, making my breath hitch with anticipation.

And then pressed against my core.

"Kaeleron." What had meant to sound demanding came out as a breathy whisper as I urged him to take me, to give me what I needed.

He inched forwards, his face strained as he released my wrists and braced his weight on his arms, and I bit my lip as he stretched me, slowly filling me, the pleasure of it so intense I thought I might come just from him entering me. Not yet. I didn't want to come yet. I wanted to feel him inside me, wanted to feel every inch of him claiming me, and wanted him to come with me.

"Breathe, little wolf," he murmured, sounding as strained as he looked.

I hadn't realised I had been holding my breath.

I let it out in a great rush as he stilled inside me, so deep it hurt, and then gasped as my body flexed around his, a greedy little thing I had no control over.

Gods, he felt good inside me.

He felt even better as he began moving, stroking me deeply but slowly, every muscle on his body tense as I placed my arms between his ribs and his arms and curled my hands over his shoulders, clinging to him as the pain became pleasure that rippled through me with each thrust of his body into mine.

Oh gods.

I moaned against his lips and he kissed me, swallowing a gasp as he grasped my hip in his left hand and lifted it, and drove deeper into me.

Heat and need coiled together inside me, pleasure building until I felt as tense as he was, straining for another reason as I rolled my hips against him as much as I could. My primal instincts howled for more, hungry for him to show me his strength.

It needed more than this gentle coupling.

It needed it wild and fierce, a display of dominance and strength.

I met his gaze as he pulled back, his gaze searing mine, a questioning look in it.

"Harder," I uttered. "Mate me."

I thought he wouldn't understand, that he would make me spell it out, but then he pulled out of me and flipped me onto my front, and hauled my hips up, forcing me onto my knees. Before I could catch up, he rammed into me from behind, thrusting deep and fast, filling me in a blinding flash.

His hand twisted in my hair, pulling my head back, and then shifted lower. He claimed hold of my nape, holding me in place as he took me. I angled my head, looking back at him as best as I could as I moaned, rocking forwards with each punishing plunge of his cock.

Oh my gods.

I had never seen anything so delicious.

So perfect.

Kaeleron was on one knee, his other foot planted beside me, his hand gripping my nape while the other held my hips, holding me in place for his pleasure. His handsome face was dark as he took me, a sneer on his lips as he worked his hips, each flex of them making his corded muscles dance in a powerful symphony.

I moaned and pressed back against him, the need he ignited in me twisting into a demanding thing within me, making me push him. He gripped me harder, his strokes growing longer, making me feel all of him as he held my nape, as he uttered my name.

"More," I whispered on a moan.

He shoved me down against the fur, spreading my thighs with his knees, holding them off the rug as he fucked me harder, taking me out of my mind and making me rumble with a low growl of satisfaction. Close. I growled and groaned, tried to move but he wouldn't let me.

Short claws pressed into my nape to pin me.

And my entire body exploded into a shower of stars.

I howled his name as he pressed deep into my quivering body and spilled, hot seed scalding my core with each deep, short shove of his cock as he grunted in time with each one.

Darkness encroached as blissful coolness followed the heat wave, as I sank into the fur and savoured the feel of his climax and my own. I wasn't sure how long we stayed like that, intimately entwined, his body coming to rest on top of mine, his breath skating across my damp back and his claws still pressed into my skin. I mourned the loss of him when he pulled out and left me, and shivered as he gently washed me between my thighs.

"I should not have been so rough with you, little one," he murmured.

"I wanted you rougher," I admitted, not scared to voice that, not if it would ease his mind that I had wanted him to be rough with me, had needed it to break my mating heat.

But maybe next time, we could do it gentle and slow.

His low chuckle warmed my limp limbs and I smiled lazily

at him as he lifted me in his arms, turning me towards him, and carried me to the bed.

He stepped up onto it, kicked the covers out of the way, and set me down on it, and then he did the most delicious thing yet as sleep overcame me.

He stretched out beside me and pulled me into his arms, tucking me close to his chest.

And stole another piece of my heart.

CHAPTER 46
SAPHIRA

Kaeleron's scent of wild storm swirled around me as I rolled onto my side. I burrowed my face into the soft pillow beside me, breathing deep of his smell that was on it.

And on me.

In me.

I was too damned satisfied to be mortified by what he had done or how I had acted last night. I stretched beneath the soft covers, arching more like a cat than a wolf, and most certainly feeling like I had gotten the cream. The ache between my thighs was blissful, and the calm that lived within me, filling every fibre of my being, was heavenly.

I wanted to stay here in the cottage, floating in this bed and replaying everything we had done, but I'd had the strangest dream.

One of a vast dark grey desert and a glittering crimson crystal lovingly held aloft on a plinth crafted of bleached bones.

And I wasn't wholly sure the dream had been mine.

Neve had pushed those images into my mind while I slept

and it was open, unguarded. I was sure of it as I shuffled from the bed and bundled my robe into a tight ball, tying it with the belt, my mind turning towards my task of finding the location of An'sidwain for Kaeleron. I would grab breakfast in my rooms and then I would head straight to the library.

I opened the door, taking only a moment to breathe in the dewy kiss of morning as I stepped out of the cottage, and then closed the door behind me, shifted and grabbed the bundle of my robe with my fangs. I let my paws fly over the long grass, my ears twitching as I listened to the forest waking up, seeking any sign of predators so I could avoid them, and then thundered into the trees, my strides lengthening as their canopy shaded me, stealing that beautiful sky from my eyes.

The run to the castle was shorter than I had expected, and I quickly found the path from the glade, picking up the trail and following it towards the garden.

And scented someone familiar ahead of me.

I ducked behind a tree and shifted back to my human form, and quickly untied the black robe and donned it, wishing I had something a little less flimsy to cover me. The next time I decided to lose my temper, I needed to strip before anger got the better of me and I ended up ruining another set of clothes.

Riordan was just walking past as I stepped out from the trees, and he whirled and bared fangs, his eyes crimson and pupils elliptical as his hands came up in a defensive move. He huffed when he saw it was me and lowered his hands, the ruby bleeding from his irises.

"I didn't mean to scare you." I checked the belt of my robe was tied tightly enough and that the garment covered all of me, feeling uneasy to be in such a state of undress in the garden. The servants were going to speak. Worse, the high-born would be talking about it for weeks if they caught sight of me.

Especially if they caught sight of me speaking with Riordan while dressed like this.

"I'm going to pretend you don't reek of sex and be all polite. Here goes. Oh, Saphira, fancy coming across you here." Riordan grinned at me and I barely resisted the urge to box his ears as my cheeks heated, and then he relaxed and shoved his hands into the pockets of his fitted black pants. "I heard you met Mal."

I nodded. "I don't think it went well."

He shrugged, shifting his black tunic. "Don't take it personally. Mal is a little twitchy around the whole slavery subject since he went through it himself and lost pretty much everything... including his sanity for a while there. Sometimes, still his sanity."

"If I had known. I wouldn't have said what I did."

"How could you have known? Mal wasn't meant to be back until today. Last report he filed to me had his return as this evening, and that's what I told Kaeleron. Our royal highness probably wants my head for that. Vyr says he wanted to prepare you before you met Mal."

"That would have been nice," I said and fell into step beside him as we took the pale stone steps down to the main garden. "I'm on my way to the library... via my room to bathe and have breakfast. Maybe I'll see Malachi there. He seemed rather at home there and I suspect that the chair I've been making my own was his all along."

Riordan's expression pinched and he scrubbed his neck. "No library time for Mal today. He's with Kaeleron in the great hall, greeting our unwanted guests."

"Unwanted guests?" My mind leaped to my pack, my heart racing even as I told myself it wouldn't be them. It was probably just another court come to visit.

"I'd steer clear if I were you." Riordan waved as he broke away from me. "Vyr is with them so I need to handle the training for the recruits today. I'll catch you later."

I hurried into the castle and up to my rooms, somehow making it there without being spotted by anyone else. I made fast work of bathing, and when I left the bathroom my breakfast was waiting, and I blushed as I saw it was almost double the usual amount, as if Kaeleron had told the cooks I would be extra hungry this morning.

Bastard.

I devoured the food anyway, not leaving a single bite, and drained the tea pot before quickly dressing in a fresh pair of black leathers, a cream blouse and a supple dark brown suede under-bust corset, and boots.

I braided my hair as I left my room.

Intending to go straight to the library.

But what Riordan had said slowed my steps and had my focus turning towards the floors below me.

What if the unwanted guests *were* wolves? What if it was Lucas?

I told myself to go straight to the library, but somehow found myself on the ground floor instead, sneaking towards the arched doors of the great hall at the end of the broad entrance corridor. They were ajar and I strained to hear what was happening inside.

And flinched and reared back as someone unleashed a shrill cry of pain.

I shoved the right door open, bursting into the room, my heart in my throat as my hackles rose.

But it wasn't anyone I recognised kneeling on the marble floor before Kaeleron.

Malachi was a deadly shadow in head-to-toe black leather,

blades sheathed along his ribs and his onyx wings spread as he loomed over one of the trio of blond males, one of his small knives buried in the male's chest as he pinned him to the floor.

All three of the males were young, the oldest looking no older than nineteen to my eyes. They were just boys.

Kaeleron turned glacial silver eyes on the middle male and growled, "Speak your reason for being in my court."

When the young male hesitated, shadows rose around him, sharp lances poised to strike as his green eyes darted to them and he shrank into himself, his arms coming up to shield his vital organs. As if that would save him.

"Speak," Kaeleron boomed, the command echoing around the cathedral-like chamber, ricocheting off the carved black columns that supported the vaulted ceiling.

The male hesitated still, and I flinched away as those shadows flew at him, as they stabbed him one by one, piercing only deep enough to inflict pain rather than a fatal wound. The fae unleashed a blood-curdling scream as his body jerked and twisted with each shadow that struck him. Malachi lifted his head and shoved off the one he had stabbed, his onyx gaze alight with reddish-purple fire as he looked at the one Kaeleron was torturing.

I looked at Kael.

At the cold male who stood on that dais at the end of the aisle, dressed in black armour and a thorny crown, ice coating the hard lines of his face and his eyes empty, soulless pits that revealed no emotion as he stared at the fae he was striking with his shadows, not even giving him a chance to speak.

"Stop!" I stepped further into the room, my heart pounding as I forced myself to do something rather than stand by and let him do this, let him torment these fae, and maybe part of me didn't want to see this reminder of the male he could be.

The cold, ruthless unseelie king.

The fae closest to Malachi made the mistake of trying to move towards his companion, and Kaeleron made a small gesture with his hand, a flicker of something twisted and predatory in his eyes as he watched the two fae. Malachi immediately caught the male around the throat and shoved him back against the floor, his blade against his throat this time, poised to cut it.

Kaeleron's lips stretched in a satisfied smirk as the fae in the middle cast a terrified look at the younger male Malachi had pinned, his face crumpling as tears lined his pale lashes.

"Wait." That word was garbled and the male coughed, bringing up blood that trickled down his chin as he reached for the male beneath Malachi. "Stop. Wait. Do not harm my brother."

I gasped as I looked between the two of them, and then looked at Kaeleron.

And saw only darkness in his eyes.

Victory.

He had found a weakness among them, and was going to harm the brother to make this male speak.

I stared at Kaeleron, hating this brutal reminder of who he really was, a male so different to the one who had come to me last night, who had taken care of me and had held me in his arms while I slept.

"Stop," I said and stepped further into the room.

Kaeleron's eyes lifted to me, his expression dark and unreadable, and then he gestured to someone off to his left, his voice cold as he ordered, "Remove her from the room."

Jenavyr nodded and stalked towards me, her face as cold as her brother's as she closed the distance between us.

I shot Kaeleron a hard look. "You're harming innocents."

He snarled, baring jagged fangs, the lines of his face hardening with it as he stared me down. "The only innocent in this room is you, and you are a blind fool if you believe I will show mercy to these wretches simply because you asked it of me. I have no mercy to give. Take her to her room and lock her in it."

Jenavyr seized my arm and I started, entire body tensing before I recognised who had me.

With a withering glare in Kaeleron's direction, and sickness brewing in my stomach as I glanced at the sobbing, cowering fae before him, I bit out, "It appears the seelie aren't liars after all. You're as much a monster as they paint your kind to be."

I wrenched free of Vyr's grip and stormed from the room.

Kaeleron's roar shook the castle and fear flashed through my blood as I broke into a run, fleeing from him, afraid of him even when I knew deep in my soul that he would never harm me.

Jenavyr closed the door of the great hall behind me but didn't chase me down the corridor as I expected. I glanced back at her, finding her standing with her back against the ornate wooden doors, her beautiful face still as dark as night.

I didn't stop running until I was in my room, my heart thundering as I closed the door and locked it behind me, my limbs shaking as the adrenaline wore off and my mind cleared.

And I realised I was going to pay for my outburst later, that I'd had no right to intervene when I didn't know why those fae had been brought to Kaeleron, and no right to believe them innocent simply because they had been young. I had overstepped, but I hadn't been able to stop myself. I couldn't stand by and watch that sickening display of power—and anger—and *hatred*—without saying something.

I struggled for air as I went to the balcony, as I pressed my hands to the stone balustrade and looked out at the city that seemed darker now when it had been a source of light for me just an hour ago, while I had enjoyed my breakfast, all of me warmed by my night with Kaeleron.

I wasn't sure how long I stood there, trying to reconcile everything that had happened, torn between polar feelings as I thought about Kaeleron.

It was only when the lock on my door snicked and it opened slowly that I realised afternoon was fading into evening, and I had been stood on my balcony for hours, lost in thoughts of the male who entered my room on a wave of power that curled around me in a gentle embrace rather than crushed my bones to powder as I had expected.

I looked over my shoulder at him as he stopped in the centre of my room, his gaze downcast, his air withdrawn rather than raging and furious. The stillness of him was more terrifying than his rage would have been.

"You cannot understand the burden I bear—the choices I must make. You do not understand how the things I have done —the things I must do—affect me." He slowly lifted his emotionless silver gaze to meet mine. "You would rather watch a world go to hell than bloody your hands."

I curled those hands into fists at my sides, hating the kernel of truth in his words.

"I pray you never have to discover what it is like to face that choice—to have to decide whether to run or fight—to decide whether to bloody your delicate, soft hands, or let those you love die a horrible death and watch them ripped from you."

I swallowed, a feeling growing within me. He was talking of his past now. I hung on every grim, painful word, because he was right. Faced with such a choice, I wasn't sure if I would fall to my knees and beg and plead for the lives of my family, or rise to my feet and do whatever it took—no matter how bloody and terrible—to save them.

Kaeleron heaved a sigh as he walked to the arched window

closest to me, his broad shoulders shifting with it beneath his black tunic.

"You do not know what I would do for my court." He gazed out of the window at it, his shoulders rigid, heavy with that invisible burden. "Or the lengths I would go to in order to keep my people safe... and if that makes me a monster, so be it. I would embrace all that is dark—that is violent—in my blood to save them."

I believed that softly spoken vow.

His eyebrows lowered and pinched as his gaze dropped to the city and he whispered, "A king does not remain in control of a kingdom by being everyone's friend, little wolf. You cannot rule with kindness. Not in this world. In this world, you need to keep everyone in line. You need to be firm. You need to do what you must to protect your people... even if those people cannot understand your actions."

I leaned my right side against the stone arch of the door to the balcony as those words touched me deeply, connecting with a part of me that could understand his actions and his reasons for being as vicious and cold as he had been in the great hall.

"I know a little of what you speak about," I said and then cleared my throat, putting more force behind my trembling voice. "Alpha wolves have to be strong and fierce, and rule with an iron fist if they're to remain in power. The moment they show softness—weakness—another would rise to cut them down and take their place. My world and this one aren't so different. They're both brutal. Violent at times."

I exhaled softly as I thought about my pack, lowering my gaze to Kaeleron's legs as he turned towards me, his eyes on me now.

"My father rules with kindness and warmth, supporting our pack members and keeping them happy that way, doing his best to be a good alpha. But sometimes he needs to put people in their places. Not that it happens often. But sometimes... sometimes he has to be fierce, unyielding, to keep people in line." And he had often sheltered me from that side of pack life, sending me away to the cabin so I didn't witness it, as if he feared me seeing it would change my opinion of him.

Sour my love for him.

And maybe that was why Kaeleron had sent me away.

He hadn't wanted me to see the darker, more brutal side of him, the ruthless king he needed to be at times in order to keep his position and keep his court safe.

But I had seen it.

And gods damn me, but it hadn't changed my opinion of him.

My growing love for him.

I frowned at his clothing, a simple black tunic and pants, not the intimidating armour he had been wearing in the great hall. No crown on his head. No mask in place. This male before me wasn't the wrathful king of the Shadow Court.

He was just Kaeleron.

A freshly bathed Kaeleron, judging by his damp black hair.

He had bathed before he had come to me, washing the stain of what he had done from his body and softening his appearance. I could still hear the way that fae had begged him, could scent their terror and feel their fear.

"Were they—" I started.

"They were of the Silver Court," he finished for me, his voice soft but gaining a hard edge it often did whenever he spoke of his enemies.

"A seelie court," I whispered, recalling the position of it from the map in the war room. It was south of the Summer Court, and only the mountainous Black Pass separated it from the Shadow Court.

He nodded, still holding himself at a distance from me.

"What were they doing here?" I stepped into the room, hating the distance between us, wanting to erase it and bring things back to how they had been last night, aching to feel that closeness to him again.

"They were sent to my court to gather information to report to their king." He met me halfway and then took hold of my arm, his touch gentle as he gripped it and led me back onto the balcony.

"Spies." I mourned the loss of contact between us as he released me. I moved to stand beside him, almost shoulder to shoulder with him as he stared at his city. His court. And then his silver gaze was on me again, open and calm, a flicker of warmth shimmering in its depths. I looked west, towards the border there. "Were they the ones spotted in Wraith Wood?"

He inclined his head, his gaze distant as it drifted back to the city.

Beyond it, I realised.

He was looking at the rest of his kingdom—to the point where these fae had infiltrated his borders—concern growing in his eyes that drummed within me too.

How much information had they been able to gather in the time they had eluded capture? What kind of things could they have taken back to their king had they escaped? Kaeleron's spies told him of troop movements and other valuable information, and were likely key when planning an invasion. Could the Shadow Court have come under attack if they had returned to the Silver Court?

I was beginning to doubt any accord between the high kings would stop the courts if they really wanted to go to war. They would find a way.

"What—What happened to them?" I looked up at him, gaze tracing his noble profile as his expression hardened, the black slashes of his eyebrows dipping low and his silver eyes glacial again.

"I was merciful. Their deaths were swift." He turned to me at last. "They were not innocent, little wolf. They were spies—wolves clothed as bleating lambs. Trained from a young age in espionage, honed for this purpose. Had I let them leave, they would have reported everything of my kingdom back to their king. I did what I must to protect my people."

"I know." But I was only just understanding how these courts worked and what this world was like, and I was only just realising that I didn't understand what it was like to rule a kingdom, to have the welfare and safety of tens of thousands of people constantly on my mind.

Or the things Kael needed to live with, choices he had to make whose repercussions still echoed through his life now.

I had compared him to an alpha once, but he was so much more than that. His life was so much more difficult and challenging.

Not just the constant meetings, checking on his men, visiting border outposts, ensuring his legions were trained sufficiently, and ensuring thousands of people had all they needed in terms of food and safety. It was the scars even his immortal body couldn't heal and the wars he had fought in that I had read about in the library. Those were the things that made me realise how different our lives had been.

I had been sheltered. So had my pack, and even Lucas's pack. None of us had ever really had to fight for our lives, to protect everything, not like Kaeleron had. He wasn't what I had thought a king would be. There was no waiting in the rear. No. In every account I had read, he had been at the front of the battle, in the thick of it, commanding and watching over his men.

He was a hard, cold bastard at times, but maybe that was

for the reason he had said. It was the way he had to be, so everyone survived, so they could live as they did in the city. Safe. Quiet. Without fear of attack. And while they longed for their families, while they secretly resented their king for closing the borders, it was that closing of the borders and warding them with magic at great cost to himself that kept them safe, that meant they didn't need to fear they would be attacked.

I looked at the city, seeing a flash of what might have happened had those seelie walked free, had they been able to report to their king. Fire. Destruction. Death. Everything good and beautiful rendered to ash.

I couldn't imagine what it was like to fight for your life and be in a battle. I just couldn't. My mind refused to conjure how terrifying it would be, the choices people had to make, the sounds and the *smells*.

Kaeleron had fought in many, had survived them all, but as I looked at him, as he stood proud beside me, surveying his court—a court that was safe thanks to him—I could see those invisible scars each battle had left on him.

The life of a king was so different to that of an alpha. Kaeleron's life made them look like pampered princes.

I glanced between him and the city, trying to find a way to break the thickening silence, wanting him to know that nothing had changed between us, that I wasn't angry or afraid of him, and that while some of the townsfolk might not appreciate the things he did, that I did. He had been right back in the library. He was a very good king. One who was willing to make an enemy of himself to keep his people safe.

"I'm planning to visit the library today to research An'sid-wain for you." I knocked my knuckles against his, trying to get his attention.

The touch only lasted a split-second yet a thrill bolted up my arm at the contact.

That thrill became warmth and light as Kaeleron shifted his hand so our knuckles were in contact again, keeping it against mine as he spoke, as if he needed the connection as much as I did.

"Neve had another vision. An'sidwain lies within the Forgotten Wastes."

I savoured the contact between us as I lifted my gaze to his face. "The Forgotten Wastes. I saw something in my dreams. Glittering dark grey sand. A plinth of bones. A red crystal. And I was terrified by the sight of it."

That last part hit me out of nowhere, something I hadn't recalled until I had replayed my dream.

"Exactly as Neve saw it." Kaeleron huffed, his mood darkening. "Neve meddles. She should not force her visions upon you."

"Why does she do it?" I had wanted to ask how, but that question had come out instead. "It's not the first time she has."

"She believes it is a way of keeping you here... of encouraging you to do as she needs or has seen." He glowered at the city.

"She showed me this world... because I was afraid and wanted to go home. She showed me pieces of it, enough to make me want to stay and see it. And now she's shown me the Forgotten Wastes and An'sidwain... But I don't know why."

His lips flattened, the corners turning downwards as shadows restlessly twined around the carved stone spindles of the balustrade. "Because she wishes me to take you with me, and I will not."

"If I have to go, then I'll go," I said. "I'm not afraid."

He gave me a look that said I might not be afraid, but he was. He didn't want to take me there, meaning the Forgotten Wastes had to be a dangerous place, and going there might get me killed.

"Tell me where it is anyway, and maybe I can help research a way to get it." I wouldn't let him shut me out, wouldn't be kept in the dark any longer, not when I felt I could be of use to him and could help him.

"An'sidwain is in the last place I would ever take you."

His gaze locked with mine, warm yet dark as his words sent a cold shiver down my spine and filled me with dread.

"The home of an ancient lich."

CHAPTER 47
SAPHIRA

The evening light felt good on my body as I walked through the garden, eyes tired from spending the day with my head stuck in books in the library.

Malachi had been there when I had arrived, and had politely apologised for what had happened. I knew he meant every word he had said, but my wolf side had been snarling within me from the moment I had set eyes on him, and whenever I had glanced his way during my time in the library, I had wanted to growl, warning him away from Kaeleron.

And maybe once or twice I might have actually growled at him, the soft snarl slipping from me before I could contain it.

Despite my frosty attitude towards him, he hadn't been scared away and had kept me company for hours, a brooding tower of silence in his armchair. As the day had worn on, the mood between us had softened. It might have helped that he had gone to the kitchens and returned with a tray of tea and sweet things, and a few meat pies with some cold cuts and bread and butter. When I had eyed the pies and meat, he had confessed he had run into Kaeleron and had been given intelligence on me.

I had been tempted to find Kaeleron and growl at him too, but had shrugged it off and devoured the peace offering instead.

Malachi had helped me rearrange the furniture, moving a smaller wingback armchair into position opposite his near the fireplace and adding a low wooden table next to it where I could keep my stack of books and cups of tea.

Today, I had scoured the books for any mentions of lich, wanting to know what I might be up against if I managed to wear Kaeleron down.

According to Malachi, Neve had received another vision, one that had again seen both me and Kaeleron in the Forgotten Wastes, hunting for An'sidwain, and had warned Kaeleron that if he didn't take me with him that his mission would fail.

And Kaeleron had decided to recruit Malachi in my place regardless.

That had stung a little, and I wasn't proud of myself for refusing to speak to Malachi after he had announced he would be going with Kaeleron instead, dropping that little bomb on me just as I had been growing comfortable around him, or how I had spent a good hour plotting ways to make Kaeleron pay for doubting my strength and my courage.

I sighed as I leaned against the wall in my favourite spot in the garden, my gaze taking in the magnificent wall of white water that thundered into the bay below and then the ships that bobbed on the gentle waves, heading towards the port.

A few minutes later, Kaeleron came to rest beside me, his body braced on his elbows on the balustrade and his eyes on the ships too. I ended up watching him instead, the silence we shared comfortable. Too comfortable. I was beginning to feel at home by his side, as if it was where I belonged, and I was sure that wasn't a good thing.

"I looked into the Forgotten Wastes today, and also into the lich." I picked at the stone wall, but managed to keep my gaze on his face rather than obeying the urge to avert it and avoid him as I said, "I still want to go with you. Neve told you that you had to take me, and I'm not afraid. I'm not."

He just heaved a long sigh at that.

"You haven't come to train me. I get that you're busy, but—"

"Your training is on hold for now," he interjected.

Earning a frown from me. "Because you want an excuse not to take me."

He arched an eyebrow at me. "Because I am busy."

"You're too obvious," I muttered and jabbed at the stone wall, my mood taking a dark turn. "Of course I would see through it. You can blame it on being busy all you want, but I'm not stupid, Kaeleron. I know you stopped it so you can use my lack of training as a reason not to take me with you. Is it really so dangerous for me to go to the Forgotten Wastes?"

He exhaled again, as if his patience had a puncture and I was squeezing all the air out of it, and looked over my head at the mountains to our left. "Yes."

That wasn't answer enough for me. Before I could press him for an explanation, he continued.

"I found Neve in the Forgotten Wastes, long ago. She was near mad from her time there, trying to evade the beast who hunted her. A starving, vicious little thing that tried to kill me when I came upon her in a cave, fearing I was in allegiance with the one looking for her and terrified that I would lead the creatures that roamed the Wastes to her if I was not." His handsome face darkened, his silver gaze distant as he kept it fixed on the jagged maws of the mountains. "She had been brutally beaten by those creatures, had brushed with death more than once before she had holed herself up in that cave, too terrified to leave it. Neve fears that land. You would be wise to fear it too."

I shrugged, trying to let images of beautiful, powerful Neve all broken and scared roll off my back. "I get what you're saying—that no one in their right mind should want to go there—but I can handle myself."

He scoffed and shook his head. "It is not a matter of handling yourself. The Wastes are dangerous, and I did not want to take you there before. Now that I know the dragon stone is in the possession of an ancient lich, I have half a mind to reinforce the wards that shield my court from that wretched land and prevent you from even thinking about heading there. I will find another way, one that does not involve taking you there."

"You mean taking Malachi?" I glared at him as he tensed, eyes widening a fraction. "I heard about that plan, and again… Neve saw you taking me. Not the demon. Finding An'sidwain is important, yes? Vital?"

"Neve seems to believe so." He didn't look pleased that the dragon had decided the stone was necessary, or that I was insisting on going with him, determined to find a way to break his resolve and make him agree to take me, or that his spymaster had been so quick to divulge their little secret.

"Then we should go and find it."

His silver eyes narrowed on me. "Why are you so invested in this?"

"Because I'm coming to realise how important vengeance can be… how it can give you a form of closure that just letting it all go can't sometimes."

He growled, "You speak of the wolf who sold you."

I nodded and prodded at a small worn dip in the stone before me, my focus on it now as anger simmered in my veins, as I thought about Lucas and my wolf side didn't howl in pain.

It snarled in rage, hungry to sink fangs into the bastard.

He faced me, a wall of muscle that radiated darkness as his shadows twisted around his legs and forearms, and caressed his shoulders, his handsome face hard and fierce. "What lengths would you go to in order to have your vengeance—"

"Anything." I cut him off, my voice a thick growl that startled me. I had never sounded so vicious, so dark. "I'd do anything to make him pay."

He lifted his right hand and feathered the backs of his fingers down my cheek, concern breaking through the steel in his eyes, his voice low as he said, "Vengeance is a dark and bloody path, one that requires you to cut out parts of yourself and not one I would recommend."

I fell silent as I looked at him, deep into his eyes. How much of himself had he cut out, and how little would be left of me if I followed in his footsteps?

His gaze lifted to the garden and then the castle. "I built this castle here because of the view—this vantage point over the entire kingdom. I knew the moment I saw the view from up in these mountains that I would build my home here, but I had not expected to move the capital to this location."

Because he hadn't expected to rule.

"I thought the castle was old... built centuries ago." I looked at it too, at the colossal black towers that rose from it, at the arched windows and beautiful carvings on columns and around some of the doorframes.

He slid me a look, a soft and amused one. "It was. I completed work on it around four hundred years ago. It took half a century for the court's finest craftsmen to build the palace, and another half a century to complete the town to the point you see it today."

I looked at the monument to darkness, a castle designed to strike terror into the hearts of his enemies, but one that managed to still feel like a home. I had the feeling the sense of this being a home had taken time to take root, that at first it had been a cold and merciless place, much like its master had felt.

"How old were you when you became ruler of these lands?" I shifted my gaze to him, catching the pain my question caused in his eyes before he concealed it, lowering his mask once again.

"I was a boy... No more than sixty. I looked as you might have at the time." His gaze fell to me, a hard edge to it, as cold as a blade of ice, and I wondered what terrible things he was remembering as he drifted away from me, falling into the darkness of his past.

He would have looked like a teenager. A boy barely as old as his brother had been in that painting. The brother that should have ruled this court.

"What happened to your family?" My voice wobbled as I asked that, betraying the nerves and the feeling I shouldn't have asked, that it was rude of me to bring it up and make him relive the pain.

He turned his cheek to me, his face hardening once more and the air around him growing cold, and a glance at his fingertips revealed they were stained inky black at their tips. He flexed them, revealing a thin line of fae markings that ran down their undersides to his palm.

"They were murdered by seelie." His deep voice was empty, emotionless. "And my brother was taken."

I looked from him to the castle he stared at, a monument to his pain and rage, and then reached for his hand. "I'm sorry."

Before I could make contact, he pushed away from me, heading for the castle.

"I do not need your pity," he snarled over his shoulder. "I need revenge."

He stopped at the entrance of the white wooden pergola

and looked back at me, darker and more menacing than I had ever seen him as his crimson eyes met mine and he growled.

"Can you give me that?"

I didn't like how I felt in that moment as I looked at him, as I saw all that pain and that violent need for vengeance in his eyes, and I wanted to do it for him, despite the fact I knew he wanted the heads of those he believed responsible for his parents' deaths and his brother's abduction.

When I failed to find my voice to answer him, he disappeared in a swirl of inky night glittering with gold and silver stars.

Leaving me alone.

I looked at the city, at the home he had built for himself and his sister, for his people, abandoning the one he had shared with his parents.

Deep in my heart, I felt the truth of him.

He had run away from his pain—his grief—and had moulded it into a hunger for revenge rather than dealing with his hurt. He had built a castle to escape it, so he didn't need to see the constant reminder of the warm home and loving parents he had lost. He had locked it all deep inside him, using it as fuel for his wrath.

How would he feel when he found the fae who had murdered his family and killed them?

Would he find the closure he needed in their brutal deaths or would he find only a hollow kind of victory, one that wouldn't ease the pain he continued to carry in his heart?

Like a festering wound that was slowly poisoning him.

I looked back at the castle, desperate to understand him, to understand the strength of the hunger that consumed him and had done for *centuries*.

And I wondered.

What would I do if my parents were taken from me?

CHAPTER 48

KAELERON

Malachi checked his weapons, a tower of black leather and muscle, the silver blades glinting in the warm torchlight in the great hall as he cleaned and sheathed them against his ribs one by one. "I still wonder whether it was wise to teach the wolf to fight when you did not know what she might be. For all Neve can see, she might be your future enemy, and now you have made her stronger."

We had been going over this argument for the last fifteen minutes, since I had mentioned resuming my training of Saphira once we returned from the Wastes, a way of smoothing things over with the little wolf and hopefully taking the edge off the mood that would no doubt hit her the moment she realised I had gone ahead and left for the Wastes with Malachi instead of her.

"If we are meant to fight one day, I will deal with it when it happens, but I was not going to leave her unable to defend herself when there was something I could do about it." I tucked rolls of gauze into the leather satchel and two vials of liquid the physicians had prepared for us—one to speed healing, the other to reverse any poison that hit us. A third vial followed it, this one gifted to me by my royal necromancers, an elixir that would remove any necrotic effects should the lich we were due to fight manage to hit us with any of his dark spells.

"You could have locked her away again." Malachi did not even glance my way as he said that, his words as cold and carefully crafted as the steel he carried.

I pushed my hair back and neatened the top half, the black leather of my light armour creaking as I retied it, aware where this was going. "She was in the cell for barely a few days, until I had made sure it was safe to allow her out."

Mal grunted, "Until Vyr wore you down."

I did not deign that with a response.

Thunder rumbled in the distance and the scent of rain covered the subtler smells in the castle as the temperature dropped a few degrees.

"Neve believes you should take Saphira." Malachi tossed a change of clothes into his own pack.

"Has she recruited you to her side too now?" First it had been Saphira, and then my sister had been intent on bringing up what Neve had seen, and now Malachi was going to push me in a direction I did not want to take—one I had considered just this morning, when Neve had told me bluntly that my vengeance would fail without Saphira at my side.

Lightning struck in the mountains, the thunder echoing around them, rattling the castle, and the sound of heavy rain reached us even in the heart of it.

A summer storm.

That bad feeling that had been nagging at my gut all day grew stronger, but I continued to shove things in my pack, ignoring it. I would not take Saphira to the Wastes. It was far too dangerous.

Malachi straightened and looked towards the entrance to the great hall as footsteps sounded. Hurried footsteps.

A guard halted at the threshold, his black armour dripping water all over the floor as he pressed his hand to his chest and his words fell like a death knell.

"My king, there is a visitor at the gatehouse."

A traveller.

I stilled right down to my breathing as thunder rattled the windows again, as I stared beyond the guard to the end of the long hallway and the rain that pelted Falkyr so hard that it was like a mist, obscuring everything from view.

A traveller in a summer storm.

Malachi looked at me, as tense as I was.

A bad sign.

Millennia ago, a traveller had come to an unseelie court in a summer storm, seeking shelter. That traveller had ended up murdering the king who had offered him refuge.

And now a traveller had entered my court unnoticed, crossing the border into my kingdom unseen and had managed to reach my door.

Dread trickled down my spine beneath my black armour.

"Send him away," I growled.

The guard hesitated.

"What?" I barked and rested my hand on the hilt of my sword, the unease rippling through me becoming waves that rocked me as he refused to carry out my order.

"My king, the visitor… is wolven."

My breath left my lungs as they constricted.

As the need to send the male away only increased a hundredfold and I strode for the guard, ready to seize hold of him and shake him until he did as I ordered.

Was it the one who had sold her to me, come to take her back?

Two guards appeared beyond him, a soaked and bedraggled male held between them, his dark checked shirt and black jeans plastered to his muscled frame. Stormy grey eyes locked onto me, narrowing fiercely as his lips compressed.

Grey eyes. Brown hair.

I growled through emerging fangs as I realised who this male was.

Morden.

Saphira's protector.

The one she had spoken of with light in her eyes and a bright smile, who she had grown angry with me over when I had used past tense for their relationship, accusing me of making it sound as if they would never see each other again. I held the male's fierce gaze, unflinching as he broke free of my guards and stormed towards me, his heavy leather boots loud on the marble floor. It would have been better had it been the wolf who had sold her come to try to take her back.

Then I could have slaughtered him without restraint.

This traveller visiting me in the midst of a summer storm felt more like the blade of fate, come to cut her away from me.

"Where is she?" Morden snarled, baring short fangs, no trace of fear in his scent as he approached me, ignoring the guards' attempts to block his path.

He shoved them aside, knocking them away from him, snapping fangs in their faces before his unwavering gaze landed back on me.

"Where is she?" he bit out, harder this time, his eyes taking on a hard edge, one laced with disgust as he looked me over, his lip curling. "What have you done to her?"

This male thought me a beast, a monster who would take her against her will and hurt her.

"She is safe, no thanks to you," I growled back at him, my aim true as the male flinched at the reminder of what had happened to her on his watch and how he had failed to protect her.

I had felt very few things in recent years that were as satisfying as taking this overbearing wolf down a peg or two.

Morden halted a few metres from me, gaze dark and promising death, as if that paltry distance would be any sort of hindrance if I wished to disembowel him. The wolf had come to a world of monsters without preparing himself, had no doubt rushed in to save his little pack princess without sparing a single moment to discover what kind of creatures lived in this world he now found himself in.

My world.

My court.

"How did you pass through my court unseen?" I growled at him, staring him down as I studied him. I sensed no magic on him, no method of concealing himself, meaning he had traversed my kingdom in the open.

His right eyebrow lifted. "Easily. It's heavily wooded. It wasn't difficult to avoid the locals, and with my wolf sight and hearing, it was a simple matter of listening in from the shadows near a few taverns and inns to find out the name of your capital and then following the signposts at night, when I wouldn't run into anyone. Any hunter could have done it."

Hunter.

The male thought to make himself out to be an apex predator when he was in the presence of one far superior to him.

But still, I would dispatch a few of the stronger members of my court to strengthen the barrier magic, reinforcing the detection spells. I had the feeling that the Silver Court seelie who had crossed the border had tampered with the spells somehow, leaving them open to this wretch before me, and that was the reason he had gone undetected.

"I want to see her. I want to see she's unharmed." The wolf stood his ground, back ramrod straight, gaze never straying from me even as my guards formed a line behind him, ready to seize him at my signal.

Malachi casually toyed with one of his knives, a looming shadow at my back.

The wolf was outnumbered, and seriously out of his depth, yet he dared insinuate that I would harm Saphira, risking not only my wrath but that of my men.

"The little wolf is fine. She has no need of your assistance. Return to your pack, wolf." I tipped my shoulders back as I stared him down, looking down my nose at the bastard as he continued to remain where he was, dripping all over my floor.

Trying to take my little wolf from me.

Lightning flashed crimson behind the wolf, throwing his shadow out long before him, and it writhed as fury curled through my veins, as darkness clouded my mind, whispering how easy it would be to eliminate this fool before he even knew what had hit him. My shadows would make swift work of him.

And then the threat to Saphira would be gone.

But fate was against me.

And the dread pooling in my chest only grew stronger as Saphira strolled into the room through the side door, muttering about the rain as she wrung out her long silver braid.

"I thought I might find you here," she said. "About An'sidwain—"

Her eyes widened as they landed on Morden, shock dancing across her beautiful face as she noticed him, followed by something terribly like relief and happiness as her eyes lit up.

And *my* heart froze solid.

She ran towards the wolf, fracturing the sickeningly fragile thing in my chest.

I stepped forward, almost blocking her path to the male, and she drew up short and looked at me.

"Return to your room," I said in the fae tongue so the wolf could not understand me and wove magic to make her words come out in the same language, concealing our conversation from him.

"But this is Morden... my protector. The one I told you about. I can't believe he's here, that he's come for me!"

That was a blade in my chest, slipping into the fracture in my heart and twisting to prise it open. "You believe this male has come for you... to take you from me. To save you. Do you feel you need saving?"

She blinked at me and then frowned. "No, of course not."

Shadows rose and rippled around me as I looked from her to Morden. "You wish to leave with him."

She hesitated, and then shook her head. "No, but—"

Morden slipped his hand into his pocket and withdrew something—a silver chain. Saphira's blue eyes lit up again at the sight of the bracelet, as if it meant the world to her and so did the male who had brought it to her.

"I thought I would never see it again." Joy shone in her eyes, brightening her face, her happiness so fierce that something within me snapped, hissing at the sight of it and how she took several steps towards the wolf.

A wall of shadows shot up between her and the male, keeping them from each other, and she glowered over her shoulder at me.

I held her gaze, darkness pouring through my veins in response to that insidious, poisonous thing that writhed in my chest, snapping fangs at Morden as he glared at me from beyond the veil of shadows.

"Take our guest below." I did not take my eyes from Saphira's as I issued that command to my guards and to Malachi.

Hurt flashed in her blue eyes, revealing she knew what I meant by that. I was sending Morden to the dungeon. That hurt morphed into anger as she stared me down.

And bit out, "You mean to stop me from seeing my friend?"

Friend.

I despised that word.

I had not missed how the wolf had looked at her before I had stepped into her path, halting her. I had not missed the banked heat beneath the relief as his gaze had swung her way and taken her in. I had not missed his desperate attempt to take her attention away from me by producing something he knew would steal it and bring it to him instead.

"Until I know more about this wolf—this threat—the male will be staying somewhere he cannot harm anyone." I watched as Malachi seized hold of the male and the wretched wolf fought admirably as a black hole opened beneath them and they fell into it together, Mal teleporting him to the dungeon.

Saphira's glare was withering. "Morden wouldn't hurt anyone."

She said it with such confidence, as if she knew this male so well that she could say what he would and would not do. But she did not know him. Morden wanted to take her from me. Morden wanted to hurt me. It had all been there in his eyes when I had been speaking with her, when he had been seething with a need to make her look at him instead.

She went to walk away from me.

I grabbed her arm with one hand and my pack with the other.

And teleported.

She stumbled from the suddenness of the teleport as we landed on a sliver of plateau high on Noainfir, close to the peak of the black mountain, the loose gravel crunching beneath her boots as she turned on me.

"Why did you do that? What will happen to Morden?" She looked from me to the castle far below us, and the treacherous stretch of jagged rock, steep cliffs and loose shale that formed the only path back to it.

I growled, "Malachi will deal with him."

She whirled to face me again, her damp silver braid swinging with the sharp motion, and scrubbed the rain from her face so she could glare at me. "Mal? The same Mal that helped you hurt those seelie?"

I slid her a black look as the storm pelted us, because she knew I had needed to deal with those seelie, that by entering my court, they had not given me a choice. They had known the second they had crossed my border that being caught was a death sentence.

"Answer me," she bit out as worry and anger clashed in her eyes. "What will happen to Morden? Are you going to have him killed? He's my friend!"

"Friend? Or lover?" I gritted from between clenched teeth.

She reared back, her eyebrows shooting high on her forehead. "You're jealous."

"I am not." I adjusted the pack on my shoulder, hoping to draw her attention there instead. "It was simply time to leave. Malachi will deal with your friend."

"The same Malachi you had been preparing to take with you instead of me?" She clenched her fists at her sides as the rain soaked her flimsy navy blouse and saturated her leather corset and pants, clothing that gave her far too little protection for where I was taking her, and I arched a brow at my astute little wolf as she tipped her chin up. "Just give me a moment with Morden. Five minutes. That's all I'm asking."

She was asking for five minutes too many. I was damned if I was going to take her back to that wolf.

I shook my head, sending cold rain slithering down my

neck. "I have waited too long for my revenge as it is. You can wait a day or two to see your *friend*."

"Will he even be alive when I return?"

I growled now, rounding on her, my mood taking a dark turn as she averted her gaze, her air growing awkward and a flicker of regret crossing her face.

"I am not a monster, little lamb. Your precious *friend* will remain unharmed." Despite the dark urge I had to remove his head from his shoulders.

"Promise?" she whispered and glanced up at me, her brow furrowing as worry glittered in her eyes.

She worried so much for this wolf. This friend of hers. Her precious Morden.

Would she worry so much for me if I were missing, if we did not see each other for a time? I doubted it, and I did not care. Saphira was a tool in my arsenal, the key to my vengeance, that was all. Morden's arrival was nothing more than a timely reminder that I had a goal that required my attention, one I had been working towards for too long now to get distracted by nothing more than a female.

I stared down at her, not revealing anything I felt as I built a wall around my heart, replacing the one she had been tearing down stone by stone. Closing it off just as she had accused me of doing.

"The wolf will live." I pivoted away from her, hardening my heart, trudging up the barely visible path that would take me around the jagged peak of Noainfir.

I tracked her with my senses through the lightening rain, and when she did not move to follow me, I looked over my shoulder, the part of me I failed to kill fearing she might attempt to return to the wolf, abandoning me.

She stood with her back to me, gazing down at the world as the rain cleared, as the storm rolled south-west towards Belkarthen, crimson lightning striking at the sweeping farmland beyond Falkyr.

"Where are we?" She glanced over her shoulder at me, her expression soft, no trace of anger remaining in her blue eyes as they met mine.

"You stand upon Noainfir, the sacred mountain of the Shadow Court, on Dagger Overlook. This is as far as I can teleport us. We must walk down the other side until we are beyond the magic wards on the border and I can teleport us again." I opened the pack slung over my shoulder and pulled out the one thing I knew would make her believe I had considered bringing her rather than Malachi with me, revealing I had been torn between them until the last moment.

She stared at the dagger I offered her.

Her dagger.

Her hand shook a little as she reached for it and gripped it tightly, drawing it to her and looking between me and the weapon I had made for her.

"Try not to stab me in the back with it." I turned that back to her, heading for the path to the border.

Only she did not move to follow.

When I looked back at her this time, she clutched the dagger to her chest, her eyes on my court.

"Come," I said, and she still did not move.

I walked back to her and came to stand beside her on the narrow plateau, studying her as she surveyed my kingdom, her lips parting as she drank it all in, from the western Wraith Wood and the mountains blazing with an orange glow beyond it, to the southern shores of Belkarthen, and then down at Falkyr where it nestled among woods and water below us.

"If you are considering traversing the mountain to reach your friend, I would advise against it. This side of the mountain is rather unforgiving," I said.

No reaction.

I could not decipher that look in her eyes as she stood silently above the world at my side—above my world.

"Saphira." I risked murmuring her name, one I had used so rarely, rather than calling her by a pet name I had created to keep space between us, to tease and keep her distant from me.

"It's beautiful," she breathed.

I looked at the Shadow Court, trying to see it through her eyes, my kingdom laid out before her, ensconced by treacherous black peaks on three sides and an ocean on the fourth, the rolling lands stretching out beneath the aurora-kissed sky.

Her gaze shifted to me, soft and warm, and filled with a light I could not name.

One I found bewitching.

"Now I understand why you built your castle on the side of this mountain."

The wall I had been erecting around my heart crumbled a little as she said that, as she gazed at my court and called it beautiful when many in this world found it frightening and dark. But then she always had seen things differently to many in Lucia.

Things including myself. She had never truly been afraid of me.

Her gaze lowered to the dagger. "I don't intend to stab you in the back, Kael. And Morden is just a friend."

Kael.

The wall did not just crumble upon hearing Vyr's name for me on her lips, it exploded into dust, leaving my heart far too exposed.

Part of me wanted to ask her what she saw me as if Morden was only her friend, if she called me by a nickname my sister had given me. Something more than a friend?

Her lover?

Or something even more than that?

I lost my nerve when she looked up at me, averting my gaze to the dagger she gripped.

"You seem to like it," I said instead of the words that wanted to leave my lips, ones that would leave my exposed heart far too vulnerable, and ones I should not even be considering. I reminded myself that Saphira was a tool of vengeance. A tool.

Not a beautiful, bewitching wolf.

"It's not every day a dark fae king gives you a dagger crafted by his own hands." She toyed with it, her words warm with a teasing edge.

"I am not sure whether you are more pleased by the fact I gave you a dagger, a weapon you could easily wield against me, or that I made it for you." I turned my cheek to her, taking in the view of the Shadow Court, easily able to pick out the blacksmith in Falkyr where I had made the dagger with her in mind.

"Probably the latter. Maybe the former." She smiled at me when I glanced at her and shrugged. "I don't know. I honestly never thought someone would give me a weapon, let alone the training to wield it."

"Training you deserved, and training we shall resume when we return." I looked at the dagger in her hand and wondered if she knew how precious it really was. "The blade is a smaller twin to the one I forged for myself centuries ago."

I drew that blade from the sheath hanging from my waist, showing it to her, and her eyes darted over the grip and markings that matched her dagger.

"The metal used to make it is the same as my armour and crown, and Vyr's weapon and armour too. It comes from this sacred mountain, and each ingot is blessed and reserved for royalty."

She almost dropped the dagger, fumbling with it as her eyes clashed with mine.

"I don't deserve something like this." She tried to push it into my hands, shoving it against my chest when I refused to take it. "Give it to Vyr or someone special."

I reached out and swept my knuckles across her cheek, my eyes locked with hers and my voice softer than I had heard it in a long time.

"There is none more deserving of it than you, Saphira."

CHAPTER 49

SAPHIRA

Morden was here in Lucia, and he had my charm bracelet.

It could only mean one thing—my pack knew what had happened to me.

I kept glancing back over my shoulder as I followed Kaeleron along the narrow rocky track, heading down a steep incline towards a glittering sea of dark grey sand punctured by the twisted bleached bones of dead trees.

What was Malachi doing to Morden right now?

I wanted to ask Kaeleron that, but I had poked that bear enough times that whenever I so much as mentioned Morden's name, he grew feral.

Near rabid.

Jealousy.

The same acidic feeling had scoured my insides whenever I had been around Elanaluvyr, so I could easily recognise it in him. He might pretend otherwise, might even be oblivious to the emotion that had him snapping fangs whenever I dared to even think of that male, blaming it on a need to protect his kingdom or some other bullshit, but he was jealous.

No doubt about it.

And it shouldn't warm me, but by the gods and my ancestors it did.

Because it made me feel I wasn't alone in my emotions, in my desires.

I toyed with the dagger sheathed at my hip, my gaze on Kaeleron's back as he carefully navigated a particularly brutal stretch of the path, where the narrow worn track fell off into a sheer drop that would most likely kill me. It might kill Kaeleron too. I wasn't sure if he could teleport yet or whether we were still within the bounds of the magical ward that protected his court.

One that had been breached in the west, allowing seelie into his lands.

I didn't lead my pack, but I still grew as angry as my father whenever another wolf shifter crossed into our territory without permission.

When I looked back over my shoulder this time, it wasn't the castle I was looking for, it was the mountain itself. The peak loomed above me like a great shard of obsidian. A sacred mountain. Kaeleron had called it that, and had said the metal mined from it was precious and rare, and reserved for royalty. This was the mountain I had read about in the library.

Some part of me still didn't believe I deserved the dagger he had crafted for me, not now I knew the metal used in it came from such a rare source. I wasn't royalty. Not even close. I was just the daughter of an alpha, fated to another alpha, raised to act not as his second in command but as his peacekeeper and baby maker.

"You practically vibrate with tension," Kaeleron grumbled and glanced over his shoulder at me, his feet somehow still keeping to the path with a confidence I didn't share, not when it was so narrow and treacherous. "Is this about the wolf?"

I shook my head. "No. This dagger is feeling a lot heavier than before."

He chuckled. "Do you wish I had not given it to you now?"

My eyebrows pinched as I considered the answer to that question. It came easily.

"No. But a heads up might have been nice. Like... hey, Saphi, I made this dagger for you and you might get some strange looks because people in the castle can recognise the metal I used should only be used for myself and my sister, but I figured what the heck, have it anyway, you're totally special enough."

His chuckle grew warmer and he stopped at a bend ahead of me, slowly turning to face me. "You believe I would say it like that?"

"No. You'd sound more haughty." I stopped close to him when he didn't move and angled my head up, my legs trembling a little as I took my gaze away from the deadly drop to my right.

His smile hit me like a fist in the chest.

Knocking the wind from me.

Good gods, he shouldn't be allowed to smile, not when he put his heart and soul into it, when the mask fell away to reveal a hint of the boy I had seen in that painting, one who looked as if he had made a career out of causing trouble and had spent most of his time laughing.

"But would I still call you Saphi?"

My legs trembled for another reason as he murmured that, his silver gaze intense and fixed on mine, a flicker of heat in its depths. He rarely called me Saphira, and I wasn't wholly used to that yet, so switching to calling me by a pet name, one that sounded so intimate on his lips, far too romantic, had my world tipping on its axis again.

"Maybe. Maybe not." I shrugged.

Kaeleron pulled me into his arms, the movement so swift I squeaked as he tugged me against his hard chest, my palms landing on the firm leather of his armour. Darkness swirled around me, glittering with golden stars, and then my feet were on solid ground again. Or at least soft ground that shifted beneath my boots as I moved my weight.

But Kaeleron didn't release me.

He stared down at me, his face so close to mine, and for a heartbeat, I thought he might kiss me again.

"Who is that wolf that he came all the way to Lucia to take you back?" His gaze lowered to my mouth, darkening by degrees before it lifted to lock with mine again, his voice a deep rumble like thunder as he studied me closely. "Your lover? Your fated one?"

I pushed out of his arms on a scowl and snapped, "You *bought* me from my *fated mate*."

The sand beneath my boots trembled and I looked at it, at the ripples that emanated from beneath Kael's boots as shadows twisted and snaked through the grains. The air chilled around me, raising goosebumps on my skin, and I wrapped my arms around myself.

Only I wasn't sure it was to keep the chill in the air off my skin.

It was to chase away the chill in my heart—in my soul.

"Lucas—" I started and then swallowed, my wolf side howling with a blend of rage and agony, a terrible sound that filled all of me and made me want to tip my head back and unleash it. Whatever hurt, whatever grief, I had felt when Lucas had rejected me was long dead, scorched away by this burning rage that whirled within me, a fire that kept my need for vengeance strong. I lowered my gaze to my boots, unable to look at Kaeleron as I confessed this, some misplaced sense of shame rolling up on me as I took that brave step towards him and away from my past. "Lucas is my fated mate, and I stupidly fell in love with him... and then he not only rejected me on the night we were to be mated, but he shut me in a cage and forced me to watch... to watch him with another."

The ground didn't just tremble now, it shook so violently I feared I would lose balance, and the stars above began to fall, slowly at first but then faster and faster, bright streaks of white that blazed to their deaths one by one, lighting up the world.

Vyr had warned that when Kaeleron lost his temper, he was so powerful that this entire realm could pay the price, but I hadn't imagined this.

He was tearing stars from the sky.

Was turning the sand into a violent sea, with great waves that rolled outwards from him and broke against the bones of the trees.

Because I had poured out my pain to him, had finally told someone what had happened that night.

Kaeleron's crimson-to-silver eyes blazed as brightly as the falling stars against their backdrop of black, his skin as white as those stars as his dark lips peeled back off his jagged fangs.

"I already wanted to kill him for selling you," he growled, his voice as dark as the night closing in above us, as terrifying as those stars that continued to fall, that slammed into the sand of the Wastes around us, throwing it into the air. "Now I will kill him slowly. He will beg before I end his life... beg for your forgiveness... and you will give him none. Do you hear me? *None*. Because such a wretched, blind male is unworthy of having you as his mate."

His black-tipped fingers brushed my cheek, the touch gentle and careful, a mere whisper of his claws against my skin.

Darkness reigned in his eyes, a fierce hunger that echoed within me as I leaned into the touch, needing more, needing firmer contact between us as I cherished his dark vow.

How strongly I wanted that beautiful vision he had painted in my mind should have startled me and even shocked me, but rather than feeling horrified by it, I embraced it. Lucas would pay for what he had done, and if I unleashed Kaeleron upon him, I would only find satisfaction in his bloody end.

"Kael," I murmured as my brow furrowed and my thoughts turned to Morden again, and what his appearance might mean. "I'm afraid my pack might be in danger. Lucas is... He's strong and cruel with it. Since he became alpha of his pack, they've been growing violent, many of the males going to other nearby packs to gather females for their own. I thought it was just because Lucas was grieving and that he would get them under control, but I'm beginning to suspect that he's letting them do those things... might even be encouraging it. I'm worried that if Morden is here, and he has my bracelet with him—a bracelet Lucas took from me—that either Lucas came to my pack or my pack went to him. What if—"

I couldn't bring myself to say it, to voice my fear that my pack were now at the mercy of Lucas and his men, some part of me feeling that I would only make it come true if I put it out there.

Kaeleron's skin darkened to light tan and the shadows around his eyes melted away as his irises returned to silver and his hand remained on my face, cupping it now, his palm warm against my chilled skin.

"We shall recover the heart quickly and then you can speak with the wolf." His thumb brushed my cheek close to my eye, his gaze so earnest that it stole my breath and all I could do was nod in agreement.

His hand lowered to my arm and he skimmed it down the length of it, and surprised me by taking hold of my hand.

"Come, little wolf." He gently tugged me forwards and as he walked, the sand settled and the sky stilled, and all the stars were back in their places, twinkling among the aurora.

The raw power of Kaeleron sent a shiver coursing through me and I thought about his promise, about how fierce and angry he had been, and something deep within me stirred in response, as if it had been slumbering and his wrath had awakened it.

Or maybe it was this strange world and the connection I felt to the lands, how strongly they called to me, its dark power seeping into me and affecting me.

Because I wanted Lucas on his knees, begging forgiveness.

Only I wanted to be the one who had put him there.

CHAPTER 50
KAELERON

I could not get my mind off what Saphira had told me. Rage simmered in my veins, barely leashed and in danger of stealing control from me as we trekked through the Wastes, teleporting ahead a few miles whenever the magical field that coated the land here allowed me to use that power.

Her own mate had humiliated and sold her.

A male she had clearly loved.

No wonder she had been in so much pain when I had met her, and had been lost to darkness at times, grappling with a hunger I could name.

Vengeance.

No wonder she had grown withdrawn at Beltane, on edge and tormented by the festivities.

I catalogued every moment I had glimpsed her pain, her darkness, and her trauma, filing them away because for every second she had suffered, I would make Lucas suffer a lunar cycle when I found him and dragged him to the Shadow Court. I would make him weep. Beg. I would make him so desperate for death he would plead me for it rather than his life.

The stars blurred above me and I reined in the darkness howling within me like a storm, pulling it back under my control before I did something reckless, like teleporting to the nearest waygate to the human world and hunting this male down, leaving Saphira undefended.

I still could not believe that someone, especially a shifter who were known for being so possessive and protective of their fated one and felt strongly about their mate bonds, would do this to her. To someone so pure and kind, so loving and beautiful. Someone who deserved a male who would worship her, would strive to take care of her every need, and would destroy the world to defend her.

I could only imagine how deeply the betrayal had cut her, and how that wound festered.

And how she must have despised me for buying her.

I had saved her from a far worse fate than she would have had if another at the auction had bought her. That was my only consolation as she continued to walk beside me, lost in her own thoughts.

Her fated one was unworthy of her, and destiny had been cruel to bind her to a male who had not only treated her so abominably, but did the same to other females. I had done my research as best I could in the limited time I had to act between Neve's vision and the auction. Saphira had not been the first female Lucas had sold. He had been making a name for himself in the seedy underground as the place to go for virgin females.

My gaze strayed to her, that distant look in her eyes unsettling me and making me want to find a way to bring her back to me. She needed time. Patience. I could be patient while she fought through the mire of her thoughts and her feelings for this male, while she clawed her way back to me and vanquished the wolf, banishing him from her mind.

And her heart.

I was not sure how I could make things better for her. I wracked my brain as I sensed the magic around me weaken and gripped her hand and teleported us again, landing us barely a mile deeper into the Wastes this time, and hitting upon a way I could help her.

"When we return, we shall resume our training, and I shall school you in the art of war."

Her dull eyes brightened as they lifted to me.

The thought of her seeking vengeance upset the balance of something within me, igniting a war between a need to shelter her and a need to teach her. I knew the price you paid for treading that path, and I did not want Saphira to lose the woman she was—her warmth and her kindness—by bloodying her hands.

I wanted to help her.

I wanted to be her sword and her shield, if she would let me, even as I recalled how angry she had been when I had stepped in last time, acting as her weapon against the fae female who had hurt her.

"I'd like that," she murmured and surveyed the glittering sands stretching around us. "It's strangely pretty here."

"It was more beautiful once." I looked at the ashy land punctured by spiny shards of lifeless trees—a barren land where only the strongest and most violent creatures could survive now.

Saphira's gaze landed on me, curiosity shining in it, no trace of her pain or her doubts now as she waited for me to tell her more.

I obeyed her silent command.

"It was once a verdant, green kingdom, ruled by beasts and nature. A land no fae had a right to and one that was greatly sought after. Fae courts do so enjoy expanding their lands, equating the size of them with their power and wealth."

She frowned. "But you don't?"

I shook my head. "My court is among the smaller, and yet there are few fae as feared or as powerful as I am."

"Or so modest." She smiled slightly.

I chuckled. "I speak only the truth. That truth is that a court is only as powerful as its king."

"And that means the Shadow Court is ranked number one."

It was my turn to shake my head. "There are others more powerful than I in this world, but I am one of the strongest."

"What happened to this place then? Was it war?" She looked at the lands that stretched as far as the eye could see and the magic thickening the air faded again, allowing me to teleport us another mile or two deeper into the Wastes.

"It happened long before I was born." I flexed my fingers against her hand, enjoying the feel of it in mine. "It was a magical cataclysm, but not like the one that caused the Wrathborn Scar in the south lands."

"Wrathborn Scar. That sounds delightfully ominous. What happened there?" She looked south, as if she might spy it, but it was hundreds of miles away.

"A war that went too far."

"What were they fighting over?" Her eyebrows rose high on her forehead.

She was going to love the answer to that question, I knew it before it left my lips.

"A female."

"I'm beginning to think fae males are worse than shifters. So ready to destroy everything for a female." Her little smile warmed the space in my chest that had grown cold the moment Morden had shown up in that storm and for the first time since he had arrived, I felt she would not leave the Shadow Court.

Or at least, she would come back.

If I asked it of her.

"I need to know more about that. When we're back at Falkyr, I'm going straight to the library to look it up." She was partly teasing, but it pleased me that she placed learning more about my world above running to Morden. "But you were telling me about this place and what happened here. A magical cataclysm doesn't sound like a good thing. Is that why the air reeks of it?"

I nodded. "It is in the sand… the remains of everything that was here when the explosion happened and obliterated it all."

She shivered and cast a nervous glance at the sands. "And we're safe here? It's not going to go kaboom again?"

"You are safe, little wolf." I would never take her anywhere I felt she was in real danger, where I felt I could not handle whatever came at us. "The residual magic in the sand simply dampens my abilities at times."

"Hence the short teleports."

I nodded.

She looked over her shoulder. "So how did the Shadow Court survive unscathed? If this explosion was big enough to be called a cataclysm and wiped out everything, how did it not affect the surrounding courts?"

I glanced back in the direction of my court too, my voice growing softer as I thought about the stories I had been told, and the one responsible for saving that court. "My father… he took measures to protect the border of the Shadow Court using magic—at great expense to himself—and so the mountains only bear scars."

She looked at those scars, great curving cuts into the faces of the mountains that formed sheer walls of rock.

"What happened to him?" she said quietly, as if sensing my shift in mood, the sombreness that welled up in me as I thought about him.

"I am told he was unconscious for weeks, that the court feared he would not recover. He had no heir at the time. It was before he met my mother. My uncle was poised to take the throne and had been acting as steward, closing in on it. The day before he was due to be crowned king, my father awoke. My uncle went back to the legions, returning to acting as his general."

I teleported with her again.

When we landed, she said, "Was your uncle a good man? Would he have made a good king?"

"No." It was easy to answer that question as I thought of the days following my parents' deaths, as I recalled him closing in on my throne, challenging my fragile hold on it as I grieved.

"What happened to him?" That question was cautious, as if she already knew the answer.

"He is dead."

She did not press me to expand on that, to tell her the bitter truth—that my first act as king had been to order his death as punishment for failing to protect my parents.

I should have executed myself for the same reason.

But Vyr had needed me.

And so I had moulded myself into a blade sheathed in shadow, one strong enough to cut down anyone who sought to hurt her again.

I teleported with Saphira, managing to shift us further this time, and stilled as we landed, immediately drawing her closer to me and down into a crouch behind the thick bleached trunk of a fallen tree. She peered over it at the tower that loomed ahead of us.

A tower of bones.

It looked as if some dark power had raised all the bones buried in the sands and drawn them here, constructing this grim monument to death. Bones as big as dragon femurs formed columns on each level, smaller bones laid horizontally between them to fill the gaps. Around the windows, skulls had been placed, fae mostly around the curved sides, but at the peak of the arches, they were the skulls of horned beasts. At the top of the three-storey tower sat a crown of huge fangs, each taller than I was.

"That looks inviting," Saphira muttered beside me. "You should be taking notes. You could make some serious improvements on how formidable your castle looks if you cherry picked aspects of this tower. Wouldn't want to be outdone by a lich."

I chuckled low at her humour, a weapon she often employed when nervous, and studied the tower, covering all the angles and looking for a sign of life. Power radiated from it, one unfamiliar to me, but it was strong, coming in waves.

Like a beating heart.

A cold sense of dread spilled through my veins as I felt that beat, as I looked at the tower, and felt the warmth of Saphira beside me.

This was too dangerous, and not only for myself and Saphira.

Neve and this dragon stone were connected somehow, in a way she refused to tell me, and taking this crystal to her might place her in danger, might change everything in a way I did not want, drawing the gaze of the one who hunted her towards my court.

Exposing her again.

But I had to take it.

Neve herself had asked me to go through with it and bring her the stone. If she was prepared to face whatever happened when it was back in her hands, then I could be too.

I just needed to get my hands on it.

A breeze kicked the sand up around me as I studied the tower, cataloguing the entrance and the piles of bones that encircled it. Guards. This lich was strong enough to command a creature to rise and do its bidding even when it was only bones.

That was not good.

The lich in my court were powerful, but even they were limited to reanimating corpses whose deaths had been less than a lunar cycle ago. I stared at the bone piles. Their forms were not that of someone who had died and then their flesh had rotted or had been picked off the bones. These things had been nothing more than bones when they had been released from the lich's hold, falling into a crumpled heap until the lich summoned them again.

"Kael." Saphira tugged at my arm, her grip firm. "What's that?"

My head whipped towards her, adrenaline shooting through my veins as I instantly readied for battle, but it was not an enemy she stared at across the sea of sand.

It was a storm.

The great whirling wall of sand was travelling at speed, heading straight for us.

I gripped her hand and pulled her to her feet as I quickly scanned our surroundings, my pulse kicking up a notch and the urge to get her somewhere safe before the storm hit us at the helm, driving me to move with her, to protect her.

"There." I pointed to a cavemouth barely visible beyond a crag of black rock at the base of one of the mountains that surrounded the western flank of the Forgotten Wastes and began running in that direction with her.

I could not risk a teleport, not with Saphira in tow.

Already the magic in the air was thickening, a cloying blanket that dampened my power, whipped up by the wind that tore at the sand and unleashed the magic buried deep within it.

It would be a while before I could use magic again.

Not good.

I pulled her along with me as I ran, heart thundering at the thought of Saphira being caught out in the storm. She stumbled on the sand, losing her footing, and I tugged my arm upwards, stopping her from falling. Rather than running with her, I swept her up into my arms, carrying her tucked against me like the precious load she was as I set off again.

She wrapped her arms around my neck and breathed urgently against my ear.

"Faster! It's closing in on us."

CHAPTER 51

KAELERON

We made it to the cave before the sandstorm reached us and I set Saphira down and pushed her ahead of me into the darkness, my senses scanning the tunnel that curved just ahead of us, banking right. Nothing moved. Nothing breathed except us. My heightened vision allowed me to make out the sandy floor and the few bones scattered around it, old enough that I breathed a little easier. Whatever had called this place home once had long since moved on, and there were not enough bones to create anything that could be used against us by a lich. We were safe for now.

Wind howled across the cave mouth, a blur of sand and magic that had me urging Saphira deeper into the shelter of the cave, around the corner where we would be out of sight and safe from the storm.

I guided her to the back of the cave and set the pack down.

"I can't see a thing," she muttered and groped along the wall, moving into a crouch as she followed it downwards, and then patted the sand and slumped onto it.

I opened my pack and rooted around in it until I found the single candle I had bought with me. I placed the base of it into the sand, pressing it deep so it stood upright, and then lit the wick. Warm light blazed outwards, chasing back the darkness, revealing Saphira where she sat huddled in the corner, her knees tucked to her chest.

"You're like a scout. What else do you have in there, Mr Prepared-For-Anything?" She leaned over and tugged the pack towards her, her eyebrows rising as she plucked out packages of dried meat, a bottle of water, the rolls of gauze and the ointments. She put it all back in. Except the meat. She kept hold of that and when I arched a brow at her, she tucked it close to her chest. "This is mine now. Don't even think about taking it. You should have packed some for yourself."

I held my hand out to her. "And you need to learn how to share."

She opened the packet and pulled a strip of meat out. "I've spent enough of my life sharing. For once, I'm being selfish. I'm doing all the things I want to do."

"Is that what you think you are doing in my court—being selfish?" My eyebrows dipped low as I plucked one of the pieces of meat from the packet as she offered it to me and searched her eyes. "You have not been selfish once in the time I have known you."

"I am selfish. If I wasn't... I don't know. I just feel selfish for... for enjoying my time here." She picked at the meat she held, tearing small pieces from it as she looked at it, her brows lowering to shadow her blue eyes.

"It is not selfish to enjoy something, especially when it comes at no cost to anyone. I was right about your pack being a cage, one I am surprised you want to return to with that wolf." I broke a piece of meat off and popped it into my mouth.

She glowered at me. "That wolf has a name, and... if I want to return, it's because I need to know my family are safe, Kael."

She kept calling me that, and each time my heart constricted and I had foolish thoughts, like keeping her with me.

Like making her stay.

I owned her after all.

"And what happens then?" When a confused crinkle marred her brow, I added, "When you return to your pack and see they are safe, what happens then? Do you allow them to place you back in a cage, or will you fly free?"

She frowned at her meat, the candlelight playing across her delicate features, dancing in her silver hair.

"I don't know. I haven't figured that out yet." Her answer was quiet, softly spoken, and I believed her, because I knew the truth she refused to face.

She wanted to see her family were safe, but she did not want to subject herself to the life she had lived with them again. She wanted more than they would give her. Her fingers brushed the ring I had placed on her finger and she toyed with it as she watched the flame flickering on the candle, drifting away from me, deep into her thoughts.

So I drew her back to me.

"The bracelet the wolf had, it is special to you?"

She frowned and nodded, and then lifted her gaze from the ring, settling it on my face as she smiled. It wobbled. And pain had her eyes glittering.

"Everlee gave it to me. It's a charm bracelet. You add things to it. Treasured memories. You buy little silver charms, like tiny metal carvings that represent the things you see, and add them to the bracelet. She gave it to me when I told her how much I wanted to travel and see the world."

The bracelet I had seen had been a plain silver chain, with no adornments other than a small wolf.

"And did you see the world?" I knew the answer to that question as her expression took on a sombre edge and she toyed with the ring again, her shoulders shifting on a long sigh.

"No. My father wouldn't allow it." She nibbled the meat, darkness building in her eyes. Anger that her own flesh and blood had kept her caged long before Lucas had, before I had.

"But you have seen more than the world, little wolf. You have seen a whole new world." I reached my hand towards the candle and focused hard, pushing through the dampening fog of magic in the air to summon my own.

Her eyes widened as parts of the flame leaped upwards, becoming wolves that sprang and pranced before they disappeared into smoke, bounding free of their invisible bonds.

"Then I guess you owe me a charm for the bracelet then." She pulled another piece of the meat free of the package.

I eased back to lean against the wall as I contemplated that. "I will gladly make you one, but I am not sure what would best represent my court or Lucia."

She stood, moved my pack and set it down where she had been, and then eased onto her backside. Right next to me.

"It would need to be something special." She hugged her knees to her chest as awareness of her proximity drummed in my blood, the few inches that separated us feeling like nothing more than a wisp of air.

Her face pinched as she watched the candle, her profile to me.

"An elkyn?" I offered.

She scrunched up her nose. "Elkyn are beautiful, but I was thinking something that reminded me of... your court."

You.

She had wanted to say 'you', but had lost her nerve. I was

sure of it as I subtly leaned towards her, placing my left hand behind her backside and bracing my weight on it, and sensed her tension and scented her nerves.

"I have an idea," I said.

"What?" She tensed as I leaned towards her, reaching my right hand around her waist, my body caging her and my mouth close to hers.

And scowled when I plucked her dagger from the sheathe at her waist and held it before her as I sat back where I had been.

"A blade like this one, wrought from metal from Noainfir. A reminder of your strength, your courage, and your spirit." I gazed at it, scrutinising the details of it. "It would be a challenge, but I believe I could do it."

She placed her hand over the dagger, fingers brushing my skin. "It would be perfect."

Her words felt as sharp as the blade I gripped, cutting at my heart as I thought of her bracelet and its reminders of places she had been, and was no longer, and I found I did not want to be something she looked back on, nothing more than a memory to her.

I seized her nape, my body moving of its own accord, and brought my mouth down on hers, claiming her lips in a bruising, desperate kiss.

And rejoiced as she returned it, her lips dancing with mine, spreading heat through my body that eased the chill that had taken root in my chest.

She loosed a little moan as she shifted onto her knees, coming to face me, her hands lifting to rest on my left shoulder and right biceps. I planted one hand against her lower spine, pulling her against me, kissing her deeper as I drowned in my need of her, not wanting this moment to end. That chill lingered, marring my thoughts even as Saphira's kiss thawed it, together with the way her hands found the buckles of my leather armour.

Her lips remained dancing against mine, each stroke of her tongue maddening me, warming me, as she slowly undressed me, her fingers finding each buckle, as if she had been memorising their positions the whole time we had been travelling so she could unfastened them without looking. I untied the bow on her corset, loosening the string that cinched it closed, unravelling it until the strip of leather came away in my hands. I tossed it to one side and lowered my mouth to her throat, earning a husky moan as my reward as I stroked my tongue over the faded marks I had placed on her fair skin. She leaned into each brush of my lips as I worked my way downwards, lifting the hem of her blouse from her leathers at the same time.

When she eased back, granting me better access, I made fast work of stripping the blouse from her and helped her with my chest piece, casting both away from her before eagerly cupping her bare breasts. Her teeth sank into her lower lip and her blue gaze grew hooded as I thumbed her nipples, teasing the stiff pink peaks, and then I swooped on them, grabbing her backside to haul her up onto her knees before me. Her hands flew to my hair, fingers burying deep to cling to me as I sucked and teased one nipple and then the other, lavishing them with the attention they deserved.

"Kael," she murmured, the scent of her need maddening me.

I lowered my hand to cup her between her thighs, cursing the obstruction between us, and she mirrored me, her small hand brushing over my caged erection. I groaned low in my throat, breaths shortening as she tormented me.

Apparently, she tormented herself too, because she tore at the laces of my leathers, a frustrated little thing that pulled a husky chuckle from me. She shot me a glare and had her revenge, silencing me with her palm against my bare flesh. The heat of her scalded me as she stroked my cock, wrapping her fingers around it tightly to choke me. Her thumb grazed the sensitive head on the down stroke, stealing my breath, flooding me with need that bordered on painful and making my mind race forwards to being inside her.

I wanted to be inside her.

Deep.

Claiming her.

I reached for the fastenings of her own trousers, but she beat me to it, shooting to her feet and ripping them open, hastily shimmying out of them and kicking them aside with her boots. I was not the only one who did not want to wait.

She proved that by straddling my thighs, one hand branding my chest as she pushed my back against the rough wall of the cave, and the other reaching for my cock. My hand joined hers and together we guided my erection to her slick pussy, our moans combining as we rubbed the head through the essence of her arousal to her opening and I nudged inside her.

I kept hold of myself as her hand moved to my shoulders, as she bit her lip and eased down onto me, slowly taking me into her inch by inch. My breaths shortened as our eyes locked, as we seemed to join in more ways than just our bodies interlocking. Our souls seemed to entwine as she gazed into my eyes, as she sank onto me, taking me as deep as I could go, and she scooted closer to me.

I was falling.

I knew it as I looked at her, as I wrapped my arms around her and she began to move on me, slow strokes that rocked my entire world.

I had never been in love, but I had seen it between others, and this feeling growing within me was unmistakable. Raw. Vulnerable. A flicker of emotion and a bond that felt weak and breakable, but so dangerous at the same time as I moved with Saphira, as I drowned in the warm azure of her eyes and the feel of her in my arms.

For so long, I had been set on my path, things in motion that I had little control over despite all my power—things that would have consequences if I fell for her.

Yet I could not help myself as I leaned in to capture her lips, some reckless part of me wanting to steal more than a kiss from her.

My little wolf was bewitching, and brave, and beautiful.

And I was falling for her.

She gasped softly into my ear as she shattered, as she pulled me over the edge with her into a freefall that had me aware of only her and this feeling beating within a heart that had once been hollow but now roared to life.

I wrapped my arms tightly around her and kissed her softly, reverently, deeply.

I was never letting her go.

Saphira was mine.

And Great Mother help anyone who tried to take her from me.

CHAPTER 52

KAELERON

My senses immediately stretched towards the tower as I led Saphira towards it, my gaze rooted on the bleached bones that formed the columns and walls of it as I breathed through the rising nerves, slowly vanquishing them. Again, I sensed no life within it, but that was not a comfort. I was not sure a lich could be considered a living being. They had crossed to the other side, born behind the veil of death.

Saphira pressed close to me, her side grazing my arm, and I squeezed her hand, silently reassuring her that I was here with her and would allow nothing to happen to her. What I really wanted to do was return home with her and bring Malachi to this place instead, but the thought of leaving her alone in the castle with Morden had me keeping her pinned to my side.

Despite how uneasy I was about taking her into the tower of bones.

I glanced at her, meant only to briefly check on her, but she snared my gaze and filled my mind with thoughts of our moment in the cave. What power this little wolf wielded over me. I had held her so close and so tightly as she had slumbered, keeping watch over her as the storm had raged outside the cave, ensuring she was safe.

Afraid to let her go.

I had never feared in all my years, in all the battles I had fought that might have claimed my life, as I had in these short few months with her.

She eyed the piles of bones as we picked our way between them, whispering, "I can't sense anyone. Not a soul."

It reassured her, so I did not mention my theory that a lich might be capable of hiding from our senses, using the veil of death to conceal themselves. My court necromancers were not capable of such a thing, but they were not as old nor as powerful as the one we might face in this tower.

When we reached the arched door, I tugged Saphira closer to me.

It was open.

I signalled for her to be silent and laid the flat of my free hand against the crumbling wooden door, and carefully eased it open, pushing back the layer of glittering grey sand that covered the floor. It had piled up beneath the staircase that tracked up the curved wall too, and even coated some of the steps.

Steps made of more bones.

I glanced at Saphira to check on her and caught the fear in her eyes as she looked at those bones.

And squeezed her hand again.

Her blue eyes lifted to mine and she forced a tight smile.

I nodded to her dagger as I drew my sword, and she gripped it and pulled it from its sheath, holding it in her right hand. I was right-handed myself, but I could fight almost as well with my left, and I was damned if I would relinquish her hand to wield the weapon in my stronger one.

Sand trickled down from the point where the steps met a floor above us and Saphira looked ready to attack it as she tensed beside me, brandishing her dagger.

I pointed to the arched window close to the top of the steps, one that had a frame of bones criss-crossing it, the glass long gone, only shards of it remaining, trying to tell her it was only the wind that continued to scour the Wastes that had disturbed the sand.

Wind that might be a problem if the lich was home.

Dust from the sandstorm made the air hazy, the magic it contained dampening mine, working against me.

Good thing I was skilled with a blade as well as magic.

I tugged Saphira forwards, my steps stealthy as we ascended the bones to the first floor. I readied my weapon as I peeked to my right as it came into view and relaxed a notch when I saw only ancient, worn furniture in the large circular room. The bed was decaying, the black blanket on it rotting away, and a layer of dust covered the wooden chairs and table.

Saphira exhaled behind me as she saw the state of the room, her grip loosening a touch as we crossed it to the next set of steps. It slowly tightened as we ascended, her trailing behind me, her breathing loud in my ears as I focused on her, on that sound that told me she was alive.

Safe for now.

Flashes of a dark room crossed my vision as I led her ever upwards, of a sliver of light that stuttered, and trembling breaths sounded in my ears, far too loud.

I banished that vision from my mind, fixing my focus on my task—retrieve An'sidwain, see Saphira safely home.

I tiptoed to peek at the next floor, making sure we were alone before I continued to follow the stairs up to it. A laboratory of some kind. Wooden shelves housed colourful dusty bottles and vials, and musty tomes with yellowed pages. A curved bench took up half of the wall, covered with flecks of sand and equipment—rusty tools, more books, what looked like some kind of clamps, and a bowl of runes and bones.

Saphira stopped dead.

I looked at her and tracked her wide gaze to the centre of the room.

To a wooden table with chains and shackles attached to it, the surface scarred and stained. Blood. I looked at the tools again and then the wooden buckets lined up beneath the bench. The lich had brought his victims here to rid them of their corporeal flesh and turn them into his puppets.

That dark room flickered across my eyes again, that rough panicked breathing scraping in my ears.

Followed by screams.

I gritted my teeth so hard they hurt and clung to Saphira's hand, my heart pounding as a war erupted within me, one side demanding I take her far away from here, from danger, while the other demanded I press onwards, towards vengeance.

"Kael," she whispered.

"You are safe. Nothing will happen to you. I will not allow it, Saphira." I felt as if those words were to reassure me as much as they were to reassure her as I strode onwards, heading for the final set of bone steps, and the beating waves of power that pulsed through the tower grew stronger, beckoning me.

A crimson glow lit the top of the staircase, pulsing in time with the power coursing over my skin and sinking into my bones.

I slowed as I neared the top, gaze shifting to the plinth of white bones and the ruby crystal lovingly held aloft within two bony hands. In the middle of the crystal, a heart of fire beat in time with the waves of power.

"An'sidwain," Saphira murmured.

And reached for it before I could stop her.

The moment her fingers made contact with the crystal, darkness poured into the room.

Saphira began choking and my heart seized as she snatched the crystal and covered her mouth, her eyes watering as she turned back towards me. Not just darkness. It was poisonous.

"Run," I barked and pulled her with me, pushing her in front of me as she coughed and spluttered, still clutching the crystal tight against her chest.

She ran down the stairs ahead of me and I kept pushing her, forcing her to keep moving as black mist rolled after us. We were barely keeping ahead of it. When we hit the next floor down, I grabbed hold of her and lifted her into my arms and summoned all of my strength.

And bellowed as I forced a teleport that felt as if it was ripping my flesh from my bones.

We hit the dark grey sand outside the tower in an uncontrolled landing that ended with Saphira pinned beneath me. I rolled off her and grabbed my pack, ripping it open and snatching up the vial as she coughed and wheezed, her back arching as she struggled to push herself off the ground. Popping the lid off the vial with one hand, I grabbed her with the other, twisting her onto her back on my lap. Red streaks marred her skin, branching outwards from her lips and her eyes.

"Saphira," I whispered and her blue eyes opened, bloodshot and filled with pain. "Drink."

I tipped the vial towards her mouth and she opened for me, greedily drinking down the violet liquid I tipped onto her tongue. Her body seized, stiffening, and she jerked in my arms. I held her more tightly, pinning her arms and her legs, holding her down so she would not hurt herself. Her head launched backwards and she screamed at the top of her lungs, a scream that ended in a howl that tore at me as she shuddered.

And then her shaking subsided, the crimson veins receding to leave healthy pink skin behind.

And I could breathe again.

I pulled her to me, burying my face in her throat, breathing her in as her own breaths slowed and settled, and growled, "Fool. You should have let me take it."

Her left arm came up, wrapping around my back, and she held me gently, no doubt with all the strength she had as her body recovered from the poison and the trauma of healing so rapidly.

I pulled down another breath of her scent, pressing my nose to her hair, clinging to her as she clung to me, my heart labouring as fear trickled through my veins, whispering dark things at me. I had almost lost her.

I had almost lost her.

Power rolled over me and I eased back to look down at the crystal she still held to her chest, and frowned. This wave of power did not match the one emanating from An'sidwain.

I slowly lifted my head, my fear turning to shadows and darkness that poured through my veins as I stared at the figure standing a short distance from us.

Cloaked in tattered night.

Bound by thorny vines.

Blue fire ignited in the hollow pits of the lich's deer-skull-like head, the shimmering ghostly crown that sat between his horns distorting the jagged collar of sharp bones behind it.

"Saphira," I whispered and she looked at me, her eyes dull and tired. "Hold on tight."

I teleported with her, shrouded in black smoke and glittering stars, and grunted as I hit something solid. We fell together, and I took the brunt of the impact this time as I landed in the sand with Saphira on top of me.

Barely feet from where we had been.

The lich slowly turned to face us.

Saphira scrambled off me and I sat up, pressing my hand to the invisible barrier to my left as I kept my focus fixed on the lich to my right, between us and the tower of bones that leaked black mist.

"This isn't good," she said.

I levelled a look on her that said it was far worse than not good. I doubted our situation could get much worse.

The piles of bones behind the lich began twitching and moving, reforming into skeletons.

Or perhaps it could.

I shoved to my feet and pushed Saphira behind me as several of the skeletons launched at us, sweeping my hand out before us to form my own barrier. They slammed into it, bones scattering across the sand, each impact weakening the barrier. It would not hold long.

I handed Saphira the pack and she placed An'sidwain into it and then readied her dagger, her eyes darting over the skeletons as they reformed, their bones tumbling back together.

"Take the heart." I pressed my hand to the barrier the lich had cast, sensing it, studying it, picking it apart as I kept my eyes on the skeletons. "When I break this spell, you run."

She locked up tight. "No. What about you? You're coming with me. You're coming with me, Kael."

I glanced over my shoulder at her and she growled that demanding little growl of hers that called me a bastard and ordered me to do what she wanted.

"I'm not leaving without you," she snapped.

It was my turn to growl at her. "You are leaving. You run and you do not look back."

The skeletons slammed into the barrier before me again, and it fractured, crumbling to pieces. One made it through, launching at me, and Saphira swung the pack and struck it in the chest, the blow so fierce it broke apart.

And then she was yanking off her corset and kicking off her boots.

"What in the Great Mother's name are you doing?" I snapped at her as she stripped.

"I'm faster as a wolf." She loosened her pants and pulled her blouse over her head, flashing her breasts, and then she was a wolf hurtling towards the skeletons, a snarling blur of white fur as she tackled them to the ground and snapped their bones with her teeth.

Those she broke did not get back up again.

I followed her lead, slicing through the skeletons with my blade, making sure to cut clean through their bones to incapacitate them. Several of the skeletons jumbled together, forming a new beast from the whole bones, a gnarled monster that lumbered after Saphira as she leaped between the humanoid skeletons. Blue fire blazed in their palms and grew, stretching long before them into swords or spears.

They swung at Saphira and she kicked left, narrowly avoiding being struck.

Orbs of cerulean fire shot at her, keeping her on her toes, and I gritted my teeth and raised my hand, pulling up a wall of shadows to block them for her as she skirted around the edge of the skeletons, coming back towards me.

Too fast.

She was going too fast.

"Saphira!" A grunt burst from my lips as I tried to keep up with her as she moved back to me, as I pulled my limited magic to me and pushed through the pain.

She yelped as she reached the end of the shadows before I could finish summoning them to shield her and an orb struck her hindquarters, taking them out from under her. The scent of singed fur seared my nostrils and her gasping pants sounded in my ears.

A growl of rage tore from my lips as I turned on the lich.

The fiend raised his fiery blue staff and orbs shot from it, forming a ring around the crystal at the tip of it.

And they all shot towards Saphira, a blazing shower of shooting stars that had me hurling myself into their path to shield her, agony ripping through me as I summoned my magic and cast the spell before me.

The air there hardened, forming a barrier between her and the spell, and bright light exploded across my eyes as the stars hit it.

Saphira came around behind me, snarling as she sailed through the air and tackled a skeleton that had been coming at me in my blind spot. She savaged it, breaking bones and scattering them across the sand. When it was no longer a threat to me, she whined and licked her side, cleaning the darkened fur and burned skin.

Darkness overcame me.

I surrendered to it, letting it stain my fingertips black and sharpen my fangs, and drench the world in crimson.

On a vicious snarl, I tore through the air, sweeping around behind the lich who had hurt my little wolf, nothing more than mist and stars. The lich moved with me, trying to keep me in his sight, but I was faster, and grinned as I materialised behind him, shoving my inch-long claws into his back. Jagged vines tore at my leather armour as I plunged my hand deep into his robe to grip rotten flesh and bone, and the unearthly howl that tore from his teeth as I pulled sent satisfaction rolling down my spine.

He turned, bringing the staff around with him, and slammed the bottom of the shaft into the side of my head. Pain splintered across my skull but I did not relinquish my hold.

I pulled harder, ripping at his putrid organs.

Saphira snarled and I looked at her, freezing right down to my marrow.

Skeletons surrounded her, at least a dozen of them, forming a ring with their fiery blue swords, and she snapped at them, trying to drive them back, but they continued to close in on her.

Saphira.

I became shadow, a violent seething mass of it that shot towards the skeletons and wrenched them apart using tendrils of night, and then my bare hands as I materialised. I shattered the femur bone of one, and shoved it into the eye socket of the one beside it, before pulling it out and bringing it around in a fast arc to knock the head off a third.

Saphira rallied, attacking two more at the same time, nimbly leaping between them to snap their bones.

And then she screamed.

Screamed so loud that my heart stopped.

A blue ghostly blade protruded from her right shoulder, holding her high in the air even as she shifted back, returning to her human form.

Blood spilled down her chest.

The lich hurled her away from him, sending her tumbling across the sand, leaving a trail of blood in her wake.

No.

I launched at the male, all the rage I felt condensing to overwhelm me, to shadow my vision and my mind, and roared as I tore at him, as I weathered his blows and those of his army, uncaring of my own fate.

All that mattered was vengeance. Bloody vengeance.

The darkness caged me in my own body as I ripped at the lich, as I funnelled it all into him, pouring shadows around us to steal the light as the Wastes shook, trembling so fiercely it rattled my bones as they ached, as they hummed with power I could not contain.

And then there were soft hands on my shoulders.

Warm hands.

Trying to pull me off the male.

Trying to stop me from serving him justice, from sending him to his maker, and ensuring he never returned again.

"Kael!"

My name on her lips, yelled so desperately, so fearfully, shattered the hold the darkness had on me and light poured in, pooling within me, so bright it blinded me.

"It's over. It's over," she chanted, her hands gripping my shoulders, holding me tightly, as if she feared I might disappear.

I stared at my hands, more shadow than flesh and bone, talons tipped with razor sharp claws.

And perhaps she had a reason to hold me so tightly to keep me with her.

The shadows slowly shrank, transforming back into my hands, into black-tipped fingers that were bloodied and aching.

Beyond them, the lich was little more than shreds of cloth and scattered pieces of bone.

"It's over," she whispered.

I turned and pulled her into my arms, and her gasp ripped at me, a reminder of what had happened to her that threatened to unleash the darkness again. I eased her away from me, gaze falling to her bleeding shoulder.

I had almost lost her. I had been a fool to bring her here. I had almost lost her.

I lifted her in my arms, shadows trailing in my wake as I strode towards the pack and her clothes, the ground still trembling beneath my boots with each step I took. She leaned into me, her gaze on my face, and even when I set her down on the sand, she did not look away from me.

She took the vials I offered, one to heal her and the other to rid her of any necrotic effects, in case the spell that had speared her had been of that kind. And I carefully dressed her as she drank the elixirs, my hands shaking as I covered her dirty skin, as I replayed that moment she had been speared over and over again.

I had failed to protect her.

I had failed to protect her and she had almost been taken from me.

Killed.

My breaths shortened as my chest squeezed and darkness encroached at the corners of my vision.

"Kael," she breathed, banishing that darkness and drawing me back to her. "Are those your men?"

I looked at her face, and then over my shoulder, my eyes widening as I spotted what she had.

A wall of men marching towards us through the fog.

Vengeance.

This was the reason Neve had sent me to the Wastes, had seen me here and had believed it vital. My vengeance marched towards me, little more than a scouting party from the Summer Court, but they were heading towards my lands, and should they follow me there, I would be justified in my retaliation.

And decimation of their court.

But as their forms grew clearer, my vengeance slipped through my claws.

Not Summer Court.

They wore the deep blue and silver of the Evening Star Court, whose lands extended north of the Winter Court, separated from it by a broad channel of water.

I looked from the seelie to Saphira, torn between fighting them and retreating. The darkness in me pushed to fight, to eradicate the seelie presence from the unseelie lands, but the strategist in me demanded I fall back.

As did my heart.

I gathered Saphira to me and placed the pack on her lap, and teleported with her, as far from the seelie as I could manage.

And then I teleported again, sacrificing my strength.

My focus on Falkyr.

And getting Saphira as far from danger as I could.

CHAPTER 53
KAELERON

"Medic!" I yelled as I strode into my castle, Saphira tucked close to my chest, one of my arms cradling her back while the other supported her legs.

I kept walking, heading for the great hall at the end of the broad corridor, my gaze flickering between her and the arched double doors ahead of us.

I willed her to be strong, as strong as I knew her to be in these coming moments. The bleeding had stopped, but her blouse was wet with it, her skin stained by it, and the material concealed the wound, making it impossible for me to reassure myself that the tonic really had done its job and she would survive this wound.

Jenavyr was the first to come rushing down the stairs near to the entrance of the great hall, her silver eyes wild as they landed on me and then Saphira, and the way she looked at me, concern shining in her eyes, told me Saphira was not the only one with injuries that needed tending. I did not notice my own wounds as I carried Saphira towards the doors.

"They are already waiting for you," my sister said as she fell into step beside me, that concern in her eyes growing.

"How?" I kicked the double doors open and sure enough, the medics were waiting beside the dais, as if someone had warned them we were coming.

"Neve." It was all my sister needed to say. "She had a vision. She saw Saphira wounded. Saw your return. Kael, she... she left her home to warn us."

Dread pooled in my stomach, weighing down my insides as I strode towards the dais and gently laid Saphira down before my throne.

Her blood glistened on the leather of my armour as torch-light flickered over us, the warmth of it struggling to improve the pallid colour of her skin.

I stroked fingers through her tangle of silver hair. Fight. Be strong.

The three males dressed in black robes moved as one towards her and I paid them no heed as they made me stand and move back from her, as one checked me over while the other two tended to her. My gaze remained rooted on her, the whole of my focus narrowed to her as I willed her to be strong. Survive.

A growl pealed from my lips when they stripped her blouse from her, in danger of exposing her, and my sister hurried forwards, swatting them away until she had taken one of the cloths they had brought with them to soak up the blood and had laid it over her chest.

I stared at the wound on her right shoulder, at the reddened skin that was already healing, the wound closed but still tender looking.

And told myself she would live.

But had the wound been only inches to the left, she would have died.

Because of me.

The physicians took their leave, bowing their heads to me as they departed, and I continued to gaze down at the little wolf as she breathed slowly, easily, as if she merely slumbered rather than had succumbed to exhaustion during one of the teleports.

I grew increasingly aware that it was not only Jenavyr with me now.

Malachi loomed like a shadow close to one of the ornate pillars. Riordan casually leaned against the one opposite him. And Neve hovered, her amber eyes as bright as fire as she checked Saphira over and whispered apologies to her in the dragon tongue.

I was the one who should be apologising to Saphira. I was the reason she was injured. Not Neve. It had been my decision to take Saphira with me, a rash and reckless one born of jealousy and a dark need to keep her away from Morden.

I had endangered her, and I had endangered Neve too.

Her amber gaze was grave as she looked at me and muttered, "Do not give me that look. I saw her injured. What else was I to do? I wanted everyone to be ready for your return."

She had been worried about Saphira—her friend—and had done what she could to save her.

She had left her home, had stepped beyond the protective wards for the first time in decades, and had risked her own life by doing so.

But whatever happened as a consequence of her actions, I would keep her safe. I silently vowed that as she checked on Saphira, humming softly to her. I would keep them both safe.

Jenavyr neatly piled the pieces of my chest armour near her and then looked at me, her brows furrowing. "You will be well, brother?"

I looked down at the bandages that crossed my chest and

wrapped around my hands, and nodded. "I am healing and they gave me a draught to help. The bandages are wholly unnecessary."

And I would remove them once I was alone, would bathe to rid myself of the dirt and blood.

Saphira's blood.

"What happened?" Malachi positively growled those words. "I knew you should have taken me with you. A little wolf—"

"Saphira served me well," I growled, cutting him off, unwilling to have him belittle her strength. He did not know her. He did not know how strong and brave she was, or how she had thrown herself into battle despite her fears. "We secured An'sidwain."

I nodded towards the pack next to Saphira.

Neve scurried to it and ripped it open, scattering the contents across the flagstones, and her eyes lit up as she found what she was looking for. She cooed at the ruby crystal as she gathered it carefully into her hands and brought it to her chest, as if it was a baby. As she held it, it seemed to grow, the sides expanding outwards a little. I shook my head, sure it was fatigue making me see that, and turned to my sister.

She was already in her armour, the black metal plates covering her from her shoulders to the pointed tips of her boots. I had failed to notice that until now. Vyr had come dressed for war. She knew something more than Saphira's injuries had had me hurtling from the Wastes, expending far too much magic.

"Seelie cross the Wastes." I sank onto my throne, gaze on Saphira, monitoring her as she twitched and her face crumpled for a moment before relaxing again. She would wake soon.

"Summer Court?" Riordan pushed away from the pillar, no longer so casual.

I shook my head.

Saphira loosed a little sigh.

Her eyelids fluttered.

"Evening Star Court. A scouting party. Perhaps a hundred strong." I watched her as she woke, as her eyes slowly opened, and then she suddenly shot up into a sitting position, gasping and reaching for her injured shoulder, her eyes wide and filled with fear.

Vyr went to her, crouching beside her and placing a hand on her shoulder as she softly whispered, "All is well, Saphi. You are home in Falkyr."

Home.

If only that was the truth.

Saphira's blue gaze shifted to me, relief swamping her eyes. "What happened?"

"You passed out. I carried you here." I struggled to keep my voice cold as I said those words, fighting to raise a barrier between us again, one that might shut her light out and stop it from touching my heart.

She frowned at me, confusion crinkling her brow, and I despised myself for being so cold with her.

But it was necessary.

"An'sidwain?" she whispered.

"Neve has it." I looked for the dragon but she was gone, returned to her home in the dungeon.

No doubt she would tell the wolf there that Saphira had returned and he would demand to see her.

So be it.

It was time I took the measure of this male.

"Jenavyr, you will head to Rhyn's Gate. The Winter Court must be warned about this incursion into unseelie lands." If Rhyn would welcome any member of my court into his lands, it would be either me or my sister, and I had business that required my attention here. "Leave immediately."

Riordan stepped forwards and I stopped him with a look before he could offer to go with her.

"Riordan, gather her legion and yours. Ready them for war." I waited for the vampire to nod before I looked to Malachi.

"War?" Saphira breathed.

My gaze shifted to her. "The seelie march on the Wastes and a message must be sent to their court and their high king that incursion into unseelie lands will not be tolerated."

She frowned at me. "What kind of message?"

I held her gaze, unflinching as I said, "Their heads delivered in boxes."

Her eyes widened as she gasped.

So innocent.

I had been wrong to think her strong enough to live in my world, that she could come to understand it in time, I could see that now as a war erupted in her eyes and her lips flattened, holding back the words she wanted to let fly in my direction.

"War is brutal, little lamb. It is no place for kindness." I turned my gaze from her to Malachi. "Fly out to the Wastes. Stay high and stay hidden. I want those seelie tracked and I want a detailed report on every male."

I signalled to one of the guards now stationed at the double doors.

"Bring our guest from the dungeon."

"Morden?" Saphira brightened, her gaze flying to me, the darkness that had clouded it gone. Because of the wolf.

"Yes," I growled. "Your precious Morden. We shall see if this male you vouch for is as noble as you believe."

She glowered at me, a hint of hurt in her eyes as she righted her clothes. I waved my hand through the air, summoning another of her blouses for her, and tossed it to her. She hurried behind my throne, a rustle of material that had me glaring at the two males in the room.

Riordan and Malachi filed in behind Jenavyr as she strode from the room, leaving me alone with the little wolf.

Saphira emerged, her gaze on me as she came around me, that hurt and confusion in it cutting at me. She opened her mouth to say something and then snapped it shut as heavy boots sounded on the marble floor and her eyes darted to her left, to the end of the aisle, and the dark-haired male walking down it.

"Morden." Saphira hurried to him and he did not resist her as she wrapped him in her arms.

In fact, he signed his own death warrant by wrapping muscled arms around her and holding her just as tightly.

"Saphi." He gripped her shoulders and pushed her back, his grey eyes raking over her and brow furrowed. "Are you okay?"

She nodded. "I'm fine. I'm fine. Really. Our pack... How did you find out I was here? Are the pack—"

"I think they're fine. They were fine when I left, anyway... but I'm worried about them. I don't know what's happened to them since... Lucas..." Morden shook his head and his expression darkened, his words coming out more as a growl as he continued, "That son of a bitch. I never should have trusted him with you. We didn't hear from you for weeks and Lucas kept acting like you were fine and you didn't want to see us. Something about it all just didn't sit right with me. I know you."

He dared to brush his fingers across her cheek, his look sincere as some of the shadows in his eyes lifted for a moment.

"I knew you'd never turn your back on your pack... your family." His stormy gaze shifted to me, darkening by degrees before it dropped back to Saphira. "I went to the Hunt Pack and demanded he let me see you, and he pretended to take me to you and then Braxton jumped me. Bastard hits like a truck, but I managed to beat him, and then I went after Lucas. I caught him at his house, beat the shit out of him and made him tell me where you were. When he couldn't, I made him tell me who took you."

His fierce gaze slid back to me, narrowing and darkening again, and remaining that way as it lowered back to her.

"I saw your bracelet, and I grabbed it when I left. I went straight to Quesnel, to that witch, and I made her craft me enchanted tokens so I could use the portals and then I went to the nearest underground fae town in Whistler and hunted down information on *him*." Morden snarled that word, all the anger and hatred that burned in it blazing in his eyes as he glared at me. "Turns out it's not hard to find this fancy fae world when you ask in the right places. Some blond guy was heading to this world and helped me get to his court, and then he gave me directions over a mountain pass to this court."

I growled low in response to the male's admission that he had travelled with a seelie.

Saphira stiffened and stepped back towards me, her hands coming up protectively in front of her chest. "My family. Our pack. Do you think they're in danger?"

Morden nodded. "You know they are deep in your heart. You know Lucas. Or you do now. He'll target them as revenge for what I did. I need to get back there as soon as possible. *We* need to get back there. I'm not sure what might have happened to them, but I know it's probably not good. We have to go now."

Something dark stirred within me as I studied the male, as I recognised the desperation in his gaze, poorly concealed beneath the layers of concern and hope, and relief. He wanted to take Saphira back to his world as quickly as possible, and I did not believe that need stemmed purely from a desire to protect his pack. It ran deeper. Was more personal.

Did he have someone in particular at the pack he wanted to save?

How far was he willing to go to ensure their safety?

I did not trust this wolf.

And I was not sure Saphira did either as she hesitated despite what he had told her.

Morden produced the charm bracelet from his pocket, showing it to her, his gaze grave. "Lucas has... What if Lucas has our pack locked down, Saphi? I never should have left without warning them. Gods, I was an idiot. Chase and the others can fight, but you've seen the Hunt Pack. We wouldn't stand a chance against them, and Lucas knows that. I'm sure he's there now. We have to get back. You know what Lucas will do if he takes command of our pack."

She shook her head, her hands moving to her mouth as horror danced in her eyes. "No. My parents—"

"They're alive." He gripped her shoulders again, palming them gently, and I glared at him, silently deciding I would begin with removing those hands he touched the little wolf with so easily, as if it was nothing. "They're alive. I'm sure of it. But... if we don't get help, I don't know what will happen. I don't know what will happen to your parents... to my sister. She's the only family I have, Saphi. I can't lose her. I can't let that bastard—"

Morden cut himself off with a growl, a snarl that relayed the anger and raw fury I could sense in him as his face darkened. His sister. This was the person he wanted to save, and every instinct I possessed said her safety was paramount, that he would do anything to ensure it.

Saphira looked as if she might crumple to the floor. She glanced over her shoulder at me, her eyes watery, tears glistening on her cheeks. That look nearly felled me.

"I can't," she whispered as she looked back at Morden. "I... I can't."

"Why not?" Morden bit out and his fingers tightened against her shoulders. "This isn't a choice you get to make, Saphi. You can't decide not to do this. Your parents... my sister... everyone will die if we don't get help and get back to our pack."

She wrenched free of his hold. "You don't understand. I have a debt. The cost to Kaeleron when he—"

"Fuck that bastard," Morden snarled, flashing fangs as he scowled down at Saphira, and she flinched.

I slowly rose to my feet, gaining the male's attention, my shadows spreading down the steps of the dais like a creeping black mist. "I would caution you to watch your tongue, wolf."

I shifted my gaze from the male to Saphira.

"Come, little lamb."

She obediently backed away from the wolf, and shock rippled across his face, morphing to anger as he looked from her to me.

"You'd let her family die?" he barked.

No. I would not.

Because I was not a monster.

She turned to face me, tears shining in her reddened eyes, together with conflict and pain I could recognise, one I had felt once, long ago.

I went to her, lifted my right hand and brushed those tears away, skimming my thumb lightly along her lashes to capture them. She had almost died. I had failed to protect her. With war brewing in the Wastes, my world was about to get too violent for her, and keeping her with me would only result in her death.

And she had her own battle to face, one I could not keep her from.

She needed to protect her people. She needed to save her parents.

That desire was something I could understand, and I could not keep her with me knowing her family might die because I had failed to act and do what was right.

I lowered my head and pressed a kiss to her lips, savouring her scent and her taste, putting it to memory as I gathered my courage and built walls around my heart, layer upon layer of them that blocked out her light.

And then I released her and stepped back.

Because the thought of watching her die was more painful than the thought of her living without me, safe and free.

I sensed my sister's eyes on me and looked off to my left at her where she stood near the side entrance, concern in her gaze as she watched me with Saphira.

"You are needed in the war room," Jenavyr said.

I nodded, a heavy feeling settling inside me, one that seeped through the cracks in the shields I had constructed. "I will be right there."

Her tone was soft, and questioning. "And Saphira?"

I looked at the bastard wolf who looked as if he wanted to wrench Saphira from me and then at her, at her beautiful tear-streaked face and the pain in her eyes, and those lips I wanted to kiss just one more time, trying to crush the voice within me that screamed at me to keep her here, to keep her with me, that my vengeance was not done.

That Saphira was a tool I needed, a weapon in my arsenal that would give me my revenge.

I would find another way.

"I am done using her."

CHAPTER 54
SAPHIRA

I stared at Kaeleron as his words rang in my ears, pierced my soul and leaked poison into it.

He was done using me?

My mind raced, images of how he had been since I had awoken layering on top of each other. His icy tone. His distance. But then he had kissed me.

And even that had hollowed out something inside me, leaving me feeling bereft and cold.

I looked at him, reeling and trying to make sense of everything, torn in so many directions by my thoughts that I felt dizzy. The fragile, frustratingly weak part of me that still nursed the wound Lucas had inflicted on me rose to the fore, stripping my strength from me. Sowing doubts in my heart. He was done using me? I stared into his striking silver eyes, trying to see if any of it had been real.

Had it all been a lie?

Had I only been seeing what I wanted to see?

Because I felt something for him.

Because I had foolishly confused my first mating heat with

true attraction and desire, with a need for this male rather than anyone. Apparently, I couldn't do the emotionless mating heat thing that others in my pack did after all. I had let my emotions get tangled up in the exchange of pleasure, in the satisfying of my heat, letting myself get carried away and finding meaning in his actions.

But he had kissed me.

Made love to me.

I hadn't imagined his feelings in that moment in the cave in the Wastes—the feelings I had seen in his eyes and felt in the way he had held me. I hadn't. I knew it. I knew him. This attraction we shared wasn't one sided. He wanted me as fiercely as I wanted him.

Felt something for me that was as violent and beautiful as what I felt for him.

Hurt and anger welled within me, mingling with the confusion, and I wanted to yell at him, to lash out at him, but I also wanted to run, or shift, or escape. Escape seemed like the right word. I wanted to escape because something inside me was breaking as I looked at him, as he stared down at me, eyes as glacial and empty as they had been the day we had met.

I looked at Vyr, but she kept her cheek to me, her gaze downcast. A sign she wouldn't help me. She had told me once that her loyalty was to her brother, and it hurt now that she was shutting me out too when I had believed her to be a friend, someone who might talk sense into her brother or at least help me make sense of what was happening.

"Saphi," Morden breathed behind me, a reminder that I had an ally in this room, someone who had traversed a dangerous world to find me, to take me home.

Home.

Tears pricked my eyes as I looked at the great hall, as I looked at Vyr and then Kaeleron.

This was home.

"There is a waygate just south of the entrance to Falkyr. Guards will escort you there and you will be able to return to your world using it," Kaeleron said, each word like a dagger in my chest as he made it all the more real. This was really happening. He was just going to discard me now he had what he wanted. "Your debt is paid. You are free to leave."

He was sending me away. Done with me.

But I wasn't done with him.

"What about Neve's visions?" I curled my hands into fists and steeled my heart.

"I have An'sidwain," he countered.

"She saw more than that." I growled at him, sure that she had and wishing I had asked more about the visions she had seen now, so I would have ammunition to use against him and stop him from doing this. "I haven't paid you back anywhere near what I owe you."

The bastard held his right hand aloft and the contract I had signed in my own blood appeared in it.

When he tore it in two, I felt as if he was ripping apart my heart.

"Your debt is paid. You saved my life in the Wastes." He held my gaze, his silver eyes still cold, the mask firmly in place.

"Bullshit. That skeleton wouldn't have dented your armour before you destroyed it," I snapped at him and then shook my head, my voice softening as I whispered, "Bullshit."

"Your debt is paid," he repeated.

I wasn't buying any of this.

I might have massively underestimated my ability to keep emotions out of my mating heat and the time I spent with him, but I hadn't been wrong about his feelings. I hadn't been wrong about this attraction between us that had only grown in the last few days. It was real. It was fierce.

He had just kissed me, and he hadn't done it as a show of possession for Morden's sake because he was kicking me out of his court, setting me free and placing me in Morden's hands.

Or had he?

Ice tumbled down my spine as it hit me.

I hadn't underestimated his feelings at all. I hadn't been wrong about them.

They were the reason he was sending me away.

That kiss had been a goodbye, but also a message to Morden that I was his.

War was at his borders, at the very borders he had closed with a magical barrier when he had lost his parents and brother, sealing them in the same way he had closed off his heart. To protect it. I had been wounded in the Wastes, beyond the safety of that magical barrier, and it had changed something within him.

And I was now a liability.

Or something to be protected.

I looked him right in the eyes, staring deep into them, trying to penetrate the cold mask of indifference.

A shimmer of regret crossed his silver gaze, there and gone in the blink of an eye, a flicker of unspoken things that echoed inside me too and made me want to stand up to him, because I knew he was pushing me away on purpose, deliberately being a cold bastard so I would leave his court and return to my world, far from the danger of the war brewing here. He knew if he shoved me away, if he rejected me and prodded that lingering wound that still pained me, that I would run.

Just as he wanted.

And maybe the old Saphira would have fled with her tail tucked between her legs, with her head bowed and tears in her eyes, pitying herself and withdrawing from the fight. I would have broken down, and might have even begged or pleaded, desperately hoping I could convince him to change his mind or come with me to help me.

But I wasn't that weak little lamb anymore.

He had made me strong. He had made me a fighter.

And that strength he had seen in me rose to the fore as I stared him down, unflinching as his cold gaze penetrated my heart.

A heart that beat strong and steady, defiant and ready to go to war for what I wanted.

Him.

When I had first found myself in the Shadow Court, I had wanted my freedom.

But now?

I wasn't the winner in this game we had been playing from the moment he had bought me. Gaining my freedom didn't feel like a victory. It felt like a punishment.

One I was going to return to him tenfold.

"Send me away all you want," I growled as I stormed towards him. "But know that we're not done."

I strode up the steps of the dais to him.

Grabbed him by his nape and looked him right in the eye.

"This isn't over. We're not over. We're only just beginning and once I've dealt with my asshole fated mate, once I've saved my pack, I'm coming back here and it's going to take a lot more than a ring and a dagger to win me back."

I kissed him. Hard.

With all my fury.

With all my growing love for him.

And just as he softened and began to kiss me back, I broke contact and stepped back from him, satisfied this moment would torment him and keep me in his mind while we were apart.

"When I return, and I *will* return," I growled, holding his silver gaze, catching the glimmer of shock in it, and need, "you're going to have to do some real grovelling to win me back. On your knees."

I backed away from him, not hiding how angry I was about what he was doing. I stared at him the whole time, making him see it.

Making sure that he knew.

My words had been no idle threat.

They were a vow.

As unbreakable as his brand on my chest.

I was going to do what he wanted.

I was going to leave and return to my pack, to my world, because I was needed there, just as he was needed here. We both had a war to fight. It was time I showed my pack just how strong I had become, just how strong I had always been beneath the surface, using what Kaeleron had seen in me and honed with his training to save them from Lucas.

To end my fated mate.

I turned on my heel, a wolf on a mission as my hand came to rest on the hilt of my dagger and I stormed away from Kaeleron, his gaze a fierce caress down my spine.

But after my vengeance was done, I would find my way back here.

To Lucia.

To Kaeleron.

To this place that felt like home in a way my pack lands never had.

And I was going to make him mine.

Want more Saphira & Kaeleron?

Find out what happened that first night at the cottage in their bonus scene. Read it now at:

https://geni.us/wolfcagedbonus

The Bound to the Shadow King series continues in Wolf Hunted, coming January 2026

Thanks for reading!

If you've enjoyed this book, please consider leaving a review to help other readers decide whether this is the book for them too.

Discover more about my paranormal romance books at: https://www.felicityheaton.com

Or visit my book store at: https://authorfelicityheaton.com

About the Author

Felicity Heaton is a New York Times and USA Today best-selling author living in rural Oxfordshire, who enjoys long country walks, video games, and escaping to other worlds. She writes passionate paranormal romances and romantasy novels with detailed worlds, twisting plots, mind-blowing action, intense emotion and heart-stopping romances with leading men who are happy to grovel, might be a little grumpy, and would burn the world for their heroine if anyone so much as looked at her wrong, and leading women who don't take no for an answer, aren't afraid of monsters, know what they want and will face anything or do anything to make it theirs.

If you're a fan of paranormal romance authors Lara Adrian, J R Ward, Sherrilyn Kenyon, Kresley Cole, Gena Showalter, Larissa Ione and Christine Feehan or romantasy authors such as Sarah J Maas and Rebecca Yarros then you will enjoy her books too.

If you have enjoyed this story,
please take a moment to contact the author at
author@felicityheaton.com or to post a review of
the book online

Connect with Felicity:

Website –
www.felicityheaton.com

Direct Bookstore –
authorfelicityheaton.com
Facebook –
www.facebook.com/felicityheaton
Instagram –
instagram.com/felicityheaton
Goodreads –
www.goodreads.com/felicityheaton
Mailing List –
www.felicityheaton.com/newsletter.php

FIND OUT MORE ABOUT HER BOOKS AT:
www.felicityheaton.com

BUY DIRECT FROM THE AUTHOR AT:
authorfelicityheaton.com

Made in the USA
Middletown, DE
19 September 2025

17831305R00350